MAY 10

FABLEHAVEN
KEYS TO THE DEMON PRISON

FABLEHAVEN
KEYS TO THE DEMON PRISON

BRANDON MULL

ILLUSTRATED BY
BRANDON DORMAN

SHADOW
MOUNTAIN

✣ ✣ ✣

For the librarians, teachers,
booksellers, and readers who have made
the Fablehaven series a success!

Visit us at ShadowMountain.com

Library of Congress Cataloging-in-Publication Data
Mull, Brandon, 1974–
  Fablehaven : Keys to the demon prison / Brandon Mull.
     p. cm.
  Summary: When Kendra and Seth go to stay at their grandparents' estate, they discover that it is a sanctuary for magical creatures and that a battle between good and evil is looming.
  ISBN-13 978-1-60641-238-1 (hardbound : alk. paper)
  [1. Magic—Fiction.   2. Grandparents—Fiction.   3. Brothers and sisters—Fiction.]   I. Title.
PZ7.M9112Fa   2006
[Fic]—dc22   2006000911

Printed in the United States of America
Publishers Printing, Salt Lake City, UT

10   9   8   7   6   5   4   3   2   1

Contents

Contents

A Dying Wish

S eth knew he should not be here. His grandparents would be furious if they found out. The dismal cave smelled more rancid than ever, like a nauseating feast of spoiled meat and fruit. Almost steamy with humidity, the wet air forced him not only to smell but also to taste the putrid sweetness. Every inhalation made him want to retch.

Graulas lay on his side, chest swelling and shrinking with labored, hitching breaths. His infected face rested against the rocky floor, inflamed flesh flattened in a sticky mass. Although the demon's wrinkly eyelids were shut, he twitched and grunted as Seth drew near. Groaning and coughing, the bulky demon peeled his face away from the floor, one curled ram horn scraping the ground. The demon did not fully arise, but managed to prop himself up on one elbow. One eye opened a fraction. The other was fused shut by congealed goo.

"Seth," Graulas rasped, his formerly rumbling voice weak and tired.

"I came," Seth acknowledged. "You said it was urgent."

The heavy head nodded slightly. "I . . . am . . . dying," he managed.

The ancient demon had been diseased and dying since Seth had first met him. "Worse than ever?"

The demon wheezed and coughed, a cloud of dust rising from his lumpy frame. After spitting out a thick wad of phlegm, he spoke again, his voice little more than a whisper. "After . . . long years . . . of dwindling . . . my final days . . . have arrived."

Seth was unsure what to say. Graulas had never tried to hide his nefarious past. Most good people would be relieved to hear of his demise. But the demon had taken a liking to Seth. After becoming intrigued by Seth's unusual exploits and successes, Graulas had helped him figure out how to stop the shadow plague, and had further assisted him in learning to use his newfound abilities as a shadow charmer. Whatever crimes Graulas may have committed in the past, the moribund demon had always treated Seth well.

"I'm sorry," Seth said, mildly surprised to find he really meant it.

The demon trembled, then his elbow collapsed and he flopped flat against the ground. His eye closed. "The pain," he moaned softly. "Exquisite pain. My kind . . . dies . . . so very slowly. I thought . . . I had sampled . . . every possible agony. But now, it burrows . . . twists . . . gnaws . . . expands. Deep inside. Relentless. Consuming. Before I can master it . . . the pain increases . . . to new plateaus of anguish."

"Can I help?" Seth asked, doubting whether anything from the medicine cabinet would do the trick.

The demon snorted. "Not likely," he panted. "I understand . . . you will leave tomorrow."

"How did you know that?" His mission the next day was supposedly a secret.

"Confide . . . no plans . . . to Newel and Doren."

Seth had not provided the satyrs with details. He had just told them he would be leaving Fablehaven for a time. He had been at the preserve for more than three months, ever since he and the others had returned from Wyrmroost. He had enjoyed several adventures with Newel and Doren in the interim, and felt he owed them a good-bye. Grandpa would only let them discuss the mission in his office with spells to help prevent spying, so Seth had shared no specifics, but he probably should not have said anything at all to the satyrs. "I didn't give them details," he told Graulas.

"No . . . but I heard them mention your departure . . . as they moved about the woods. Although . . . I can't see into your house . . . I can deduce . . . you seek another artifact. Only such . . . a mission . . . would prompt Stan to risk . . . your safety."

"I can't really talk about it," Seth apologized.

Graulas coughed wetly. "The details are unimportant. If I heard and guessed . . . others may have heard. Though I cannot . . . see . . . beyond the preserve . . . I can sense much outside attention focused here. Mighty wills straining to spy. Be on your guard."

"I'll be careful," Seth promised. "Is that why you called me here? To warn me?"

One eye cracked open and a faint smile touched the demon's desiccated lips. "Nothing so . . . altruistic. I am soliciting a favor."

"What?"

"I may . . . expire . . . before you return. Which would render my wishes . . . irrelevant. After all this time . . . my days are truly numbered. Seth . . . not only . . . my physical pain . . . troubles me. I am afraid to die."

"Me too."

Graulas grimaced. "You do not understand. Compared to me . . . you have little to fear."

Seth scrunched his brow. "You mean because you were bad?"

"If I could . . . evaporate . . . into nothing . . . I would welcome death. But this is not the case. There are other spheres awaiting us, Seth. The place prepared for my kind . . . when we exit this life . . . is not pleasant. Which is partly why demons cling to this life for as long as we can. After how I lived . . . for thousands of years . . . I will have to pay a steep price."

"But you're not the person you were," Seth said. "You've helped me a lot! I'm sure that will count for something."

Graulas huffed and coughed differently than he had before. It almost sounded like a bitter chuckle. "I meddled with your dilemmas . . . from my deathbed . . . to amuse myself. Such trivialities will do little to offset centuries of deliberate evil. I have not changed, Seth. I am merely powerless. I have no drive left. As much pain as I am now enduring, I fear that the afterlife . . . will hold far greater agonies."

"So what can I do?" Seth wondered.

"One thing only," Graulas growled through clenched lips. His eye squinted shut and his fists tightened. Seth heard teeth grinding. The demon's breath came in sharp, ragged bursts. "One moment," he managed, trembling. Creamy tears oozed from his eyes.

Seth turned away. It was too much to watch. He had never imagined such misery. He wanted to run from the cave and never return.

"One moment," Graulas gasped again. After a few grunts and moans, he began to breathe more deeply. "You can do one thing for me."

"Tell me," Seth said.

"I do not know the purpose of your mission . . . but should you recover the Sands of Sanctity . . . that artifact could greatly alleviate my suffering."

"But you're so diseased. Wouldn't it kill you?"

"You're thinking of . . . the unicorn horn. The horn purifies . . . and yes . . . its touch would slay me. But the Sands heal. They wouldn't just burn away my impurities. The Sands would cure my maladies and help my body survive the process. I would still be dying of old age, but the pain would be lessened, and the healing might even buy me a little more time. Forgive me, Seth. I would not ask . . . were I not desperate."

Seth stared at the pathetic ruin the demon's body had become. "The Sphinx has the Sands," he said gently.

"I know," Graulas whispered. "Even the thought . . . that there is some small chance . . . gives me something to dwell upon . . . besides . . . besides . . ."

"I understand," Seth said.

"I have nothing else to hope for."

"Of course we're trying to get the Sands back," Seth soothed. "I can't say this mission will do that, but of course we hope to recover all of the artifacts. If we can get the Sands of Sanctity, I'll bring the artifact here and heal you. I promise. Okay?"

Discolored tears gushed from the eyes of the demon. He turned his face away. "Fair enough. You have . . . my thanks . . . Seth Sorenson. Farewell."

"Is there anything else I can—"

"Go. You can do nothing more. I would rather not . . . be seen . . . like this."

"Okay. Hang in there."

Flashlight in hand, Seth exited the cave, relieved to leave behind the humid stench and the naked agony.

CHAPTER TWO

Obsidian Waste

Kendra reclined in the comfy seat and tried to doze, but despite the hypnotically steady whine of the private jet's engines, she could not calm her mind. A string of flights had taken her, Tanu, and Seth from New York to London, then to Singapore, and finally to Perth, the capital of Western Australia, where they had boarded the private jet they currently occupied. At the various airports along the way, Tanu had them ducking into bathrooms to change outfits and taking complicated routes through the terminals. They traveled under assumed names using false identification, all in the hope of avoiding the notice of their enemies in the Society of the Evening Star.

At Perth they had met up with Trask, Mara, Elise, and a guy named Vincent. Trask sat across the aisle from Kendra, filing his nails, his dark scalp gleaming. She was glad he was leading the mission. Her past experiences with him had shown that he remained calm under duress, and he was widely considered the most seasoned field operative among the Knights of the Dawn.

Directly in front of Kendra, Tanu leaned against a window, snoring gently. The Samoan potion master had spent more time asleep than awake on their previous flights. Despite his bulk, he had a knack for dozing on planes. Kendra wished she had asked him for a concoction to help her relax.

Elise reclined behind Kendra, listening to music on a pair of noise-canceling headphones. She had new red streaks in her hair and wore heavier makeup than when she had helped Warren guard Seth and Kendra back in December. Eyes closed, she softly tapped her fingers against her thighs to the beat.

At the front of the cabin, Mara gazed out the window. A tall, athletic woman with dramatic cheekbones, Mara hadn't been talkative even before the Lost Mesa preserve fell and her mother was killed. Since greeting them at the airport in Perth, the Native American seemed quieter than ever.

Vincent, the only member of the party Kendra had not met previously, sat across from Mara. A small man of Filipino descent, he smiled a lot and had a faint accent. Grandpa had explained that Vincent had been included on the mission because of his familiarity with the Obsidian Waste preserve.

Although she could not see him, Kendra knew that Seth was up in the cockpit with Aaron Stone, the same man who had piloted their helicopter when they went to Wyrmroost. Had that really been only three months ago? It felt like a lifetime.

She wished Warren were here with them. It felt wrong to go adventuring without him. He had been with her at the inverted tower at Fablehaven, as well as Lost Mesa and Wyrmroost. But now he was part of the reason this expedition was so urgent. At Wyrmroost, Warren had been trapped inside a magical chamber. The entrance to the room looked like a regular knapsack, but inside the unassuming mouth of the bag a series of rungs led down into a spacious storeroom heaped with junk and provisions. After Gavin had revealed himself as Navarog, he had destroyed the knapsack, stranding Warren inside the storage room along with a small hermit troll named Bubda.

The room had been well stocked with food and water, but any supply was finite, and now, after three months, Grandpa and the others had estimated that Warren would be nearly out of rations. Without prompt intervention, starvation would claim him.

Not long after Kendra had returned to Fablehaven from Wyrmroost, Coulter Dixon had embarked on a campaign to discover how the Translocator functioned. The adventure at Wyrmroost had provided them with the key to the vault at Obsidian Waste, but obtaining the Translocator would be much more useful if they knew how it exerted power over space. Otherwise, it might end up like the Chronometer, a powerful artifact that they had little idea how to operate.

After exploiting his best contacts and hunches, the veteran relic hunter had returned with no new information. Kendra had never seen Coulter looking so old and defeated. Others kept searching for operational guidelines, but a couple of weeks ago, it was Vanessa who finally reported success. She had been mentally traveling out of Fablehaven into the sleeping minds of people she had bitten in the past. Her primary focus had been trying to figure out where Kendra's parents had been taken, but while working with one of her contacts inside the Society of the Evening Star, the narcoblix had uncovered long-guarded information about operating the Translocator. Once Coulter had verified that the intelligence seemed authentic, the Knights had started planning this mission, in the hope that the Translocator could help them rescue Warren and gain a new advantage over the Society.

Kendra also quietly hoped that an artifact as powerful as the Translocator might help in the search for her mother and father. Marla and Scott Sorenson had known nothing about disguised magical creatures existing in the real world. And yet, despite their lack of involvement in the affairs surrounding Fablehaven, contrary to all precedent, they had been abducted. Stranger still, there had been no contact from the Society about terms for their release. After Wyrmroost, the Sphinx and the Society had seemed to disappear.

Kendra tried not to dwell on her parents. The thought

of them made her ache. Scott and Marla both still believed she was dead. They had held a funeral and buried a duplicate Kendra and then had been abducted before the record could be set straight. A miserable emptiness overcame Kendra whenever she remembered that her parents believed their daughter to be dead and buried. All of that futile grief! Now that her parents were prisoners, would they ever learn the truth?

To make matters worse, her parents had been taken through no fault of their own. They had never even heard of the Society of the Evening Star. Kendra, Seth, and maybe Grandma and Grandpa Sorenson were the ones to blame. The abduction had to be in retaliation for Navarog's failure at Wyrmroost. The thought of her beloved parents paying for her decisions made Kendra want to scream her way to insanity.

To combat the grief, Kendra usually let it flare into hatred, a fiery coal bed of wrath that grew hotter over time, fueled by fear and fanned by guilt. Almost all of that hate was directed toward a single individual: the Sphinx.

It was the Sphinx who had waged war on the preserves for magical creatures, trying to steal the five secret artifacts that together could open the demon prison Zzyzx. It was the Sphinx who had introduced her to Gavin, a cute guy and a good friend who had turned out to be a scheming, demonic dragon. It was the Sphinx who had initiated the shadow plague, which had led to the death of Lena. It was the Sphinx who had kidnapped her and forced Kendra to use the Oculus, an artifact with amazing powers of sight that had almost devoured her mind. And it was the Sphinx who was still out there, unpunished, with her parents under his control, plotting further mischief that could lead to the opening of Zzyzx and the end of the world.

At least now she was an active part of the effort to deal the Sphinx a major blow and hopefully help Warren and her parents in the process. After months of wait and worry, it felt good to be doing something, even if it was dangerous. Under tutelage from Tanu, Coulter, and occasionally Vanessa, she and Seth had trained with swords, bows, and other weapons over the past few months, so she felt more empowered than ever. Nevertheless, although she and Seth were now both full-fledged Knights of the Dawn, she had been surprised when Grandpa, as Captain of the Knights, had included them on such a risky mission. In the end, the essential roles their abilities had played on past assignments had won out. Their presence underscored the desperate need for success.

Kendra yawned, trying to get her ears to pop. The plane was descending. Trask unbuckled his seat belt, rose, and retrieved Seth from the cockpit. As Seth found a seat, Trask stood at the front of the cabin to address everyone.

"We'll be landing in about fifteen minutes," he announced. "I've set up several spells to prevent outside eyes and ears from spying. The magic should divert anything short of the Oculus. Now would be an appropriate time to review our mission."

Trask paused, brooding eyes roving the cabin. He cleared his throat. "Most of us have worked together before, so we'll skip introductions, except for Vincent, who is a new face to some of us, though not to me."

"I'm Vincent," the Filipino man said, half rising from his seat. "I'll be your guide at Obsidian Waste. Over the past ten years, I have spent several months there."

"How do we know you're not a monster in disguise?" Seth asked bluntly.

Vincent gave a weak chuckle. "I know we've all been dealing with unprecedented betrayals lately. The Knights of the Dawn have never seen infiltration and upheaval like the past year has provided. But as Trask can attest, I'm a Knight to the core, have been since my teenage years, when my parents were murdered by the Society."

"Trust has been running thin lately," Trask acknowledged, "but I'd let Vincent watch my back any day. Part of the reason this particular group was assembled was because we have been through enough together to trust each other. I have no doubts or hesitations that Vincent belongs in this circle of trust."

Kendra gazed at Vincent. She was glad her brother had spoken up. She wanted to believe Trask. But what if Trask himself was a traitor, patiently waiting for that vital, heartbreaking opportunity? Probably not. But Kendra had learned that "probably" wasn't always good enough. From now on, she wanted to be ready for anything.

"Our object is to retrieve the Translocator," Trask continued. "I have withheld some of the specifics until now. We believe we understand how the artifact functions. If our intelligence is correct, the device can transport an individual to anyplace he or she has visited previously."

Elise raised a hand. "Can it take passengers?"

Trask gave a nod. "Thanks to Vanessa and Coulter, we understand it can transport up to three people, along with their belongings. The device is a platinum cylinder, set with jewels, divided into three rotating sections. The user twists the sections to bring the jewels into alignment, activating the artifact. Whoever holds the center section controls the destination, and needs to focus mentally on that location as the other sections slide into place. Each intended traveler would grasp a different section."

"What if not all the passengers have been to the destination before?" Seth asked.

Trask shrugged. "Based on the recovered information, Coulter thinks only the person gripping the center section needs to have been to the desired location. But we won't be sure until we test it out."

"What if you teleport into solid rock?" Seth asked. "Or a hundred feet into the air? Or in front of a speeding train?"

The jet shuddered momentarily, and Trask raised a hand to brace himself until the turbulence passed. "The device carries unknowable risks, but given the sophistication of these artifacts, we can reasonably assume that the Translocator was designed to minimize those dangers."

Elise raised a finger. "We'll go into the vault tomorrow?"

"The plan is quick in, quick out," Trask confirmed. "We'll spend the night at the main house to get over our jet lag, then proceed to the vault in the morning. Hopefully, by tomorrow evening, we'll be flying home."

"If the artifact works right," Seth pointed out, "maybe we can skip the flight home."

Trask's mouth twitched and his eyes smiled. "We'll see. Our first order of business will be to make preparations at the main house tonight."

"Do we know where the vault is located?" Kendra asked. "The vaults at Fablehaven and Lost Mesa were well hidden."

Vincent answered. "The vault at Obsidian Waste gave the preserve its name—an immense monolith of obsidian overshadowing the surrounding plain. We know the location of the vault, and even where to place the key. But no rumors hint at what dangers await inside."

"Since the vault is so obvious," Trask said, "we must be prepared for the traps inside to be all the more deadly."

"The lack of camouflage may be related to the strength of the obsidian," Vincent observed. "We're not talking about regular stone. Over the years, there have been numerous attempts to drill, chisel, and blast entrances to the vault. So far nobody has scratched it."

"Why hide when you're invincible?" Elise muttered.

The intercom from the cockpit interrupted. "We're on final approach," Aaron announced. "The air is a little choppy, so I'm going to recommend you all take your seats for the duration."

"I'll pass around some walrus butter to make sure our eyes are open to the magical creatures of Obsidian Waste,"

Trask said. "We'll speak more at the house." He returned to his seat as a prolonged vibration rattled the aircraft.

Kendra didn't need magical milk or walrus butter to pierce the illusions that shielded most magical creatures from mortal eyes, so she passed it back to Elise without sampling any. Kendra checked her seat belt and peered out the window. Down below, the shadow of the jet fluttered over uneven ground. She observed mostly flat terrain, with scrubby bushes, low ridges, and shallow ravines. A pair of jeeps caught her eye, the vehicles kicking up dust as they moved along a dirt road on a diagonal course to intercept the descending jet. She was low enough to see a figure driving each open-topped jeep, but their features were unclear.

Gazing along the road behind the jeeps, Kendra noticed a wall. Actually, it was more the idea of a wall. At regular intervals, pyramids of stones stood in lonely piles, stretching away from the road in opposite directions. Nothing connected the rock piles, so they formed a boundary without creating an actual barrier. But Kendra recognized a shimmer in the air above the line formed by the rock piles, and she realized that it must be the distracter spell shielding Obsidian Waste.

Beyond the orderly stacks of stone, Kendra could see the sweeping loops of a meandering river, and, in the distance, a huge black stone shaped like a shoe box, its rectangular lines unnaturally regular. A tremor ran through the aircraft, and for a moment the jet wobbled sickeningly left and right. Kendra turned away from the window, facing forward, her hands gripping the armrests. The plane bucked and shuddered again. Kendra felt the tingling sensation that accompanies the initial plunge of a fast elevator. She had never been on a flight with this much turbulence!

Glancing across the aisle, she saw that Trask appeared unperturbed. Of course, he was tough to ruffle, and would probably wear that same impassive expression if the airplane disintegrated and his seat were plummeting alone toward the outback. The thought made Kendra smile.

Despite a few more bumps and jiggles, a minute or two later, the private jet landed smoothly. After taxiing shortly, the aircraft came to a stop. Kendra shouldered her backpack and waited while Tanu opened a door that swung out and down to become a short staircase. Kendra followed Seth down the steps. The isolated airstrip had a single runway, a ramshackle hangar, and a small office topped by a flapping wind sock.

After deplaning, Trask, Tanu, and Vincent started retrieving gear from the luggage compartment. Mara wandered off to one side and began a fluid routine of elaborate stretches. From the door of the plane, Elise studied the area through hefty binoculars. The sun hung high and bright overhead.

"Welcome to Australia," Seth announced in his best local accent, gesturing at their barren surroundings. After surveying the area for a moment, he frowned. "I expected more koalas."

"Which way to the baggage claim area?" Kendra asked.

Seth chuckled. "Not one of the fancier airports I've seen. This is more like some smuggler's hidden landing strip."

"What do they smuggle?"

"Boomerangs, mostly. And kangaroos. Poor little fellas."

"Here comes the welcoming crew," Elise reported. "Two vehicles, each with a single occupant."

Before long a pair of jeeps rumbled into view. Painted a military green, the rugged vehicles had oversized tires and growling engines. After the jeeps pulled to a stop beside the luggage compartment, the Indigenous Australian drivers climbed down. One was a young man, the other a young woman, both in their early twenties, dark-skinned and long-limbed. The woman had white ribbons tied in her innovative hairdo.

Vincent charged over and greeted them with enthusiastic hugs. He was half a head shorter than the woman and a full head shorter than the man. Kendra and Seth drifted over for a closer look. Trask approached the drivers and shook hands with them.

"I'm Camira," the woman said to everyone, "and this is my brother Berrigan. Don't pay any attention to him. His head is full of pudding."

"At least I'm not a know-it-all with a poisonous tongue," Berrigan replied with an easy smile, one hand resting on the large knife strapped to his waist.

"We're here to escort you to the house," Camira went on, ignoring her brother. "I suggest the ladies ride with me, or his smell might be the end of you."

"I recommend the guys ride with me," Berrigan agreed, "or you'll arrive at Obsidian Waste with no self-esteem."

"You two never stop going at each other," Vincent laughed. "You're exactly as I left you!"

"And you're still about the size of a termite," Camira teased, rising up on her tiptoes.

Kendra noticed that Camira wore colorful sandals decorated with flashy stones. "I like your shoes."

"These?" Camira asked, holding up a foot. "I made them myself. They say I put the 'original' in 'Aboriginal.'"

"I say we should get on the road instead of chirping about footwear," Berrigan groaned. "These people are tired."

"Forgive my brother," Camira apologized. "We don't normally let him out of his cage when guests are present."

Working together, it did not take long to transfer the luggage to the jeeps. True to the drivers' suggestions, Trask, Tanu, Seth, and Vincent piled in with Berrigan, while Kendra, Elise, and Mara rode with Camira. Aaron stayed behind to perform maintenance on the jet.

Camira hit the gas hard, and her jeep roared onto the road first. Glancing back, Kendra saw the guys choking on their dust. Open-topped vehicles were not made for caravanning along dusty trails!

The jeep rocked and jounced as Camira sped along the imperfect road. She swerved to dodge the worst rocks and ruts, heedless of the huge plumes of dust kicked up by her wild maneuvers. The other jeep fell back, leaving room for some of the dust to dissipate before they passed through it.

Despite the bouncy ride, Kendra studied the arid landscape as best she could. The scraggly shrubs and barren rocks looked no more hospitable than the terrain surrounding the

Lost Mesa preserve in Arizona. She supposed the people who had hidden these sanctuaries would have kept an eye out for unfriendly environments that might deter visitors.

Up ahead, the row of piled rocks came into view. Kendra did not mention the rocks or the shimmer in the air, because she knew that an ordinary person would not have been able to focus on them.

"Are you sure we're going the right way?" Elise shouted over the road noise.

"You're just feeling the effects of the distracter spell that shields the preserve," Camira answered. "I feel it too. We're on the right road. As long as I focus on staying on the road, we'll be fine. The sensation will pass once we're beyond the barrier."

Kendra felt no such effects, but she knew better than to reveal her immunity to a stranger. Sure enough, once they passed the row of rock piles, everyone in the jeep relaxed.

Beyond the rocks, the terrain became more welcoming. Wildflowers brightened the ground, the shrubs looked more robust, and trees came into view. Kendra saw a few mothlike fairies flitting around on speckled gray wings. Near a muddy water hole, she spotted a pair of animals that looked like large, striped greyhounds with long tails. "What are those?" Kendra asked, pointing.

"Thylacines," Camira responded. "Tasmanian tigers. We have many of them here. They're extinct elsewhere. Some have the power of speech. Look up that slope, by those bushes."

Kendra followed Camira's gaze and saw a hairy

humanoid figure. As Elise shaded her eyes, squinting up-slope, the creature withdrew from sight.

"What was that?" Elise exclaimed.

"A Yowie," Camira said. "Kind of like a Sasquatch. They're timid, but curious. Elusive creatures. You often glimpse them, but they'll flee if you show too much interest."

"It seemed sad," Mara observed.

"Their songs are mostly forlorn," Camira agreed.

As the jeep neared the top of a gradual rise, the main house of Obsidian Waste came into view off to the left. Occupying high ground, the wooden house had numerous steep gables and a generous porch. An enormous barn was visible behind the house, along with a wide stable connected to a corral.

Ahead and off to the right, the river Kendra had noticed from the plane could now be seen, and behind it loomed the geometric form of the giant obsidian block.

"I don't recall a river in the area on the maps I studied," Elise noted.

"The Rainbow River runs mostly underground," Camira replied. "But it surfaces here at Obsidian Waste, a gift from the Rainbow Serpent."

"Rainbow Serpent?" Kendra asked.

"One of our most reverenced benefactors," Camira explained. "An entity of tremendous creative power."

The engine revved, and the jeep raced across the distance to the house before sliding to a stop. The jeep with the boys had almost caught up, and it swung in to park beside them. Kendra jumped down to the ground.

"Seth says he's hearing voices," Trask said.

"Like dead voices?" Kendra asked. With help from the demon Graulas, Seth had become a shadow charmer, which, among other things, enabled him to hear the minds of the undead.

"Exactly," Seth said, brow furrowed. "It's weird. They're not talking to me, not directly, but I can hear them murmuring, thirsting. At first the voices were distant. Now they seem to be all around us."

"Do you have zombies buried around here?" Trask asked Camira.

She met his gaze with wide eyes. Her mouth worked for a moment without speaking. "I don't know much about what's buried here. I don't like to speak of the cursed ones."

"We don't usually discuss such things," Berrigan agreed.

The main door to the house opened and a woman emerged. Her honey-blonde hair was tied back in a ponytail and she wore a khaki shirt with matching shorts. Her tan skin was lightly burnt, and although she had to be nearly fifty, she was very fit and walked with a spring in her step.

"Laura," Vincent called.

"Hello, Vincent, Trask. Welcome back to Obsidian Waste. Greetings to the rest of you as well." She joined them beside the jeeps, hands on her hips. "I trust you're all travel weary and ready for a rest."

Trask gestured at Seth. "Seth says he hears the undead all around us."

Nodding, Laura shot a brief glance at Camira. "At least one of us has some intuition," she muttered.

"Excuse me?" Trask said.

Camira scowled.

In a quick motion, Laura yanked Berrigan's knife from its sheath and plunged it into Camira. "It's a trap," Laura warned. "They're waiting for us in the house. Subdue Berrigan. Don't kill him."

As Berrigan tried to dodge away, Trask seized the young man, whirled him around, and slammed him against the side of a jeep, levering one arm into a painful hold behind his back. Laura withdrew her blade, and Camira crumpled to the ground.

"Into the jeeps," Laura commanded, retrieving the keys from Camira. "Make for the Dreamstone. Don't harm Berrigan—he's under the control of a narcoblix."

Trask took Berrigan's keys, then passed the gangly young man to Tanu, who dragged him into the jeep in a head-lock. Trask and Laura started the engines while the others scrambled back into the vehicles. Kendra boosted herself over the side without opening the door, ending up in Laura's jeep with Seth, Mara, and Vincent.

As the tires spun, spraying grit and dust, an arrow thudded into the side of the jeep, causing Kendra to look back at the house. Zombies were crashing through the windows and flooding from the door. They moved jerkily, some limping, a few on all fours. In the midst of them she recognized a tall Asian man with long, grim features: Mr. Lich.

A second arrow streaked down, lodging in a suitcase beside Vincent. Scanning the house again, Kendra saw the archer on the balcony, a striking woman with elegantly

styled blonde hair. Wearing a knowing smirk, Torina, her former captor, locked eyes with Kendra for a moment before ducking into a window to avoid crossbow bolts fired by Elise and Mara.

Through the front door came a figure clad entirely in gray, his face wrapped in fabric. He dashed toward the jeeps with astonishing speed, easily outrunning the zombies, a sword gripped in each hand.

"The Gray Assassin?" Vincent exclaimed. "Who *isn't* here to kill us? They don't want us kind of dead, they want us extremely dead!"

Dozens of zombies came out of hiding around the yard as the jeeps accelerated away from the house. Some had been crouched in holes or trenches, others beneath bushes, one in a barrel full of water. The shambling corpses approached from all directions, their hideous bodies in various states of decomposition. Trask and Laura gunned the engines and swerved to plow directly into the zombies who were attempting to block their escape. Kendra closed her eyes as grotesque bodies went flying.

A stocky zombie with curly orange hair lunged at Laura's jeep, catching hold of the side briefly until Vincent hacked off the freckled hand with a machete. Seth snatched up the severed, bloodless hand and chucked it out the back.

And then the zombies and the house were receding behind them. The Gray Assassin continued after them, but, quick as he was, he was no match for the jeeps once they got moving. Laura took the lead, with Trask close behind, as they raced toward the distant obsidian monolith.

CHAPTER THREE

Dreamstone

Seth wished he had kept the zombie hand. What a perfect souvenir from his first official mission as a Knight of the Dawn! Instead he had thrown it out of the jeep almost reflexively. Hearing all of those zombie voices must have temporarily scrambled his reason.

The voices had been creepy. Hundreds of whispery, yearning zombies, eager to strike but held in restraint by a will stronger than their drive to feed. It had sounded like the zombies were all around them, but he had seen nothing. Until the monstrosities finally lurched out of hiding, Seth had worried that he might be losing it.

Mr. Lich must have been controlling them, instructing the zombies to lay low until the opportune moment. The tall Asian was a viviblix, capable of raising and controlling the dead, and also served as right-hand man to the Sphinx. If Laura hadn't helped them make a speedy escape, they would have all been zombie food.

As the jeep zoomed across a bridge spanning the Rainbow River, Seth continued to mourn for the lost hand. He could have hidden it beneath Kendra's covers. He could have tied a string around it and left it dangling from a showerhead. He could have displayed it proudly on a shelf in his room. He quietly vowed to keep all of these possibilities in mind if a severed zombie hand ever fell into his lap again.

Enormous trees lined the far side of the river, reaching hundreds of feet into the air. "Those trees are huge!" Seth exclaimed.

"Those are karri," Laura answered loudly. "A species of eucalyptus, one of the tallest types of tree in the world."

"What happened back there?" Vincent asked.

"Camira betrayed us," Laura said bitterly. "Last night she admitted several members of the Society to the preserve, along with dozens of zombies brought by that viviblix."

"You said Berrigan is under the control of a narcoblix?" Kendra asked. "Do you know which narcoblix?"

"He's back at the house," Laura said. "His name is Wayne."

Kendra looked over at Seth, relief in her eyes. He had been concerned about the same thing, wondering if Vanessa might have been helping their enemies.

They hit a spine-jarring bump, but Laura did not slow down. Looking behind them, Seth could detect no pursuers.

As they came out from under the towering karri trees,

the obsidian monolith loomed back into view. The scale was amazing—the geological marvel looked like a black mountain that had been carved into a glossy brick.

"It shines like a rainbow," Kendra said.

"I don't see much color," Seth disagreed.

"The stone is black," Kendra said, "but the light reflecting off of it is very colorful."

"Her eyes may perceive something ours can't," Laura said thoughtfully. "We call it the Dreamstone. It is laced with deep magic."

Seth squinted at the obsidian monolith. It definitely had a bright sheen, but the gleam was white, not colorful. Why would Kendra see colors? Was the Dreamstone full of fairy magic or something? They drove toward the imposing block in silence.

Engine roaring, Laura finally closed in on the Dreamstone, piloting the jeep around to the far side. The monolith stood hundreds of yards tall, hundreds of yards wide, and the length exceeded the width by double. Seth marveled at the polished smoothness of the stone and the sharp perfection of the corners. They finally skidded to a halt near the only imperfection Seth had noticed on the unblemished surface: a bowl-shaped recess about the size of half a volleyball.

Trask pulled up alongside them. Seth watched as Tanu wrestled Berrigan from the jeep and pinned the young man to the ground. Trask trotted over to Laura. "What happened?"

"We were betrayed last night by Camira," Laura said.

"Members of the Society surprised us and captured the house. They thought the threat of harming their hostages was enough to convince me to lead you into their trap."

"There are no more hostages," Berrigan laughed. "Not after that little stunt! Your nephew is dead. So are your sister and her husband. Same with Corbin and Sam and Lois."

Laura's face went rigid. Her lip twitched. "You would have killed them either way. At least I managed to save some lives."

"You're still all dead," Berrigan assured her. "You're just prolonging your demise."

"Get out of him, Wayne," Laura snapped.

"I'm enjoying the ride," Berrigan replied. "How did it feel to kill your prize pupil?"

Laura glared. "I never would have suspected Camira."

"You heard the lady," Tanu said, laying his thick forearm across the back of Berrigan's neck. "Get out."

"You need to lay off the Twinkies," Berrigan gasped, his voice strangled.

"I can make things very uncomfortable for you," Tanu promised.

"You're not hurting *my* body," Berrigan panted. "Do what you want to Berrigan."

"Hold him, Trask," Tanu said.

Trask switched positions with the Samoan. Tanu withdrew a needle and a small bottle from his satchel.

"You going to sew me to death?" Berrigan chuckled.

Tanu dipped the needle into the bottle. "I can cause you

plenty of pain without harming your host." Tanu touched the needle to Berrigan's neck.

A full-throated scream issued immediately from Berrigan. His eyes bulged and spittle ran from his lips.

"What are you doing?" Laura asked in distress.

Tanu removed the needle and Berrigan sagged into unconsciousness. "The potion sends a message of extreme pain to the brain," Tanu explained. "It does no actual damage, just talks to the nerves." He pricked the needle against Berrigan's neck again. "The narcoblix truly has withdrawn, or he would be writhing." Tanu rummaged in his bag and pulled out another small bottle. Unstopping it, he wafted it under Berrigan's nostrils.

The young man convulsed and his eyes opened. He struggled against Trask, his eyes on Tanu. "Who are you?"

"They're friends, Berrigan," Laura soothed, crouching into view. "Be still."

"What happened?" he asked, somewhat calmer.

Laura caressed his forehead. "That narcoblix drugged you and stole your body. This is the team we've been awaiting. Answer me a question or two, to make sure you're in possession of yourself. What is your Aunt Jannali's favorite song?"

"'Moon River.'"

"As a child, what did you like in your mashed potatoes?"

"Little cubes of Spam."

"What is the farthest your Uncle Dural has thrown a spear?"

"I don't have an Uncle Dural."

"Welcome back, Berrigan. Ready to help?"

He nodded, and Tanu helped him sit up. Closing his eyes, Berrigan rubbed his temples. "My head is pounding." He opened his eyes. "What about Camira?"

"She's dead," Laura said flatly.

Berrigan gave a single quick nod, tears welling into his eyes. "Serves her right," he managed. His face twisted into a pained expression. "Serves her right. I can't believe, I can't believe she would—" He broke down into sobs.

"Grieving will have to come later," Laura said, rising. "Our foes will be on us soon." She regarded Trask somberly. "Your best hope is to reach the Translocator and teleport out of here. You have the key?"

"Certainly," Trask said. "What are the chances of us taking the fight to our enemies before attempting to access the vault?"

Laura shook her head. "Very poor. The viviblix has perhaps seventy zombies under his control. Some he brought, some were acquired here. They have the Gray Assassin, a narcoblix, a viviblix, a lectoblix, a psychic, a pair of lycanthropes, and, worst of all, a wizard called Mirav."

"I know that name," Trask said grimly. "He's an old one."

"The sun is our best ally against him," Laura said. "He cannot come out during the day. Direct sunlight would kill him. Once daybreak arrived, he was hiding in the basement."

"Agad told me that all wizards used to be dragons," Kendra interjected.

"Mirav is a real wizard," Trask said, "so yes, he was once

a dragon. He came out of India. He is truly evil, and a leader among the Society. His presence means the Society is putting everything they have into this mission."

"We won't be able to stand against a wizard and a zombie army," Tanu said.

"Agreed," Laura said. "Which is why you must hurry to the Translocator."

"You won't be joining us?" Trask wondered.

Laura shook her head. "I'll muster what help I can and try to slow them. I'm not out of allies yet. I'm confident I can take out the bridge."

"I'll help you," Berrigan offered fervently.

"No," Laura said. "You could contribute more by helping the others reach the artifact. I'll achieve the same ends with or without you."

Trask scowled. "After you take action to stall our pursuers, what are the chances you might make it to the airstrip? Our pilot could fly you out of here."

"None," Laura said. "I was caretaker here, and I failed in my charge. I'll do all I can to slow our enemies so you can retrieve the artifact. We all know that to lose the Translocator would be disaster. I will not abandon Obsidian Waste. I will hear no arguments. Tell your pilot to leave while he can. Quick, on your way, we haven't a moment to spare."

Trask began pulling gear from the back of a jeep. "You heard the lady—grab your equipment and let's get moving. Elise, call Aaron, tell him to take off immediately. We'll get out using the Translocator or not at all."

Elise produced a satellite phone and started dialing. Seth grabbed his suitcase, set it on the ground, and opened it up. He had not traveled with his weapons—they had been sent through other channels to Perth, where they had been loaded on the private jet. He found his sword and strapped it on, adding a knife as well. Looking over at Kendra, he saw her putting on the adamant mail he had acquired from the satyrs. Light and strong, the shirt had saved her life at Wyrmroost. He grabbed his emergency kit, which was now a leather satchel instead of a cereal box but still contained a variety of items that might come in handy. He still had the onyx tower and the agate leviathan that Thronis had given him. He made sure he also had the small metal flask from Tanu that could change him into a gaseous state. He was only to use the potion in a dire emergency, because Tanu had doubted whether the Translocator would work on him if he were gaseous. Kendra possessed a matching flask.

Glancing to one side, Seth saw Berrigan sitting cross-legged on the ground, looking shell-shocked. "You better get your stuff," Seth told him.

The young man stared at Seth. "My best stuff is back at the house. Besides, you think swords are going to help you in there?"

"Sure, if we find something to stab."

Berrigan grinned vaguely. "Who knows what we'll face inside the Dreamstone? Honestly, I'd prefer a clean death out here under the sky. In there, we won't know if we're asleep or awake. Most likely, some twisted combination of both."

"We have to go in, so we might as well be prepared."

"Prepare your mind, not your sword," Berrigan advised. "You're young."

Seth shrugged. "You're skinny."

Berrigan flashed a real grin. "I like your attitude."

"Sorry about your sister," Seth offered. "She seemed pretty funny."

"She was very funny. I can't believe she was a traitor. Could they have compromised her while she was away at her university?"

"Maybe it was mind control. Or maybe she was a sting-bulb or something."

Berrigan batted at the flies circling his head. "Camira was amazing. Flighty, headstrong, annoying, but amazing. I'd prefer an alternate explanation to betrayal."

"I once thought my sister, Kendra, was dead. I also once thought she was being disloyal. Turned out it was all trickery by the Society."

Berrigan reached out a hand. Seth took it and hauled the young man to his feet. Berrigan squinted up at the Dreamstone. "I've always wondered what was inside. I guess I should at least bring a knife."

Trask now held an egg-shaped iron object roughly the size of a pineapple, with irregular protuberances jutting from the top half. His stance suggested it was quite heavy. Laura and Vincent were inspecting the strange key with interest.

"You'd better hurry," Laura prompted.

Trask shuffled over to the recess in the wall of the Dream-stone, heaved the top half of the egg into the indentation, and fiddled with it until the key clicked home. Trask rotated the iron egg to the right. After he had twisted it halfway around, the top half of the key detached. Still holding the bottom half of the key, Trask discovered a smaller egg-shaped key nested inside.

"It's like a matryoshka doll," Elise murmured.

"A what?" Seth asked.

"Those wooden Russian dolls that fit inside of each other," she clarified.

"Oh, right."

"Where's the door?" Kendra asked. The key had turned, but no opening had appeared.

"I'm not sure," Laura murmured.

Trask removed the smaller key from the bottom half of the larger one. "Is there a second keyhole? This one has teeth on top just like the first."

Berrigan shook his head. "Everything else is smooth."

"Or was smooth," Tanu mused. "Opening the first lock may have created a second keyhole elsewhere."

Mara was scanning the broad expanse of the wall. "I see nothing from here. We should examine the whole Dreamstone."

Laura rushed back to the jeep she had driven. "I'll go left, you guys go right. Honk if you find something."

Trask let the empty iron shell drop to the ground, carrying the smaller egg back to the other jeep without too much effort. Everyone piled back into the jeeps they had ridden in previously.

Seth scrutinized the flawless wall for irregularities as the jeep accelerated. He scanned high and low, although if the second keyhole were up high, he had no idea how they would reach it. There were no handholds for climbing, no nearby trees, and no ladders handy.

They raced around a corner and along the side of the Dreamstone, bouncing over the uneven terrain. None of them spotted indentations, and they heard no signals from the other jeep.

Rounding the next corner to the far side of the stone, Mara pointed ahead to a large opening. The other jeep came around the far corner, and they met at the entrance to a tunnel.

"Big keyhole," Seth said.

"The first key did open a door," Berrigan said. "Just on the far side of the Dreamstone."

"The next keyhole will be somewhere inside," Trask replied. "Make ready."

Seth and the others climbed down from the jeeps and checked their gear. Kendra came up beside Seth. "Having fun yet?" she asked.

"A little. I'm excited for the zombies to catch up. The best part so far was running them over."

Kendra shook her head. "We should check if Tanu has a potion for curing stupidity."

"I'm hoping to get another zombie hand. I can't believe I threw one away!"

Kendra rolled her eyes.

Seth gazed at the shadowy entryway. It was barely large enough for a person to enter walking upright. The floor of the narrow tunnel sloped upward out of sight. He might be immune to magical fear, but natural emotions still affected him like anyone. Sick with worry and anticipation, he suppressed a shudder and composed his expression. There was no way he would let his sister see his anxiety.

Trask strode to the mouth of the tunnel and faced the others. "This is not how we planned to enter the vault. We're rushed, we're tired, and we're under duress. On the bright side, we have less time to stress out about it. We can do this. We have a perfect team assembled, and we're well equipped. I'm ready. Let's go."

Laura stood up in her jeep. "I'm leaving. Good luck."

"Laura," Trask called. "Don't throw your life away. You know this preserve. Do what you can to stall our enemies, then get away."

"I'm in no hurry to die." She swung the jeep around and started speeding away.

Tanu approached Trask. "If you're taking the lead, let me carry the key."

Trask handed the iron egg to Tanu, unslung his enormous crossbow, and led the way into the tunnel. Advancing in single file, Vincent followed, then Mara, Berrigan, Tanu, Kendra, Seth, and finally Elise.

Just like the exterior of the Dreamstone, the ceiling, walls, and floor of the passage were smooth obsidian. Seth kept glancing over his shoulder until the entrance was out of sight. Elise watched their rear, keeping her compact crossbow ready.

"Where is the light coming from?" Mara asked.

Only after the question did Seth notice that nobody had flashlights out yet, but the corridor was lit by an even glow. He could see no source for the light.

"This is an unnatural place," Berrigan said.

The corridor began to curve in different directions. First left, then right, then down, then up and to the left, then down and right, and so on. Before long, Seth lost all sense of what direction they were moving in relation to where they had entered. The corridor never branched. The only choice was forward or back.

Seth remained tense, caressing the hilt of his sword as he walked. After several minutes, Trask said, "What have we here?"

"You have to be kidding me!" Vincent added.

Seth rose to his tiptoes and leaned from side to side trying to see what they were talking about, but the corridor was too narrow and there were too many bodies between him and Trask. As he kept moving forward, the tunnel widened, allowing the others to spread out. Soon Seth had a view of the dead end.

After widening, the corridor ended with a rounded wall. Mara, Vincent, and Trask were searching the end of the corridor and the surrounding walls. Tanu clicked on a flashlight, but the added shine revealed nothing new.

"We must have missed a turnoff," Elise suggested, looking back.

"The hall ran unbroken from the entrance," Mara responded with calm certainty. "There were no gaps in the ceiling, walls, or floor, no alternate routes whatsoever."

"I didn't see another way to go," Trask added. "There must be a secret passage."

"Did anyone notice a keyhole?" Kendra asked.

"I saw nothing," Mara replied. She sighed. "It may have been disguised."

"Use your hands and your eyes," Vincent said. "Hunt for any indentation or recess."

They scoured the area at the end of the passage. The ceiling was low enough that most of them could reach it. They searched diligently, but found nothing.

"The keyhole could have been anywhere along the passage," Trask finally said.

"There is nothing here," Vincent confirmed.

"That was a long corridor," Elise pointed out.

"Then we'd better get going," Trask said. "Let's not forget who is in pursuit. Keep your eyes open."

Trask took the lead again, and the others followed in the same order as before. Seth slid his hands along the glossy wall. How might the creators of this vault have camouflaged the next keyhole? Could it be covered by a hatch? Or shielded by a distracter spell?

"Kendra?" he said.

"Yes?"

"If the keyhole is protected by some kind of distracter spell, you might be the only one who can see it."

"That's a good point, Seth," Trask called back. "Keep a sharp lookout, Kendra."

"I'm trying."

They regressed slowly along the corridor for several

minutes without finding anything suspicious. "This feels wrong," Mara murmured.

"What do you mean?" Trask asked.

"This doesn't feel like the reverse of the turns we took to get here."

"The tunnel has no forks," Trask reminded her.

"That's what I don't like," Mara said.

"It just feels different because we're going more carefully," Vincent said.

"I disagree," Mara replied.

Seth caressed the walls, searching for cracks, seams, anything unusual. He shuffled his feet to sort of feel the ground, even though Vincent was on his hands and knees examining the floor of the corridor much more carefully. There had to be something all of them were missing.

"Oh, no," Trask said.

"What?" Elise asked from the back.

"Impossible," Vincent complained.

"Another dead end," Trask answered.

Seth felt the hair rise on the back of his neck.

"What do you mean, another dead end?" Elise challenged.

"This is an unnatural place," Berrigan repeated, his voice unsteady. "We've left the real world behind. We should not be surprised. Is this any stranger than light coming from nowhere?"

Seth kept advancing until he had the same view as the others. Once again the corridor widened and then came to an abrupt, rounded conclusion.

While Vincent and Mara scoured the walls and ceiling, Trask stood surveying the area with one hand on his waist, the other holding his huge crossbow.

"Let's not waste time here," Trask said. "Stay vigilant, but let's pick up the pace. Mara, let me know if the way feels different again."

They proceeded with greater haste. Within a minute or two, Mara said that the way felt different. A few minutes after that, they arrived at another dead end, almost identical to the first two.

"I'm starting to have my first case of claustrophobia," Vincent declared, his face shiny with perspiration.

"Great place to start," Trask said.

"I think we're making progress," Mara said, sniffing the air. "Just not the way we're used to."

"Then on we go," Trask urged.

They came to several more dead ends. An occasional steep slope or odd sequence of turns made it clear to Seth that the passageway kept changing, even though they seemed to be traveling back and forth between the same endpoints.

At last, Trask let out a relieved laugh. "Look here, it seems we have found someplace else."

The passage widened again, allowing them to spread out once more, only this time it opened into an expansive chamber. They paused in the entryway, gazing at the huge room. As in the tunnels, a steady glow illuminated the room, still lacking an apparent source. The wall across from them was curved, the floor semicircular, the ceiling half a dome.

Directly across from them a large statue stood in an alcove, flanked by a pair of granite basins. Carved from a greenish stone, the figure had a long face with exaggerated features and wielded a flat, curved club. A smooth expanse of greenish clay dominated the near portion of the floor, bordered by blue and black patterned tiles. The rest of the floor was polished obsidian, unblemished except for a circular indentation near the center.

"No doors," Vincent said, "but the keyhole in the floor looks to be the right size."

Seth walked forward and used his finger to mark the greenish clay. "What's with all the clay?" Seth wondered. "It's wet."

"Could it be for drawing?" Kendra guessed. "A huge, prehistoric doodle pad? Like for mapmaking?"

Vincent shrugged. "Who knows? I don't see any instruments for drawing."

"What do you suppose would happen if we backtracked from here?" Trask asked.

"More dead ends," Mara said. "I don't believe this place allows us to go back. Can't you feel it? Each dead end cuts off our retreat, luring us in deeper, as if we're being swallowed."

"This isn't helping my claustrophobia," Vincent mumbled.

"We could double back to check," Mara continued, "but I'm not sure we'll get another chance to reach this room. The keyhole must be the way to proceed."

Tanu shouldered forward. "The rest of you wait here."

He walked around the bordered field of clay to the recess in the floor. Squatting, he studied the iron key, considered the round indentation, inserted the key, adjusted it, and turned it halfway around.

A faint tremor made the floor vibrate. A pair of spouts thrust from the wall near the statue and began pouring water into the basins. The statue raised the curved club high, as if preparing to strike. Tanu discarded an empty shell of the key and tucked a smaller iron egg under one arm.

Everyone watched the statue, waiting to see if it would attack, but it had stopped moving after raising the club. Seth glanced down at the clay on the floor and saw words inscribed in unfamiliar characters. "Look at the clay!" Seth shouted. "Writing!"

"Create a champion," Kendra read. "Time is short."

"You read Sanskrit?" Vincent asked. "Or Chinese?"

"I see English," Kendra said. "And some scribbles, too."

"Must be a fairy language," Trask said. "The message repeats in several languages. What does it mean?"

"The basins must be clepsydras," Elise said. "Water clocks."

"The clay," Vincent said. "It has to be the clay." He ran forward and plunged his hands into the moist clay up to his wrists, then started digging a hole, disturbing some of the writing in the process. "This is a pool of clay. A pit. I think we are to build a champion out of clay to contend with the statue."

"I was a failure in art class," Trask mumbled. "Who knows how to work with clay?"

"I have some experience," Elise said.

"As do I," Mara offered.

"Mara and Elise will shape our warrior," Trask directed, voice tight. "The rest of us start digging out clay for them to work with and follow their instructions. How long do we have?"

Mara dashed across the room to look into the basins. Vincent was already vigorously scooping clay out of the pool and piling it nearby. Berrigan jumped onto the clay, sinking to his ankles. Dropping to his knees, he began heaving out armfuls. Mara considered the basins for a moment. "Ten minutes," she called. "Maybe eleven. Assuming the water keeps pouring in at the same rate."

Setting the iron egg aside, Tanu entered the clay pit, brown feet sinking deep. Seth waded into the clay along with Trask and Kendra. The top layer felt loose and slimy, but the clay got more solid about six inches down. He grabbed slurping handfuls of the mushy top layer and began hurling it toward Berrigan's rapidly growing pile.

"What do we want him to look like?" Elise asked.

Nobody answered for a moment.

"Make him like Hugo," Seth proposed. "Not pretty, just big."

"I like that," Trask agreed. "Build him sturdy. Thick arms and legs. Bigger than the other statue if we can."

"We'll have to make him lying down," Mara said. "Otherwise he won't hold together."

Berrigan had cleared most of the squishy clay from his area and was now using his knife to carve out large slabs of the firmer material. As they delved downward, it soon became apparent that the clay went quite deep. Three piles grew quickly at the edges of the clay pit. Elise and Mara stole from the largest pile to work on feet and legs. Tanu started running heavy loads of clay from the other piles to the largest one.

After several minutes, arms gray-green with clay past his elbows, Vincent ran to check the basins. "Over half full," he announced. "I better help mold the figure. Tanu, help me transfer more clay to our champion. Keep fresh clay coming!"

"You heard the man," Trask growled, using a sword to carve out another huge greenish slab.

Seth noticed that nobody dug out clay faster than Berrigan. The young man moved in tireless silence, his thin limbs carrying larger loads than Seth would have pictured. Muscles burning, Seth continued to harvest clay at his best pace, reminding himself that each dense wad would add mass to their defender. He was not as effective as Berrigan or Trask, but he was moving more material than Kendra.

Elise and Mara were now working on the arms, Tanu was adding bulk to the torso, and Vincent appeared to be fashioning a large hammer. The clay warrior might actually take shape!

"Check the basins, Kendra," Vincent called.

She ran across the floor. "Getting really full. Like seven-eighths. We only have a couple of minutes left."

"Berrigan can keep digging out clay," Vincent cried, placing the handle of the huge war hammer onto the crude right palm. "Everyone else should work on the warrior. We have lots of clay piled, get it over here! We'll want a shield for the left arm, and thicken up those legs. Make the feet bigger for stability. Hurry!"

The clay pit had already been excavated to waist deep in most places. Seth boosted himself out and started transferring clay from the piles to beef up the legs. As he packed new clay against the existing clay, Seth wondered how long their warrior could survive. After all, the other statue was solid stone. Wouldn't its club slash apart the clay champion without any trouble? What use was a clay hammer against stone?

Kendra remained beside the basins. The statue loomed over her, almost twice her height. "Almost full," she called. "Maybe fifteen more seconds."

"Get away from the statue," Trask ordered.

"Don't stress about the head!" Vincent directed fervently. "I like him without much neck. More sturdy. Add to the shoulders! Quickly!"

Kendra raced back across the floor from the basins. Seth added another small slab of clay to the left foot. Mara crouched over the face, hollowing out eyes and shaping a nose.

As Seth heard the water lapping over the sides of the basins, a sudden wind swept through the room with surprising force. Staggering, Seth found himself leaning against the gale to keep his balance.

The wind died as quickly as it had risen, and the statue on the other side of the room stepped out of the alcove. The bulky figure on the ground sat up, no longer composed of clay. Like the other statue, the champion they had sculpted was now made of solid, greenish stone.

"He should have a name," Mara said.

"Goliath," Elise suggested.

"I like it," Vincent said.

"What should we call the other statue?" Tanu asked.

"Nancy," Seth said quickly.

Vincent and Trask chuckled.

Goliath tottered to his feet. He had a squarish head with no neck. One bulky leg was a bit shorter than the other. The toes on the right foot were too long and shaped like carrots. Now that Goliath was standing, his arms looked a little stubby, but they were thick, with a rectangular shield attached to one forearm and a heavy stone hammer in the opposite hand. The clay had not been properly smoothed, so irregular bulges and slabs covered his surface, contributing to his rough-hewn look. Goliath was not quite as tall as Nancy, who had a long jaw and a high forehead, but his shoulders were just as high and somewhat broader.

While the statues approached each other, Trask herded everyone back toward the entryway. Tanu scooped up the egg-shaped key. Walking backwards, Seth stared as the opponents seemed to measure one another, moving cautiously, weapons held ready. As an art project, Goliath was a failure. He looked slapped together by some careless kid. But as a combatant designed for smashing enemy statues, he had potential.

"Can we help Goliath?" Seth asked.

"I don't think arrows and swords will do much," Trask replied. "If I had brought a sledgehammer, it might be a different story."

"Couldn't we provide distractions?" Elise asked.

Trask shrugged. "We might end up as the wrong kind of distractions. The guardian statue could use our welfare to bait Goliath and force mistakes. Let's see how our champion fares. His bulk might give him a shot."

As the statues circled each other, it became clear that Nancy was more balanced and therefore moved more fluidly. The enemy statue tested Goliath by switching direction several times and making little feints. Given his somewhat lopsided construction, Goliath did not change direction very smoothly. The first strike by Nancy came as Goliath teetered momentarily on his short leg. The enemy statue darted forward, swinging the curved, flat club in a vicious arc. Connecting fiercely with Goliath's head, the top two-thirds of the club snapped off. In retaliation, Goliath swung his shield, which landed with a tremendous crack of stone against stone. Nancy stumbled backward with Goliath in pursuit.

Seth cupped his hands around his mouth and cheered.

Without looking over, the enemy statue flung the remaining length of his club toward Seth. Mara dove, tackling Seth to the floor as the broken club hissed over them before clattering down the passage.

From the cool, hard floor, Seth watched as Goliath swung his hammer several times, but Nancy managed to evade the blows with nimble footwork. As Goliath kept up the pursuit, hammer swinging aggressively, the enemy statue started looking for openings, sneaking in punches or kicks between strokes. The counterattacks proved ineffective, connecting weakly before Nancy had to dodge the next major blow.

Goliath relentlessly pressed his advantage, pursuing the enemy statue around the room, always maneuvering himself to keep his opponent away from the entrance to the passage. Seth watched with his hands balled into fists, his anxiety rising as Nancy proved to be impossible for Goliath to hit. What would they do if Goliath lost? There was no chance they could stand against the huge and agile statue. It would smash them into hamburger.

As Goliath swung high, rather than dodge, Nancy accepted the blow. The hammer connected, shattering the top half of Nancy's head in a gravelly spray. But even as the blow landed, the enemy statue delivered a strong, sweeping kick to the ankle of Goliath's short leg, sending Goliath sprawling.

Nancy knelt hard on the wrist of the hand that held the hammer, wrested the weapon free, and then took off Goliath's head with a fearsome blow. The crude, squarish head bounced and rolled across the floor, reminding Seth of dice. Half rising, moving with alarming speed and grace, the enemy statue brought another crushing blow down on Goliath's hip. Goliath grasped for the hammer, but Nancy skipped away.

Headless, with a web of cracks running through his right hip, Goliath arose. The enemy statue circled, the heavy hammer poised menacingly. When Nancy charged, Goliath lunged forward to meet him, shield upraised. The hammer whistled down savagely, bashing through the shield and demolishing Goliath's arm below the elbow. Goliath used his good arm to punch the enemy statue in the chest. Nancy fell backward, but rose to his knees as Goliath rushed forward. The stone hammer connected with Goliath's right hip once more, snapping the head off the weapon and breaking off Goliath's right leg. The enemy statue heaved Goliath away.

"We're dead," Vincent moaned.

"Keyhole," Kendra said, pointing.

All eyes turned to the alcove on the far side of the room where Nancy had originally stood. Against the back of the alcove was a circular indentation a little smaller than the recess in the floor.

"Bless you," Trask said to Kendra, setting down his cross-bow and snatching the egg-shaped key from Tanu.

"I'm quicker," Mara said.

"Not holding a forty-pound weight," Trask replied hastily. Cradling the iron key in one arm like a football, he raced out into the room.

The enemy statue instantly took notice, turning away from Goliath and rushing to intercept Trask. Seth held his breath. As Nancy closed in, Trask cut to the right, forcing the huge statue to change course. Then Trask cut back to the left at the last second, narrowly avoiding the statue's out-stretched hands as it dove at him.

Goliath was now scuttling across the floor like a wounded crab, using his good arm, his shortened arm, and his remaining leg. As the enemy statue recovered from the fruitless dive, Trask dashed for the alcove. Nancy raced to catch up to Trask, but before the statue succeeded, Goliath pounced and wrapped his thick arms around Nancy's legs. The enemy statue fell hard, then pounded and thrashed in an attempt to get free, but Goliath held firm.

A dozen paces away, Trask reached the alcove and jammed the iron egg into the recess. After fumbling for a moment, he got it locked into place and spun it halfway around.

Instantly, both Nancy and Goliath crumbled to dust. A grainy green cloud plumed out of the clay pit. The floor trembled as a gust of wind swept through the room, seeming to blow the dust out of existence. Trask returned from the alcove carrying a smaller iron egg.

"The clay pit is now a stairway," Vincent reported, standing at the edge and peering down.

Holding the iron egg in his palm, Trask curled his arm. "And I'd say our key is now under thirty pounds."

"Having fun yet?" Kendra asked Seth.

"Watching giant statues pound each other into gravel? I can think of nothing more beautiful."

CHAPTER FOUR

Passageways

Kendra rolled her eyes. Only her brother could act upbeat after nearly getting decapitated by a primitive stone club. She supposed it was better than wallowing in pessimism.

As the others gathered near the stairway to continue onward, Kendra paused, surveying the room. The seamless perfection shared by all of the surfaces inside the Dreamstone made the place feel surreal. Nothing in here looked constructed. The thought of winding through more alien corridors made her frown. After the statues and the strange dead ends, who knew what dangers might await? Berrigan was right—the rules of reality did not seem to apply completely here.

Despite her apprehension, as Trask led the way down the

stairs, Kendra fell into line between Tanu and Seth. What else could she do? There were enemies in pursuit. Not to mention that they needed the Translocator to rescue Warren and perhaps her parents.

She felt glad that she had noticed the keyhole in the alcove. Up until that moment, she had been feeling like useless baggage. Of course, a big reason she had been invited along was in case the Translocator needed recharging. If the artifact was inoperative, the magic inside of her should bring it back to life. Still, she hoped she could find ways to help beyond serving as a spare battery.

The stairway narrowed as it descended. After the stairs ended, Kendra and the others once again meandered single file through a snug, snaking corridor until they reached a dead end. Doubling back, they arrived at a short downward stairway that promptly led to another rounded termination. When they reversed direction again, they found a long stairway that curved up and up, spiraling left and right in a disorienting climb until finally the steps ended at a wide, level corridor. As they progressed along the serpentine passage, the air became balmy and humid.

The corridor descended until they reached a cavernous, flooded room. Water simmered within a few inches of the level of the corridor, heat radiating from the burbling surface. Steam hung in the air, and moisture beaded the walls. A simple wooden canoe was secured near the entryway to the room, with two paddles resting inside. A low island in the middle of the partially submerged chamber was the only destination accessible by boat besides the bases of the high, smooth walls.

"How deep is it?" Seth asked, squinting down.

"Can't tell," Mara replied. "The water is too bubbly and the surrounding stone too dark. At least fifteen feet. I would guess more, perhaps much more."

Trask leaned out over the boiling water, inspecting the room. "The next keyhole probably awaits on that island. I don't see any on the walls or ceiling. We have any canoeing enthusiasts among us?"

"I can handle a canoe," Vincent said.

"As can I," Berrigan added.

"Me too," Mara put in.

"The craft is small," Trask said. "I wouldn't trust it to carry more than two people. Vincent and Berrigan were the first to speak."

"I don't like all this superheated water," Tanu said. "We should all take one of these." He held up a small cylinder of fluid. "The potion is designed to make the user fire resistant. It will offer considerable protection against high temperatures."

"This makes me feel a little better about the rickety canoe," Vincent said, accepting a cylinder.

"You're a miracle worker," Trask said.

"I try to be prepared," Tanu replied. "I originally designed these for Wyrmroost."

Kendra unstopped a cylinder and drank the contents. The clear liquid tasted sugary at first, then spicy hot, then cool and tangy.

After everyone had downed the potion, Vincent accepted the iron egg from Trask. Tanu held the canoe steady as the two men climbed inside and got situated.

"Let's not capsize," Vincent recommended.

"Not in the mood for boiled Aborigine?" Berrigan asked.

"I could live with that," Vincent replied. "It's the side order of Filipino guy that worries me."

Tanu gave them a gentle shove away from the entrance. Vincent and Berrigan dipped their paddles into the simmering water. Kendra estimated it was about fifty yards to the damp island. Handling their paddles with careful competence, Vincent and Berrigan guided the canoe swiftly to the destination. Vincent disembarked first, one foot sliding on the shiny black surface. He steadied himself, and then Berrigan climbed out too, remaining at the edge of the island with a brown hand on the canoe.

"Hot out here," Vincent called. "You might end up with *steamed* Filipino guy."

"See a keyhole?" Elise asked.

"Sure do, right here at the center of the island." Vincent stood up straight and turned in a slow circle. "I don't see any other options. Should I go for it?"

"Time is a critical issue," Trask shouted back.

Vincent knelt and took out the iron egg. The island was high enough that they could not see the keyhole from the entryway, but they could see Vincent's posture change as he turned the key. He held up a slightly smaller key to show he had accomplished the task.

The water stopped bubbling, creating a momentary

silence. After the brief lull, a strong wind swept through the room. Vincent fell flat to avoid being blown off the island. Berrigan sprang into the canoe as the gust pushed it adrift. The small craft rocked severely, then capsized, dumping him into the water.

Kendra noticed when the sound of the wind changed, becoming fuller and more violent. The volume seemed to increase behind her, as if a gale were whooshing down the corridor. She turned in time to see a frothing wall of water hurtling down the tunnel toward her. Mara called out a warning. Kendra barely had time to close her eyes and tuck her head before a foamy explosion of water hurled her and the others into the searing pool.

The water felt scalding, although Kendra hardly noticed since the force of the flash flood kept her tumbling blindly. Hot water sluiced into her nostrils. As the colossal influx of water pushed Kendra farther from the tunnel, the turbulence diminished. Having lost all sense of direction, Kendra opened her eyes to verify which way was up, then stroked toward the surface, following the bubbles churned up by the flood. The weight of her sword made her progress slow, so, with her lungs beginning to burn, she unbuckled the weapon. When her head finally broke the surface, she coughed out water and gulped air in greedy gasps. Her clothes felt billowy and cumbersome, but she could keep her head above water. At least her shirt of adamant mail didn't exert too much downward pull.

The water seemed cooler than it had at first. Either the new water rushing from the tunnel was lowering the overall temperature of the pool or the potion was compensating, because although the water felt uncomfortably warm, it was endurable and did not seem to be inflicting physical harm.

Already beyond the island, Kendra treaded water, drifting toward the far wall of the room. She saw Seth and Tanu not far from her. Trask, Elise, and Berrigan had righted the canoe and clung to the sides as they swam toward her.

Suddenly Vincent's head shot out of the water, breathing hard. "I lost the key!" he spluttered.

"Where?" Trask demanded urgently.

"Right around here," Vincent said. "Below me. I think Mara dove for it."

"I'm on it," Elise said, disappearing under the water.

"Me too," Berrigan said, vanishing as well.

"Everyone grab the canoe," Trask instructed, towing it toward Kendra. "I'm worried we aren't out of the woods yet."

Kendra reached the canoe a moment before Seth and Tanu. The water level in the room surpassed the top of the entryway. Although the water continued to rise, the influx of water stopped making noise. They drifted in silence.

"Should I dive down?" Tanu asked.

"I saw you could barely stay afloat," Trask said. "You're like me—too much gear. Give the others a few more seconds."

Mara came up first, taking deep, controlled breaths. "Berrigan has it," she reported. "The key was too heavy. I could barely make upward progress with it."

Several seconds later, Berrigan and Elise surfaced

together. They swam over and heaved the iron key into the canoe.

"I don't know how she did it," Berrigan said, nodding at Mara. "When we found her, she was on her way up, but she still had to be forty feet under."

"The key sank a long way before I caught up," Mara responded. "I found it sliding down the underwater slope of the island. It was slow going."

"Butterfingers," Vincent lamented. "My bad. The flood caught me off guard."

"It's hard to swim with it," Berrigan said. "No harm done."

"Are we going to drown?" Seth asked, glancing up at the ceiling. The water level continued to rise.

"Good question," Trask said. "Did any of you notice an exit down there?"

Mara shook her head. "I looked, but didn't see any exits or keyholes. Of course, I couldn't see everywhere."

"Could you see the floor?" Kendra asked.

"Yes. Maybe twenty feet below the lowest point of my dive."

"Do you feel all right?" Seth asked. "Can't you get the bends from coming up too fast after a deep dive?"

Elise smirked. "We weren't that deep. Plus, decompression sickness is less of a threat when free diving. You know, with only the air in your lungs."

"Meanwhile, the water keeps rising," Vincent pointed out.

"Let's hunt for another keyhole," Trask decided. "Do I

have it right that Mara, Elise, and Berrigan are our best swimmers?" There were no objections. "You three explore underwater as best you can. The rest of us will look up. Let's find an evacuation tunnel or a keyhole."

Still holding the canoe, Kendra dipped her head under the water and watched as Berrigan, Elise, and Mara swam away and down in different directions. With her eyes below the surface, and the water no longer bubbling, the underwater scene was surprisingly clear and well-lit, although Kendra could not clearly discern whether she could see all the way to the bottom.

"The water isn't bubbling anymore," Kendra said after bringing her head up. "It feels cooler."

"The temperature is dropping," Tanu remarked. "The potion isn't stopping you from perceiving the heat. It just helps reduce the damage."

"This feels like a medium hot tub," Seth said, eyes upward.

"Won't matter what temperature it is once it fills to the ceiling," Vincent muttered.

"The ceiling is irregular," Trask said. "We've got sort of a chimney over by that corner." He pointed at a square gap in the ceiling. "Hard to say how high the shaft goes, but we should get under it. That will be our last resort."

Mara popped up near the wall above the submerged entryway. "Water is still flowing in. I checked around the entryway but found no keyhole." Without awaiting a response, she ducked back under the water.

Kendra scoured the walls and ceiling, searching with

increased intensity as the ceiling drew nearer. Berrigan, Elise, and Mara surfaced periodically, reporting no success. The temperature of the water continued to fall until it was barely lukewarm.

"Tiny perforations in the ceiling," Vincent remarked. "See them?"

"I see them," Trask confirmed.

"Those teensy holes mean this is a death trap," Vincent said. "The air escapes through the holes so the room can fill up without forming air pockets."

"I guess you don't have any anti-drowning potions," Seth said.

"Don't I wish," Tanu chuckled darkly. "We might try a gaseous potion, but the effects won't work underwater, and I don't think those holes are big enough to use as an exit, even as a gas. Your form could get too dispersed, and that would be the end of you. As a last resort, I suppose we can try. You and Kendra each have a gaseous potion, and I have three extras."

The smooth ceiling was now within reach. Trask called Berrigan, Elise, and Mara over to the canoe the next time they surfaced. All three looked exhausted and waterlogged. They positioned the canoe under the square gap in the ceiling. Kendra stared up. The sheer chimney would accommodate the canoe if they kept it at a diagonal, from one corner to the other. She could see the ceiling at the top of the shaft, a long way up, glossy and smooth. It felt like she was gazing up from the bottom of a well.

As the water level reached the ceiling of the room, the

little group drifted up into the shaft, clinging to the canoe. With considerably less volume, the shaft filled much faster than the chamber below. The canoe carried them upward at an alarming rate. The top rapidly drew near.

"I don't see holes in this ceiling," Tanu said. "So much for the gaseous potion."

"I see an offshoot near the top," Mara declared.

"You're right," Kendra agreed. "A little shaft branching off to the side."

"We'd better flip the canoe," Trask said. "It will create an air pocket. Tanu, grab the key."

Once Tanu had snatched the iron egg, Trask flipped the canoe. They all kept hold as the ceiling approached.

"Don't go under the canoe until you must," Trask ordered. "We'll deplete the oxygen soon enough."

"I'll explore the side tunnel," Berrigan said. "Give me the key." Tanu handed it over. Berrigan scrambled inside as soon as the water level reached high enough, wriggling forward on his belly due to the cramped confines. Water slurped into the little tunnel behind him. An instant later, the side shaft was flooded, and the bottom of the canoe bumped against the ceiling. Kendra raised her chin, her nose brushing the ceiling as she inhaled a final panicked breath before the water filled to the top.

Holding her breath, Kendra stared after Berrigan. He disappeared around a corner in the side shaft. The water felt cool now. Vincent swam into the overturned canoe. Trask motioned for Kendra to follow.

Her head came up in the enclosed space beside Vincent,

who was panting. The air smelled like wet wood. "This is our only air pocket," Vincent complained. "Not a bit outside. There must be holes somewhere, in the corners or something, maybe so small we can't see them." He paused as if an afterthought had occurred to him. "Or maybe the place is simply unnatural." He gave a thin chuckle. "I guess now would be a bad time to mention that drowning has always been my greatest fear."

"It was never a goal of mine," Kendra said, trying to stay brave.

Seth surfaced inside the canoe. The others surfaced as well.

"No sign of Berrigan," Mara said. "I'm going after him. There's a chance this little tunnel leads to a way out."

"Go," Trask agreed.

Mara dove into the side shaft.

Trask looked from Kendra to Seth. "Unless they return reporting a dead end, once the air goes stale, we'll follow."

Vincent had his eyes squinted shut, his lips moving soundlessly. Kendra trembled. There were too many heads inside the little air pocket under the canoe. The air would soon go bad. What would drowning feel like? Would she pass out before she inhaled water? Would inhaling liquid instead of air provide any consolation, any illusion of breathing? She didn't want to know. She tried not to think about it.

"What a way to go," Seth mumbled.

"We're not dead yet," Tanu said.

Kendra ducked under the water and stared into the shaft. Mara was already out of sight. Kendra stayed down, watching hopefully. Mara shot back into view, returning swiftly. The water level began to drop! Kendra screamed with joy, the sound distorted in the water, bubbles rising from her lips. Mara hurried forward. Kendra glimpsed Berrigan behind her. Then the water was dropping fast enough that the side shaft passed out of sight.

Kendra surfaced. Trask and Tanu righted the canoe, and everyone grabbed hold. Mara dropped from the shaft, entering the water with her toes pointed and without hitting anybody. A moment later, Berrigan hit the water the same way, plunging through a tight slot between Vincent and Trask. Soon Mara and Berrigan clutched the canoe as well.

"There was a keyhole at the end of the tunnel," Berrigan said, holding up a smaller iron egg. "This place was designed by very cruel people."

The canoe dropped out of the shaft, and the water level continued to fall rapidly. Despite her excitement, Kendra's teeth began to chatter. The water was becoming truly cold.

"The water is flowing out faster than it came in," Mara said.

"Just what I need," Vincent griped, "to get sucked down a giant drain."

Kendra watched the walls, hoping a new tunnel would come into view. The water level kept plummeting.

"The water's getting really cold," Seth said.

"Too cold," Trask agreed. "Something is wrong."

"It's going to freeze," Mara predicted.

Trask heaved Kendra into the canoe. Tanu boosted Seth. Berrigan dropped the key inside.

"To the island," Trask ordered.

The island did not yet exist. The water level was still too high. Kendra watched as the others frantically stroked toward the center of the room. As the tip of the island came into view, a fragile skin of ice formed on the surface of the water. Tearing through the film of ice, Mara reached the island first, followed by Berrigan. The water level continued to drop, revealing more of the island. Elise scrambled onto the slick, black rock. Trask and Tanu followed, their bodies crashing through the thickening crust of ice until they lunged out of the freezing water.

As the surface became solid, the water level stopped dropping. The ice pinned Vincent. His head, shoulders, and arms stuck out of the frozen surface just a couple of yards shy of the island. As he tried to boost himself up, chuckling and gasping, the ice around him shattered. He disappeared completely under the water, and before he came up, the surface had refrozen.

Below Kendra, the canoe cracked, squeezed by the swelling ice. Mara sprawled forward onto the ice, over the place where Vincent had gone under, hatchet in hand, Berrigan gripping her ankles. The ice held her without cracking. She hacked at the surface, chopping chips of ice free.

After a moment she paused. Moving to one side, she wiped away stray wedges of ice and stared down. "It keeps freezing deeper and deeper," she reported. "Vincent is panicking. He keeps pushing off the ice to avoid getting trapped, which is driving him farther from the surface. There must be more than four feet of ice between us already. I can barely see him. Now I can't."

Kendra and Seth climbed out of the canoe onto the solid ice. Tanu, Trask, Berrigan, and Elise joined Mara in attacking the ice, using knives and swords. Seth drew his sword and chiseled at the ice as well.

Kendra had lost her sword. As the others diligently burrowed, she monitored their pathetic progress in shock, trying not to dwell upon the unseen tragedy happening below her feet. Was Vincent already encased in ice, trapped motionless? Was he conscious? Was he frantically diving deeper, seeking to escape the inevitable as his breath ran out? Were they even digging in the right spot? After passing out of sight, he could have moved off in any direction.

"This is like trying to dig through concrete," Seth growled in frustration.

"The ice seems unnaturally hard," Mara grunted, swinging the hatchet with urgent determination.

Kendra sank to her knees, feeling the cold of the ice through her wet pants. Minutes passed. Kendra shivered. Did the others really believe they would rescue Vincent? He was gone. Hopelessly gone. It wasn't fair, or nice, but it was true.

Scanning the room, Kendra noticed a new passage where one had not existed before. Despite the tragedy, all she could think was that they had to hurry and move on before Torina and the zombies showed up and Vincent's sacrifice was wasted. She felt numbly detached, watching the others scrape up ice shavings. With hysteria gnawing at her numbness, she wanted to stay detached.

At last Trask stood. They had barely carved their way two feet down. "Rescuing Vincent is a lost cause," he sighed.

"A new tunnel has opened," Elise said softly.

"We had better move on," Trask advised reluctantly. "None of us would want the mission to fail in a vain attempt to retrieve our corpse."

"I should have moved faster," Mara hissed, still chopping with her hatchet, eyes fixed on the slowly growing crater in the ice. "He was above the ice. He had almost made it. If I had reached for him an instant sooner—"

"You may well have plunged through the ice with him," Trask finished. "It happened too quickly and caught all of us off balance. I should have boosted him into the canoe with Kendra and Seth."

"Which might have swamped the canoe," Tanu said. "We could have lost all three."

"If we're not going to dig, we need to get going," Elise warned. "This trap cost us a lot of time."

"She has a point," Berrigan agreed, looking around as if he mistrusted the walls and ceiling. "This is a deadly place. The sooner we move on, the better."

Tanu hustled over to the canoe and retrieved the key. Peeling her wet pants away from the hard ice, Kendra arose and crossed the room with the others to the new passage. Her soaked clothes shifted and clung as she moved. Tiny bumps erupted on her skin.

The air in the passage felt warmer than the air in the icy

room. Trask led the way, crossbow in one hand, sword in the other. The passage narrowed until they had to proceed once again in single file. Kendra clenched her jaw to keep her teeth from chattering.

The passage was rarely level, sloping up or down. After they had advanced for some distance, the corridor forked. Trask called a halt.

"This could be trouble," Elise said from the back.

"What do we do?" Trask asked.

"Experiment," Mara answered.

"Anybody have a sense of which turn to make?" Trask asked.

"Not yet," Mara said. She was studying the walls and peering down the corridors.

"Then I'll choose the right," Trask said, leading them forward. The passage wound until they reached a dead end. When they returned down the passage, they met with a second dead end. Doubling back, they paused at a wider area where the passage diverged in three directions.

"This is going to be bad," Elise moaned.

"A magically shifting maze full of branching passageways," Seth muttered. "Not exactly a time saver."

"We could get lost in here forever," Berrigan cautioned.

"I could scout ahead," Mara said. "I could run."

"If you found a way through, there might be no way to return to us," Trask warned.

"Then we should all run," Mara said. "Let me guide us. It may take some trial and error, but I can figure this out. I have a fairly good sense for where we are inside the Dreamstone.

As I get a feel for these tunnels, I believe I can lead us through."

"Any other ideas?" Trask asked.

"I could leave markers at the intersections," Elise offered.

Mara shook her head. "That might encourage our pursuers. I certainly won't forget any intersections. Trust me. Staying oriented is my biggest strength. I was born for this."

Nobody spoke for a moment. "You take the lead," Trask decided. He faced the others. "Holler if the pace gets too rough."

Mara started loping down the center passage. Kendra was glad they were jogging. The exertion helped drive away the chill. They reached a T, and Mara went left. Then they reached three dead ends in a row without turning before arriving at a small room where the corridor branched in five directions. Mara picked a corridor without pause.

Kendra was happy that all she had to do was follow. She could not imagine how Mara could keep her bearings through these twisting, cramped passageways. The sameness of the smooth walls and floors and ceiling made it almost impossible to distinguish one tortuous corridor from another. As time went on, they continued to reach dead ends and intersections. Every now and then Mara would call back that they were in a hall they had traveled before, or at an intersection they had previously visited. Most of the time, Kendra had no idea whether Mara was correct.

Eventually, despite how the pace of the jog had flagged somewhat, and even though she was used to regular exercise, Kendra found herself out of breath. She did not want to be the weak link who begged for a slowdown. But from the way the others were panting, she judged she was not the only person running out of gas.

It was Tanu who finally called for a walk. Nobody complained. Kendra's clothes were now damp from sweat as well as from water. They walked for several minutes before attempting another jog. They hurried back and forth between dead ends, reaching intersections now and again. Trask, Berrigan, and Elise added comments as they recognized features in the passages or positions of the intersections, always deferring to Mara.

At length, Trask called a break to eat. Kendra sat beside Seth, munching a partly squished sandwich, her back to the cool wall. She wondered how much faster they would move if they could hear their enemies coming.

"The scary thing in here," Seth said around a mouthful of food, "is that we could lose ground with a wrong turn and run right into the zombies."

"We must be ready for that," Trask said. "Let's hope Laura managed to slow them."

"Outside the sun is about to set," Mara noted.

"Then we'll have the wizard joining the chase," Berrigan reminded them.

"Do you think we're getting close?" Kendra asked Mara.

"Where the end may lie is hard to judge just yet," she replied. "We've eliminated several routes as dead ends or pointless loops. Time will tell."

"Time is what we lack," Elise grumbled.

"We'll press on as if our lives depended on it," Trask said, "because they do. And countless other lives as well."

"You're a good leader," Seth said pensively. "How do you prepare for an adventure like this?"

Trask huffed. "You can't fully prepare. You do your best to acquire diverse skills. You try to learn from your successes and mistakes over the years. You try to assemble a team with varied talents and expertise. Mostly, you strive to stay calm enough to think clearly even under extreme pressure. You try to use the adrenaline for focus rather than panic. You stay on your toes, ready to improvise. And you hope for the best."

They ate in silence until Trask told them it was time to move on. Again Mara jogged in the lead, and again they trotted and walked down endless passages, reversing at numberless dead ends. Mara became increasingly frustrated as it seemed she recognized nearly every intersection they reached.

Finally, when the latest corridor had led them to an intersection that forked in three directions, Mara brought them to an exasperated halt. Kendra had trouble recognizing most intersections, but she remembered this one.

"Maybe I was wrong to lead us," Mara apologized. "By my reckoning, all three of these halls will take us into networks of loops and dead ends that will eventually lead us back here. I must have missed something. I don't know how to go forward."

Kendra had never seen Mara this unsettled. An idea occurred to her. "Mara, maybe we have to treat this intersection like a dead end and go back down the passage that brought us here."

Squinting her eyes shut, Mara rubbed her knuckles against her forehead, a grin spreading across her face. "Of course, of course, that has to be it. I've only experimented with doubling back from dead ends, never at intersections."

"Good thinking, Kendra," Trask acknowledged.

"I was about to say the same thing," Seth complained.

Mara led them back the way they had just come, and they reached an area where the tunnel forked in two directions, one slanting up, the other down. "This is new," Mara said with renewed vigor. "Follow me."

They continued onward, running and walking, seldom pausing, passing some of the same intersections several times. From time to time, Mara had them double back without reaching a dead end. Kendra felt her eyes growing heavy. Her legs felt leaden. When she jogged, her muscles burned. Only fear about their urgent mission kept her from curling up on the floor to fall asleep.

When they next halted to eat and drink, Kendra guzzled water, then slumped against the wall to rest her eyes. Tanu had to wake her when it was time to proceed. He hoisted her to her feet, apologizing.

"It isn't your fault," Kendra said, slapping her cheeks to make herself more alert.

Not long after that, Mara started loping forward with greater vigor, claiming she could sense a change in the air. Kendra struggled to keep up. Tanu ran beside her, one supportive hand against the small of her back.

Kendra tried to let Mara's hope become contagious. Could this be the end of the unrelenting labyrinth? Might they actually escape before collapsing from exhaustion? After a final intersection and a few dead ends, the passage opened into the largest room they had encountered so far.

"Well done," Trask enthused, clapping Mara on the back.

"We're in the belly of the Dreamstone," Mara said. "The hollow center."

The vast, empty space of the rectangular room had dimensions proportional to the Dreamstone itself. Polished expanses of dark obsidian formed the floor, walls, and ceiling, illuminated by the same mysterious light prevalent throughout the convoluted passageways. Three strange devices patrolled the far side of the otherwise vacant room: two mechanical bulls and one mechanical lion.

Composed of overlapping iron plates, the elephant-sized bulls tossed their heads as they rolled around the floor on four wheels, their metal legs dangling decoratively. The artfully rendered bronze lion, slightly larger than the bulls, prowled about on huge paws, moving with a sinuous grace inconsistent with its clockwork appearance.

"Are these the guardians of the artifact?" Seth wondered.

"I hope so," Elise said. "I've had my fill of this place."

CHAPTER FIVE

Translocator

I don't see any keyholes," Kendra remarked, eyes roving the walls, floor, and ceiling.

"Me neither," Mara said.

"We'll find one on those animals," Trask predicted.

The mechanized bulls had turned and were rumbling toward the entryway, their bulky shapes reflecting darkly in the polished floor. The lion continued to prowl the far side of the room, copper mane gleaming.

"Let's go see what we're dealing with," Trask said, striding forward. "Judging from their design, my guess is the bulls can't turn very well. We should be able to dodge them if we keep on our toes. The lion looks like a different story. The bulls seem to be defending it, so I'd bet we'll find the keyhole on the lion. Kendra, Seth, hang back at the entrance with Elise. Who has the key?"

"Got it," Tanu said, following Trask onto the floor.

"Spread out," Trask said. "Make them work."

Mara went the farthest left, Berrigan the farthest right, while Trask and Tanu advanced across the center of the room several paces from each other. The bulls veered slightly and increased their speed, both wheeling at Tanu.

"I think they know I have the key," Tanu said as the bulls hurtled toward him.

"How heavy is it now?" Trask asked, moving farther from Tanu.

"Maybe six or seven pounds."

"Throw it here," Trask said.

"I could wait until the last second?"

"No, now."

Tanu tossed the key underhand to Trask. Having sheathed his sword and slung his crossbow over his shoulder, Trask caught the iron egg in both hands. The bulls swerved, altering their course to run down Trask rather than Tanu. Trask stood his ground as the bulls approached, wide horns lowered. Kendra gasped as he dove out of the way at the last instant, the tip of one horn missing his leg by inches.

The bulls started curving around to come at him again, careening as they turned. Trask now ran toward the lion, his long legs eating up ground. Mara ran alongside him, paralleling his course. Berrigan did likewise on the other side of the room. Tanu hustled valiantly, trying to keep up.

"They're swinging back around," Elise warned, as both bulls charged Trask from behind.

"Use me," Mara called.

Without breaking stride, Trask flung the key over to Mara, who caught it one-handed, staggering a bit until she regained her balance. One bull swerved after Mara; the other stayed on Trask.

"They're not so dumb," Seth said.

Mara came to a standstill, facing the onrushing bull, showing little concern. As the bull drew near, she vaulted nimbly aside, performing a one-handed cartwheel. Trask managed to dodge his bull as well.

The lion roared, mechanical jaws quivering. One of the bulls went for Berrigan, who adroitly skipped out of the way. The other bull came around for Mara again, who threw the iron egg to Trask before using a lowered horn to gracefully swing astride the speeding bull. The iron bull tossed its head, metallic parts squealing, but Mara rode it effortlessly.

Kendra resisted a smile. Her friends seemed to have the situation under control. It looked like they were battling giant metal puppets.

Tanu had stopped in the middle of the room, kneeling. He pulled what looked like a large silken sheet from his pack, then swallowed the contents of a bottle. Yanking off his shoes, he began to expand, promptly shredding whatever clothing he failed to remove. The Samoan swelled to more than twice his former height, his meaty body growing broader and thicker to remain proportional. He tied the sheet around his waist. With the transformation complete, he stood head and shoulders above the lion and bulls.

Apparently sensing the threat, the bull not ridden by Mara charged Tanu. The other bull streaked toward Trask, while the lion pounced at Berrigan. Tanu stood his ground like a matador, danced aside to avoid the horns, then lunged at the side of the bull, lowering his shoulder. The impact overturned the mechanical bull, and the iron body squealed as it slid across the stone floor.

From astride the other bull, Mara called for the key, and Trask tossed it up as he leapt out of the way. When Mara leaned out precariously to catch the imperfect toss, the iron egg grazed her fingertips before falling to the floor with a resounding clack.

As Berrigan tried to flee, the bronze lion swiped him with a paw, sending him sprawling across the floor with parallel gashes in his back. Tanu rushed over to help, and the lion turned to confront the new threat.

Suddenly, beside Kendra, Seth stumbled abruptly forward. He turned to face her, his expression shocked. It took her a moment to notice the arrowhead protruding from his chest.

Elise and Kendra whirled to see Torina at the far end of the hall behind them, setting another arrow to her bowstring. Zombies staggered into view around her. One of the leading zombies was clearly recognizable as Laura, her hair disheveled, her outfit tattered and bloodied. Another was Camira.

Torina looked giddily triumphant. Back at the house, she

had been too far away for Kendra to view her clearly. The lectoblix appeared even younger than when Kendra had last spoken with her, and more athletic as well, like a woman who obviously knew her way around a gym. Her sporty outfit accentuated her fit physique. She grinned as she pulled the arrow back.

Before Kendra could react, the arrow struck the center of her belly, jostling her backward as it rebounded off the adamant mail beneath her shirt. Seth had given her that armor. It was rightfully his. Had he been wearing it, he would not have an arrow through his rib cage. Light blue eyes holding Kendra's gaze, Torina gave a disappointed pout.

After fumbling momentarily with her crossbow, Elise launched a quarrel at Torina. The lectoblix ducked behind the jumbled mass of emerging zombies, and the quarrel lodged in the hip of a rotting, balding man.

"We've got company!" Elise called, seizing Seth's shoulder and rushing him around the side of the entryway, out of sight from the passageway. Staying low, Kendra followed them out of the entryway into the huge chamber.

On the other side of the room, Tanu had wrestled the lion onto its back. Mara had dropped from the bull and recovered the iron egg. Trask faced the entryway, huge crossbow held ready, a pair of long quarrels waiting to take flight. The bull Tanu had toppled lay motionless on its side, but the other was coming back around to attack Mara again. Berrigan rose unsteadily to his feet.

"The keyhole is under his chin," Tanu boomed.

Wincing, Seth plopped down on the floor. The feathered

shaft of the arrow protruded from his back, the cruel arrow-head from his front. He scrabbled in his emergency kit, withdrew a flask, then handed the satchel to Kendra. "Keep it safe," he rasped.

"You'll be all right," Kendra assured him hysterically. Everything was happening too fast!

Seth unscrewed the lid of the flask. "She got me," he wheezed. "I'm a shish kebab."

"You can't go gaseous," Kendra insisted. "You might not be able to teleport with us!"

"Better than bleeding to death or getting zombified." He fingered the arrowhead. "I'm useless like this." He coughed wetly into his fist, then chugged the contents of the flask. His body and clothes became hazy as Seth transformed into a ghostly, vaporous version of himself. The arrow in his chest became gaseous as well.

Elise grabbed Kendra, hustling her farther from the entrance. Kendra allowed herself to be led. The spectral form of her injured brother followed at a much slower pace.

Up ahead, grimacing fiercely, sweat glistening on his brow, Tanu held the squirming bronze lion in a wrestling hold as Mara drew near. The iron bull was rapidly closing in on them, but Mara reached the lion first, climbing hurriedly. She hastily stabbed the key into a socket and twisted. Both of the bulls and the lion fell apart in clangorous heaps of metal scraps. The parts from the moving bull tumbled and slid across the glossy floor, colliding with the wreckage of the lion.

As zombies shambled into the room, Trask fired a quarrel

from his huge crossbow, then set the weapon down, drawing a sword. Tanu and Berrigan flung aside metallic plates and ornaments, searching frantically. Blood oozed from ragged stripes and ugly punctures on Tanu's arms and shoulders. Elise raced toward the demolished lion with Kendra.

A melodically chanting voice caused Kendra to glance over her shoulder. The zombies had parted to let a glaring man with golden skin stride into the room. The slender stranger wore a cape and a turban. Beads, bones, and bits of twine decorated his braided beard. He held up one hand clenched in a fist. With every step, he left behind a flaming footprint burning blue and green. His chant rose to a shout as he pointed across the room at Tanu. In a flash, the giant Samoan shrank back to his normal size.

"I have it!" Mara cried, holding up a platinum cylinder. "It was inside the key."

"Use it!" Trask barked.

Tanu, Mara, and Berrigan all took hold of the Translocator. Nothing happened.

Not far from where Trask stood with his sword, Kendra and Elise ran side by side, still about forty yards from the fragmented lion. Tanu took a step away from Mara and Berrigan and flung the Translocator like a desperate quarterback. The cylinder flew in a high arc toward Elise and Kendra, turning end over end. Elise stopped rushing forward, took several steps to one side, and made a diving catch.

Trask lifted his crossbow, aimed, and let loose another quarrel. The wizard waved a hand, and the quarrel turned into a harmless stream of twinkling dust. Behind the wizard, the Gray Assassin stalked confidently into the room, swords unsheathed. Trask ran toward Kendra and Elise.

Elise handed Kendra the cylinder. Symbols embossed the silvery casing. Tiny white gems sparkled. Kendra felt the Translocator hum to life when the device came into contact with her fingers. Noting its three segmented sections, she could see where she would twist it, but she hesitated, waiting for Trask to reach them.

Back by the entrance to the chamber, the wizard was chanting again. He opened a small, samite sack, and thick-linked chains slithered out rapidly, clinking against the polished floor. The chains were much too long to have fit in the small sack without the aid of magic. Torina emerged from the entryway, bow held ready, along with a fierce creature that looked halfway between a wolf and a bear. Zombies continued to stagger forward.

Trask grabbed the middle section of the Translocator. Kendra held the left, Elise the right. They twisted the device as Torina let loose an arrow.

Kendra experienced a brief sensation like she was folding into herself, as if she were collapsing down to a single point somewhere in her midsection, and then the odd sensation passed, and she was standing in a tidy apartment. Daylight streamed through the windows. Out on the street, somebody honked a car's horn.

"Where are we?" Elise asked.

"My apartment in Manhattan," Trask said, tossing his crossbow onto a nearby couch. "First place that came to mind. Let go of the device. I have to go after the others."

Kendra and Elise released the device. Trask twisted it and vanished. For a moment, Elise and Kendra stood together in silence. The refrigerator hummed as the compressor kicked on.

"He'll be back, right?" Kendra asked.

"He'll be back."

"Is there a chance he'll get Seth?"

Elise stared with wordless sympathy. "He'll try," she finally said.

Elise started to pace. Kendra folded her arms. The apartment was stylish, with leather sofas, a sleek flat-screen television, a glass coffee table, black-and-white photographs framed on the walls, and designer lamps. Kendra disliked the suspense of waiting. "When do you—"

Trask reappeared suddenly, along with Tanu. Chains cocooned the Samoan from his ankles to the bottom of his chest. An arrow jutted from Trask's shoulder.

"Can't go back," Trask panted. "Can't lose the artifact."

"What about the others?" Elise asked.

"Mara and Berrigan are wrapped in chains," Tanu said. "The wizard cast a spell and sucked Seth into a bottle."

Kendra whimpered involuntarily, her hands going to her mouth. "What will happen to him?"

"Inside the bottle, he won't be able to revert to his normal state," Tanu explained. "He'll be preserved as a gas until released, theoretically for years. He's been imprisoned."

"It could be worse," Trask said gently. "The wizard could have scattered and destroyed him. At least this means they want him alive."

"And as a gas, his wound won't get any worse," Tanu added.

Kendra nodded, trying to act brave as tears leaked down her cheeks. It felt like her heart was being squeezed. First her parents, now Seth! What else would the Sphinx take from her? Rage flared up, helping her resist the grief. She ground her teeth.

"Couldn't I pop in, grab Mara, and pop out?" Elise asked.

Trask shook his head. "I barely made it back. They're ready now. They'll get you. We have to choose a better time."

Elise turned and hugged Kendra. "Seth will be all right. We have a powerful new weapon in our war against the Society. We'll use the Translocator to get your brother back, and your parents."

Kendra wasn't sure how much she believed the words, but they were nice to hear. "Warren," Kendra said softly. "We should get Warren."

"Shouldn't we return to Fablehaven first?" Tanu said.

"No, in case he's starving," Kendra protested, wiping tears from her cheeks. "We've left him there long enough. It should be safe. He's in a room cut off from the rest of the world. I'm not sure what could be less risky. I should teleport to him right now."

"I'll go with you," Elise said.

"I can start treating my scratches and Trask's shoulder," Tanu said, unwinding the chains from his abdomen.

Trask gave a nod. "Go bring him back."

"I just picture the room?" Kendra asked.

"I just pictured my apartment," Trask replied, handing her the Translocator.

Elise held the left side of the Translocator. Trying to calm her fatigued mind from the shock of losing Mara, Berrigan, and her brother, Kendra envisioned the storage room, picturing the heaps of junk, the slate floor, the adobe walls. She twisted the center of the device, felt the swooning, folding sensation, and then she and Elise were standing in the very room she had visualized.

An electric lantern illuminated the scene. A small troll with an oversized head, greenish skin, and a wide, lipless mouth whirled to face Kendra and Elise, sniffing suspiciously. Near the troll sat a man in grimy clothes, his face obscured by a beard and long hair.

"How you get here?" Bubda asked, his posture becoming less aggressive.

Kendra held up the Translocator. "A magical transporter."

Warren rose to his feet warily. "Who are you?" he asked, unsmiling.

"You know who I am," Kendra said.

Warren narrowed his eyes, one hand straying to the knife in his belt. "Forgive me if I don't run over and hug you. What kind of game is this?"

Kendra realized that the last time Warren had seen her, Navarog had taken her prisoner before sealing the room by destroying the knapsack. For all he knew, she and Elise might be stingbulbs. To him, their sudden arrival seemed too good to be true.

"It's really us, Warren," Elise said. "You won't need that knife. We're not holding weapons."

Warren smiled sadly. "I'd love to believe you. How'd you escape the dragon, Kendra?"

"Raxtus ate him," Kendra said.

"The little guy who tried to heal me?" Warren exclaimed incredulously. "Word of advice: If you're going to lie, make it somewhat believable."

"We were trapped in that narrow cave," Kendra explained. "Raxtus could fit inside as a dragon, but Gavin couldn't change to his true form."

The corners of Warren's mouth twitched. "I'd love to believe it. How about a quick test? The Society might be able to mimic your form, but not your abilities." He leaned forward and grabbed the electric lantern. "Nobody move. I'm going to shut this off." He clicked a switch, and the light went out.

Kendra supposed that the room was in total darkness for the others. To her it just looked dim.

Warren held up four fingers. "How many fingers am I holding up?" he asked.

"Four," Bubda answered.

"Not you, Bubda," Warren complained. "I already know *you* can see in the dark. Okay, how about now?"

"Still four," Kendra said. He changed it to two fingers. "Now two. Now three."

Warren clicked the light back on. He looked hopeful.

"If the Society knew how to get in here, they wouldn't need to use subterfuge," Elise said.

"Trask and Tanu are waiting for us," Kendra said. "They're injured."

"So you got the . . ." he paused, glancing at Bubda, "the, um, thing we wanted to get with the Wyrmroost key?"

"At a dear price," Elise said. "Seth, Mara, and a man named Berrigan were taken captive. And Vincent Morales lost his life."

"I'm so sorry," Warren said.

"How are your injuries?" Kendra asked.

Warren flexed his hands. "I'm fine. Tanu left me with enough medicine that I healed up before too long. I'm a little malnourished. I've been rationing. I was getting close to trying the rancid goop Bubda lives on."

"My goop better than granola," the troll said, making a disgusted face.

"You look like you're in good shape," Elise noted, not without admiration.

"Not much to do here," Warren said. "I've been exercising. And playing Yahtzee. So much Yahtzee. I'm surprised we haven't worn the spots off the dice."

"You go now," Bubda said, making a shooing motion with one hand. "Bubda no want roommate."

Warren chuckled. "You have to come with us, Bubda. There's no way out of here. Eventually you'll run out of food, even the kind you can stomach."

"Bubda no leave. Bubda finally have peace."

Warren put his hands on his hips. "Come on, don't be like that, I wasn't so bad, was I?"

Bubda scrunched his face. "You could be worse. Not as bad as granola."

"What about all the Yahtzee we played?"

"If Bubda play alone, Bubda always win."

Warren turned to Kendra and Elise. "I got seven Yahtzees once in a single game. Seven!"

"He cheat," Bubda mumbled.

"For the millionth time, how was I supposed to cheat? You were right there! You watched me roll the dice!"

"You cheat," Bubda said. "Too much luck."

"What about that time you got five Yahtzees?" Warren reminded him.

"That skill," Bubda said smugly.

"I hate to interrupt," Elise said, "but we need to get back to Tanu and Trask."

"Lady right," Bubda said. "Lady only smart one. You go."

"Bubda, you have to come," Warren insisted.

"Bubda stay. Bubda relax. You go. Take granola."

Warren looked to Kendra and Elise for support.

"We can come back anytime," Kendra said. "Even in an hour or two. But we should get back to Trask and Tanu. We need to get them to Fablehaven."

"Where are they now?" Warren asked.

"Trask's apartment in New York."

"He have anything in his fridge?" Warren asked hopefully. He swiveled to face Bubda. "I'm not abandoning you, Mr. Hermit Troll. Enjoy your break, because I'll be back. We'll find you an even better home. Someplace with lots of moist food. Nothing dry or crunchy. No granola."

Bubda turned away, grumbling unintelligibly.

Warren walked over to Kendra. "If this is some kind of trick or trap, well played, you got me. What do I do?"

"Just grab the cylinder," Kendra instructed.

Elise held the left side, Kendra kept hold of the middle segment, and Warren gripped the right end. "Can't say I'm going to miss this place," he murmured.

Kendra imagined Trask's apartment, twisted the cylinder, and a moment later they were standing between a leather sofa and a glass coffee table. Tanu crouched over Trask, applying ointment to his shoulder.

"You guys never get a break," Warren quipped.

"All in a day's work," Tanu replied.

"You look like you were marooned on a desert island," Trask said.

"I wish. I would have given anything for an ocean breeze." Warren stroked his beard. "Kendra, how about you teleport us to a barber shop?"

"We should get to Fablehaven," Trask said. "My apartment has certain protections, but nothing like the walls of a preserve. You three go first."

"Want to swing by a burger joint on the way?" Warren asked out of the side of his mouth.

"I'm sure Grandma will whip up something," Kendra replied, twisting the cylinder. A moment later, she, Warren, and Elise were at Fablehaven, standing together in the kitchen. Nobody else was in sight.

"Hello?" Kendra called.

"Kendra?" Grandpa answered. It sounded like he was in his study.

"I'll be right back," Kendra told Elise. Twisting the cylinder, she returned alone to Trask's apartment.

"It worked all right?" Trask asked.

"We went straight to the kitchen," Kendra said.

Trask nodded. "Good. I'm not surprised. But I'm more impressed that the Translocator could leap through the defenses of a preserve than I am that it can take us to the other side of the globe. Let's go."

Once Trask and Tanu had taken hold of the Translocator, Kendra teleported them to Fablehaven. When they appeared in the kitchen, Grandpa, Grandma, and Coulter were already there. They looked subdued.

"Get this, Stan," Tanu said. "The key we retrieved from Wyrmroost had smaller keys inside, like a nesting doll. And guess what we found at the center? The Translocator."

"The key was the vault," Grandpa said.

"Elise told us about Seth and the others," Coulter said.

Grandma caught Kendra in a tight embrace. "We'll get him back," she promised.

Kendra nodded, eyes stinging. She didn't trust herself to speak.

CHAPTER SIX

Living Mirage

S eth could hardly think. He could hear nothing. He could smell nothing. All he saw was muted grayness, which almost seemed more like oblivion than pure blackness would have. When he tried to move, there was no physical response, no sensation, as if all his nerves had been disconnected.

Time had lost all meaning. His sense of self had begun to diminish. His mind seemed sluggish, half asleep. He did not dream, but when he focused, he could remember.

He remembered looking down at the arrowhead, remembered the horror on Kendra's face. He remembered feeling angry. What a cheap shot! Right in the back! Taking a few steps had proved that he was useless, dying.

He had instantly thought about the gaseous potion. The

concoction wouldn't heal the injury, but it would put him in hibernation, prevent the wound from worsening. In the meantime, he wouldn't be a burden. They could fight without having to drag him around, perhaps killing him and themselves in the process. He recalled thinking that if his friends could somehow win the battle, maybe they could rescue him later.

Seth remembered giving Kendra his emergency kit. That was important. The tower was inside, and the leviathan, and some other less precious items he didn't want to hand over to the enemy if he were killed or captured.

After becoming gaseous, he had moved slowly, drifting in whatever direction he chose. Having lost the ability of speech, he had watched wordlessly as Kendra used the Translocator to escape with Trask and Elise. He had watched the magician send chains after the others as zombies crowded into the room.

Then Trask had returned, trying to help Tanu, and, without warning, Seth had felt effervescent rushes of bubbles tingling through his wispy body. That was when the grayness had overtaken him and most physical sensations had ended.

Had his mind been separated from his body? Somehow stolen out of the gas? It felt that way. It was tough to focus on the present. There was nothing to focus on.

He caught himself slipping into trances. It was hard to say for how long. Whenever his mind kicked back into gear, becoming self-aware instead of coasting, he would fight the emptiness with memories, people he knew, places he had been, fun things he had done. Anything to keep his mind from shutting down and merging with the nothingness.

Thanks to his addled state, Seth could not say how long he had been adrift in gray oblivion when sensation returned in a rush. There came a sense of motion, of tiny bubbles coursing through him, and then he was flesh and blood again, lying on his side on a plush rug, his chest aflame with agony.

Turning his head, Seth looked up into the dark eyes of the Sphinx. The gaze of his enemy was warm and gentle. The Sphinx gestured to the wizard who had attacked his friends inside the Dreamstone, the man with the braided beard and the turban. The man pointed at the arrow protruding from Seth, and it dissolved into smoke, although the deep pain of the wound persisted. When the wizard waved a hand, Seth's sword and knife evaporated as well.

"Welcome back," the Sphinx said to Seth. He glanced at the wizard. "Leave us."

The gold-skinned man nodded and moved out of view. Seth heard a door open and close. The intense pain in his chest remained. He was afraid to move, afraid blood would gush out of the wound. He could smell incense burning.

The Sphinx produced a bright copper teapot in the shape of a cat, the tail forming the spout. He upended the teapot over Seth, and dust streamed out. Seth's wounds tingled momentarily, and then the pain was gone. The Sphinx set the teapot aside.

"The artifact from Fablehaven," Seth said.

"You should be glad I have the Sands of Sanctity," the Sphinx said. "Your injury was mortal."

"Where was I? What happened?"

"While you were in your gaseous state, Mirav trapped you in a bottle. The effects would have been disorienting."

Seth stood up, groggily brushing dust from his shirt. "Kendra got away."

The Sphinx smiled. He was a handsome man with short, beaded dreadlocks and very dark skin. He wore a white ribbed shirt and loose jeans. His feet were bare. "You're taller."

"Tanu and Trask got away too, right? And Elise. What about Mara and Berrigan?"

The Sphinx regarded Seth with fathomless black eyes. "There is something different about you, Seth Sorenson." His faint accent was hard to place, but hinted at tropical islands. "You have been consorting with demons."

Seth felt his face grow warm. "I'm a shadow charmer."

"I can see. I had heard rumors. Congratulations."

Seth frowned. Getting congratulated by the Sphinx was no compliment. "Tell me about the others."

"We have Mara and Berrigan. The others got away with the Translocator. We should have had all of you. Laura, the caretaker at Obsidian Waste, demolished a bridge and led a counterattack that stalled the pursuit."

Some of the tension went out of Seth. At least the others really had escaped. The mission was a success. He glanced around the room. There were no windows, and just a single door. Filmy veils hung from the ceiling. Tapestries and other hangings softened the walls. Rich rugs blanketed the floors. Cushions and pillows of various shape and size took the place of furniture, although Seth noticed a traditional desk in one corner, next to a divan. "Where are we?"

The Sphinx sat down on a cushion. He motioned to another cushion nearby. "Please have a seat."

Seth sat down. "No Foosball table?"

The Sphinx smiled. "I am glad to see you again. I've missed you."

"Didn't you get my Christmas card? I drew it myself."

"A shadow charmer is not made every day," the Sphinx said, his demeanor growing serious. "You intrigue me as much as your sister does. I would like to have an honest conversation."

"How about an honest answer as to where we are?" Seth pressed.

The Sphinx studied him. "When masters play chess, there often comes a point, sometimes many moves before checkmate, when the outcome is decided. Sometimes the inevitable loser will resign. Sometimes the doomed participant will continue until the final move. But beyond that pivotal point, the drama is over."

"Is this your way of saying you've won?" Seth asked. "They're not dumb enough to trade everything for me!"

"I am not yet claiming victory. Zzyzx is not yet open. I'm saying I am well beyond the point where my victory is certain."

Seth squirmed. "What you're trying to do is a little more complicated than a game of chess."

"A lot more complicated."

"I think you'll find we still have a few tricks up our sleeves." Seth hoped it was true.

"I'm sure you're right. Underestimating an opponent can be lethal. Seth, I'm not trying to boast or to intimidate you. I am telling you that I am so confident of victory, and so certain that you will leave here only at my whim, that we can actually have an honest, open conversation. Ask me anything."

"Okay, for the third time, where are we?"

"We are in Eastern Turkey on a preserve called Living Mirage. At least, that is the closest English translation. Some have dubbed it the Grand Oasis. Your friends and family refer to it as the fifth secret preserve. I call it home."

Seth could not conceal his astonishment. "You live at the fifth preserve? The one nobody can find?"

"I have dwelled here for a long time."

"This is where the final artifact is hidden."

The Sphinx smiled. "It was the first artifact I recovered, many lifetimes ago."

Seth paled. "Then you have three. The Sands of Sanctity, the Oculus, and . . ."

" . . . the Font of Immortality."

"Is that how you've lived so long?"

"When we first met, you asked whether I was an actual sphinx. I am not the avatar of a sphinx. I am a human being who has prolonged his life through ownership of the Font of Immortality."

Seth regarded the Sphinx skeptically. "You're also a huge

liar. A master con artist. How do I know whether a word you just told me is true?"

"Deception has been an inseparable companion," the Sphinx conceded. "Strange. I have guarded these secrets for so long that it almost surprises me to have them disbelieved. But you're right. We could be anywhere. I could be anyone, or anything. Keep in mind, I just healed you with the Sands of Sanctity. The Oculus rests on my desk, which is how I know nobody could possibly be overhearing this conversation. And the Font of Immortality is in this room as well, though I suppose you could dismiss it as an elaborate prop."

"Let's see it," Seth said.

"Why not?" The Sphinx stood and walked to the desk. Seth followed, noticing the flawless, multifaceted crystal resting upon a cushion on the desktop, refracting light into little rainbows. The Oculus looked exactly how Kendra had described it.

The Sphinx pulled aside a tapestry, opened a hidden cupboard in the wall, and removed a tall object. Seth recognized the straight, pearly spiral of a unicorn horn, although this one was much longer than the horn he had recovered from the centaurs. The horn served as the long stem to an alabaster goblet, embellished with shimmering enamel. A sturdy base was attached to the other end.

"That's the Font of Immortality?" Seth asked.

"I can't prove it in the short term," the Sphinx replied, "but if you sip from this goblet once a week, you will stop aging."

"Is that a unicorn horn?" Seth asked.

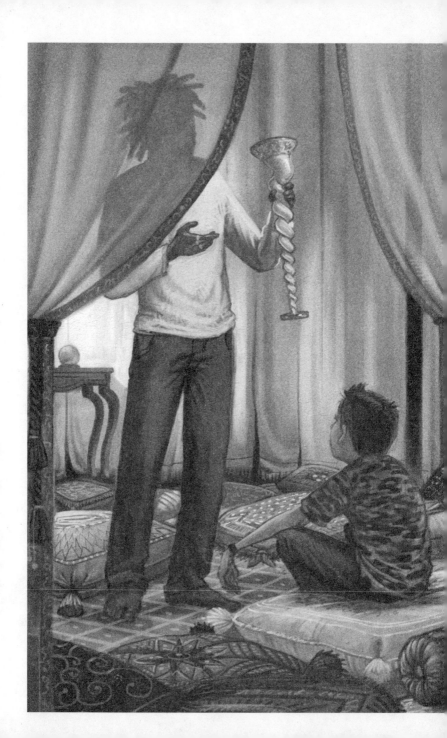

"You've seen one before," the Sphinx recognized. "You needed it to enter Wyrmroost. What you handled was a first horn. This is the third and final horn of a unicorn." The Sphinx replaced the artifact in the cupboard and inclined his head toward the desk. "Unlike the Font, if you touch the Oculus, you will instantly experience its authenticity."

"I'll take your word for it," Seth hedged.

"Sit," the Sphinx invited. "I did not mean to disturb your comfort." Seth complied. The Sphinx remained on his feet. "I can do no more to persuade you of my sincerity. It will be up to you to believe or disbelieve, as you choose. Understand, I have concealed myself for centuries. The only way to really keep a secret is to tell no one. But my identity, my life story, is no longer a secret. It is merely history. You will never escape here with this information. And if you did, it would not matter. I no longer have a motive to lie."

"How did you find this preserve?" Seth asked.

"I did not find Living Mirage. Living Mirage found me."

"Is that supposed to be a riddle?"

"As a child, I was brought here as a slave."

Seth frowned. "That's horrible. Where were you from?"

"Ethiopia."

"The caretaker had slaves?"

The Sphinx started pacing. "This was long ago. Not all caretakers were good men like your grandfather. There were many slaves here. Through their labor, those who ran the preserve lived like kings. No, like tyrants. The preserve was deadly. Slaves were employed for many high-risk duties.

When they died, it was not considered a loss of life, just a depletion of resources."

"I can see how that would make you bitter," Seth said.

"I was a bright child and a hard worker. I realized that, given my circumstances, the best chance for a good life was through diligent obedience to my masters. The slaves who resisted were punished and ended up with dangerous assignments. The rebellious never lasted long.

"I went out of my way to be the ideal servant. Many of the other slaves despised me for it. As my talents and devotion were recognized, my work took me indoors. My masters never loved me, but they appreciated my usefulness, my reliability. As I grew older, I became an administrator. Head slave, if you will.

"What my masters did not know, what the other slaves could not guess, was that I was the most dangerous person at Living Mirage. Deep down, beneath the pleasant demeanor and quiet competence, in the invisible self that nobody knew, I was a rebel to the very center. Furious. Ambitious. Vengeful. But I was a patient rebel. I watched. I listened. I learned. I plotted. I did not want to rebel in some symbolic way. I had no interest in a futile act of defiance that would lead to my destruction. I wanted to turn the tables on my captors. I craved victory.

"There is great power in harboring a single goal. With my words and actions, I excelled at my daily tasks. But with my thoughts I planned my coup. I constantly sought opportunities for my eyes and ears to acquire the knowledge I required. I learned that Living Mirage was a secret preserve, known only to a few outsiders. That was important. It meant that if I could stage a coup, I might have a chance to truly take ownership of the preserve, to hide my victory from possible external enemies. When I learned about the artifact, my ambitions grew. What if I could destroy my captors, become master of Living Mirage, and then live forever? That would be vengeance indeed.

"I was a young adult when I first learned of my future mentor, the most feared demon at Living Mirage, perhaps the most feared demon in the world: Nagi Luna. The demon resided inside a Quiet Box in the lower extremity of the Living Mirage dungeon, below the great ziggurat."

"What's a ziggurat?" Seth interrupted.

"A huge old temple, a step pyramid."

"Step pyramid?"

"We're in one now. A terraced pyramid. Picture a pyramid that recedes a little at each new level." The Sphinx pantomimed the shape of a stairway.

"Got it. Sorry, go on." Seth reconsidered the room. Beneath the soft hangings and mellow lamplight, the walls were made of stone.

"The Quiet Box of Nagi Luna was kept in the bottommost cell of the dungeon, a room accessible only through a hatch in the ceiling. Only the chief jailer and the head caretaker had a key that could open it. Months after learning the location of Nagi Luna, I received the task of punishing an elderly slave, a man called Funi. I clearly remembered Funi from my childhood, a crass character who mistreated the weak.

"One of my regular duties included supervising the slaves assigned to labor in the vast dungeon below the great ziggurat. In the course of those duties, I had forged a relationship with the chief jailer. He was a hard, private man, but somewhat predictable. I told him I wanted to give Funi a scare by taking him down to the catacombs where the undead were housed. The key to those catacombs was the same key to the cell where Nagi Luna languished.

"The jailer should not have let that key out of his possession. But nobody could imagine me as a threat. In addition, the jailer disliked me, and he assumed I would receive as big a scare as Funi. He knew that it was possible I would have an accident that could cost me my life or my job, and it amused him to imagine the uppity slave getting humbled. I knew the jailer would not voluntarily go anywhere near the undead prisoners. As I had expected, he lent the key to his assistant and ordered him to admit me to the catacombs.

"I brought Funi, and, with the assistant at my heels, we descended into the forbidden levels of the dungeon. When we reached the door to the catacombs, I caught the assistant in a stranglehold until he passed out. Then I made Funi help me drag the man deeper into the dungeon, until we reached the lowest cell. I opened the hatch, lowered the assistant jailer into the room with a rope, ordered Funi to climb down, then climbed down myself.

"Who did you put into the Quiet Box?" Seth asked breathlessly.

"The assistant," the Sphinx said, his voice becoming

quieter. "It was the greatest risk I have ever taken, even though a ring of constraint surrounded the Quiet Box."

"Ring of constraint?"

"A magical prison at least as strong as the Quiet Box. It essentially marked the domain at Living Mirage where Nagi Luna was permitted to roam, a steel circle on the floor with a thirty-foot diameter."

"Kind of like the area at Fablehaven where Graulas lives," Seth said. "Or where Kurisock lived."

"Much like that," the Sphinx agreed. "But considerably stronger. I made Funi put the assistant jailer into the Quiet Box while I watched from outside the ring. It took some effort, because he was old and frail, but Funi managed to place the unconscious body inside and close the door. The box turned slowly. The instant the Quiet Box opened, Funi turned and attacked me."

"Mind control?" Seth asked.

"Very good. Yes, before stepping out of the box, Nagi Luna took instant control, and Funi came at me like a man possessed. Although I was ready for such an eventuality, having retained the assistant jailer's truncheon, the vehemence of the assault nearly overwhelmed me. Funi was smaller, thinner, and older, but he fought with inhuman strength and ferocity, heedless of injuries. By the time I had quelled the attack, he was unrecognizable."

"Gross. Then Nagi Luna came out? What did the demon look like?"

"Harmless. A tiny, toothless, hairless, hunched old woman, no taller than my waist. Her purple skin drooped in moist creases. A white chain led from a manacle on her ankle to a stone tablet inscribed with arcane characters, which she dragged along behind her. As her lips mumbled nonsense, she spoke to me with her mind, trying to lure me inside her ring of constraint. When I refused, she spoke in her actual voice, commending me for resisting her invitations. I explained my situation. She explained her hatred of her confinement. We decided to help one another."

"What did she do?" Seth wondered.

"First she asked to see the key to her cell. After I held it up, she crouched, scraped together dirt from the floor, and transformed it into an exact replica of the metal key. She set the key at the edge of the ring of constraint, and I removed it with the truncheon. Then she produced a needle, spat on it, and gave it to me in similar fashion. She explained that whoever I pricked with the needle would die the following morning. We had a long conversation. In the end, I climbed out of the cell, hauled the remains of Funi up, and returned to the jailer."

"You left the assistant in the Quiet Box?"

"Correct."

"How did you explain that?"

"With a fabrication. I said the assistant jailer had joined us in the catacombs, that Funi had shoved him against a cell door, and that the wraith inside had devoured him, body and soul. I explained that I had killed Funi as punishment. I had the needle ready, but there was no need to use it that day. The chief jailer wanted to cover up his injudicious sharing of the key, so we made some alterations to my version. We decided that Funi had attacked and killed the assistant, hurling him into a deep shaft, so I killed Funi, and that became our story. But I digress into obscure details."

"I don't mind," Seth said. "It's interesting."

"I used my counterfeit key to visit Nagi Luna from time to time. She taught me what I needed to know to overthrow the preserve. And she made me into a shadow charmer."

"You're a shadow charmer?" Seth exclaimed, rising to his feet.

"There are not many of us, Seth. In fact, you and I may be the only ones who remain. My abilities as a shadow charmer, and the alliances Nagi Luna helped me forge, proved essential to my taking over Living Mirage and eventually uncovering the Font of Immortality."

"I'm evil," Seth said numbly, plopping back down on his cushion.

"We're not evil," the Sphinx said.

"Demons are evil."

"Yes."

"Where is Nagi Luna now?"

"Still down in her cell, hemmed in by her ring of constraint. I can't release her yet."

"Why not? Aren't you the guy who wants to release all the demons in Zzyzx?"

The Sphinx sat down beside Seth, his wrists resting on his knees. "Here is what I have learned, Seth. Here is what life has taught me. The best way to avoid being the slave is to be the master."

"Okay . . . that kind of makes sense."

"You believe that I hate you. That I hate your grandfather."

"Seems that way."

The Sphinx furrowed his brow. "You must understand: I do not view Stan Sorenson as my enemy. He is merely my opponent. I like your grandfather. He is a good man. And he is an obstacle. I have to best him. We do not see eye to eye on the opening of Zzyzx."

"You keep getting people killed," Seth said, sick of his enemy's pretenses.

The Sphinx sighed. "I go out of my way to avoid killing those I respect, including you and your sister. But yes, this is a bloody business, and sometimes people have to perish. To be honest, in the end, if killing Stan is what it takes to open the demon prison, I will kill him. He would do no less in order to stop me. This is not because I hate Stan, but because he stands in opposition to my cause, and I believe in my cause."

"Releasing demons? You admitted they were evil!"

"Zzyzx cannot stand forever," the Sphinx explained. "That which has a beginning must have an end. When wizards try to make anything permanent, it becomes brittle, fallible. Invincibility is impossible. Attempts to attain it always fail. So instead of creating an impregnable prison, they created a nearly impregnable prison. That made the prison as strong as possible, but it also means that eventually somebody will open it. I have spent my long life preparing myself to be the right person to release the demons on strict conditions, and rule over them. Heed my words: With or without me, eventually that prison will be opened. Where others would fail and unleash ruin upon the world, I will succeed. In time, I will use the power of my position to reinstate balance in the world so magical creatures won't have to cower in preserves and prisons. By virtue of my position, I will use evil to bring about good."

Seth lowered his face into his hands. "Let's pretend everything you're saying is straight from the heart. How can we possibly trust that you're the right person to open the prison? Wouldn't it be safer to try to make sure it never gets opened?"

"Only in the short term," the Sphinx said. "Eventually, even if it is well beyond our lifetimes, the prison will be opened. It is inevitable. And if the prison does not open on my terms, it may well mean the end of the world."

"But you can't live forever," Seth said. "Even with a Font of Immortality. It breaks your rule that everything with a beginning has to end. If you release the demons, what happens when you die?"

The Sphinx grinned. "Good thinking. I will live as long as I can. But if a full week ever passes without a sip from the Font, I turn to dust. No matter what precautions I take, given infinite time, that will eventually happen. Which is why I must set up a system, a kingdom, a new order, that can persist long after I am gone. It is all part of my plan."

"Grandpa Sorenson doesn't trust that you're the guy to do this. And neither do I."

"Which is your right, and his," the Sphinx acknowledged. "I would not trust anyone besides myself to do it, so I can understand how others might not trust me. This is why I don't hate your grandfather, why I simply view us as being in a state of disagreement."

Seth balled his hands into fists. "You get that he's right, don't you? You get that you're overestimating yourself, that the demons will trick you or overpower you? If you succeed in opening Zzyzx, you're going to destroy the whole world!"

"I have confronted these doubts and overcome them," the Sphinx said calmly. "I have prepared. I am certain. I have been a slave, Seth. As master, I will release the prisoners and create a world without slaves."

Seth shifted on his cushion. There was something disconcerting about the Sphinx's expression, an overzealousness. "Here's what I don't get: if you open Zzyzx, when do you get to negotiate with the demons? Once they're out, where's your bargaining power?"

"A reasonable concern. There is a time before the prison fully opens when communication will be possible. If they will not agree to my terms, I will close the gate. I am fully prepared to walk away, and they will know this, and so they will compromise."

Seth studied the Sphinx suspiciously. "How much of this is Nagi Yoma's idea?"

"Nagi Luna. It was her aim from the start, from our first conversation, to eventually free herself and the other demons."

Seth sat up straight. "Then how do you know she didn't trick you into feeling so confident about it? How do you know she didn't brainwash you?"

"I have done all the research myself," the Sphinx said. "It has taken many lifetimes, but I am sure of my course."

Seth shook his head. "How much do you rely on her?"

"Very little, although more lately than in a long while. She is the key to my use of the Oculus."

"You have her look for you?"

"No. Your sister inspired my method. When Kendra gazed into the Oculus, she found a mentor who helped her awaken from the seeing trance. She claimed it was Ruth, but I believe she was fibbing. At any rate, Nagi Luna is extremely clairvoyant, although within her prison her sight is limited. When I need to awaken from gazing, I look to her, and she brings me back."

"You trust her that much?"

"Insofar as our goals remain aligned."

Seth filled his cheeks with air and blew out slowly. "So this is what the guy who will destroy the world looks like."

"After I succeed, Seth, I will be generous to those who doubted or opposed me. When I speak of a world without prisoners, that includes you and your family."

"Sounds like a good policy. Why not start right now?"

The Sphinx smiled enigmatically. "Some ends are worth enduring any means. For now, hostages, deceit, treachery, and even killing are tools to accomplishing the greatest good for the greatest number. For the moment, Seth, you are in the way. A devoted member of my opposition. Hopefully, after I establish my new order, we can work together. You can help me manage my empire, and I can help you achieve your potential."

"We can sit around and talk to zombies," Seth mumbled.

"Don't undervalue your gifts," the Sphinx chastised. "Mr. Lich is probably the most powerful viviblix in the world. He can create and control undead servants. But he cannot hear their thoughts, their voices."

"I guess I should count my blessings," Seth said dryly.

"You have not yet understood the advantage of that gift. The undead feel utterly alone. Their communication with each other is limited or nonexistent. They have no communication with the living. But with you and me, they can sense our minds, as we can sense theirs. We become a link to life, and they would do anything to preserve that link."

"I've had strange creatures offer to serve me," Seth admitted.

"Creatures who would serve no other man would serve us. Commanding them must be done with caution, because any of the undead can turn on you. But whereas, at his best, Mr. Lich can issue simple commands to zombies, we can employ wraiths, shades, phantoms. Demons and their kind will pause to hear our counsel. The undead can supply us with knowledge. And that is only one aspect of our powers."

The Sphinx raised a hand and the room plunged into darkness. The temperature began to drop. The floor tilted and spun. And then the lights came back on, and the dizzy spell passed.

"You did that?" Seth asked.

"So can you, and much more, with instruction and practice."

Seth pressed his lips together. "I'm not going to pretend

that isn't cool." He paused, hands folded in his lap. "All right, you've convinced me. I want to join your cause. I don't agree with what you're doing, but I don't see how anyone will stop you. If you're going to open that prison, for the sake of the world, you'll need all the help you can get."

The Sphinx licked his lips. "We both know you're lying. I appreciate the attempt."

"No, I'm serious. What, you think I would betray you? How? I'm barely a teenager!"

"I have told you some of my secrets," the Sphinx said. "I asked for an honest conversation. That works two ways. I take it your grandfather has not yet discovered how to use the Chronometer?"

"They're working on it," Seth said vaguely. He didn't want to reveal anything the Sphinx might find useful. "I never promised to give you secrets."

"And the Chronometer remains at Fablehaven, correct?"

"No comment."

"To think, both of the final artifacts are together in one place. Even if they are moved, both are now in play, and I have the Oculus." The Sphinx studied Seth intently. "Tell me about Vanessa."

Seth closed his eyes. "Just because you're willing to spill your guts doesn't mean I have to join in. I'm not like you. I don't have this figured out like a chess game. I don't know what information is crucial to the outcome of all this, so I'm keeping my mouth shut."

After several seconds ticked past without a response, Seth opened his eyes. The Sphinx held his gaze with grim intensity. "Very well. You have already told me enough. More than you know. This interview is at an end. We'll speak again after Zzyzx is open."

"Wait," Seth said. "Seriously, I have one more question. Where are my parents?"

The Sphinx's expression softened slightly. "They are safe, Seth."

"Why did you take them?"

"I wanted to ensure that you and your grandparents would not go into deep hiding with the Chronometer and the key to the Translocator. I wanted to motivate you to remain active and involved. And, in the event of an emergency, I wanted bargaining power. That is all I can share at the moment. You are now my prisoner. Behave, and you will not be mistreated." The Sphinx crossed the room and opened the door. "Mirav! Please escort the prisoner to his cell."

The wizard with the braided beard and golden skin came into view. The man looked wrong, not quite human. Seth tried to keep his face from revealing the apprehension he felt. He stood up, feeling tense. Was there any point in trying to fight? What if he rushed to the desk and flipped it over? Might the Oculus shatter? He doubted it. Was it worth a try? He didn't want to slink meekly to his cell like a trained poodle.

"You want to come quietly," the Sphinx assured him, as if reading his thoughts. "Any resistance you could offer would be embarrassingly futile. I do not always use Mirav to escort prisoners to the dungeon. Consider it a compliment."

Hating himself for not resisting more, Seth obeyed.

CHAPTER SEVEN

Doomsday Capsule

The fairies kept the grounds around the main house of Fablehaven in bloom all year, but as Kendra wandered the perimeter of the yard, the blossoms seemed extra bright, as if springtime lent added splendor even to enchanted gardens. The flowers looked bigger—tulips the size of coffee mugs, roses the size of soup bowls, and sunflowers larger than dinner plates. The colors seemed more vibrant, the grass shockingly green, the flower petals vividly ablaze with electric shades. Fresh perfumes mingled in the air, light and dewy. Gleaming fairies fluttered everywhere, basking in the vernal glory.

Kendra felt certain her perceptions of the garden's enhanced beauty had nothing to do with her mood. It had been three days since the group had returned from Obsidian

Waste, and they still had no leads on finding Seth. Warren, Coulter, and Tanu had teleported around the globe using the Translocator, Vanessa had reached out to her best contacts, and Grandpa had tried every method he knew to hail the Sphinx, but none of their efforts had yielded results. The Translocator could take them places they had been before, but it was becoming increasingly obvious that in order to find Seth and her parents, they would have to venture someplace none of them had ever visited.

As Kendra drank in the springtime splendor, she imagined her parents, tied up in a sunless cell, confused, hungry, and ill. While a fairy used sparkling magic to enliven the highlights of a delicate orchid, she pictured her brother, imprisoned in a bottle like some genie in a lamp. Or worse, out of the bottle, dying from a severe chest wound. How was it possible that she was roaming a glorious garden while the rest of her family suffered?

"Hey, grouchy face, is your brother around?"

The voice came from the woods. Looking up, Kendra saw Newel and Doren standing beyond the border of the lawn.

"Seth can't play," she informed them. "He was captured by the Society of the Evening Star."

"The Society?" Doren said. "Oh, no!"

Newel let loose a roaring laugh, slapping his furry thigh and elbowing Doren. "Don't be daft, Doren, it's April Fool's Day. Good one, Kendra!"

Kendra paused. The satyr was right, today was the first of April. Without Seth around to fill the sugar bowl with salt or stick bouillon cubes in the showerheads, she had completely forgotten. "No, I'm really not—" Kendra began, but Newel raised a hand to silence her.

"Before you go on," Newel chuckled, "I have very important news. Doren and I were strolling past the hill where the Forgotten Chapel used to be, and it has split wide open. Muriel emerged astride Bahumat, and we tailed them as they proceeded to wake up Olloch the Glutton. They're all heading this way! Quick, fetch Stan!" Newel grimaced with mirth, shoulders quivering with suppressed laughter.

Doren rapped Newel with the back of his hand. "I think she means it. Look at her face."

Newel put one hand on his hip and held out the other toward Kendra. "It's called acting, dunderhead. She's staying in character to try to sell the joke. Which is bad form, by the way, Kendra. Once you've been exposed, you're better off starting fresh with a different ploy later. Don't try another on me, of course. Hard to kid a kidder."

"But she was pacing the yard looking all sour before we hailed her," Doren reminded his friend.

"Acting!" Newel shouted. "She must have seen us coming. She was laying groundwork for the joke. She'd do well on a soap opera. She's plenty pretty. Kendra, give me a glare like I threatened your boyfriend. Why are you rolling your eyes? Give it a shot! Pretend I'm a casting director."

"How did it happen?" Doren asked, ignoring Newel.

"A lectoblix shot him with an arrow," Kendra said, her patience thinning. "Seth took a gaseous potion and ended up trapped in a bottle by an evil wizard. We don't know where they took him."

Newel winked. "A good lie is all about the details. Quirky details can help sell a tall tale, but there's a line where quirky crosses over to ridiculous."

"Newel would know," Doren said. "He lives on the ridiculous side."

Newel turned to face the other satyr, raising his fists like a boxer, hips swaying. "And you, my friend, have just crossed over to the dangerous side."

Doren didn't take the bait. "This isn't an April Fool's prank. She lost her parents to the Society, and now her brother, the very best human we know."

"I wish it were a prank," Kendra said.

Newel dropped out of his fighting stance, uncertainty flickering across his features. Then his knowing look returned. He pointed at both Kendra and Doren. "I get it, you're both in on it, going for the hard sell. As soon as I soften up and buy it, you have a good laugh. Not bad— somewhat lacking in subtlety, but not bad."

"Here comes Warren," Doren said, gesturing toward the house. "He can settle the issue."

"Can he, now?" Newel said knowingly. "And I suppose he isn't in on the sham as well? You're a devious lot, I'll grant you that much. Next you'll march in a notary with signed documents."

Kendra could hardly believe she was having this conver-sation. She waved at Warren. He looked much better shaved and with his hair cut short. "Any news?"

"Nothing new on Seth yet," he answered. "But your grandparents want to see us. These two hitting you up for batteries?"

"They're reminding me that it's April Fool's Day," Kendra said.

"Good day, Warren," Newel called. "You're just in time. The shadow plague has started up again! The centaurs are on a rampage!"

"What do Grandma and Grandpa want?" Kendra asked.

"They weren't specific," Warren said. "Something in the attic."

"Sorry, guys," Kendra said to the satyrs. "I have to go."

"Let us know if there's anything we can do," Doren said.

Kendra gave a nod. "I will."

"Are you guys filming this?" Newel chortled, eying the surrounding foliage suspiciously. "If so, you're wasting resources. I am not going to fall for it."

"See you later," Kendra called, joining Warren.

"Hey, Kendra," Newel said. "Before you go, could you lend me a handkerchief? Or some other personal token? I want to get a rise out of Verl, pretend you've fallen for him."

"Oh, that could be good," Doren snickered.

"Don't you dare," Kendra warned over her shoulder. "That isn't funny, it's cruel."

"No crueler than pretending my best friend was kidnapped!" Newel countered.

"What am I?" Doren asked in a mildly offended undertone.

"You're more like family," Newel said. "I meant my best human friend. Yours too."

"He really was kidnapped," Doren asserted. "She's not joking."

"Twenty percent of me believes you," Newel replied. "I'll ask again tomorrow."

"Does this have anything to do with Seth?" Kendra asked Warren as they walked toward the house. "If they heard something bad, I'd rather hear it now."

"This isn't bad news," Warren said. "I think they need your help deciphering an inscription."

Kendra followed Warren into the house, up to her grandparents' room, and over to the bathroom closet. The heavy door to the secret side of the attic looked like it belonged on a bank vault. Warren spun the combination wheel, hauled the door open, and then pulled it shut behind them as Kendra started up the stairs.

Grandma, Grandpa, Coulter, and Tanu awaited Kendra. A workbench stretched along one wall; wooden cabinets lined the others. Unusual objects littered the room—tribal masks, a mannequin, a huge globe, a timeworn phonograph, a birdcage. Trunks, boxes, and other containers were stacked everywhere, accessible by narrow aisles.

Grandpa smiled at Kendra. They all smiled at her. They had all been smiling a lot since Obsidian Waste. Kendra appreciated their intentions, but the attention felt too much like pity, and only served to emphasize her loss.

"How are you today?" Grandpa asked.

"Is this an April Fool's joke?" Kendra asked. "If so, don't

bother, Newel and Doren already reminded me about the holiday."

"We're not here to jest," Grandpa said. He glanced at Grandma. "However, it is peculiar that we'll be opening the capsule on April first."

"What capsule?" Kendra wondered.

"There are a few secret doors and compartments in this attic," Grandma explained. "One hidden door leads to a turret. Patton left a time capsule inside the turret, a secret passed down by previous caretakers."

"Does it have a timer?" Kendra asked. "If it's set to open today, maybe it *is* a joke!" Prank or not, she would love to hear from Patton. It was strange to have met him, to have worked alongside him to save Fablehaven, and to know he had passed away long before she was born.

"Patton didn't call it a time capsule," Grandpa said. "He called it his Doomsday Capsule. As caretaker of Fablehaven, I was left with instructions not to open it unless the end of the world appeared imminent."

"You never mentioned this before," Kendra said.

"It was meant to remain a secret," Grandpa replied. "But I think the time has come to crack it open. Your grandmother agrees. We've run out of leads. We desperately need whatever help we can get."

"What about Vanessa?" Kendra said. "She's still keeping secrets."

Grandpa sighed. "She has hinted that her big secret might be revealed soon. She insists it's in our best interest for her to keep silent about it a little longer."

Grandma scowled. "Whatever reasons she gives, I say she's holding out until she gets her freedom, trying to preserve leverage—assuming there was ever a real secret to begin with."

"She has steadily provided us with useful info," Tanu said.

"Useful but not vital," Coulter huffed.

Grandma took Kendra by the hand. "There are some characters on the outside of the canister that we cannot read. We believe they offer further instructions that may help us finalize our decision."

"You need me to translate," Kendra said. "Where is it?"

Coulter led them over to one of the many tall cabinets lining the walls, pulled open the doors, then stepped inside and opened the false back. "We normally keep this cabinet full of junk," Coulter said. "We recently cleaned it out, since we've been weighing whether to open the capsule."

Kendra passed through the cabinet and down three steps into the cramped, round room of the turret. A steel cylinder rested in the center of the floor, almost as tall as her waist. To Kendra, the writing engraved in the sides of the container looked like English.

Coulter, Grandpa, and Grandma filed into the room, filling the available space around the capsule. Warren and Tanu watched from the cabinet. "Can you read it?" Grandpa asked.

"*Open only in a time of utmost crisis pertaining to Zzyzx and the end of the world*," Kendra read. "*The key to the capsule must be turned by one who shares my bloodline, and an umite candle must be burning in the room, or else the capsule will destroy itself.*"

"Anything else?" Grandpa asked.

"That's all I see," Kendra replied, inspecting the capsule from all directions. She ran a hand along the curved metal surface, feeling the grooves of the writing below her fingers.

"We didn't know about the candle," Grandma said. "That could have ended badly."

"Nor did we know that whoever turned the key had to be related to Patton," Grandpa said.

"Pays to read the instructions," Coulter grumbled.

"You have the key?" Kendra asked.

Grandpa held up a long, black key with elaborate teeth. "Your grandmother will have to do the honors."

"Or Warren," Grandma added.

"I'll fetch a candle," Coulter offered, exiting the turret.

"Where's Dale?" Kendra asked.

"Keeping the preserve running," Grandpa said.

Grandma folded her arms. "What would we do without Dale and Hugo?"

"What do you think we'll find inside?" Warren wondered.

Grandpa shrugged. "Information, probably. A weapon, perhaps. Nothing would surprise me. Knowing Patton, it might hold the final artifact."

"Are you worried about whether the Sphinx will watch us open it?" Kendra asked.

"This attic is well shielded from prying eyes," Grandpa said. "Of course, nothing can totally divert the Oculus. If the

Sphinx happens to be looking hard at us right now, he'll see what we're doing. But we can't let his possession of the Oculus paralyze us. He can't possibly spy on us all the time."

"Even if he could watch us constantly, we would need to remain active," Grandma said. "As long as the Sphinx holds the Oculus, we'll need to be as discreet as possible, and hope for a little luck."

Coulter returned with the candle already lit. "Do I just hold it?"

"Stand near the capsule," Grandpa instructed. "Ruth, would you do the honors?"

Grandma inserted the key in the top of the capsule and turned it. After hearing a click, Grandpa helped her unscrew the top of the canister. Grandma set aside the round lid. Kendra held her breath as Grandpa reached inside.

Grandpa withdrew a rolled scroll from the capsule. He peered inside, then felt around for a moment. "Looks like this is all he included." He unrolled the scroll and raised his eyebrows. "We'll need Kendra to read it."

Kendra took the scroll from Grandpa. Just like the characters on the container, the message looked written in English. At the bottom was a labeled diagram of the Chronometer.

> *Greetings, current guardians of Fablehaven.*
>
> *You may not be reading this very long after I visited you. From the evidence I beheld in your time, the Society was in the final stages of their plot to open Zzyzx. I have more information that might be of use*

to you, but did not want to risk writing all of it down. I will share what I can. I have learned how you can use the Chronometer to send up to five people back in time. The Chronometer will only transport mortals, and will only take you as far back as the day of your birth. To clarify, the device will transport any group of mortals as far back as the day the eldest member of the group was born. Traveling back in time, you will not be able to bring any items with you.

Below you will find instructions on how to set the Chronometer to take you to September 24, 1940, at half past eight in the evening. If Coulter remains with you, he should be just old enough to reach that day. If not, you will have to find a willing participant of the appropriate age.

Should you elect to use the Chronometer to visit my time, do so in the attic. I look forward to perhaps seeing some of you again. I would be thrilled to discover that my advice is not required.

Yours always,
Patton Burgess

Kendra read the message to the others.

"If we ever needed advice from Patton, now would be the time," Grandpa said.

"You five go," Tanu suggested. "Patton will want to see his relatives. I can hold down the fort."

Coulter looked overjoyed. He had Kendra translate the Chronometer instructions and decipher the labels to the diagram. He kept smiling and nodding. Having spent months trying to figure out how to operate the Chronometer, he seemed to absorb the meaning of the instructions without hesitation, although to Kendra the directions sounded extremely confusing.

"The Chronometer is here in the attic," he said once Kendra had finished. "No time like the present, right?"

"I see no advantage in waiting," Grandpa agreed.

They passed out of the turret into the main part of the attic. Coulter retrieved the Chronometer, a golden orb etched with engravings and bristling with little buttons and dials. Coulter fiddled with the switches and dials, asking Kendra to retranslate a few instructions from the scroll. Applying the settings did not take him long.

"This should do it," Coulter announced. "Everyone who is coming needs to place a hand on the device. And I need to slide this lever, then flip this little switch."

Kendra felt her heart racing. This was all so sudden. Was she really about to see Patton again? Might he have advice that could help them out of their bleak predicament?

The others had placed their hands on the orb. Kendra added hers.

"Here goes nothing," Coulter said. He placed a finger on what looked like an embossed symbol, slid it along a groove, then toggled a tiny switch.

Kendra felt like somebody kicked her in the stomach. She doubled over, the air violently escaping her lungs. She looked up, unable to inhale. Coulter, Grandma, and Grandpa had collapsed to the attic floor, hands around their midsections. Warren crouched with his hands on his knees. She averted her eyes, because none of them had clothes on.

Coulter made a miserable croaking sound. Warren started coughing. Kendra let out a little burp, then found she could inhale again. Her temporary panic melted as her lungs continued to function.

A robe was gently placed over her shoulders from behind. Kendra turned. It was Patton, his hair white and wispy, his head liver-spotted, a roguish smile enlivening his withered face. A faint scar that Kendra did not recall slanted diagonally across his forehead. He seemed slimmer and shorter, his frail shoulders stooped.

"Just breathe, Kendra," he said, his voice familiar though less hearty. He gingerly patted her back.

Taking shuffling steps, Patton distributed soft white robes to the others. Warren helped Grandma and Grandpa arise. Coulter beamed as he accepted his robe. "Nice to see you again, Patton."

Patton nodded and shuffled over to a rocking chair. Kendra did not remember the chair, but was surprised by how similar the attic looked, still cluttered, although some of the items and containers looked less timeworn. Using the armrests to brace himself, Patton sat down carefully.

"Well, I know I'll be dead within a year," Patton said.

"What do you mean?" Warren replied.

Patton rubbed his nose with the back of a finger. "I update the scroll every year, pushing the date when you can visit closer to your time. Since you finally made an appearance, it means I've made my final update. I had hoped to reach one hundred. Nice round number. I suppose I can't complain. I'm glad I lived long enough for Coulter to bring you here. One less headache for you to worry about."

"A few more years and I could have brought us," Stan said.

"I didn't explain everything in the note," Patton said. He pulled out a pocket watch and a monocle, using the lens to check the time. Satisfied, he put them away. "We only have half an hour together. You'll notice that the Chronometer did not travel with you. In half an hour, if you stand in approximately the same spot where you entered this time, you will be drawn home to your proper era. If not, you'll become trapped in my time. If we need to talk longer, you'll have to come again. Coulter, that would mean giving knob C-5 three-quarters of a turn."

"Gotcha," Coulter said.

Patton leaned forward. "Let's get right into the serious stuff. Does the Sphinx have the Oculus?"

"Yes," Grandma said.

Patton scowled. "I knew I shouldn't have left it in Brazil. I debated about going after it, but I was already past my prime . . . well, water under the bridge. At least in this time, the Sphinx does not have it yet, so we can converse with confidence. Does he have the Translocator?"

"We have it," Grandpa said.

Patton brightened. "You retrieved the key from Wyrmroost?"

"Wasn't easy," Warren said. "We have Kendra to thank more than anyone."

Patton regarded her warmly. "Well done, my dear. The Sphinx still has the Sands of Sanctity?"

"Right," Grandpa said.

"What about the Font of Immortality?"

"We're not sure," Grandma said. "We haven't been able to find the fifth secret preserve."

Patton scowled thoughtfully. "I never found the fifth preserve either. Or the Font of Immortality. You know, then. The Sphinx surely has been around a long time."

"You think he already has it?" Grandpa asked.

"Can't say for certain," Patton admitted. "That would be my best guess. I'm downright talented at finding things. But the fifth preserve and the Font of Immortality completely eluded me. In all my days, I never heard a believable rumor about either."

"The Sphinx captured Seth," Kendra said, trying to keep her voice steady. "Members of the Society grabbed him at Obsidian Waste. They also kidnapped my parents."

Patton sat up straighter. "Did your parents finally learn the truth about Fablehaven?"

"No," Grandpa said. "Apparently the Sphinx abducted them regardless."

Patton narrowed his eyes, fingers gripping the armrests of the rocker. "I would trade just about anything to have words with that maniac. I don't reckon wishing will do me much good. Do you know whether he has learned to use the Oculus effectively?"

"Yes," Kendra said. "At Wyrmroost, the Fairy Queen confirmed that she saw him using it. He needs assistance.

Someone else helps him free his mind from the grip of the Oculus when he wants to quit."

Patton gave a quick nod. He lowered his head, hands folded on his lap. For a moment, Kendra thought he had dozed off. Then he looked up. "If the Sphinx can use the Oculus, your plight is indeed dire. He will be very difficult to stop. The hardest part about opening Zzyzx is acquiring the necessary knowledge and locating the appropriate items. Mastery of the Oculus will lead the Sphinx to success."

"What can we do?" Grandpa asked.

"Guard the artifacts you have," Patton said. "There may be times when it would be prudent to use the Translocator, but not many. The Sphinx is patient and intelligent. If he anticipates a location you might visit using the Translocator, and manages to steal it, all is lost."

"Is there a better place to hide the artifacts than at Fablehaven?" Grandma asked.

"I don't like the idea of having two artifacts in the same place," Patton said. "But I like the idea of transporting them even less, especially since the Sphinx has the Oculus. The closest thing to a wizard I might trust is Agad at Wyrmroost. He understands the stakes. Some of you could get there instantaneously with the Translocator. Almost no location is as well defended as a dragon sanctuary. If all else fails, Wyrmroost might serve as a last resort. You'll have to apply your best judgment."

Patton studied their faces before going on. "In the event you lose all of the artifacts, you may need to know where to find Zzyzx. Are you aware of the exact location?"

Nobody responded at first, then Grandpa shook his head.

"Zzyzx is located in the Atlantic, on an island southwest of Bermuda. Shoreless Isle." He recited the latitude and longitude. "As you might imagine, it is nearly impossible to find. Hence the name. Massive distracter spells drive away attention, along with other defenses. Ships have a history of vanishing in that vicinity."

"The Bermuda Triangle," Coulter murmured.

"Have you been there?" Grandpa asked.

One corner of Patton's mouth quirked up into a lopsided smile. "Why would I go and do such a foolish thing? Unless there were a shrine to the Fairy Queen on that island, and I had decided to visit as many of her shrines as I could reach."

"Can you tell us anything useful about Shoreless Isle?" Grandma asked.

"Beautiful place," Patton said. "They should have chosen an uglier spot for the prison. Maybe the island was uglier back when the wizards founded it. What I saw was a waste of paradise. The island is bigger than you might guess. Zzyzx lies inside the central mountain, a huge dome of rock. The shrine is on the east side. Reaching the island can be problematic."

"How did you get there?" Kendra asked.

Patton regarded her with a twinkle in his eye. "A ghost ship. But that was a one-way trip, fraught with peril. I rode home on a giant bird."

"What kind of bird?" Coulter wondered.

"Something similar to a thunderbird," Patton said.

"Temperamental to ride, not highly recommended. I brought it with me on the ship."

"What else can you tell us?" Grandpa pursued.

"If the Sphinx has the Oculus, depending on his mastery and knowledge, sooner or later he'll be going after the Eternals. Have you caught wind of them yet?"

"The Eternals?" Warren asked.

"Five of them," Patton said. "One associated with each artifact. They are part of the lock that holds Zzyzx closed, debatably the final obstacle. They were once regular humans, but the wizards who founded Zzyzx made them virtually immortal. The artifacts can't open the prison until all five are dead."

"I've never heard of this," Grandpa said. "Not even a whisper."

"Me neither," Warren added, a hint of jealousy in his voice.

"Took some digging," Patton said. "Serious digging. It is one of the secrets I never wrote about. Anonymity has historically been one of their best forms of protection."

"Does anybody know where they are?" Warren asked.

"Not likely. I tried to find them. I believe I met one in Japan, years ago. A man, middle-aged, always had an exotic bird with him. He could be anywhere now. But if the Sphinx searches for them with the Oculus, anonymity will no longer shield them. They must get behind sturdy walls."

"Is there any way we could find them without the Oculus?" Grandpa asked.

Patton shrugged. "It would be tough. The trail is cold.

You might pay the Singing Sisters a visit. Or take a stroll in the Hall of Whispers. Or try to get the Totem Wall to speak."

"The Singing Sisters?" Warren asked Grandpa dubiously. "The Hall of Whispers? Are those real?"

"Shady magic," Grandpa said. "The kind that usually comes with a steep price."

"I'm not claiming to have convenient solutions," Patton said. "You asked, I'm telling what I might try."

"How can they be killed?" Kendra asked. "You said the Eternals are nearly immortal."

"They don't age, they don't get sick, and they don't die easily," Patton said. "From what I understand, they are somehow connected to the magic of the artifacts, especially the Sands of Sanctity and the Font of Immortality. To slay them would require dragon breath, phoenix fire, a mortal wound from a unicorn horn, or some weapon of similar potency."

"Anything else to tell us about Zzyxz?" Grandpa probed.

Patton frowned. "Not right now. Come again if things get worse, and I might share a few truly desperate ideas. Hopefully we'll never have that conversation. Before you go, let's talk strategy. You have worked every angle to find Seth and his parents?"

"Everything," Grandpa said.

"Everything short of the Singing Sisters," Grandma added.

Patton shook his head. "Stan is right, the Sisters are dangerous and unreliable, a last resort. You have found no leads?"

"None," Warren said. "It's like they've fallen off the planet."

Patton scratched his cheek. "Ever get that secret out of Vanessa?"

Grandpa flushed slightly. "Not yet. She claims she'll reveal it soon."

"Until you have that secret, you have not exhausted all leads. Get her to talk. Kendra, have you spoken with the Fairy Queen lately?"

"The shrine at Fablehaven is ruined," Kendra reminded him.

"Might be time to find a shrine to visit," Patton said. "Even if it takes some effort. The Fairy Queen is a mortal enemy of the Demon King. This threat will get her attention. You are in need of allies. Who knows how she might be able to help? You mentioned she could perceive the Sphinx using the Oculus?"

"Right."

"That doesn't seem right," Patton said. "Even a powerful outside entity would normally have to be invited to connect to the Oculus. Using the Oculus would make the Sphinx vulnerable to powerful minds, but he would have to let down his guard for them to really gain access."

"I might have invited her when I used it," Kendra replied.

"You used the Oculus?" Patton exclaimed.

Kendra explained about getting kidnapped by Torina and being forced by the Sphinx to use the Oculus. She told how the Fairy Queen helped her break free from the hold the Oculus had on her mind.

"I see," Patton said. "Through you, as you willingly

reached out to her, the Fairy Queen found a link to the Oculus. If she has preserved that link, she may have new information about the Sphinx. You must follow up on this."

"We will," Grandpa promised.

Patton nodded. "Let's discuss priorities. As I mentioned before, your first priority is to retain the artifacts you have. The Society cannot succeed without them. Second priority is to get the Oculus away from the Sphinx. Until that happens, destruction will constantly loom. My hunch is that if you find Seth and his folks, you'll find the Sphinx and the Oculus. Use the possible leads we discussed, especially Vanessa. You may want to task some of the Knights with locating and protecting the Eternals. No small assignment, but worth the effort. Since stealth no longer provides the protection that the Eternals expect, you must alert them that an enemy has the Oculus and try to direct them to safety."

Grandpa rubbed his mouth and chin, lost in thought. Raising his eyebrows, he locked eyes with Patton. "I wish we had a man like you in our time."

"You've done great work, Stan," Patton said tenderly. "You have surrounded yourself with more quality people than I've ever encountered." He switched his gaze to Warren. "I would not be surprised to learn that many of you surpass my accomplishments. Let's face it, Stan, you are dealing with greater challenges than I ever had to weather." He gave a perturbed smile. "Most of my hardships were self-inflicted."

"Speaking of quality people," Kendra said, "is Lena around?"

"Lena is fantastic," Patton replied. "More radiant than ever. How she can fake affection for an old bag of bones like me defies explanation. She is downstairs as we speak, with strict instructions not to disturb me. She has learned to indulge my senile whims."

"We can't see her?" Kendra asked.

"No, because time travel is rare, dangerous magic," Patton said. "I have no reason to believe Lena ever laid eyes on you until the day you first came to Fablehaven. In theory, I don't believe a time machine can really alter the past. I believe that anyone who tries will just discover that whatever actions they take were already part of the past. But I'm also not sure the wizards who designed the Chronometer fully understood the powers they were tampering with. I doubt paradoxes could be created, but I'm not eager to take any risks. As much as you all would enjoy seeing Lena, she knows none of you yet. She will, in due time. Perhaps it would be best to leave it that way."

"If the Chronometer can't change the past, what's the point?" Kendra asked.

"We know the Chronometer can affect the present," Patton said. "Your present. Like when I visited you during the shadow plague. And like I am trying to do now, by sharing information. The Chronometer can also make use of the past to affect the future. For those who wish to access Zzyzx, it is a necessary tool."

"You're starting to break my brain," Warren said.

Patton chuckled. "Mine too." His face took on a wistful expression, his eyes moistening. "I wish I could have done more, somehow averted all of this. I spent my life trying. I honestly gave it my best."

"You did more than we could have hoped or imagined," Grandma said, laying a hand on his.

Patton winked at Grandpa. "You married a good one."

"Course I did. She's a Burgess."

Patton pulled out his pocket watch and his monocle. "Time has a way of slipping by. You should have a few minutes still, but it might not hurt for you to move toward your original positions. You remember the latitude and longitude of Zzyzx?"

Coulter repeated the coordinates. Kendra went and stood where she had been when she had crossed into this time period. The others did likewise.

"Anything else you want to review?" Patton asked.

"We may visit you again," Coulter said. "If we want to come again, I'd give knob C-5 a three-quarter turn."

"You got it," Patton said. "I should have had Lena make refreshments. I did that for the first few years I waited for you. I guess I started to believe I might really make it to a hundred."

"It was good to see you," Kendra said, trying to keep from choking up. Her emotions were a mess lately.

Patton rocked himself to his feet, came over, and gave her a hug. "That brother of yours will be fine. Don't be surprised if he shows up on your doorstep with the Oculus in his hip pocket."

Kendra hugged Patton back. He felt bony.

"Not too tight," Patton laughed. "I've gotten brittle. I'm

glad I got to see all of you again. Sorry it took the end of the world to provoke a reunion."

Warren and Coulter chuckled bitterly.

"Do something nice to Lena for me," Kendra said.

"I'll think of something special," Patton promised, stepping away.

"Thanks, Patton," Grandma said.

"My pleasure, Ruth."

They stood in silence. Kendra hated the tension, waiting for Patton to be gone. Part of her wanted to stay, to somehow hide from all the heartache waiting back in the present.

"Seth is going to be mad he missed this," Kendra said.

"Send him my very best," Patton said.

"I think he—"

All the breath went out of Kendra. The robe was gone, her clothes were back, and she was doubled over, trying to breathe. Once again, Grandpa, Grandma, and Coulter had fallen down.

"Are you all right?" Tanu asked. "What happened? Did it work?"

Warren got his breath back first. "We spoke with Patton for half an hour."

Tanu shook his head, helping Grandma up. "You guys didn't even flicker. Coulter flipped the switch, and you all crumpled like somebody slugged you in the gut. Was it productive?"

Grandpa gave a curt nod. "We have work to do."

CHAPTER EIGHT

Bracken

S eth sat on the rickety cot in his gloomy cell, watching faint torchlight flicker through the barred peephole in the door. On the far side of the stone enclosure, water dripped with the regularity of a metronome, forming a puddle that slowly seeped into the cracks of the floor, perhaps to drip down to a deeper cell. Beside him sat the latest meal, a brick of tough meat, a wedge of moldy cheese, and a greasy mound of purple mush. He had gnawed at the scabby meat, unsure what he was eating. The stinky cheese had a sharp flavor. He had failed to convince himself that the mold was supposed to be there. The purple pulp had not tasted bad, almost sweet, but the texture was unbearably stringy, as if long, coarse hairs had been a deliberate ingredient.

This was not the dungeon at Fablehaven. This was the real thing. They had marched him along dank passageways, down crumbling stairs, and through a series of guarded iron doors. The smells were earthy and old, pungent odors of rot, mildew, filth, and stone. The wooden door to his cell was five or six inches thick. Meals arrived on woven mats through a slot at the bottom. A new meal did not come unless he made the previous mat accessible.

From time to time the echoes of distant screams interrupted the monotonous dripping. Less often, a deep voice would croak sad songs about the sea. Occasionally he would hear footfalls and see a torch pass by his peephole, the direct firelight seeming very bright.

Seth had not seen another person since he was locked in his cell. He longed for a conversation. How many days had it been? Several meals. He wondered how many times a day he received food.

Climbing off the cot, Seth crawled across the rough stone floor to the flimsy pan of water near the door. Without a cup, he had to drink on all fours like a dog. The pan was so broad that lifting it meant he would almost certainly spill, and he only got a refill with each meal. He had discovered that puckering his lips and sucking worked best. The water tasted flat and gritty, but it was wet and, together with whatever food he could stomach, would hopefully keep him alive.

Seth visited the small hole in the front left corner of his cell. The smell rising from it made him want to retch. After a brief hesitation, he decided to relieve himself later.

Alone with his thoughts, he returned to his cot. He

wondered if the Sphinx had truly convinced himself that opening Zzyzx was a good thing. It had to be an excuse he gave to others. Nobody could really believe something so insane.

Seth wondered about his family. His parents might be imprisoned in this same dungeon. Judging by the many halls he had passed and the several levels he had descended on his way to his cell, the dungeon was immense. He tried to imagine the deepest cell, where Nagi Luna still lurked.

He tried not to imagine getting rescued. What were the chances that Kendra or Grandpa or anyone would ever find this place? People had been looking for the fifth preserve for hundreds of years. A rescue was highly unlikely. He would do better simply to hope that the others would not be captured as well.

How long would this cell be his home? It really might be for the rest of his life. Then again, if the Sphinx opened Zzyzx, the rest of his life might not be very long.

He picked up the brick of meat, nibbling at a salty corner. Would he learn to tolerate this food? Look forward to it?

Seth wondered if he could convince the Sphinx he wanted to be his apprentice. If he served him, eventually he might find a chance to escape, maybe even swipe an artifact or two. It would be worth a try, although the Sphinx seemed too clever to be conned that way.

The creepiness of his surroundings was his only defense against boredom. Over time, as worry and fear distracted him less, his boredom grew. Yes, the cell was miserable, but he was getting used to it. He wondered if eventually he might actually die of boredom.

A rumble from behind startled him. This was new! From the back wall of his cell came the low, heavy grating of stone grinding against stone. A portion of the wall slid open, and a mellow white light shed soft luminance into the room. A young man stepped through the opening, holding the white light in his hand.

Seth picked up the brick of meat, the closest thing he had to a weapon. The intruder froze in the doorway, a hand held up defensively. "Please, don't assault me with that meat amalgam," the stranger said. "It would surely cause an infection."

Seth lowered the mystery meat. The young man wore ragged clothing. Improvised moccasins covered his dirty feet. The white light in his hand was clearly magical, some kind of glowing stone. The illumination gave his grime-streaked skin a pearly sheen. Tall and lean, he had silver-white hair down to his shoulders and a handsome, open face.

"Who are you?" Seth asked.

"A fellow prisoner," the young man answered. Seth estimated he was around eighteen. "May I come in?"

Seth considered the stranger. What kind of prison had secret passages that allowed inmates to visit each other? This guy had to be an enemy sent by the Sphinx to squeeze information out of him. Still, at the moment, Seth would be willing to talk with just about anyone. Anything to relieve the loneliness. "Sure, I guess."

Turning, the young man retrieved a small three-legged

stool from the corridor. He brought it into the cell and sat down. "Welcome to Living Mirage."

"Am I really supposed to believe you're another prisoner?" Seth said.

"I don't blame you for doubting," the young man said. "I have a similar concern about you. I'm Bracken."

"Seth."

"They stashed you down deep. That means either you're dangerous and they're done with you for the foreseeable future, or else you're a spy."

Seth fidgeted with the brick of meat, turning it in his hands. "And how am I supposed to know you're not a spy? What sort of prison has secret passages between cells?"

"This dungeon is old," Bracken said. "It has been expanded and rebuilt so many times that nobody knows all the half-buried corridors and sealed-up chambers. Centuries of tunneling prisoners have added to the abandoned shafts and forgotten cavities. I helped excavate some of these passages personally, but most existed long before I came here. Nothing leads out, mind you. Not even close. But we've connected many of the deep rooms."

"Nobody has caught on?" Seth said incredulously.

"We're not fooling anybody," Bracken replied. "If we're really obvious about our activities, they seal up some of our excavations and administer punishments, but later we chip our way through again. Our tunneling is relatively harmless, and it keeps us occupied, so if we stay quiet about it, our captors mostly look the other way."

"You talk like you've been here a long time," Seth said. "How old are you? Like seventeen?"

Bracken gave a wry smile. "I'm a tad older than I look. You would weep for me if you knew how long I'd been here."

"So when are you going to start investigating my secrets?"

"Still don't trust me? At least you're not stupid."

"Don't give me too much credit. I'm here, aren't I?"

Bracken studied him shrewdly. "Yes, you are here. And you are clearly a shadow charmer, which makes you such an obvious spy that I wonder why the Sphinx would bother."

"How can you tell I'm a shadow charmer?"

"I can tell more than that," Bracken said, moving the stool closer to the cot. "Mind if I conduct a little test?"

"Depends on the test."

"Nothing painful," Bracken assured him. He tossed the glowing rock onto the cot. "Just take my hands." He held them out, palms up.

"This is weird," Seth said, keeping his hands in his lap.

"I just want to ask you a couple of questions. If I ask something you don't like, go ahead and punch me in the face."

Seth set his meat brick aside and took Bracken's hands. Bracken gazed into his eyes. "Tell me your name."

"Seth Sorenson."

"Tell me a lie."

"The food here is terrific."

Bracken grinned. "Tell me something true."

"Centaurs are jerks."

The grin broadened. "Are you a friend of the Society of the Evening Star?"

"Nope. I'm the opposite. A Knight of the Dawn."

Bracken released his hands and scooted the stool back. "I believe you. In fact, I know some things about you. You have friends here."

"My parents?" Seth said hopefully.

"Your parents might be here, but not in a cell we can access."

"So what are you, a human lie detector?"

"I'm good at reading people. I wanted a close look at you. They've sent down stingbulbs before. Now I know you're not a stingbulb, or a changeling. More important, your friends might have been mistaken about your allegiances. Hard to believe a shadow charmer could be on our side. But now I'm convinced."

Seth folded his arms. "I'm glad I passed your test. Do you have something I can hang on my fridge?"

"I left my stickers in my cell."

Seth rubbed his hands together. "It still doesn't prove whether I should trust you."

"Agreed. I'd question your judgment if you did. For starters, why don't I take you to visit one of your friends?"

"Sure. Do I have lots of friends here?"

"A few." Bracken grabbed the glowing stone.

"Where did you get the light?"

"I made it." He led the way to the gap in the back wall of the cell. "I'm pretty close to powerless these days, but I still know a trick or two."

"What are you, a wizard?"

Bracken chuckled, closing the gap in the wall. Then he started along a narrow corridor. "A wizard stuck in cells like these would be a sorry wizard indeed. I'll tell you more about myself once you know you can trust me. Let's go quiet for a stretch. The walls are thin up here, and a guard is posted nearby."

Bracken closed his fist around the stone so that only a little light escaped. Seth followed him up an incline, treading lightly. The floor felt slick.

The narrow passage eventually tapered to an end. "This part is a little tricky," Bracken whispered. He put the glowing stone in a pocket and pointed up. A tiny globe of light the size of a ping-pong ball leapt from his fingertip, hovering upward. The ball rose into a hole in the ceiling, which turned out to be a tall shaft.

Bracing himself against opposite sides of the passage, Bracken spidered up until his feet were well above Seth's reach. The sure swiftness of his movements made the maneuver look simple. "There are rungs in the shaft," he stage-whispered down, pulling himself into the vertical crawl space.

Seth chimneyed up toward the hole in the ceiling, bracing himself and then scooting upward in increments. The walls were spaced too wide to make the ascent comfortable. Arms quivering, he gained only a few inches with each movement. When he reached the mouth of the shaft, he braced with his legs and quickly reached up to a rung, then followed Bracken upward. At the top of the damp shaft,

Bracken raised a wooden hatch. Seth followed Bracken out into the new passageway. The top of the hatch was disguised to match the floor after Bracken carefully closed it.

Bracken recalled the floating ball of light, snuffed it out, and took the stone from his pocket. Seth followed him down the passage, through a hidden door, and along another passage until Bracken stopped.

"Here we are," Bracken said, his voice less hushed. "This character keeps his cell locked from the inside." Bracken used the rock to tap against the wall—four slow beats, two quick ones, a pause, and then three quick strikes. A moment later, an arrangement of stone blocks pulled inward, leaving a space large enough to crawl through. Bracken entered first.

"You bring him?" inquired a familiar voice as Seth crawled through. "There he is!"

Seth looked up in surprise. "Maddox?"

The burly fairy trader beamed down at him. "I'm sorry you're here, Seth, but it's good to see you." Offering a meaty hand, Maddox hauled Seth to his feet.

"You're alive!" Seth said. "The last time I saw you, it was an impostor."

"A stingbulb," Maddox said gravely. "I hoped you all would manage to see through the charade."

"Not at first," Seth said. "It did a good job. But we figured it out before any real harm was done."

"The stingbulbs come from here, you know," Maddox said. "The last known stingbulb trees are on this preserve. I'll be honest, if I ever managed to bust out of this dungeon, I'd be tempted to stick around and explore. This is an ancient preserve. Who knows what supposedly extinct species I might encounter!"

Seth scrunched his brow. "How can I be sure you're not a stingbulb?"

"Good boy!" Maddox bellowed. He glanced over to Bracken. "This one thinks like a survivor."

"My sentiments exactly," Bracken agreed.

"Bracken can tell," Maddox told Seth. "But I'll wager you don't trust him yet, either."

"I want to trust you guys," Seth said. "I just don't want to be an idiot."

"A stingbulb would have my memories," Maddox said. "There isn't much I can do to prove my authenticity. For now, it'll have to suffice that we won't press you for secrets."

"I'm not sure I have any in the first place," Seth said. "The Society already knows everything I do."

"Now, don't think like that," Maddox said. "You never know what odd detail might offer the Society an advantage. Keep those lips sealed."

"All right."

Bracken picked up Maddox's empty meal mat. "Cleaned your plate again, I see!"

Maddox gave an awkward smile. "I'll be honest, I've eaten worse."

"Worse?" Bracken laughed. "Where? Was it uncooked and decomposing? Seth, this guy wolfs down everything they serve here. He's put on a good twenty pounds since they brought him in."

Maddox reddened, smoothing his hands over the ratty

skins covering his belly. "I'm not saying I would choose this grub over home-cooked lasagna. I was starving when they brought me here."

"I can't even bite the meat," Seth said.

"It's like a salt lick," Bracken said. He jerked a thumb at Maddox. "This guy chews it up."

"You can find fracture points if you probe for weaknesses," Maddox said.

"What about the hairy paste?" Seth asked.

"I'm not sure those are hairs," Bracken said solemnly. "Might be veins."

"Laugh it up," Maddox grumbled, waving both arms at them. "Mind my words. Best to store up a little extra when given the chance. You can't be sure when you'll see your next meal."

"I know when I will see it and what it will be," Bracken challenged. "I've been here a long time. Twice a day, like clockwork, we're served a compressed blend of dog, rat, and hobgoblin."

Seth laughed and gagged at the same time. "I hope you're kidding."

"Torch coming," Bracken said, crouching and covering the light from his stone. He stealthily backed toward the gap through which he had entered, and Seth did the same.

"It's not mealtime," Maddox whispered.

The faint light through the barred peephole shifted as footsteps approached. A torch swept past the small, rectangular opening, and the heavy footsteps continued along the corridor.

Bracken remained tense and quiet until the footfalls passed out of hearing. "They almost never come into the cells," Bracken said. "But with my luck, I try to be ready for exceptions."

"Say, Seth," Maddox began awkwardly, "I know I shouldn't press you, but have you had any non-secretive word from my brother, Dougan?"

Seth's face fell. Maddox didn't know about his brother.

"Uh-oh," Maddox said. "Bad news?"

"The worst news," Seth said.

Maddox's mouth twisted and trembled. He gave a quick nod. "Right. Did he go bravely?"

Seth nodded vigorously. "It was at Wyrmroost. A dragon got him. Dougan helped to save Kendra and the mission."

Maddox drew a ragged breath. "What dragon?" Despite his grief, he was already thinking about vengeance.

"Navarog. But then Navarog got killed while in human form."

"Navarog is dead?" Bracken exclaimed. Glancing at Maddox, he managed to restrain his obvious excitement.

Maddox plopped down on his creaky cot. He seemed to have suddenly aged. "We play a deadly game. Something like this was bound to happen."

Seth thought about Vincent. He worried about Kendra and his grandparents. Spending time in a dungeon might be safer than what they would face in the coming days and weeks. He had to find a way to help them.

"What are our chances of busting out of here?" Seth asked.

"Bleak," Bracken replied. "I've been trying for hundreds of years."

"Hundreds of years?" Seth exclaimed.

"Some of us never get used to the food," Bracken lamented.

"We can move around down here," Maddox said, "but we've found no way to the upper levels, nothing close to a way out."

"I've searched long and hard," Bracken assured them. "Tunneled plenty as well."

"What about beating up a guard?" Seth asked.

"Even though our doors rarely open, I've tried a few times," Bracken said. "There are too many checkpoints on the way up, too many locked doors. And once the alarm sounds, the Sphinx musters too many powerful servants."

"What if we mobilized a bunch of prisoners?" Seth asked. "A big group effort?"

Bracken shrugged. "That probably has the most potential. It has been decades since I've orchestrated a big, riot-style breakout. Both of my prior attempts ended badly. The way up just has too many bottlenecks. One time they kept a magically reinforced iron door locked until we surrendered due to starvation. Another time we were subdued with noxious gas. As you might imagine, our captors are not kind to us after such attempts."

"You can make stuff glow and read people," Seth said. "Do you have other magic that could help?"

"Not much," Bracken said. "I could help run communications. And I have some skill at healing. My powers are relatively weak. What about you, shadow charmer? You might have more useful skills than mine. Can you shade walk? Quench fire? Disengage locks?"

"I can shade walk," Seth said. "Some shadow charmers can open locks?"

"With their minds," Bracken said. "You'd have to be a real pro, though. Several of the main doors are secured with spells."

"Is he really a shadow charmer?" Maddox asked.

"Undoubtedly," Bracken replied.

"I don't know much about it," Seth confessed. "It happened by accident." He explained about the grove with the nail and the revenant, and then how Graulas had sealed his powers.

"I've heard of Graulas," Bracken said. "Never crossed paths with him."

"He's right on the brink of death," Seth said. "Because his death is so near, he doesn't care about allegiances anymore, so he sometimes helps me out of boredom."

Bracken looked pensive. "Graulas may have been of service in the past, but don't let yourself get comfortable around him. Demons are evil to the center. It is their nature to take advantage of others. Good never comes from them."

"You sound like Grandpa Sorenson," Seth said. "Graulas doesn't pretend to be good, but he really did help me."

"He's just saying to be careful," Maddox said kindly. "Bracken has some experience with demons. They may offer help when they see a selfish advantage in it, but they're always scheming. In the end, bad trees tend to give bad fruit."

"Well, he might be dead by now anyhow," Seth said. "He was pretty far gone last time I saw him. Tell me your story, Bracken. What powers did you used to have? Why do you know so much about demons?"

"We'll get into it some other time," Bracken said, averting his gaze.

"No need for modesty!" Maddox bellowed. "Tell the boy what you are!"

Bracken stared at the ceiling, as if wishing he were elsewhere. "He doesn't even know whether he should trust us yet. This is premature."

"I won't be spilling sensitive information anytime soon," Seth said, "but I think I trust you enough. My instincts say we're on the same side. By the way, you said you could show me other friends."

"I barely met your friend Mara," Bracken said. "She doesn't know me any better than you do. And I know how to reach your friend Berrigan as well. It's kind of a tricky climb. He's injured. I've been helping him heal."

"You have to tell me who you are," Seth insisted. "I'm really curious. You can't dangle stuff like this and then take it back. You're torturing me!"

"I'm a unicorn," Bracken said.

Seth laughed. "No, seriously."

"He's serious," Maddox said.

Seth considered Bracken skeptically. "Don't unicorns

usually have horns? And, you know, hooves and fur and all that?"

"This is my human form," Bracken said.

"Some unicorns have avatars," Maddox said. "You know, like dragons."

"Can you switch back into your horse shape?" Seth asked. "My sister would be so jealous."

"I can't," Bracken said. "I surrendered my horn, and thus am stuck as a human."

"Don't unicorns have three horns?" Seth asked.

"Right," Bracken replied, appraising Seth as if impressed by his knowledge. "Sort of like humans with baby teeth. We have one horn as a child, then shed it for a larger horn in adolescence, and in turn shed that for our permanent adult horn."

"But yours wasn't permanent," Seth said.

"It should have been, but I surrendered it."

"Why? Did somebody defeat you or something?"

Bracken's eyes flashed dangerously. "I would never have surrendered my third horn to an enemy!"

"Steady," Maddox soothed.

Bracken calmed, his shoulders sagging slightly. "I gave up my third horn on purpose. I surrendered it to the wizards who made the demon prison."

"Wait," Seth said, forming a connection. "So the Font of Immortality is made from your horn?"

Bracken glanced at Maddox. "Not bad."

"He's a bright kid."

Bracken returned his focus to Seth. "That is correct.

How did you know the Font is fashioned from a unicorn horn?"

"The Sphinx showed it to me," Seth replied.

"He what?" Maddox spluttered.

Bracken looked skeptical. "Voluntarily?"

"Yeah, after he healed me with the Sands of Sanctity."

"He used the Sands on you!" Maddox shouted.

"A little less enthusiasm," Bracken scolded. "We don't need to tell the whole dungeon. I get it now. It makes sense. You're a shadow charmer, so the Sphinx hopes to groom you. He wants to win your trust."

Maddox balled his hands into fists. "I wouldn't trust that skunk to scrub my toilet."

"Me neither," Seth promised. "But we were talking about Bracken."

Bracken cleared his throat self-consciously. "Right. Well, after I gave up my third horn, I could no longer revert to my true shape. I still had my second horn, which I could use as a weapon, and which helped me retain many of my powers. But in the end, the Sphinx trapped me, forcibly took my remaining horn, and cast me into this dungeon."

"You must really hate the demons to have given up your permanent horn to those wizards," Seth observed.

"My kind exist in opposition to demonkind. We are protectors and creators. They are exploiters and destroyers. Where we would bring light, they bring darkness. In addition, I had . . . personal motivations. The wizards convinced me that my horn was essential to make the demon prison as impervious as possible. They were not lying to me, but you can imagine my distress that my sacrifice might soon be all for naught."

Seth pounded a fist into his palm. "Which brings us back to my goal. We have to find a way out of here. You may have tried in the past, but it has never been more urgent."

Bracken and Maddox exchanged a glance.

"What do you think?" Maddox asked.

Bracken sighed. "All right. Since the world is about to end, why not give an impossible jailbreak one last try?"

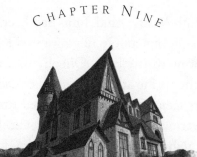

CHAPTER NINE

Assignments

Kendra knew the sun was up, but she hid under her covers nonetheless. She missed Lena. She missed Patton. She missed her parents. She missed her brother. And she was hesitant to confront a new day.

The conversation with Patton the day before had galvanized her grandparents. Grandpa had been contacting Knights of the Dawn, Grandma had been researching in the attic, and everybody was busy making plans.

Kendra had a role to play in those plans. She had put on a brave face, enthusiastically accepting her responsibilities, but they made her nervous. What if she failed? There was so much riding on her participation.

This morning after breakfast, Kendra, Warren, and Tanu would use the Translocator to visit a Scottish preserve called

Stony Vale. Both Warren and Tanu had been there before. As Patton had prompted, Grandpa wanted Kendra to have a conversation with the Fairy Queen, and, thanks to the Translocator, the shrine at Stony Vale was readily accessible.

The others seemed to take for granted that Kendra and the Fairy Queen were Best Friends Forever. In reality, the Fairy Queen might very well strike Kendra down for treading on hallowed ground if she found the intrusion unwarranted. Of course, Kendra had been cautioned to trust her instincts on the matter of whether a visit was appropriate, and she felt confident the Fairy Queen would agree that this was a genuine crisis. As an archenemy of the Demon King, the Fairy Queen would be anxious to keep Zzyzx intact.

But just because Kendra might have access to the Fairy Queen, that did not mean she could cajole the mysterious personage to provide actual help, as her family expected. Kendra worried that she would let everyone down, including herself.

Her second assignment made Kendra even more nervous than the first. The others had determined that she had the closest relationship with Vanessa, and hoped that Kendra's genuine grief over the abduction of Seth and her parents might finally persuade the narcoblix to divulge her big secret. Again, Kendra understood the reasoning behind the task, but it was too much pressure! She was supposed to speak with Vanessa after returning from Stony Vale.

Within the close space beneath her covers, Kendra reluctantly accepted that procrastinating these challenges would not make them go away. If she tried, she might fail, but hiding in her bed would certainly not bring her family home. Still, if she stole a few more minutes of sleep, her problems might temporarily melt from her mind . . .

No! She kicked off her covers and rolled out of bed. The mere act of standing up helped her feel a little more ready to tackle her upcoming obligations.

After showering and getting dressed, Kendra found Warren and Tanu enjoying a pancake breakfast. Spatula in hand, Grandpa hovered over the griddle, and he encouraged Kendra to have a seat.

"Nobody came and got me?" Kendra asked, taking a couple of pancakes from the stack and placing them on her plate.

"We heard you in the shower," Grandpa explained. "I have some hot ones coming if you want to wait a second."

Kendra tested the spongy surface with her finger. "These are still warm." She poured maple syrup over them.

Coulter strolled into the room. "Uh-oh, Stan is fixing pancakes! Must be time for another death-defying mission!"

"Way to ease the tension," Warren muttered.

"Can I have some?" Coulter asked. "Or are they only for the condemned?"

"No pessimistic geezers allowed," Warren declared.

Chuckling quietly, Coulter took a seat at the table. Tanu tried to pass him some pancakes, but Coulter held up a dismissive hand. "I'll wait for those hot ones."

Kendra cut into her pancakes with the side of her fork, speared two pieces, put them in her mouth, and relished the sweet, fluffy perfection. "Good job, Grandpa," she said. "These are delicious."

Warren smeared homemade jam on a pancake and took a bite. "You'll like Stony Vale, Kendra."

"It's very picturesque," Tanu agreed.

"The caretaker is one of our most reliable Knights," Coulter said, accepting fresh pancakes from Grandpa's spatula.

"He won't know we're coming," Warren clarified. "This is a secret operation, in and out, quick and quiet. We'll teleport away at the first sign of trouble."

"If you have to travel," Coulter said, "I can't think of a better way than the Translocator."

"I know, I'm getting spoiled," Warren replied. "I'm not sure I'll be able to do airports ever again."

Tanu nodded. "No customs, no checked bags, no tiny seats for ten hours at a time."

"What are you griping about?" Warren said. "You hibernate like a grizzly on those long flights."

"I sleep to escape the torture," Tanu maintained.

"There's my problem," Warren said, tossing up his hands. "I haven't learned to sleep during torture."

Tanu grinned. "Helps if you're a potion master."

Kendra ate quietly, content to enjoy the banter. Hearing the others joke and tease helped the day feel more normal. To make the meal last, she tried to pace herself, but after a few pancakes and some orange juice, she could stomach no more.

Warren checked his wristwatch. "It's five hours later in Scotland. We might as well get rolling."

"You ready, Kendra?" Tanu asked.

Kendra took a deep breath. Part of her wished they had opted to spring this assignment on her at the last minute. Planning it yesterday had given her too much time to worry. She tried to shake off her insecurities. "Ready as I'm going to get."

"Relax, Kendra," Grandpa said. "If anything feels wrong, just have them bring you right back here. That's the beauty of instantaneous travel."

"We'll watch your back," Warren assured her, buckling a sword around his waist. "You'll do great."

Grandpa opened a drawer and took out the Translocator.

"You're keeping it in a kitchen drawer?" Kendra asked.

Grandpa shrugged. "Just for this morning. I wanted it handy."

"He wants you in Scotland before the post-pancake euphoria wears off," Coulter said, wiping his chin with a napkin.

"Something like that," Grandpa admitted, passing the Translocator to Tanu.

"Are we going straight to the shrine?" Kendra asked.

"We've both seen the shrine at Stony Vale," Warren said. "We've never actually approached it, or we wouldn't be here. But I've stood as near as any sane mortal would dare. We'll start you out very close."

"I haven't been quite as close as Warren," Tanu said. "Probably because I'm a little saner."

"Considerable thought went into this," Grandpa assured Kendra. "We selected Stony Vale because the preserve is secure and you'll have extremely convenient access to the shrine."

Kendra stood beside Warren. "Let's get this over with."

Tanu gripped one side of the Translocator, Kendra the other, and Warren twisted the middle. Kendra felt like she was folding in on herself. When the vertigo passed, she was standing in tall grass surrounded by knobby, gray trees. She realized she had been braced for her breath to get knocked out of her, but of course this was the Translocator, not the Chronometer.

Ahead through the trees, she beheld a large, glassy pond wrapped like a horseshoe around a narrow peninsula that gradually widened as it stretched farther from the shore. At the end of the peninsula were two rough, rectangular standing stones spanned by a third heavy stone. The formation instantly brought to mind pictures of Stonehenge.

Kendra heard the ring of steel as Warren drew his sword. Tanu clutched a crossbow in one hand, the Translocator in the other. It was past noon in Scotland, but the sun was still high, shining through a partly overcast sky. The still air felt cool but not cold. Beyond the pond and the surrounding trees, Kendra glimpsed low, rolling hills.

"Is the shrine on that peninsula?" Kendra asked softly.

Tanu gave a nod. "We can't venture out there with you, but we'll stand guard near the shore."

Flanked by Warren and Tanu, Kendra started forward. As she neared the peninsula, her companions hung back.

She felt generally peaceful about proceeding, and decided the absence of an identifiable warning meant the Fairy Queen would welcome her visit.

A pair of tall women stepped out from behind the trees, blocking her path. One had flowers braided into her auburn hair; the other had leafy vines twisted into her dark plaits. Their layered gowns reminded Kendra of springtime foliage shimmering with dew. Each woman held a heavy wooden staff.

"Where did you come from?" asked the woman with dark hair, her voice a resonant alto.

"You tread on sacred ground," warned the other.

Warren and Tanu hustled up beside Kendra. Tanu was a large man, but these women stood half a head taller.

The woman with dark hair arched an eyebrow. "Would you threaten us with weapons?"

From both sides and behind, other dryads emerged from the trees.

"We are friends," Kendra said. "I have urgent business with the Fairy Queen."

"This one has a queer aspect," whispered the dryad with the auburn hair.

"Indeed," the other dryad whispered back, "and she speaks our tongue."

"I speak many languages," Kendra said.

The dryads looked stricken. "Even our secret dialect?" asked the one with auburn hair.

Kendra stared up at them, hoping her eyes displayed

more confidence than she felt. "I am fairykind, a servant of the Fairy Queen. These are my companions."

The dryad with the dark hair narrowed her green eyes. After a moment, her posture became less threatening. "I apologize for our abrupt greeting. These are troubled times, and it has long been our task to protect this shrine. We've heard of you, but did not recognize you. We have never encountered a mortal quite like you. We now see that you belong among us."

"Thank you," Kendra said. "My friends can't come to the shrine with me."

The dryads stepped aside. "We will see to it that no harm befalls them," said the dryad with the auburn hair.

"I couldn't really follow the conversation," Warren whispered. "But good job."

"They won't bother you," Kendra told them. "I'll be back in a minute."

Tanu lowered his crossbow, Warren sheathed his sword, and the dryads assumed more relaxed stances. Kendra passed between the tall dryads and strolled out onto the peninsula. She sensed many eyes following her progress but did not look back.

Kendra studied the ground, looking for the tiny shrine, not wanting to miss it and be forced to double back. She found nothing until she reached the stacked megaliths at the end of the peninsula. Beneath the primitive structure, beside a burbling spring, rested a carved wooden bowl and a tiny fairy shaped from pink, speckled stone.

As Kendra knelt beside the spring, a sudden gust of wind

disturbed the still air, bringing rich smells of freshly turned earth, ripe fruit, damp bark, and a hint of the sea. The Fairy Queen spoke with the familiar voice that Kendra heard with her mind rather than her ears. *I am pleased you came.*

"The Society is getting nearer to opening Zzyzx," Kendra said quietly, not wanting the dryads to overhear her end of the conversation. "The Sphinx has kidnapped my parents and my brother. We're worried the Sphinx will use the Oculus to collect everything else he needs. Do you know what we should do? Can you help us?"

My connection to the Oculus has waned. The Sphinx and his mentor, a demon called Nagi Luna, became aware of my prying and shut me out. They possess firm minds. Now, only when they turn their gaze to the realm where I dwell can I glimpse their thoughts. Aware of this, they have refrained from directing their attention toward me. Yet I have felt how they covet the realm I protect, and I fear for all creatures of light.

"What have you learned since we last spoke?" Kendra asked. "Tell me about Nagi Luna."

Nagi Luna is the entity who helps the Sphinx wield the Oculus. Her heart and mind are black. Darkness overcame Kendra, as if she had been struck blind. With the darkness came deep, abiding despair. Her ability to see returned as quickly as it had departed. It was always an adjustment getting used to how the Fairy Queen communicated with words, images, and emotions. *Before their minds closed to me, I sensed certain aspects of the relationship between Nagi Luna and the Sphinx. She is confined somehow, her powers constrained. While guiding the Sphinx from her confinement, Nagi*

Luna has been using him to connect to the Oculus and expand her mental reach. Her communications were inscrutable to me, for she used the secret language of demons, but I am sure she conversed with others of her kind. With the aid of the Oculus, she may even have reached some of those fell entities inside of Zzyzx.

A feeling of wrath swept over Kendra, vengeful and furious. For a moment, she felt as though she could level the surrounding forest with a sweep of her hand, or split open the ground with a shout. After a moment, the outrage passed. Kendra struggled to remind herself that these emotions were not her own.

Both the Sphinx and Nagi Luna feel certain that victory is near, but their versions of victory are not aligned. Each seeks to use the other to different ends. The Sphinx has a tightly woven plan to release the demons of Zzyzx on his terms. I failed to uncover the particulars, but I feel certain that to some degree he means well, misguided as his intentions may be. But Nagi Luna has a scheme of her own, a vision of unbridled darkness and mayhem like the world has never known. The Sphinx is no fool, but I fear her cunning may be superior.

"Could you tell where they are?" Kendra asked.

It was unclear. Too much was unclear. But I have seen enough to believe the opening of Zzyzx is imminent. Whether it is the Sphinx or Nagi Luna who succeeds, we fail. The consequences will be cataclysmic.

"We have two of the artifacts," Kendra said.

Safeguard them, if you can. I will seek to lend aid. My feud with the demons is ancient and eternal.

"Raxtus told me they destroyed your husband."

Grief washed over Kendra, so deep and forlorn that she felt she would drown in it. When the sensation passed, she gasped for breath.

My struggle against the demons predates the downfall of my consort. Our enmity is fundamental to our natures. I will always oppose Gorgrog and his minions, as they will always oppose me. My first priority is to protect my realm and my followers. This includes defending your world. The connection my realm has to your world gives it life. If your world should fall, my realm would essentially become a prison, unattached to any living sphere. For both of our sakes, we must thwart the opening of Zzyzx.

"I'm willing to do anything to help," Kendra said. "My friends and family feel the same. What do you recommend?"

There came a pause. The world seemed utterly at rest, no wind, no sound. When communication resumed, the words came slowly.

Three of my astrids perished to protect you at Wyrmroost. For ages, they have clamored for the chance to redeem themselves for failing my consort. Perhaps that day has come at last. I will reestablish communication with them. Drink from the spring.

Kendra took the wooden bowl, dipped it in the water, and drank. Sunlight gleamed off the surface of the water, dazzling her. The clear liquid tasted thick as honey, light as bubbles, rich as cream, tart as berries, and fresh as dew. For a moment, Kendra felt conscious of the tremendous reservoir of magical energy inside of her. She felt like a thundercloud charged to release a blazing onslaught of lightning.

Then a breeze wafted over her, calming, soothing. A

profound emotion of comfort and well-being made her drowsy with serenity.

As you encounter my astrids in the world, touch them and command them to be restored. I abolished three of my shrines to grant you this power.

"Don't destroy your shrines!" Kendra cried.

The hour has come to unite and make sacrifices. We must oppose the release of the Demon King and his unsavory followers from their confinement. The fate of our worlds hangs in the balance. Go, Kendra. Be brave. Be wise.

With a final nudge of hope and peace, the presence of the Fairy Queen withdrew, and Kendra found herself alone, kneeling on soggy turf. Rising, she returned along the peninsula to where the dryads waited with her friends. The regal women regarded Kendra with solemn reverence.

"Any luck?" Warren asked, wary gaze shifting from dryad to dryad.

"She didn't know where the Sphinx has my family," Kendra said. "But she understands the danger if Zzyzx gets opened, and she wants to help." Kendra turned to the dryad with auburn hair. "Are there astrids on this preserve?"

The dryad stepped forward. "A few migrate through from time to time, but we have not seen one here for many years."

Kendra nodded and turned to Tanu. "Do we have some at Fablehaven?"

"Astrids go where they please," Tanu said. "They're odd creatures. I haven't seen any at Fablehaven since the shrine lost its power."

"We should go home," Kendra said. She waved to the

dryads. "Thanks for welcoming us. Good luck protecting the shrine."

The dryads gave slight bows in response.

Kendra, Warren, and Tanu laid hands on the Translocator, twisted it, and, after the folding sensation, they were back in the kitchen at Fablehaven. Grandma had joined Grandpa and Coulter.

"You're all right?" Grandma asked anxiously.

"No problems," Warren said.

Grandma looked relieved. "I'm sorry I missed seeing you off."

"How did it go?" Grandpa asked.

Kendra related her conversation with the Fairy Queen, including what she had learned about Nagi Luna, and her new mission to restore the astrids. The others listened intently until she finished.

"I've never heard of this Nagi Luna," Grandma said with a scowl. "I'll try to uncover what I can."

"It might be difficult," Grandpa said. "I'm sure she'll be ancient."

"Who would have guessed we would ever end up chasing astrids?" Warren said.

"I always knew they had some significance to the Fairy Queen," Grandpa said. "But until Kendra reported her conversations at Wyrmroost, I had no idea they were once her most prized soldiers."

"The Fairy Queen had a major grudge against them," Kendra said. "The fact that she is restoring them means she's really worried about the Sphinx succeeding."

"Can't you call the astrids telepathically?" Warren asked.

"I can hear their thoughts," Kendra replied, "but I'm not sure how close I need to be."

"How many astrids are we talking about?" Tanu asked.

"There are eighty-seven good ones left," Kendra said. "Six gave up on the Fairy Queen, and three died protecting me from Navarog."

Tanu whistled. "Eighty-seven, huh? It's a big world."

"There were twelve at Wyrmroost," Kendra said.

"When last you checked," Coulter said. "Astrids move around capriciously."

"I got a sense those twelve had been there for some time," Kendra insisted. "It might be worth transporting to the shrine at Wyrmroost. They seemed to stay near it."

Grandpa frowned. "Let's reserve outings to dragon sanctuaries for another day. Tanu and Warren can run the preliminary investigations for tracking the astrids."

Kendra took a steadying breath. "Then I had better go speak with Vanessa."

Warren gave her half a grin. "You know, you've earned a short break. Have a snack! An apple, maybe?"

Kendra shook her head. "I'm feeling good after talking with the Fairy Queen. I want to talk to Vanessa while I'm on a roll, before I psych myself out."

"I'll take her down," Grandma offered.

"I'll tag along," Coulter said.

"Very well," Grandpa agreed.

Kendra followed Grandma Sorenson down the stairs and waited while she unlocked the door to the dungeon.

Grandma rested a hand on her shoulder. "This will work best if we leave you alone with her."

Kendra nodded. If Grandma hadn't made that suggestion, she would have asked. Grandma got along with Vanessa worse than anyone.

"We'll be right outside the door," Coulter assured Kendra. "Call out if you need us."

"She'll behave," Grandma said. "Whether friend or foe, Vanessa doesn't want to resume her stay in the Quiet Box."

"I'll be fine," Kendra said, almost meaning it. She had not spoken with Vanessa alone for some time. At the moment, the prospect of social awkwardness daunted her more than anything.

Grandma led her to the nearby cell, inserted the key, and opened the door. Kendra entered. The door closed behind her.

Vanessa was on the floor doing complicated sit-ups, hands laced behind her head as she touched alternate elbows to the opposite knees, her legs bending and extending without ever quite touching the floor. "Be with you in a moment," Vanessa panted.

Her cell looked cozy. Thick carpeting covered the floor, shaded lamps shed gentle light, and impressionist paintings brightened the walls. Potted plants of various sizes served to further soften the atmosphere. Vanessa had a refrigerator, an exercise bike, a suede beanbag chair, and an impressive sound system. Grandma and Grandpa had clearly gone out of their way to make her comfortable.

Vanessa finished her exercises and rolled to her feet.

"Here for some calisthenics?" she asked. Even sweaty and dressed in boyish exercise clothes, she had an effortless, exotic beauty.

"Your room gets better every time I visit," Kendra said.

"As prisons go, it could be worse." Vanessa walked over and took a seat behind the desk by her bed. "You here to wrench my secret out of me?"

"Could it help me find my family?"

"Are we playing twenty questions? Yes, it could."

"What is the secret?" Kendra blurted desperately.

"Haven't you played twenty questions before?" Vanessa scolded gently. "You can't ask what the secret is, just questions about it."

"Is it bigger than a bread box?"

Vanessa laughed lightly. "Now you get the idea. Actually, yes it is."

"How big is a bread box?"

"That would be relevant. Picture a container for holding a few loaves."

"Animal, vegetable, or mineral?"

"Animal."

Kendra folded her arms. "Is your secret a person?"

Vanessa returned her gaze intently. "This game is over."

"It is! Why do you have to be so secretive about it?"

Vanessa leaned back in her chair. "Hard to say. Maybe because the Sphinx could be watching us right now, and if this secret gets out, we will have no chance of stopping him."

"Is it really that important?" Kendra asked, not daring to believe it.

"You'll know soon."

"How soon?"

"It would be dangerous to say." Vanessa leaned forward. "Kendra, I'm not trying to torture you. I'm not even trying to torture your grandparents, who I like a lot less. At first I held on to this secret because it mattered, and I knew it might provide leverage to get me out of here. But ever since the Sphinx recovered the Oculus, I have been so grateful that I kept my mouth shut. My silence just might save us all. My secret represents our last, best chance to stop the Sphinx and recover your family. That will have to suffice."

"We could use the Chronometer," Kendra said. "Talk to Patton about your secret in a time the Sphinx can't see."

"You've figured out how to use the Chronometer to journey back in time?" Vanessa exclaimed. "Good news! We may do just that when the right moment arrives. Until then, letting others know the secret merely provides opportunities for somebody to slip up. Believe me, I'm on your side. This is for the greater good."

Kendra sighed in frustration. "All you care about is getting out of here."

Vanessa's expression hardened. For a moment, Kendra thought she might lose her temper. Then the narcoblix relaxed, brushing back an errant strand of hair. A forced smile appeared.

"I understand your frustration and your distrust. In fact, you have reason to trust me far less than you do. But please realize, if all I cared about was getting out of here, I have missed literally dozens of opportunities. You think this cell could hold me when I can control Tanu in his sleep? Fortunately for you, I truly am on your side, and most of what I can do to help can be done from here as well as anywhere. That may not always be true. The current situation is dire. At some point, your grandparents should release me so I can provide more active assistance."

Kendra had no reply.

Vanessa stood up. "I have been patient this long. I can wait a while longer. So can you, believe it or not. Knowing the secret will hasten nothing." Vanessa raised her arms and stretched. "By the time I reveal all I know, I might even earn Ruth's trust."

"I'm not getting anything else out of you, am I?"

"Sorry, Kendra. Vanessa Santoro may not be perfect, but she knows how to keep a secret."

CHAPTER TEN

Nagi Luna

The coin flared bright enough to awaken Seth. Temporarily disoriented, wiping sleep from his eyes, he pawed for the source of the blinding light. As his fingers closed around the coin, the brilliance dimmed, and words sprang to mind.

There you are! I was just alerted that the Sphinx is descending into our section of the dungeon. All things considered, he's probably coming for you. Don't relax around him. Keep your guard up. I'll extinguish the coin.

"Thanks," Seth whispered, trying to push the answer mentally toward Bracken.

Don't mention it. And you don't have to concentrate so hard, just let your thoughts flow to me. We'll talk later.

The coin went dark, and the connection to Bracken's

mind dissolved. After the recent brightness, the cell seemed pitch-black. Seth smacked his lips, trying to get the sleepy taste out of his mouth. His eyes began to adjust. The coin remained in his hand. It had been a gift at the end of his previous meeting with Bracken. Not only did the coin normally serve as a light source, it also functioned like a magical walkie-talkie.

Seth still did not wholly trust the supposed unicorn, but deep down he would be shocked to learn that his new friend was a fraud. Bracken hadn't tried to ferret any information out of Seth, and, by all appearances, he had been busily planning an uprising with Maddox and others.

Seth absently rubbed his thumb against the foreign coin. It felt good in his hand, somewhat larger and thicker than a quarter. More like a half-dollar. Minted from silvery metal, the tarnished currency displayed a griffin framed by unfamiliar glyphs. With the Sphinx coming, he should hide the coin. Relying on touch as much as sight, Seth lifted his cot and set the coin under one of the legs.

What could the Sphinx want with him? Had he arranged some sort of prisoner exchange? Was that too much to hope? Did the Sphinx want to grill him for information? Torture him?

The sound of approaching footsteps increased his anxiety. Maybe the Sphinx had other business down here. Bracken could not know for certain that the Sphinx was coming for Seth.

A guttering torch appeared outside Seth's peephole. A

key rattled in the lock. The door opened. The Sphinx entered, surveying the room.

"Not the grandest accommodations," the Sphinx said.

"Great toilet, though," Seth responded.

"You are, after all, a prisoner," the Sphinx said. "Come with me. Somebody wishes to speak with you."

"I'm not feeling very chatty today," Seth said. "Rain check?"

"Not a good day for jokes," the Sphinx said. "Don't make this less pleasant than it has to be."

The Sphinx sounded serious. Deciding he would rather walk than get dragged to their destination, Seth followed the Sphinx out of the room. A pair of torchbearers accompanied them, large men dressed in leather armor studded with iron. Unless Seth was mistaken, the direction they were taking would lead them deeper into the dungeon.

"Where are we going?" Seth inquired.

"Nagi Luna wishes to meet you in person," the Sphinx said.

Seth slowed. "That sounds bad."

The Sphinx shrugged. "I see little value in the exercise, but she insisted."

"She's still in the same place?" Seth asked. "In the bottommost cell?"

"She has resided there a long time," the Sphinx said.

They reached a filthy iron door. One of the torchbearers thrust in a key. The hinges protested as it opened.

"Do you come down here much?" Seth asked.

"While at Living Mirage, I can speak with Nagi Luna mind to mind, so there is little need."

"Is she always in your head?"

"No more than I allow."

They descended a long staircase and passed down a hall, around a corner, and through a formidable iron door with three locks. After another flight of stairs, the corridor grew narrow and winding. They passed many tangled intersections, the floor sloping constantly downward. At last they reached a squalid chamber with a grate in the floor.

"Leave us," the Sphinx told the guards, accepting a torch from one of them. Both guards looked pale. One was shivering. Both men hurriedly retreated down the hallway out of sight.

"Is this the place?" Seth asked.

The Sphinx spoke with quiet gravity. "For your sake, be polite, and say no more than you must. You are about to address an ancient being of incomprehensible power. Although I have dealt with her for centuries, I never enter her presence lightly."

Seth nodded. Even without the warning, he already felt apprehensive. As the Sphinx unlocked the grate, Seth fought to suppress a queasy nervousness.

The Sphinx lifted the heavy grate and unrolled a rope ladder. He started down first, the torch in one hand. Seth struggled a little getting onto the ladder, but once he started moving, the descent was no problem. Dust fumed up from where his feet landed. The cool room smelled musty. Several sets of oxidized manacles dangled from the rough stone walls.

Seth's eyes were drawn to the Quiet Box. Although it looked older than the Quiet Box at Fablehaven, the knothole-riddled wood unvarnished and unornamented, the cabinet appeared solid. On the flagstone floor, a metal circle, half obscured by dust, created a perimeter around the Quiet Box.

"Where is she?" Seth whispered, eyes sweeping the room.

The Sphinx nodded toward the Quiet Box. A small, shriveled woman shuffled out from behind it, a woolen shawl draped over her hunched shoulders. She did not look quite human. Her blotchy skin was purple and maroon. Thin earlobes sagged almost to her shoulders. Gray claws tipped her gnarled hands, and her yellow eyes had a strangely slanted shape.

Nagi Luna tottered to the near edge of the circular boundary. Only then did she fix her fierce eyes on Seth. "What are you called, boy?" she croaked, her voice a hoarse whisper.

"Seth."

She sucked her withered lips against her gums, making an unpleasant, wet sound. "Do I frighten you?"

"Sort of."

She grinned, showing ragged, inflamed gums. Her eyes darted to the Sphinx. "We were right, of course. This one is most unusual."

She glared at Seth, nose wrinkled, lips twisted. *What*

business do you have as a shadow charmer? The venomous shout struck his mind with unnerving force.

"It was an accident," Seth said.

It was profane! It was lunacy! Seth took a step back. He wished he could block out her awful telepathic shouting. The snarling words jarred his thinking. *This is clearly the work of Graulas. His mark lingers upon you. The lackwit always showed an unbalanced interest in humans.*

"Stop yelling at me," Seth demanded.

Or what?

"Or I'll throw rocks at you."

Seth heard the sharp intake of breath from the Sphinx. Nagi Luna cackled, a shiny strand of saliva connecting her top and bottom lip. The wild, throaty laughter echoed insanely in the large room.

You have courage, I will concede that much. The words remained abrasive, but they came with less force. She gestured toward the Sphinx. *This one disgusts me. His naked fear makes me ill. Come, we are both prisoners here, run to me. Enter my circle and we will unite against him.*

Seth shook his head.

Grant me permission to hear your thoughts. I will forge a connection so we can confer in private.

"No way."

You would deny my aid? The words arrived more forcefully than ever. Seth put his hands over his ears, but it did nothing to muffle the mental tirade. Darkness seemed to gather around her. *Some of the greatest figures in history have knelt before me! I have drowned navies! I have founded plagues! I have toppled monarchies! Who are you to deny me?*

"I'm the guy outside your circle," Seth said, resisting the urge to crouch and start gathering stones to throw.

The voice in his mind became gentle and slippery. *Very well, you have a will of your own, I can respect that. How is Graulas? I expected he would have perished by now.*

"He's dying."

In his season, he was quite powerful. What a waste. He became so pathetic. So soft. An embarrassment to his kind, fascinated by an inferior species, a student of their trite philosophies. He doted on his human pets, at times favoring them over demons! The weakling deserves a miserable demise. Nagi Luna glanced at the Sphinx. *I do not want our captor eavesdropping on our conversation. He cannot hear my current thoughts. I can open and close my mind to him. Answer me with only yes or no. Let Nagi Luna do the talking.*

"I can't imagine what we would talk about," Seth said, watching her cautiously.

Perhaps we should not converse. Perhaps I should speak with our captor, tell him a tale of passageways and glowing coins.

Seth tried to keep his worry from showing. "No."

When I condescend to speak with a mortal, he had better listen. More especially a hapless whelp like yourself. I made our captor everything he has become. I could do much more for you. You could eclipse him. You have more native potential. There is great power inside of you, but you do not know how to use it. You want out of here. So do I. We can work together to overthrow our jailer.

"Then what?"

A world without boundaries and cages. You could lead that world. Rule it.

"Not interested."

You could free your family. Protect them. You could keep Zzyzx locked forever.

Seth scowled. He glanced at the Sphinx, who was staring at the floor, hands behind his back. "That doesn't make sense. Why would you help me that way?"

You think I care about opening the prison? Ha! That is the dream of our captor! You know what dwells inside of that prison? Competition! If I had my freedom, I would be the most powerful demon in the world! Why would I want to spoil an advantage like that?

"You'd be my biggest enemy," Seth said.

No, no, no. You lack understanding. Before either of us goes free, I will train you. As you mature into your powers, you will find I am no threat. We will protect one another, link our destinies. You will become the greatest hero the world has known.

"You might as well save it, lady. I may be young, I may even be stupid, but not this stupid."

Fool! Ingrate! The barbed words lashed his mind, full of spite. *Men a hundred times your superior would trade everything for an offer like this! You imagine that you matter, that your sister matters, that your family and your friends matter! You are inconsequential, and doomed to remain so. Go! Away with you! Take whatever smug pride you can muster in denying me! You have sentenced your family to death and your cause to failure!*

Seth kept his composure. He said nothing else. Nagi

Luna was dangerous. Not the type of person to provoke more than necessary. The idea of having someone like her as a partner or teacher filled him with horror. He couldn't stand her in his mind for a few minutes, let alone a lifetime. By contrast she made Graulas seem like a big teddy bear. He glanced at the Sphinx, who impassively stared at the wilted demon. She returned his gaze with raw malevolence. Seth assumed they were communicating.

Seth tried to imagine himself as a miserable slave with no options. Under those circumstances, might he have accepted Nagi Luna's offer? He hoped not.

"No," the Sphinx said with finality. He turned to Seth. "This interview is over."

Nagi Luna flailed a frustrated hand at the Sphinx, as if bidding him good riddance. Hissing and gurgling, she spat on the floor. The Sphinx climbed the ladder first. Seth followed.

At the top, he helped the Sphinx shut the grate.

"She wanted your help to overthrow me?" the Sphinx asked.

"She made all sorts of offers," Seth said. "I don't see how she hasn't driven you crazy."

"Nagi Luna is a manipulator," the Sphinx said. "She employs every available tactic to find leverage. What she most desired was access to your mind."

"Were you rooting for her?" Seth asked.

"Had you been foolish enough to offer such access, I would have taken advantage of the opportunity."

"She seemed mad at you."

"She has her reasons."

"Like what?"

The Sphinx switched the torch to his other hand. "She wanted me to force you into her ring of constraint."

"Why didn't you?"

"That was not my purpose. She thought meeting you might yield useful information. I was willing to give her an opportunity to study you. But not to destroy you."

"Do I have to go back to my cell?"

"I'm afraid so."

Seth said nothing more as the Sphinx rejoined the torchbearers and they caravanned back to his cell. One of the guards opened the thick door and Seth entered.

"Home sweet home," Seth said, rubbing his hands together. "This was fun, we should do it again."

"Stay out of trouble," the Sphinx said. He gave a nod, and the guard closed the door.

Seth approached the peephole as the torches moved away. He cupped a hand beside his mouth. "Hey, I don't know who does your maintenance, but I've got a leaky roof in here." No response came. "You might want to pass that along." Still no answer. "I'm not sure where the water keeps coming from. Seems to be a limitless supply."

The torches were growing distant. A moment later, he heard a door open and clang closed. Only the indirect glow from a single unseen torch threw illumination into his cell.

Seth stepped away from the door. "Back to normal," he mumbled, patting his hands against his sides. He felt alone. "Hello, cell. How are you? Still dank and horrible? Sorry to hear it. Me? I've decided to take up a new hobby. Talking to my room. It's a lot like talking to myself, but slightly more pathetic."

As if in response, the wall at the back of the cell rumbled. A moment later, Bracken came through, bringing a white glow.

"Did you hear me?" Seth asked.

"Hear what?"

"Talking to myself?"

"No," Bracken said. "But don't worry, most of us end up chatting with ourselves on occasion. All part of the fun. How did it go?"

"He took me to meet Nagi Luna."

"You're teasing."

"I wish."

"Are you all right?"

Seth shrugged. "They didn't beat me or anything. She kept screaming in my mind. She can talk like you, telepathically. She acted like she wanted to team up against the Sphinx. What she really wanted was to get inside my head. Wait a minute."

"What?"

"When I use that coin, you can read my thoughts, can't you?"

"Yes. Mostly just the thoughts you send to me."

Seth went and plopped on the cot. It swayed and creaked beneath his weight. "How do I know that's true? How do I know you're not scouring my brain for secrets?"

"I guess you don't," Bracken said. "You don't have to use it."

"What's with everybody reading minds around here?"

"You could hear her, but she couldn't read your mind unless you let her."

"Like I let you."

"I see your concern."

Seth leaned back on his cot. He placed his hands behind his head. "Now I feel like I'm talking to a psychologist."

"Tell me about your childhood," Bracken joked.

"I've heard wraiths and zombies in my mind," Seth said. "But I've never mentally talked to a friend. Kendra used to describe what it was like talking to the Fairy Queen."

"Your sister? She spoke with the Fairy Queen?" He sounded keenly interested.

"Whoops. Maybe I shouldn't get into that. I guess it's no big secret anymore. The Sphinx knows that she's fairykind."

"You mean fairystruck?"

"No, fairykind. The Sphinx was the first to diagnose her, actually. I probably shouldn't talk about that stuff. Sounds like Maddox and the others haven't."

Bracken reached out a hand and hoisted Seth to his feet. "Whether or not the Sphinx knows about your sister, you're right that you should keep that kind of information to yourself. As a unicorn, I know the significance of a human becoming fairykind. That status is very rare, and shows a tremendous amount of trust from the Fairy Queen. She has never bestowed trust easily."

"Do you know her?"

Bracken looked inexplicably uncomfortable. "All unicorns know the Fairy Queen." After a brief pause, he smiled and clapped Seth on the arm. "Come with me, I want to show you something. I figured you could use some cheering up after your interlude with the Sphinx."

Seth followed Bracken out into the passage. They travelled the opposite direction from when they had visited Maddox. Bracken guided Seth through a secret door, up a crude stairway, through a crawl space, out a hidden hatchway, and down a cramped hall. Near the end of the hallway Bracken stopped.

"I'm about to show you my favorite place."

"Okay," Seth said, suitably curious.

"I mean my favorite place in the dungeon."

"I get it."

Bracken simultaneously pressed and turned two stones, and a section of the wall swiveled open, turning on a central pivot. As Bracken led the way through the entrance, he extinguished his stone and felt along the wall. He flipped a switch and overhead lights turned on, along with a few lamps and a pair of ceiling fans.

"No way," Seth breathed. Five pinball machines lined one wall. Three dartboards hung on another. A pool table helped fill the middle of the room, balls racked and ready. Nearby stood a ping-pong table and a Foosball table. On one side of the room, three leather couches huddled around a flat-screen television. A large weight machine dominated the far corner of the room, flanked by a treadmill and a rack of free weights. A huge jukebox stood to one side of the secret entrance.

Seth wandered over to the Foosball table. Indians versus cowboys.

"Recognize it?" Bracken asked.

"Why?"

"Because you went straight to it, and it just barely showed up."

Seth nodded. "I think I played Foosball against the Sphinx on this table when I first met him. Or one just like it. Kendra did too."

"This room is our best evidence that the Sphinx knows we sneak around down here," Bracken said. "In fact, with what you mentioned about the Foosball table, we can consider it a certainty. He uses this room to incentivize good behavior. If we act up, things disappear. Sometimes the room is left empty. As we behave, items show up. It has never been openly acknowledged that this place exists. Welcome to the dungeon rec center."

"Does the TV work?"

"Everything works. The TV gets lots of channels."

"How did he get electricity down here?"

"Wires?"

"Right." Seth walked over to a pinball machine. He tapped the flipper buttons.

"The yellow button starts the game," Bracken advised.

"Who has the high score?"

"Me. On all of them."

Seth turned to face Bracken. "I'm going to take you down."

"I'd like to see that," Bracken chuckled. "I have pretty good reflexes, and I've been playing them for almost forty years."

Seth frowned. "I bet you're pretty good at pool."

"I've had a little practice."

Seth shrugged. "I can live with getting schooled. It would sure beat sitting on my cot listening to the water drip."

"Agreed."

Seth ran a hand along the pool table. "If we start a riot, all of this will go away."

Bracken crossed to a rack on the wall and selected a cue. "This room will be empty for years. And they'll do their best to seal up as many passageways as they can find."

Seth selected a cue for himself. "Do we have a chance of succeeding?"

Bracken chalked the tip of his stick. "Not much. But I'm not willing to let the world end without a fight so I can keep playing ping-pong."

"Then we should probably enjoy this room while we have it."

Bracken twirled the cue stick expertly. "My sentiments exactly." He crouched over the table and sent the cue ball rocketing into the others.

CHAPTER ELEVEN

Vanessa's Secret

Kendra swam in a shallow, syrupy lake. The viscous liquid made it a challenge for her to keep her head up, but she didn't want to touch the bottom, either, populated as it was with slimy, squirmy creatures that might bite or sting. The brownish scum on the surface pulled and wrinkled as she carved a slow path through it, arms and legs churning awkwardly. She could not see the shore. Her only landmarks were dead limbs protruding from the mire.

Grandma jostled her shoulder, and Kendra jerked awake, relieved to be free of the uncomfortable dream, but somewhat confused because she saw no evidence of daybreak. A glance at the clock on the nightstand confirmed that it was 3:22 A.M.

"What's going on?" Kendra asked, fear dispelling her drowsiness.

"No great emergency," Grandma soothed. "We're about to learn Vanessa's secret."

Kendra bolted upright. "What is it?"

"Visitors," Grandma said. "Stan, Tanu, and Warren are meeting them at the gate."

"It could be a trick," Kendra warned. What if they admitted a pair of dragons in human form? Or that wizard Mirav?

"Vanessa whispered the secret to Stan about an hour ago," Grandma said. "Apparently she has been in communication with somebody important, and that person is coming here tonight. Stan was satisfied with her explanation. He'll be careful. You should get dressed."

Kendra slid out of bed and started changing her clothes. "You don't know the details?"

"Not yet. The plan is to discuss the situation back in time."

"And I get to come?" Kendra asked hopefully.

"Vanessa suggested that you should be there."

Kendra felt delighted to be included. Who were these mysterious visitors? Kendra could not formulate a reasonable guess. Dare she hope it might be her parents? Or Seth? Would that need to be a big secret?

Dressed in jeans and a comfortable top, Kendra followed Grandma down to the entry hall. The door opened as they arrived. Grandpa entered, followed by a masked figure of medium height wearing a loose, hooded cloak. The cartoonish rubber mask depicted a scowling man with squinty eyes, fat lips, and fleshy cheeks. A shorter person, perhaps a young child, entered as well, wearing a mask like a grinning dog with the tongue lolling out. Warren and Tanu brought up the rear.

"I'm glad you're up, Kendra," Grandpa said. He gestured to the stairs. "This way."

Kendra and Grandma joined the procession to the secret side of the attic. Kendra still had no guess regarding the identity of the disguised visitors. She hoped Grandpa knew what he was doing, letting these masked strangers into the most secretive room in the house.

When they reached the attic, Coulter awaited them with the Chronometer. "We're set for a night ten years ago. The attic should be empty."

"Well done, Coulter," Grandpa said. "Kendra, Warren, and Ruth will be joining me and our taller visitor. The other visitor will await us here."

"Won't be much of a wait for the rest of us," Tanu said.

"Right," Grandpa said. "Our conversation will seem like a blink to those who remain behind. The advice from Patton helped Coulter crack the code for setting the Chronometer. We'll do as many sessions in the past as it takes to bring everyone up to speed."

Kendra felt excited to be part of the first group to learn the secret, although she wasn't overly eager to have the breath knocked out of her again. She, Grandma, Grandpa, Warren, and the mystery guest gathered around the Chronometer.

"For the sake of modesty," Grandma said, "I submit you all keep your eyes shut while I track down some blankets."

"Sounds sensible," Grandpa agreed. "Everybody place a hand on the device."

They complied. He slid a symbol along a groove and flipped the switch.

Kendra braced herself, tightening her abdominals, but it did nothing to thwart the alarming sensation of the breath rushing out of her lungs. Eyes shut, Kendra clutched her midsection, shoulders heaving as she tried to jump-start her breathing. After a weak cough, air began to flow in and out.

She heard Grandma moving around. The stranger would be completely uncovered. Kendra resisted peeking. She would know soon enough.

She heard and sensed a light click on. From behind, Grandma placed a soft comforter over Kendra's shoulders. Kendra wrapped the comforter around herself.

"Okay," Grandma said after a moment. "Open your eyes."

Kendra did, and gazed at the visitor. She felt like the wind had been knocked out of her a second time. The stranger was Grandma Larsen.

"I'm so sorry," Grandma Larsen said gently, eyes on Kendra.

Grandma Larsen was dead! She and Grandpa Larsen had asphyxiated together! Kendra had attended the funeral, had seen her embalmed corpse in her casket!

"How is this possible?" Kendra asked numbly, disbelief impeding her happiness. Could this really be Grandma

Larsen, who snuck her candy and took her to the park and made cheese empanadas? The grandmother who had actually been there while she and Seth were growing up?

"You should be able to guess, Kendra," Grandma Larsen said. "Your family buried stingbulbs."

Kendra made a sound, half laugh, half whimper. Tears of relief sprang to her eyes. Her joy was tinged with a sense of betrayal. How could her grandparents put all of them through this? With a stab of guilt, Kendra realized this was a glimpse of how her parents would feel when they learned they had not actually buried their daughter.

"Incredible," Grandma Sorenson murmured.

"What about Uncle Tuck and Aunt Kim?" Kendra asked.

"Sadly, they really died in that trailer," Grandma Larsen said. "We used the opportunity of their demise to stage our own deaths alongside them."

Grandpa pulled his blanket more snugly around himself. "Then what happened?"

"Let me try to summarize," Grandma Larsen said. "Your grandfather and I have long worked as spies for the Knights of the Dawn. This was while the Sphinx still served as Captain, so masks were worn, and almost nobody knew us. Stan and Ruth were exceptions. As our assignments became more sensitive, Hank and I pretended to retire. The Sphinx knew that we remained active, as did our Lieutenant, but neither had ever met us face-to-face. We communicated with our leaders via coded messages, using false names. Several other spies for the Knights behaved in similar fashion. After all, once your cover is blown, your career as a spy is over. Anonymity is everything. Unlike Stan and Ruth, who were busy as caretakers, Hank and I were able to live dual lives, spending time at home between assignments."

"You went on vacations pretty often," Kendra remembered. "They weren't real?"

"Usually not. In the months leading up to our staged deaths, the Society of the Evening Star became more active than ever. Around this time, your grandfather received the opportunity to become assistant caretaker at Living Mirage."

"Living Mirage?" Warren asked.

"The fifth secret preserve," Grandma Larsen said. "The Sphinx is the caretaker."

"Oh, no," Grandma Sorenson gasped.

"Accepting the position of assistant caretaker would make Hank the most deeply placed spy in enemy ranks. The catch was that going to Living Mirage meant never leaving. Only an inner circle of five Society members are allowed to come and go from Living Mirage, which is how the secret has been preserved. Even within the Society, almost nobody knows that Living Mirage exists."

"So you faked your deaths," Kendra prompted.

"Part of it was to explain why Hank would disappear, perhaps for the rest of his life. Part of it was to prevent any chance of our enemies tracing us back to our children and grandchildren. The Society does not know Hank and I are married. To them, he is Steve Sinclair and I'm Clara Taylor."

"When did you last see Hank?" Grandpa asked.

"Three days before he left," Grandma Larsen said.

"Around the time of our mock funeral. I didn't know where Living Mirage was located, because he didn't know. I had not heard from him until a few weeks ago."

"What were you doing all that time?" Kendra asked.

"Establishing deeper trust with the Society elite," Grandma Larsen said. "I have been out of touch with the Knights for years. The Society sees me as one of their most devoted members. Your grandfather and I decided to insinuate ourselves as deeply into the Society as possible, so we could serve as a last line of defense in a worst-case scenario. Good thing we did, since that worst-case scenario is about to transpire."

"How long have you known about the Sphinx?" Warren wondered.

"He covers his tracks very well," Grandma Larsen said. "I didn't know he was leading the Society until last year. And I didn't know he was Captain of the Knights until he was revealed through your efforts."

"How did Vanessa become involved?" Kendra asked.

Grandma Larsen exhaled with exasperation. "Vanessa found me out years ago. She had worked with me once back when she was a false Knight. Even though I had been masked when we met as Knights, and I also typically wear a mask when dealing with members of the Society, she somehow recognized me at a Society event, although she kept the secret to herself at the time. While doing research prior to coming to Fablehaven, she got her hands on a home movie of me and Hank with you and Seth. That was when she connected me to my true identity."

"That girl does her homework," Warren said with admiration.

"Vanessa is a very talented operative," Grandma Larsen said. "In the past, she has caused me more distress than anyone. We should be most grateful that she has defected to our side. And we should take every precaution to prevent her from betraying us again."

"You don't trust her?" Grandpa asked.

"It would be unwise," Grandma Larsen said. "At least not until this crisis has passed."

"But didn't she bring you here?" Kendra asked.

"She has been very helpful," Grandma Larsen said. "She has been in contact with me from time to time using sleepers she had previously bitten. In fact, it was Vanessa who alerted me that you had been abducted by Torina."

"Did you help me get free?" Kendra asked.

"I watched you use the Oculus."

Kendra furrowed her brow. Then she remembered that not long before she had used the Oculus, a masked figure had entered the room with Mr. Lich. The identity of the masked onlooker had never been revealed. "You wore a mask."

"That's right. Thankfully, I almost always conceal my face when I work with the Society. I'm sure you would have had a hard time hiding your surprise. There was nothing I could do in the moment except hope you survived the Oculus. Any action I took would have hopelessly compromised both of us. But afterward, I slipped the knapsack and the stingbulb into your room."

"You gave me the knapsack!" Kendra exclaimed, her mind reeling. "I've wondered who helped me."

"Finesse is everything in my line of work," Grandma Larsen said. "I wish I could have done more. I did what I felt gave us the best chance for success. I was relieved that you were able to do the rest."

"That knapsack was my home for a few months," Warren mentioned.

"Navarog destroyed it and trapped him inside," Kendra explained. "We used the Translocator to rescue him."

"Then you must know Bubda," Grandma Larsen said.

"Both Kendra and I do," Warren said.

"Is he all right?" Grandma Larsen asked.

"He's still inside that room," Warren said. "Stubborn little guy doesn't want to leave, but eventually he'll starve unless we extract him."

"I understand about Bubda not wanting to leave," Grandma Larsen said with a knowing chuckle. "That was why I left him in there in the first place. He loves his home, and, as hermit trolls go, he is extremely mild and sociable. I saw no real harm in letting him continue to reside there."

Grandpa coughed softly into his fist. "We're beginning to stray. How are we on time?"

Grandma Sorenson checked a watch she must have acquired when she had gathered the blankets. "Fifteen more minutes."

Grandpa rubbed the edge of his blanket between his thumb and forefinger. "I know I can speak for all of us when I say we're shocked and relieved to find you alive, Gloria.

I'm sure you have more to tell us. You mentioned that Hank contacted you recently."

"Once Hank learned that Scott and Marla were in custody at Living Mirage, he began planning a rescue. When Seth showed up there, Hank hastened his efforts."

"Seth's alive?" Kendra exclaimed. "You're sure?"

"The Sphinx healed him with the Sands of Sanctity," Grandma Larsen said.

"He and my parents are all at Living Mirage," Kendra muttered. "Where is it?"

"Eastern Turkey," Grandma Larsen answered. "We have a way in. The plan is to recover as many artifacts as we can while rescuing our lost family members."

"Tell us more," Grandma Sorenson said.

"Hank risked everything to get information out of Living Mirage. The Sphinx's preserve remains his most closely guarded secret. He derives his immortality from the artifact he discovered there centuries ago. But in recent months, as the Sphinx has grown certain of victory, his caution has finally begun to slacken. Hank runs the logistics of Living Mirage, and he has built up enough trust that when the Sphinx is absent from the preserve, Hank becomes the de facto caretaker.

"In his first communication, which arrived via homing canister, Hank told me that if we acquired the Translocator, he had a way to smuggle us in. The day I learned you had recovered the Translocator, I sent word to Hank, journeyed to a predetermined location in Istanbul, and found a dwarf awaiting me."

"The dwarf you brought here tonight," Warren said.

"Correct. His name is Tollin. The dwarf used to work at Living Mirage. Hank smuggled him out. With Tollin and the Translocator, we can penetrate Living Mirage."

"Who else knows about this?" Grandpa asked.

"Only the dwarf, Hank, and myself," Grandma Larsen assured him. "Not even Vanessa knows that Hank is at Living Mirage. His communiqués have arrived untampered with, bound by cryptic seals as verification. Hank released the canisters just outside the gates of Living Mirage, and the messages flew directly to me. I have traveled in disguise, employing a brand-new set of masks. Tollin and I have worn masks the entire time since Istanbul. We got back to the United States through illegal, untraceable means. No passports, no credit cards."

"Our greatest risk is the Oculus," Grandma Sorenson said.

"Which is why we've constantly worn the masks," Grandma Larsen said. "I destroyed the messages as soon as I received them. All the Oculus could have seen so far, had the Sphinx even known to look in my direction, is masked figures travelling. This is the first time I have discussed our plans aloud."

"Is Hank confident we can trust the dwarf?" Warren asked.

"As sure as he could be," Grandma Larsen said. "It's a small miracle Hank got him out. One man at Living Mirage drives a truck to a local town when supplies are needed. Making supply runs has been that man's job for hundreds of years. Hank ordered a supply run and, unbeknownst to the driver, smuggled Tollin out in the truck. The dwarf then made his way to Istanbul. Hank has never given the Sphinx any reason to distrust him. Nor have I, until I came to Fablehaven tonight. Hank has worked closely with the dwarf, and he feels confident that Tollin, along with most of his kind, would welcome the arrival of a new caretaker at Living Mirage."

"We'll have to act swiftly," Warren said. "Every moment we spend back in our proper time increases the chance that the Sphinx might catch on. What are the chances the Sphinx will notice Tollin is gone?"

"Hank manages the dwarfs," Grandma Larsen said. "Living Mirage is an immense preserve. He doesn't expect anyone to notice Tollin missing for weeks, and can cover if they do. But I agree that we need to move swiftly. The Oculus is powerful, and it is often focused at Fablehaven."

"What do we know about the layout of Living Mirage?" Grandpa asked.

"Along with several outlying buildings, there are three main ziggurats," Grandma said. "The Sphinx has his head-quarters in the Great Ziggurat, with the dungeon under-neath. He stores the artifacts in his office. Hank will secure the artifacts. He sent duplicates of all the relevant keys with the dwarf, along with a map to the Great Ziggurat, includ-ing rarely used service tunnels."

"We might have a chance," Warren said.

"We really might," Grandma Larsen agreed. "Secrecy has protected Living Mirage for so long that security inside the compound has grown rather lax. Hank even sent official paperwork for us to retrieve Scott, Marla, and Seth if we want to try to bluff our way into the dungeon. The great advantage with the Translocator is that once we get to the prisoners, we don't have to figure out an escape. The escape is instantaneous."

"And we can abort the mission at any point," Grandma Sorenson said.

"With nothing to stop us from trying again later," Warren added. "Although we need to get it right the first time in order to take advantage of the element of surprise. How large of a strike force should we gather?"

Grandma Larsen shrugged. "That is open to debate. The Translocator carries only three people at a time. A small team can move in and out more easily, but a larger team could split up and might have a better chance of fighting their way through obstacles."

"The dwarf will obviously have to bring in the first pair," Grandpa said. "Then we can shuttle in whoever we want."

"We mustn't let the Sphinx get the Translocator," Kendra reminded them.

"Somebody reliable should have the Translocator at all times," Warren agreed. "If things go wrong, their top priority must be to teleport away."

"We don't necessarily have to leave the Translocator with the strike force," Grandma Sorenson considered. "Of course, without the Translocator on hand, escape from Living Mirage will be much more complex, even if we coordinate with satellite phones and establish rendezvous points."

"Whoever goes into the dungeon needs the Translocator," Grandpa said. "They'll be lucky to make it to the prisoners, let alone get back out. Warren is right—if all else fails, they can abort and jump away."

"This is risky," Grandma Sorenson said.

"Any option we have left is risky," Grandpa said. "This scenario is much more promising than any option I had hoped to encounter. If it pays off, we could rescue Seth, Marla, and Scott, and retrieve the other artifacts."

"And if it fails," Grandma Larsen cautioned, "we could lose the Translocator, and soon thereafter the Chronometer."

Kendra's insides fluttered nervously. "She's right. The Sphinx has been to Fablehaven. So has Mr. Lich. If they had the Translocator, they could come straight here, and that would be the end of everything."

Grandpa pinched his lip absently, eyes far away. "Gloria, you've had much more time than us to think this through. What would you recommend?"

"A team of six," Grandma Larsen said. "Two fighters and I rendezvous with Hank. The dwarf leads two other fighters to the dungeon. The dungeon strike force should keep the Translocator and leap home with the prisoners. Tollin has had some prior access to the vicinity of the dungeon, so those who go there with him will be able to teleport somewhat on the way to their objective. After the captives are secure, a designee will return to a prearranged rendezvous to claim us and the other artifacts."

"How will Hank know when to move?" Warren asked.

"He'll check from his window at two in the morning every night until I send him the signal. Which means we'd want to launch the assault around 6:30 P.M. our time to account for the seven-hour time difference."

"I would propose an extra participant," Warren said. "The dwarf should drop off an extra man first, a good distance from the others. He can serve as a fail-safe, to clean up the mess if the mission goes awry. A human insurance policy. For now, let's call him . . . Warren."

"Are there fairies at Living Mirage?" Kendra asked.

"I'm sure," Grandma Larsen said. "We can ask Tollin for details."

"Fairies have to follow my orders," Kendra explained. "I should come."

Grandpa reddened. "Absolutely not. The idea is not to jeopardize the entire family."

"I've had a little success in the past," Kendra reminded him. "The idea is to make this work, right?"

Grandma Sorenson nodded thoughtfully. "Maybe she could enter with us at first, issue commands to some fairies, then leap directly home."

"Do you have other participants in mind?" Grandma Larsen asked.

Grandpa cleared his throat. "I'd lead the assault force to the dungeon. Trask can accompany me with the dwarf. Elise and Tanu can join you to help Hank."

"And I sit at home knitting and fretting?" Grandma Sorenson said.

"Why don't you escort Kendra?" Grandpa proposed. "Help her find some fairies, set some assistance in motion, then teleport back to Fablehaven before I head for the dungeon. We'll leave Coulter back home as interim caretaker, and let Dale keep running the logistics, but I'd feel much better knowing more than one of us remained at home."

"That sounds reasonable," Grandma Sorenson admitted reluctantly.

"Where will the dwarf insert us?" Grandpa asked.

"Near the nest of a roc," Grandma Larsen said.

"A roc?" Warren exclaimed.

"A rock?" Kendra asked.

"An enormous bird that preys on elephants and aurochs," Grandma Larsen clarified. "The inhabitants of Living Mirage generally stay away from the nesting area, but the nest lies within fifteen minutes on foot from the Great Ziggurat. During maintenance errands, Tollin has ventured right up to the nest itself. He will teleport us to a sheltered location with enough proximity to the roc to provide us with privacy."

"Sounds sensible," Grandpa said. "I expect you want this to happen this evening?"

Grandma Larsen gave a nod. "The quicker we set this in motion, the less chance we have of getting discovered."

"Should be simple to bring Trask and Elise here with the Translocator," Warren said.

"We'll get word to them," Grandpa said, "but we won't reveal details or bring them to Fablehaven until the last possible moment. Surprise will be the difference between success and failure."

"The Sphinx won't know what hit him," Grandma Sorenson murmured.

"I suggest you return Vanessa to the Quiet Box until this is over," Grandma Larsen said. "You should probably place Tollin and me in the dungeon. We'll keep our masks on. Should the Sphinx glimpse us, we want him confused about our presence here."

"I believe we have the outline of a plan," Grandpa said. "We'll get to work on the particulars. First order of business will be to bring Tanu, Coulter, and Dale in on this to help flesh out details. We'll hold all meetings back in time. No discussion of this otherwise. Not a word. This has to succeed."

"We'll make sure it does," Grandma Larsen said staunchly.

"How are we on time?" Grandpa asked.

Grandma Sorenson checked the watch. "We should probably get into position." None of them had moved much since coming back in time.

Kendra studied her Grandma Larsen. It was so wonderful to have her back. At the same time, Kendra felt she hardly knew her. It was hard to reconcile her memories of Grandma Larsen with this no-nonsense spy before her.

Grandma Larsen caught Kendra's eye. "I'm sure this is a lot for you to digest."

"Kind of."

"You and your brother are well-known among the Society. You've been in much more danger than I would pre-fer, but I've been so proud of you both."

The compliment made Kendra feel awkward. "Thanks."

"I'm sorry Grandpa Larsen and I have missed the last couple of years. I suppose it's fair that Stan and Ruth got a turn to know you. Hopefully we'll all have lots of time together in the future."

"I hope so too," Kendra said.

CHAPTER TWELVE

Rescue

The next day, peering out the kitchen window, Kendra spotted Hugo sitting on the lawn, legs straight out, shoulders slumped, big hands folded in his lap. In harmony with the springtime atmosphere at Fablehaven, the golem looked more colorful than usual, with an abundance of wildflowers, blossoming creepers, and tufts of grass sprouting from his earthen body. Dale stood beside Hugo, hands on his hips. Kendra realized she had never seen the golem sitting down before.

Kendra went out the back door and crossed the lawn to Dale. "Something wrong with Hugo?" she asked.

"Hey, Kendra," Dale said, wiping his damp brow with a handkerchief. "I've never seen him like this. The big guy has been sluggish all day. Then I came out of the barn to find him picking grass."

Kendra noticed the small pits and discarded divots in front of the golem. "You okay, Hugo?"

The big head swiveled toward her, cavernous eyes regarding her solemnly. "Hugo okay," he said wearily. His gravelly voice was becoming more expressive and intelligible every day.

"Well, get up then," Dale prodded. "We have chores to do. You're making everybody nervous." Dale looked uncomfortable.

Kendra wondered if Dale missed the way Hugo used to be. In the past, Hugo had done nothing but follow orders. But after the fairies had tampered with him, the golem had developed a will of his own. He still almost always followed commands, but on occasion he would deviate or improvise.

With a grunt like rolling boulders, Hugo rose to his feet, mouth bent in a frown. He looked down at Dale.

"That's the spirit," Dale said, as if encouraging a child. "Let's go see to those stables."

Powerful arms at his sides, Hugo bent at the waist and then toppled forward. His head hit the ground hard, digging a short furrow in the lawn. Propped up by his head and feet, he rigidly held his bowed position, arms at his sides, rear end pointing skyward.

"What's wrong, Hugo?" Kendra asked. Could the golem be ill? He looked absolutely pathetic.

Heaving with his arms, Hugo rocked back to a sitting position. "Seth gone," he said, a forlorn rumble.

"You miss Seth?" Kendra said. "He'll be back."

Hugo shook his heavy head. "Seth taken."

"Who told you Seth was taken?" Dale asked.

"Doren."

Kendra blinked. Suddenly Hugo's behavior made much more sense. He was concerned about Seth.

"Is that what has you out of sorts?" Dale asked. "You miss your buddy?"

Hugo patted his chest. "Miss buddy."

"Seth will be all right," Kendra said encouragingly. "He's survived tough situations before." She wished she could fully believe her words.

Hugo regarded her with an unnerving, eyeless gaze. "Hugo want help."

"Best way you can help is to keep Fablehaven running," Dale urged. "Otherwise there won't be a preserve for Seth to come home to."

Once again, Hugo stood up. He gazed down at Kendra. "You help Seth."

"We'll figure out something," Kendra promised. She couldn't explain that they already had a rescue planned. They were only allowed to discuss plans in the past. Maybe the golem needed a distraction. "Want to play catch, Hugo? Or hit a baseball? You can throw me in the pool."

The golem forced a craggy smile. He rubbed his stony chest. "Not feel right. Maybe later. Stables first."

"I've never seen him all emotional like this," Dale muttered out the side of his mouth.

"It's sweet," Kendra said, fighting back tears.

"Come," Hugo said, picking up Dale and cradling him in one arm. The golem gently patted Kendra on the shoulder, then turned and loped out of the yard.

Kendra was left standing alone. She sat down on the grass, which had been squashed flat by the golem's rump. The rescue operation would commence within the hour. Trask and Elise had still not arrived. But they were ready. Warren would teleport them to Fablehaven at the last moment.

A quartet of fairies fluttered over and began replacing the grassy divots into the corresponding pits. Kendra focused on the nearest fairy. She had short blonde hair and wore a simple shift the color of sunflower petals. Her translucent butterfly wings ended in fanciful curled points. Kendra marveled at the tiny hands packing the clod of earth back into place. How strange to quietly observe a beautiful woman the size of an insect!

Aware of the attention, the fairy glanced up at Kendra, her expression uncertain as she brushed soil from her dainty palms. The miniature woman checked her radiant slip for stains.

"You look lovely," Kendra said.

The fairy beamed, twirled, and leaped into the air, flitting off toward the nearest rosebush. The other three fairies smoldered with jealousy.

"You all look fabulous," Kendra assured them.

The other fairies took flight as well. "And *you* said she was too big and clumsy to recognize style," one chirped to another.

Kendra smiled. This unlikely, magnificent world of magical creatures was certainly worth protecting. She could understand why her grandparents had devoted their lives to the cause. She just wished the job came with less danger.

Kendra considered how she might use the fairies of Living Mirage to help the assault force. Since the fairies would obey any order she gave in the name of the Fairy Queen, Kendra took the responsibility seriously. Her commands could cause innocent fairies to perish without any choice in the matter.

The fairies of Living Mirage could at least provide assistance as guides and sentries. Since stealth was the key to this mission, that extra guidance might give the strike force the edge they needed. Kendra ran a hand over the grass the fairies had just replaced. The repaired portions blended seamlessly with the rest of the lawn. Fairies possessed strong restorative magic. Kendra wondered if fairy magic could somehow benefit the upcoming mission.

Wearing a dark outfit, Warren came out of the house and vaulted the back porch railing. "Meditating?" he asked.

"Something like that," Kendra answered, rising.

"I just set up Bubda in a storage room in the dungeon," Warren said. "I left him with a deck of cards, taught him how to play solitaire. Little guy really resisted leaving the knapsack room. But as soon as he dug into a bag of overripe tomatoes, he was feeling much better."

"How did Vanessa take her transfer to the Quiet Box?" Kendra asked.

"Like a pro," Warren said. "She may not love the idea,

but she gets it. With a bunch of us heading off to Four Pines, she knows we can't have her loose."

They had decided to pretend that several of them would be teleporting to a preserve called Four Pines in Canada. All of their preparations were discussed in this context in order to explain why they were gathering so much gear, and to misdirect the Sphinx's attention. The idea had come from Coulter.

"It will be interesting to see a new preserve," Kendra said.

"You'll like it," Warren said. "Ruth sent me out to call you for dinner."

"What is it?"

"Italian," Warren said. "Pasta, lasagna, pizza, salad—the works. I cheated and used the Translocator to pick it up from my favorite restaurant. You'll love it."

Kendra thought about how they had tried to use pancakes to calm her before the visit to Stony Vale. Would pasta be a last meal for any of them? She tried to push away the morbid thought.

She followed Warren into the house, where Coulter and Tanu were removing plastic containers of food from bags. Grandma Larsen would not get to participate in the meal. Kendra had hardly seen Grandma Larsen since their discussion back in time. Her grandmother and the dwarf kept silent while in the present, and were currently residing in a dungeon cell.

Warren was right about the food. The spicy lasagna was so delicious that she actually got distracted from the upcoming mission and ate a hearty portion. She had cannoli for dessert, and they tasted divine as well.

Grandma and Grandpa Sorenson came to the table last. She had on a light gray sweatshirt and jeans. He was clad in black. Kendra supposed that since she and Grandma would be at Living Mirage for only a few minutes, they didn't require much camouflage.

Kendra eyed the clock while her grandparents ate. Minutes ticked by. At 6:20, Tanu went to bring Grandma Larsen and the dwarf up from the dungeon. At 6:25, Warren used the Translocator to retrieve Trask and Elise. He was back within seconds.

Everyone started checking gear and shouldering packs. Tanu examined his potions. Trask fiddled with his weapons. The dwarf gobbled up no fewer than six cannoli, stuffing them under his mask.

"Four Pines should be secure," Trask announced, sliding a dagger back into its sheath, "but we can't be too careful." Warren would only have just whispered to him the actual destination.

Grandpa clapped Coulter on the shoulder. "We'll be back soon."

"I'll be waiting," Coulter said.

"Now?" asked the dwarf.

"Me first," Warren said, holding out the Translocator. "You know the drill."

Tollin twisted the middle portion and they winked out of sight. Kendra knew Warren had conferred with the dwarf to select an alternate location for him to be inserted at

Living Mirage, but was not privy to the details. A moment later the masked dwarf returned without Warren.

Trask and Grandma Larsen grabbed opposite ends of the Translocator and vanished with the dwarf. Grandma Larsen reappeared and collected Tanu and Grandpa Sorenson. A moment later, Grandma Larsen was back for Elise and Grandma Sorenson.

"Take care," Coulter said to Kendra. "See you soon."

She gave a distracted nod. Her mouth felt dry, her palms damp.

Grandma Larsen returned. "Ready?" she asked, voice muffled by her mask.

Kendra took hold of the Translocator. Grandma Larsen twisted the device, and suddenly she and Kendra stood in a warm, dark grove of olive trees. A bright array of stars glittered in the moonless sky. Grandma Larsen raised a quieting finger to the lips of her mask.

"Trask, Elise, and Tanu will scout the area," Grandpa whispered. "We have five minutes to locate a fairy or two. At that point, whether or not we've found one, Kendra and Ruth will return home and we'll proceed."

Tollin had removed his mask. Sweat matted his gray beard. The dwarf tapped his temple and curled a finger at Grandma Larsen, miming for her to crouch. Grandma Larsen removed her mask and bent an ear down to the dwarf. Quick as a mousetrap, he snatched the Translocator from her grasp, twisted the center, and disappeared.

During the stunned pause that followed, Kendra felt her insides sink and shrivel. They were doomed.

"Scatter!" Grandpa cried.

An instant later, weighted nets started falling from the sky.

Kendra heard the twang of bowstrings and the hiss of blowguns. Hoarse shouts echoed from all directions. Somewhere above and behind, the roc shrieked with enough power to rival the roar of any dragon. Amid all the commotion, Kendra recognized the eerie chanting of Mirav the wizard.

The members of the strike force tumbled to the ground as they sought in vain to flee, tangled in nets, drugged by darts, and hampered by spells. Frozen with terror and despair, Kendra watched as the others fell. She glimpsed Trask slashing a net with a short sword. She heard Grandpa growling with effort, dragging himself a short ways along the ground before slumping into unconsciousness.

Dazedly, Kendra realized that she remained unscathed. Perhaps her inaction amid all the commotion had prevented their enemies from targeting her. Perhaps she was perceived as the least threatening member of the party. Perhaps it was dumb luck. She fleetingly wondered if she could be enjoying some form of magical protection. No, they were trespassers here. Their protection had been secrecy, and the dwarf had betrayed them.

Collapsing to the ground, Kendra faked unconsciousness. Maybe if she was sneaky, she could crawl away while the others were being rounded up. Nobody could see better than she could in the dark. If she could slither free, she might be able to find a way to help.

She heard rapid footsteps approaching, voices whispering, bushes rustling. Should she move? Should she wait?

"This one is awake," said a dry voice above her.

Kendra opened her eyes and found herself staring up at Mirav. Reaching out a long-nailed hand, he sprinkled glittering powder in her face.

Kendra felt an insistent tickle, as if she had to sneeze, but the sneeze refused to come. Instead, the world rocked, then spun, then darkness enfolded her.

※　※　※

Kendra awoke reclining against a plush, squarish cushion. The Sphinx sat opposite her, cross-legged on a mat. Kendra pushed herself upright. They were on a wide, tiled, torch-lit balcony. A glorious mist of stars sparkled overhead.

"Welcome to Living Mirage," the Sphinx said pleasantly.

Kendra felt surprisingly alert. No grogginess lingered from her unconsciousness. Here she sat, alone with the man who had sabotaged her life and stolen her family. "Where is everyone?"

"All four of your grandparents are in my custody," the Sphinx said. "As are your parents, as is your brother, as are many of your friends."

"Is everyone all right?" Kendra asked.

The Sphinx offered a kind, white smile. "None of them were harmed, and this despite several of them attempting to fight. Only Warren has not yet been captured, but Tollin told us where he left him. We will have him soon."

She despised his smile. She hated his friendly demeanor. "The dwarf betrayed us."

"Do not blame the dwarf," the Sphinx said. "All of this was orchestrated. The dwarf was merely a piece in the puzzle, an anxious servant willing to bring honor and comfort to his people."

"You saw us with the Oculus?"

"When your grandfather Hank sent his first message to his wife, your cause was ruined. I am very, very slow to trust, Kendra. My assistant caretaker was a competent man, but decades away from earning any real credibility. Steve, as Hank called himself, was constantly monitored. I cannot describe my excitement when I heard he had sent a homing canister. A spy who does not realize his cover has been blown can be a most valuable asset. My elation increased as I dug into his past and discovered he was a desperate spy, eager to rescue his relatives. Using the dwarf to spoil your incursion was simple. Even I was surprised by all we gained. I did not expect you to be joining them. May I offer you refreshments?"

Kendra's gaze strayed to a nearby low, round table crowded with food and beverages.

"No, thank you."

"The figs are exceptional."

"I just had a bunch of Italian food."

"Water, perhaps? Juice?"

"I'm fine. What are you going to do with us?"

The Sphinx folded his hands in his lap. "Your only task

in the near future will be to relax. Your role in the coming events has concluded."

"You're really going to open Zzyzx?" Kendra asked.

The Sphinx fingered his grin. "It was inevitable. There is amazing power in single-mindedness."

"You're going to destroy the world."

The grin faltered. "You and your loved ones have fought hard because you believe that is the case. I bear you no malice. In the end, you will be released."

Kendra looked around the balcony, noticing the potted ferns and inhaling exotic fragrances. "Why have you brought me here?"

"I showed your brother the same courtesy. You children fascinate me. Your potential is extraordinary. Are you sure you will not have some food? The fare in the dungeon is not quite so fine."

"Is that where you're keeping us?"

"Consider it a mark of respect. Many of you are dangerous opponents. The stay will be temporary, I assure you. Our plans are nearing fruition."

Kendra walked over to the table and sat down on a mat. "Maybe I'll have some water."

The Sphinx joined her at the table. "Try the pear juice. It is very light." He removed a chilled carafe from a bucket of ice and poured the clear fluid into a goblet.

Kendra sampled the drink. The Sphinx was right. The cool liquid had a subtle, fresh flavor.

"Have you any questions for me?" the Sphinx asked.

"Not that you would answer," Kendra huffed.

"Try me. I made a similar offer to your brother. This is finally over. Some details are not yet tied up, but the game is done. I may not be an expressive man, but I am celebrating, Kendra. It relieves me to finally lay down the burden of my secrets."

"Okay, then tell me your next move," Kendra said, not expecting an answer.

The Sphinx compressed his lips. "I like to think that once you and your family truly understand me, your hatred will evaporate. My aims are noble, and my means are no more unsavory than necessary. Would you like to know the remaining steps to opening Zzyzx?"

"Sure."

The Sphinx selected a piece of fruit and took a bite. "I do not foresee how telling you this information can cause me harm. Yet it goes against my instincts to expose my plans."

"You told me to ask."

"I'm aware. And in many ways, I cannot wait to part with these secrets. Secrecy has been necessary for so long that the habit resists my tampering. If I reveal this information to you, as a token of goodwill, will you at least promise to consider the possibility that I am truly an ally?"

She wanted to fling the pear juice in his face. But no matter how hopeless their cause might seem, and no matter how confident the Sphinx was of victory, there was always a chance that this information could prove useful. "Sure, I promise."

The Sphinx studied her for a prolonged moment. "Do you really hate me so much?"

"Put yourself in my position."

"I understand." He straightened and grew serious. "Our first task will be to retrieve the Chronometer from Fablehaven. Do not worry, we should be able to accomplish this without harming any of your other friends there. Next I will go back in time with two companions. Only mortals can use the Chronometer."

"Okay."

He munched thoughtfully on his fruit. "I'm about to sum up centuries of research. To share secrets men would kill for. Secrets I have killed to protect. So enjoy. Zzyzx lies on Shoreless Isle in the Atlantic. The gateway into Zzyzx lies within a virtually impregnable stone chamber, a hollow hill. The stone of the chamber is enchanted, much like the Dreamstone at Obsidian Waste. In other words, a direct nuclear blast would harm it no more than a breeze, just as a meteor strike would fail to scratch it. There exists but a single weakness. The stone chamber on Shoreless Isle opens for a single day every thousand years."

"When did it open last?" Kendra asked.

"The late fifteen hundreds. So I can either wait almost six hundred years to open Zzyzx, or I can travel back in time."

"You're going to open it in the past?" Kendra exclaimed, horror seeping into her voice.

"That would be convenient," the Sphinx said. "Unfortunately, the masterminds who engineered Zzyzx did not design it with convenience in mind. Quite the opposite, in fact. The Chronometer will not transport objects into the past, and the other keys are required to open the prison, so opening the gateway in the past is impossible."

Working at the problem, Kendra scrunched her brow. "So you'll go back in time to the day the chamber was open, enter it, then return to the present and use the Translocator."

The Sphinx beamed. "Very good, Kendra. That was quick. Since the Translocator can take me anyplace I have been, it should provide easy access. My expectation is that I will then be able to open the stone chamber from the inside."

"Doesn't sound too hard," Kendra lamented.

"It is only the beginning," the Sphinx said. "A virulent plague resides inside the chamber. After we enter it, we will have to get back to the present quickly to be healed by the Sands of Sanctity. Then, in the present, I will use the Translocator to transport some seeds inside. The plants that sprout will scrub the air and eradicate the plague."

"Wait a minute," Kendra said. "Before any of this, won't you have to get to Shoreless Isle? You'll have to go back in time from there, right?"

The Sphinx grinned. "One of the benefits of a long life. Mr. Lich and I are perhaps the only living men who have visited Shoreless Isle. The Translocator will take me directly there, along with the Chronometer and the Sands of Sanctity."

Kendra sipped some pear juice. "The five artifacts are also actual keys?"

The Sphinx nodded. "They are actual keys to the great

door of Zzyzx. But they all serve dual purposes. Access to the great gateway would be impossible without them."

"I get the purpose behind the Chronometer, and the Translocator, and the Sands of Sanctity," Kendra said. "What else does the immortality artifact do?"

The Sphinx held up a finger. "I believe it is an item of practicality. The Font of Immortality enables a mortal to live long enough to solve this gigantic puzzle."

A realization struck Kendra. "And it lets you live long enough to go back in time far enough to get inside the chamber."

"Or to live long enough to wait for it to open again," the Sphinx added. "Kendra, if this were a job interview, I would hire you immediately."

"I'd have to turn you down," Kendra said. "What about the Oculus?"

"In many ways the Oculus is the most important item," the Sphinx said. "It helps locate the other items. And it will help me track down the Eternals."

Kendra had been hoping he might not know about them. She decided to play dumb. "Eternals?"

"Five mortals who must be killed before Zzyzx can be opened," the Sphinx explained. "I have already found and eliminated two of them."

"You have!"

"I found one before I had the Oculus. I eliminated another recently. Without the Oculus, finding them all would be nearly impossible."

"So once the Eternals are dead . . ."

"Once the title *eternal* no longer applies to them, and once I have access to the chamber and have scrubbed the air of disease, I must only wait for the morning after a full moon to insert the keys and set the gateway ajar. Then I will negotiate with Gorgrog the Demon King. If he will not heed my terms, I will not fully open the door. He wants out. He will eventually agree. And a new age will dawn."

"And the name of that age will be *The End of the World*."

Smiling sadly, the Sphinx shook his head. "No, but it will be the end of prisons, and the end of inequality."

"Honestly, I hope you're right. Because I don't see how anyone will stop you. I'd take just about anything over the end of everything."

"Relax, Kendra. I have the minutia figured out. All you need do now is wait. Have you any other questions?"

Kendra plucked a grape and popped it in her mouth. "My brain is fried. I can't think of anything."

"Have you eaten your fill?"

"Yeah, I guess."

"Then the hour has arrived for you to become acquainted with your new accommodations. I will try to put you someplace where you may cross paths with your brother. I'm afraid the comforts are few, but unless I am mistaken, your stay will be brief." The Sphinx clapped his hands, and four armed guards came out onto the balcony.

"Don't do this," Kendra sobbed, surprised at the sudden surge of emotion. "You can still stop all of this. You should be protecting these artifacts, not using them."

"Be still," the Sphinx said. "I cannot be swayed. Do not waste your energy. I am fortified by the power of certainty."

A guard helped Kendra to her feet. "I hope somebody stops you," she said.

The Sphinx poured himself some pear juice. He took a sip, swallowed, and then spoke gently but firmly. "Hope for something else."

CHAPTER THIRTEEN

A Promise Kept

Seth rested on his cot, staring at the web of cracks in the dim ceiling, listening to the constant dripping, wondering about the time. In the dungeon, there was no sunrise, no sunset, no way to keep his internal clock calibrated. Bracken, however, seemed to know innately when it was day or night. Some time ago they had separated to sleep. Seth had slept. Later he had wakened. And he now had no idea if it was time to get up or the middle of the night.

He had not slept well in the dungeon. For days he had dozed in odd stretches, more an irregular series of naps than any normal slumber.

At the moment, if he knew it was morning, he felt awake enough to get up. He could also probably fall back to sleep if he tried. He considered calling Bracken with the coin, but decided he should wait rather than risk rousing the unicorn for a trivial concern.

The door to his cell opened without warning. He heard no footsteps approach, no key rattle in the lock. By the time he sat up, the door had banged shut.

"On your feet," a harsh voice called through the peep-hole in a loud whisper. "Have a look."

Seth jumped out of bed and hurried to the door. He pushed against it but it wouldn't budge. Beside the door sat a canvas sack. Seth pressed his face to the peephole, looking up and down the hall as best he could. Dim and silent, the only movement in the corridor came from shadows jittering in the wavering torchlight.

Returning to his cot, Seth retrieved his coin from under one of the legs. Running a finger clockwise along the edge caused it to start glowing. Coin in hand, Seth returned to the sack. He could hardly believe his eyes when he looked inside and beheld a copper teapot shaped like a cat and a narrow, segmented platinum cylinder set with precious stones. Along with a handwritten note and a cube of walrus butter, the shabby sack contained the Translocator and the Sands of Sanctity!

This had to be a trick. Still, he grabbed the note and started reading hastily.

Take these artifacts and escape from Living Mirage at once. Just twist the center of the Translocator and think of home. An attempt to rescue you has failed, and these were the only artifacts I managed to pilfer. Time is short. Leave immediately. Take nobody. Thanks to your time in the dungeon, you can help lead rescues later. Everything depends on you leaving immediately with these items.

I am the last spy the Knights have within the Society. I will contact you soon. Do not delay.

The note was unsigned.

Why was the Translocator here? Something must have gone terribly wrong. Could this be a trap? What kind of trap would grant him access to anywhere he wanted to go? What kind of trap would give away two of the artifacts essential for the Society to accomplish their objectives?

He popped the walrus butter in his mouth, chewed, and swallowed. Maybe the artifacts were fake. But what would be the point of that? They sure looked authentic.

Rereading, he tried to process the message. There had been a rescue attempt, but it had failed. Who would have participated? Trask? Tanu? Whoever had been captured would need his help. But right now he didn't even know where to start looking.

Should he follow the advice in the note and teleport straight home to Fablehaven? What about his friends? He pressed his thumb against the griffin on the glowing coin. "Bracken," he whispered.

What is it, Seth? The answer came swiftly. He doubted Bracken had been asleep.

"I have our ticket out of here. Somebody just slipped me the Translocator."

Are you serious?

"Where are you?"

In my cell.

Seth had not yet visited his cell. "Have I been near there?"

Not really. They keep me down deep.

"The Translocator came with a note. It said I should escape immediately. How long would it take you to get someplace I've been?"

At least ten minutes. That's too long. Obey the note. I've gotten word that there has been some sort of disturbance here tonight. A bunch of people captured. You should get out of here while you can. If you have the Translocator, you can come back for me anytime.

"Be in my cell tomorrow at midnight. I'll be back, I promise."

Just take the coin with you. It should work even over great distances. We can devise a plan.

"Gotcha. See you soon."

Good luck.

Seth heard many heavy footsteps running down the corridor. Had he ever heard guards rushing in the dungeon? Not that he could recall. Heart pounding, Seth slid a finger counterclockwise along the edge of the coin, then slipped it into his pocket. He pocketed the note as well. Tucking the teapot under one arm, he grabbed the Translocator.

If he pictured Fablehaven, and twisted, he would be home. But what about Maddox? He pictured Maddox's cell and twisted. For an instant, Seth felt like he was folding into himself, shrinking down to a tiny point. Then he was standing in Maddox's cell. His friend was not there.

"Bad time to go exploring, Maddox," Seth muttered to

the empty cot. He consoled himself that when he made plans with Bracken, he would figure out how to save Maddox and the others as well.

As he prepared to twist the Translocator again and return to Fablehaven, a realization stopped him. He had been to the Sphinx's office. He knew right where the Oculus was sitting, knew the location of the secret compartment that held the Font of Immortality. What if he returned to Fablehaven with all of the lost artifacts?

Mind racing, Seth tried to weigh the pros and cons objectively. If he went straight to Fablehaven, they would have three of the five artifacts. But once the Sphinx knew Seth had escaped, he would certainly relocate the artifacts Seth had seen in his office. If Seth went directly to the Sphinx's office, he might win the war with one fell swoop. Without the Oculus, the Sphinx would lose his biggest advantage. And without the Font of Immortality, he would be dead within a week.

Of course, if Seth got caught, all would be lost. But how could he get caught? If somebody was in the office, he would teleport right out.

Seth pictured the office where he had conversed with the Sphinx and twisted the Translocator. To his relief, the office was empty. He quickly observed that the Oculus no longer rested on the handsome desk. Crossing to the desk, he hastily scrabbled through the wooden drawers, but found no multifaceted crystal. Turning, Seth tore aside a tapestry, triggered the catch he had seen the Sphinx use, and tugged open the hidden cupboard in the wall. Empty.

At that moment, the Sphinx stormed into the room. Recognizing Seth, he stopped short in genuine astonishment. With the door at the far end of the office, forty feet, two dozen cushions, and a few gauzy veils separated them. The Sphinx's gaze flicked down to the Translocator. He pointed at Seth, outrage distorting his features. "Put that down," he roared. "Seth, you don't—"

Seth twisted the Translocator, and the Sphinx disappeared. After a momentary folding sensation, Seth stood on the roof of his elementary school. He had climbed up there once on a dare, and afterwards had used it as a place to escape when he wanted to be alone and think. For some reason, it was the first place that had sprung to mind.

It was a calm, cool evening. The sun had recently set, painting the cloudy horizon with warm, vivid colors. Seth sat down, his hands shaking. Nobody could have anticipated that he would receive the Translocator, and even if they did, nobody would guess that he would come here. It was hard to believe, but for the moment, he was actually safe.

Seth had never seen the Sphinx lose his façade of calm control. The Sphinx had entered the room as if aware of an intruder, but seemed shocked when he saw it was Seth. He supposed that made sense. If the Sphinx had just captured the Translocator, he had probably been off celebrating his victory. It must have blown his mind to find Seth in his office with two of the artifacts!

A pebble sat on the roof near his foot. Seth picked it up and tossed it off the edge, hearing it clack as it hit the pavement below. His next step should be to return to

Fablehaven. Even if Tanu and some of them had been captured during the failed rescue, surely Grandma and Grandpa were still there, and probably Kendra.

A single concern prevented Seth from teleporting immediately to the house at Fablehaven. Tracing a finger along the copper teapot, Seth considered his commitment to Graulas. He could clearly picture the old demon languishing in agony, hoping for some way to reduce the anguish of his impending death. Seth had never witnessed such extreme suffering. With the Translocator, he could easily pop in and heal the demon before returning the artifacts to the house. As far as Seth knew, Graulas could already be dead, or he could presently be right at the brink of death. If he didn't heal Graulas now, Seth expected Grandpa would forbid him from doing so later.

Seth had promised the demon he would heal him. Graulas had no other hope for aid. He might have lived an evil life, but the demon had helped Seth multiple times.

Seth fingered the Translocator. Could this be a bad move? What if Graulas turned on him? Of course, even in his weakened state, the demon could have killed Seth upon any of his previous visits. If Seth healed him, Graulas would probably be more grateful than ever. Maybe the cunning demon could suggest strategies to stop the Sphinx, or provide insight about Nagi Luna. After a dusting from the Sands of Sanctity, the demon would still be old and dying, but curing the disease would reduce the pain and maybe buy Graulas a little extra time. And Seth would keep the

Translocator handy. If all else failed, he could always teleport away.

Seth hesitated. He would prefer to take this action with permission from Grandpa Sorenson, but he felt certain Grandpa would never agree to it. Grandma and Grandpa hated demons. And they would worry too much about his safety. Seth scratched his arm. As long as he acted before returning home, he would not really be disobeying a direct request. Sometimes it was easier to get forgiveness than permission.

Envisioning the cave where Graulas lived, Seth twisted the Translocator. The stench of putrefying flesh hit him like a physical blow. Gagging, Seth covered his nose with one hand. The demon sprawled on the floor, flies buzzing around his many weeping sores. His wheezy breathing came quick and shallow, like that of a panting dog.

Seth slid the Translocator into his pocket. "Can you hear me, Graulas?"

Grunting, the demon raised his head, festering eyes squinting in not quite the right direction. "Seth?"

"I brought the Sands of Sanctity," Seth announced.

"The pain . . ." Graulas moaned through cracked lips, his voice trailing off.

"Hang on, I'm here to heal you." Striding forward, Seth upended the teapot over the dying demon. Golden sand poured out, snapping and hissing like water on a hot griddle as it contacted the inflamed flesh. Acrid fumes rose from the pathetic, bloated form. Pacing and swinging the teapot, Seth

dusted the limitless supply of sand all over the demon until the sizzling smoke subsided.

"Oh-ho," Graulas said, sitting up, the tone of his voice deeper and richer than Seth had ever heard. In place of infected skin, short gray fur covered his arms. The drooping wattles had vanished from his face, leaving him with the head of a ram to match his curled horns. His misshapen body had become symmetrical, and now appeared muscular rather than lumpy. He stretched his thick arms forward, examining them. "Oh-ho-ho-ho!" he laughed exultantly.

"Feeling better?" Seth asked.

Graulas pounced at him, seized a shoulder with a hairy hand, and hoisted Seth off the ground effortlessly. Before Seth could react, the demon quickly tore the Translocator from his pocket, then dropped him on a pile of rubble. Landing roughly, Seth lost hold of the teapot, and the demon snatched it up. From his supine position, Seth stared up at the broad, bestial figure towering over him.

"Honestly?" Graulas rumbled. "This is the best I've ever felt." His rejuvenated voice had more growl to it than before.

"What are you doing?" Seth cried. His elbows were bleeding, and his back ached where a wooden knob had jabbed it.

"Many things, now, many things, thanks to you." The demon flung sand from the teapot over Seth, and his injuries vanished. "After all of these years, against all odds, I am now free! She was right. She may not be utterly sane, but she was right."

"Who was right?"

"Nagi Luna."

It took Seth a moment to find words. "You know her?"

"She contacted me using the Oculus," Graulas said. "She has not yet held it herself, but she can borrow some of its power when her captor uses it. Which is often. She harbored hopes of an opportunity like this for a long while, but only felt certain after she met you."

"What have I done?" Seth mouthed.

The demon grinned better than any actual ram could. "You still don't fully understand. Of course you don't, or this would never have happened. Seth, this disease has plagued me for thousands of years. It is what slowly ruined me. The sickness was my prison much more than this cave. Only the Sands of Sanctity could have healed me. I am old, yes, but now I am far from dying."

"And you have the Translocator."

"You begin to see. This area was designed to hold me in my weakened, diseased state. Now that I'm whole, I could probably defeat the barriers that contain me. But thanks to your thoughtful tribute, that will not be necessary."

Seth groaned, hiding his face in his hands. "Why am I so stupid?"

"Not the common breed of stupidity," the demon corrected. "You're too trusting. Too independent. Too good of a friend, even to one who is by nature your enemy. These attributes were used against you."

"What happens now?"

"I will acquire the Chronometer and return to Living

Mirage. I have been there before, you see, centuries ago. And at the end of his long years of scheming, the Sphinx will lose control of his endeavor. Before long, the demons of Zzyzx will be free according to my terms."

Seth still felt off balance. "Wait—wasn't the Sphinx behind this trick?"

"Certainly not. Use your intellect. All the Sphinx needed to do was use the Translocator to collect the Chronometer. Why give it to you and risk losing it? Mirav the wizard left the artifacts in your cell, under strict orders from Nagi Luna. She communicates with him through the Oculus as well. Since the gambit paid off, I will go to Living Mirage in my full strength, free Nagi Luna, and take leadership of this endeavor. Tonight you have ushered in an age of demonic rule!"

Seth hugged himself miserably, gripping handfuls of his shirt. He wished he could stop existing. He had ruined everything!

"I will leave you with your life, Seth."

"Why bother?" Seth moaned.

"Because I sponsored your elevation to shadow charmer, and because you did me a great service. I owe you a debt of gratitude, and for that I will spare you, even though I know you will never serve me."

"Let's be honest," Seth said. "I'll try to stop you."

"Let's be honest," Graulas countered. "Resourceful as you are, there is nothing you can do about this. Not a thing. You would be wise to put it out of your mind."

"Please," Seth said, fighting back tears of desperation.

"Please, I healed you. Don't punish my family for it. Don't punish Fablehaven. Go free, do whatever, but if my aid meant anything, don't take the artifacts."

"My dear boy," Graulas said. "You do not comprehend the nature of demons. Your grandfather does, and some who work with him. It almost surprises me that you remain so naive. Did I ever bother to lie about my nature? I do not believe I did. Nagi Luna stretched the truth, perhaps, to make me seem more pitiable, and I acted somewhat more infirm than I felt, but I never misled you on this issue. Let me leave you with a final lesson. I am what you would call evil. Pure, deliberate, evil. I am aggressively self-serving. I take great pleasure in destruction. At times I cause harm to get gain, and at times I cause harm for the sheer enjoyment of breeding mayhem. So, will I take the artifacts? Seth, without a twinge of remorse, I will use them to unlock a season of devastation like the world has never witnessed. And, mark my words, I will revel in it."

Grinding his teeth, Seth tried to think of something to do. He saw one possible option. "Take me with you."

"No, no, my boy. Shadow charmer or not, I fully understand that you could never be my servant, except perhaps as part of a clumsy deception. Our destinies are no longer entwined. Should we meet again, it will be as enemies, all past debts settled. You will not be bored without me, Seth. There will be work enough to do here."

"What do you mean?"

Snarling, Graulas dragged his claws across the earthen roof of the cave, dislodging wormy clods of dirt. "I intend to pay my respects to this despicable zoo by overthrowing the foundational treaty and leaving a suitable amount of havoc behind. Like Bahumat, I never officially consented to my incarceration here. The treaty has no direct claim on me." Graulas sniffed the air, eyes narrowed to slits. He spoke in a lower tone, as if to himself. "I would free Bahumat, but the fairies buried him deep and sealed him well. There will be time to unleash him later. Kurisock is gone, Olloch more stomach than mind. I will take none of my brothers with me, but like any respectable demon coming out of retirement, I shall leave a great deal of chaos in my wake."

Graulas held up the Translocator. The device looked tiny in his huge hands.

Crouching, Seth snatched up a stone and flung it at the device. Graulas blocked the rock with his forearm. Baring his fangs and leaning forward, the demon struck Seth with a furious backhand. The blow sent him flying into the cave wall. Bones snapped, and he landed in a heap of agony, dirt and blood in his mouth.

"Do not irritate me," the demon growled. Chuckling softly, he sprinkled sand from the copper teapot over Seth. "The Sands of Sanctity bring amazing new possibilities to the field of torture. Imagine shattering bones over and over and over. Such alluring options . . ."

Bones mended, cuts closed, and Seth sat up. He glared up at the demon with helpless fury, no words left to say.

"Final piece of advice?" Graulas offered. "Run away, Seth. Forget this backward circus of a preserve and flee to the farthest, most barren portion of the globe. Hide there for the rest of your life. Pray we do not meet again."

Graulas twisted the Translocator and vanished.

"No!" Seth yelled.

Scrambling to his feet, Seth ran toward the mouth of the cave. He had to warn Grandpa! Graulas had certainly never been inside the main house. The demon had probably never been in the yard, either. He could not teleport directly to the Chronometer. First the demon would have to contend with the magical barriers protecting the yard and house.

Out in front of the cave, sunset was dwindling, the first stars already shining. "Hugo," Seth shouted, cupping his hands around his mouth. "Anyone! Help! Emergency! Help!"

Nobody answered, but he knew the way to the house from here—he had only to follow the rutted road. Seth took off running. The exertion felt good, kept him busy, provided the illusion that he was accomplishing something. After his gut-wrenching mistake, the last thing he wanted to do was think.

But it was hard to shut down his guilty mind.

Why didn't he see this coming? Grandpa had consistently warned him to stay away from Graulas! Seth had assumed his grandparents didn't understand the unique relationship he had with the demon. The dying demon had seemed so weak, and so helpful, that Seth had begun to consider him safe. Now the relationship had culminated in nightmarish betrayal, just as his grandparents had foreseen. If he had gone directly home with the artifacts, his family would be in a solid position in their war against the Sphinx. Now the opposite was true! He had befriended evil, and he had gotten burned.

Seth tried not to imagine all of the effects that would flow from his blunder. He tried not to envision Graulas slaying his family. He resisted visions of demon hordes rampaging across the globe.

Maybe he could stop it. Maybe he could beat Graulas into the house.

His breathing became more ragged, and his heart hammered, but Seth kept his legs churning. How much longer to the house if he kept up this pace? Ten minutes? More?

Something huge came crashing through the bushes off to the side of the road. Seth slowed, confident he recognized what was approaching. A moment later, Hugo loped out from under the trees. "Seth!" the golem bellowed, raising both arms.

"Hugo!" Seth exclaimed.

The golem picked Seth up, tossed him disturbingly high into the air, and caught him gently. "Seth not taken!"

"Whoa!" Seth laughed. "Good to see you, too! Hugo, we have an emergency. Graulas got loose and is headed for the house."

"Graulas?"

"I visited him and he tricked me. We have to hurry!"

The golem cradled Seth in one arm and bounded into the woods, cutting cross-country. Still panting from his run, Seth tried to calm his mind. Getting a lift from Hugo would let him reach the house much faster. But what would he do when he got there? Could Hugo defeat Graulas? Probably not. The demon was bigger and had unknown powers. What if the golem could at least wrestle away the Translocator? It would be worth a try. If that failed, they would have to try to escape somehow with the Chronometer. Where could they go?

From up ahead, Seth heard ferocious roaring. Bursts of light interrupted the deepening twilight.

"See that, Hugo?" Seth asked.

"Demon attack house," Hugo replied, pounding through the forest.

The golem trampled a path through the lush, spring foliage, tearing branches aside and bulldozing through shrubbery. Minutes passed like hours. Flashes of light accompanied feral growls and distant sounds of demolition. Realizing that he was unarmed, Seth wished for his emergency kit.

When the yard came into view, the barn was already ablaze. Devouring flames raged up most of one wall and across much of the roof. Mooing like a foghorn, eyes rolling in terror, the immense form of Viola the cow stamped across the yard, giant hooves leaving deep impressions in the lawn. By the nightmarish light of the burning barn, Seth could see that half the house had collapsed, smashed in as if by some natural disaster. He did not see Graulas, but could hear glass breaking and wood splintering within the house.

"To the house!" Seth shouted.

Hugo took off across the yard with leaping strides. A great crash sounded within the house. The golem vaulted onto what remained of the back porch and entered the ruined house, striding over the remnants of missing walls.

"Coulter," Hugo said in a concerned rumble. The golem waded through rubble-strewn rooms to the entry hall, where they found Coulter pinned beneath a beam. Dust covered his mostly bare scalp. His little tuft of gray hair was matted with blood. He was mumbling, semiconscious.

"Get the beam off of him!" Seth cried.

The golem gripped the heavy beam, shifting rubble as he raised it. Grabbing Coulter beneath his arms, Seth slid him out from underneath. Coulter jerked his head toward Seth. "Run!" Coulter urged weakly.

"Demon gone," Hugo said.

Coulter clutched at Seth. "Seth? He got it. Graulas got the Chronometer. He also had the Translocator. He destroyed the foundational treaty. He used a spell to summon the safe that contained it. It hurried to him like a trained dog. He destroyed the documentation and undid the magic. I couldn't stop him. He smashed through the defenses in no time."

"It's my fault," Seth admitted wretchedly. "I was a prisoner at Living Mirage, and somebody snuck the Translocator and the Sands of Sanctity into my cell. I'd promised Graulas I would heal him if I could, so on my way back here, I stopped by his cave. As soon as I healed him, he stole the artifacts before I could react. He was so quick!"

Coulter closed his eyes, one cheek twitching. "I see." When he spoke again, he sounded more in control of himself. "Seth, you must listen to me. I don't have much time."

"Don't talk like that," Seth said.

"Hush," Coulter insisted. "I'm no tenderfoot. I've had plenty of injuries in my time, and I know what this is. Things got crushed, parts deep inside. I have minutes, maybe seconds. Listen. While Graulas attacked the barn, I grabbed the Chronometer. As he tore into the house, I watched from a window, trying to formulate a strategy. After I glimpsed you at the edge of the woods with Hugo, I used the Chronometer."

"Used it how?" Seth asked.

Coulter coughed wetly. "I visited Patton. Told him the Chronometer was about to be taken. Told him you were around."

"You should have run!" Seth said.

"I did run. Visiting Patton cost me no time. I didn't even make it to the front door. There was no escaping what happened. Graulas is too powerful. But listen. Since we knew you were around, Patton promised to leave you some advice. A passageway beneath the old manor leads to a secret grotto. Down in the cellar, beneath the manor, you'll find a fireplace against one wall. Step inside and say, 'Everybody loves a show-off.' That will open the way."

"Then what?" Seth asked.

Coulter grimaced, his breath hissing through clenched teeth. "We hope Patton has an idea."

"Where are the others?" Seth asked urgently. "Where is Grandpa?"

Coulter shook his head. "Gone. If they lost the

Translocator, they were all captured at Living Mirage earlier tonight."

"All of them?" Seth asked incredulously.

"Stan, Ruth, Kendra, Tanu, Warren . . . all of them. I was . . . holding down the fort. Vanessa is still here, down in the Quiet Box. Maybe she could help. Use your judgment." Coulter gasped and coughed. "I'm on my way out," he grunted. "Do your best."

Hot tears flowed freely down Seth's cheeks. "I'm so sorry, Coulter."

The old relics collector patted his hand. His eyes cleared for a moment and locked with Seth's. He seemed intent on speaking, but the words resisted. "Not your fault," he finally sputtered. He gripped Seth's wrist. "You're a good boy. They tricked you. You were . . . showing mercy. Maybe we can get them yet."

"I will. I promise, I will, I really will."

Coulter laid his head back, closing his eyes. His chest shook as if trying to cough, but only a faint strangling sound came out. His eyelids fluttered. His hands jerked.

Seth looked up at Hugo. "What do we do?"

Coulter exhaled one last time and then went limp and silent. Seth felt for breathing at his mouth and tried to find a pulse in his neck and chest. There were no signs of life. Trying to recall the first-aid basics he knew, Seth started rhythmically compressing Coulter's chest. Then he pinched Coulter's nostrils shut and breathed into his mouth a couple of times. He repeated the compressions and the breathing exercise, but Coulter remained inert.

"Coulter gone," Hugo rumbled heavily.

Seth backed away from the corpse of his friend. Despite the words of comfort from Coulter, he could not avoid the conviction that he had caused this. Sure, the demons had designed and carried out the plot, but Seth had been the idiot they could design it around. Both Graulas and Nagi Luna had known he would do the wrong thing, and he had, and now Coulter was dead, Fablehaven was in ruins, and the artifacts were gone.

The weight of his regret threatened to crush him. Thanks to his lack of judgment, the Society of the Evening Star now had all the keys to the demon prison.

CHAPTER FOURTEEN

An Unexpected Ally

There seemed to be some confusion regarding where to put Kendra. She spent a lot of time waiting in smoky guard rooms as men and goblins haggled. When her escorts had finally resolved on a cell, just as she was being ushered inside, a stumpy goblin with squinty eyes and a face like a catcher's mitt showed up waving a written order. A tall, armored man and a potbellied goblin with a severe underbite studied the parchment.

"Came straight from the top," the squinty goblin rasped importantly.

"I can see that, pugface," snarled the goblin with the underbite. "Why that cell? We haven't had a chance to properly examine it yet, what with all the commotion."

"You telling me no?" the squinty goblin challenged.

"I'm saying it don't add up," the other goblin groused.

"Not our place to do the math," advised the armored man. "Boss always has his reasons."

"There's some sense," applauded the squinty goblin.

"This way," the armored man said to Kendra.

They escorted her deeper into the bowels of the dungeon, finally opening a thick wooden door. The potbellied goblin motioned for her to enter.

"You're sure?" Kendra asked.

"Don't get smart," the goblin spat.

The door banged shut behind her and the guards tromped away. When she had first been led away from the Sphinx, her captors had made her take off her shirt of adamant mail. She felt much more vulnerable without it. Feeble torchlight seeped in through a peephole, but Kendra didn't need it. To her eyes, even the deepest shadows of the room were dim, not dark.

The only furniture in the dank space was a flimsy cot. Water dripped steadily in one corner. A hole in the floor appeared to serve as a latrine. What most caught Kendra's eye were the messages scratched on the wall. She roamed the cell, reading the crudely inscribed phrases.

Seth rules!

Welcome to Seth's House.

Seth rocks!

Seth was here. Now it's your turn.

Seth Sorenson forever.

Enjoy the food!

If you're reading this, you can read.

All roads lead to Seth.
Is it still dripping?
Seth haunts these halls.
You're in a Turkish prison!
Seth is the man!
Use the meal mats as toilet paper.
And so forth.

Cold, hopeless, and alone, Kendra found herself giggling at the messages her brother had scrawled. He must have been so bored!

Kendra sat on the cot. Where had her brother gone? One of the guards had mentioned that the cell needed to be inspected. Did that mean Seth had escaped? It fit the discussion she had overheard, but seemed too much to hope. Escaped to where? After all, they were on a hostile preserve in Eastern Turkey.

Should she search for a way out? Could Seth have dug a tunnel? He had been captured less than a week ago. Unlikely or not, it seemed faithless not to look. She probed the walls and floors, tapping, pulling, trying to dig her fingers into cracks. She scooted the cot aside, in case it helped mask some kind of false panel. Her attempt at optimism began to wane. If Seth had excavated an escape tunnel, could he possibly have hidden it so well?

The Sphinx had suggested she might cross paths with her brother. What had he meant? Remembering the bickering guards, she assumed that the Sphinx had taken an active role in selecting her cell. Was the point for her to see the messages on the walls? That was sort of like crossing paths.

Would he have deliberately assigned her to a cell with an escape tunnel? Not likely.

She began to really worry about Seth. If he hadn't escaped, what had they done with him? Could the cell be faulty in a dangerous way? Would she cross paths with her brother by dying from the same type of accident? She studied the stone roof, half expecting it to cave in at any moment.

Search as she might, the dismal room offered no clues. She detected no means of escape, and perceived no particular threats. Maybe Seth had had the right idea. Maybe her time would be best spent scratching messages on the walls for the benefit of the next occupant.

From the back of the cell came a deep grating of stone on stone. Kendra watched in startled awe as a portion of the wall slid aside. Had she inadvertently stepped on a hidden trigger?

An unapproachably attractive young man with a white light in his hand ducked through the gap left by the sliding wall. He froze when he saw Kendra, wincing and tilting his head away. He raised a hand to shield his eyes.

"Who are you?" Kendra challenged.

"One of the neighbors," the stranger said. "I thought my sources must be mistaken when I heard they had already filled the vacancy here."

"You know who was here before?"

"I do. Can you turn it down a little?"

"Excuse me?"

"Hit the dimmer or something? You're shining like a

lighthouse." Blinking away tears, he made brief eye contact with her.

"Most people can't see my light," Kendra said. "Including me."

"Right, give me a second, my eyes will adjust." Blinking frequently, he turned his head toward her more and gradually widened his eyes. "Okay, I think I can handle it." His wincing expression diminished, replaced by something more like wonder. "Wow, you'll never be dim."

They stared at each other for a moment. His threadbare clothes hugged an athletic build. He had thick, longish hair; expressive, silver-blue eyes; and flawless skin. His boyishly charming features would look much more at home on a magazine cover than in a prison.

"I'm Bracken," he said.

"Does the Sphinx send you to all the new girls?" He was way too good-looking to be anything but a spy.

He held up his hands as if to calm her. "You're wise to be cautious."

"Believe me, I've learned caution. Tell the Sphinx to let me rot in peace."

"Now, don't write me off just yet. I'd have the same suspicions about you, but you're obviously fairykind. Which must mean . . . you're his sister?"

"Whose sister?"

"Seth's."

Kendra resisted getting excited by the mention of her brother. Of course he knew about Seth. He was just trying to push her buttons. "Where is my brother?"

Folding his arms, Bracken regarded her appraisingly. "He never mentioned you were so . . . bright."

Kendra felt herself blushing. "Answer the question." Her voice was hard.

Again Bracken raised his palms. "Sorry. I will. He's gone. I'm not sure where. Probably Fablehaven."

"What?"

"Somebody brought the Translocator to him and he teleported out of here."

"How is that possible?"

"Your guess would probably be better than mine. Hopefully he'll contact me before long."

Kendra huffed in exasperation. "Are you guys pen pals?"

"I gave him a coin that lets us communicate telepathically. I know he's far from here, because I can't hail him. Once he uses the coin to reach out to me, we should be able to speak."

Kendra frowned. "A magical telepathy coin? Who are you? At least, who are you pretending to be?"

Bracken chuckled and shook his head. "The truth sounds absurd."

"Try me."

"You don't even believe I'm an actual prisoner; you're not going to believe this."

"Give it a shot. You might want to stutter—that could help sell it."

"Stutter?"

"Long story."

He glanced away. "I'm a unicorn."

Kendra's jaw dropped. It took her a moment to recover. "Did you just say a unicorn?"

Eyes hesitant, he shrugged using hands and shoulders. "I warned you."

Kendra laughed incredulously. "Look. Bracken. You need to go back to spy school. In fact, maybe you should just try a different career path. You obviously weren't hired for your brains."

"Maybe you're right. I would be a suspiciously lousy spy."

"What, you're saying I should believe you because you're incompetent? Or just because your story sounds crazy? I don't suppose you can prove that you're actually a horse?"

"I'm stuck in human form. I lost my horn."

Kendra covered her eyes with one hand. "This is actually worse than feeling lonely."

"You're fairykind. Can't you perceive my aura?"

She looked at him. He was undeniably handsome. That was all. "I've never been good at seeing that stuff."

His eyes lit up with an idea. "I am now speaking the secret fairy language. Can you understand me?"

"Yes."

"Can you tell I am no longer speaking English?"

Kendra tried to focus. She heard English, but something did feel different. "I interpret intuitively. Keep talking."

"What should I say? I suppose it doesn't matter. I'm trapped in a dungeon with a girl who thinks I have lost my mind."

"I can tell you're speaking another language," Kendra

said. "But I can't tell the difference between the various fairy languages."

"At least it's a start," Bracken said. She perceived that he had reverted to English. "I can take you to visit some of your friends. Maddox, for example. Mara."

"The guards just let you roam free? Don't they know you're sneaking around in the walls?"

"Our captors look the other way if we stay unobtrusive. I've been here for a very long time. This dungeon is vast and ancient, riddled with forgotten tunnels and unused spaces. The rest we dig—*we* meaning the prisoners."

"What about my parents?"

"I know of no accessible route to their cell. I looked into it for Seth."

"But they're here?"

"I believe so."

"I'd love to contact them. They think I'm dead."

"Wish I could help. Hopefully Seth will show up soon and rescue us. He can vouch for me."

Kendra considered the statement. "It might take more than Seth's endorsement."

"Don't underestimate your brother. He was careful. He didn't trust me right away. In fact, maybe he still doesn't really trust me. I hope he uses the coin."

"If you gave him a magical toy, he'll use it."

Bracken sighed. "I can't believe you're fairykind and you can't recognize a unicorn. You know, the sooner you trust me, the sooner we can play ping-pong."

"Huh?"

"Nothing. Lousy joke. It'll make sense later. Unicorns aren't very social creatures. I'm doing my best."

"You're fine."

"Doesn't help that you're so . . . brilliant."

"Is that sarcasm?"

"I meant brilliant as in shiny. Should I stop talking?"

She was starting to entertain the possibility that Bracken might be legitimate. Wouldn't the Sphinx's dungeon be full of good creatures like unicorns? Many of his prisoners should be potential allies. Of course, every time she started trusting a stranger, it seemed like she got burned. Gavin had seemed great before his true nature was revealed. She would be slow to offer any real trust. "You're saying you could take me to Maddox right now?"

"I'm saying—" he stopped. Suddenly he looked stricken. "I don't believe it," he muttered in a completely different tone.

"What?" Kendra asked.

"I have an intruder in my cell." He sounded astonished.

"How do you know?"

Bracken turned to face the gap in the rear wall. "I created a magical detection system that would signal me if anybody entered while I was away. It has never alerted me before. Nobody ever visits my cell."

"What does it mean?" Kendra wondered.

"I have no idea. This has been the most eventful night this dungeon has seen in decades. I have to investigate. My cell is some distance away. Care to join me?"

If he was an enemy, she supposed he could harm her as

easily here in her cell as out in some secret passageway. "Sure."

He smiled. "Follow me." His expression seemed so play-ful, Kendra found herself wanting to please him.

They slipped through the gap and Bracken closed the sliding wall. Using the light from his stone to guide them, he led Kendra on an elaborate path, through hidden hatchways, down stairwells and ladders, along tight crawl spaces. They headed mostly downward, until at last they reached an area that looked like a natural cave, with no clear path and glis-tening rock formations that appeared half melted. Soon they sat and scooted down a cramped incline of oily stone. No wonder Bracken's clothes looked so ragged!

Just before the bottom of the incline, he directed Kendra into a branching passageway. They hurriedly proceeded along a crudely excavated stretch of tunnel and finally reached a dead end. Bracken held a finger to his lips. Leaning his mouth to Kendra's ear, he whispered, "My visitor awaits us inside." He produced a short, sharp knife. "Stand back."

Kendra stepped away. Bracken waved a hand and sang a few unintelligible words, and a portal opened. Glowing stone in one hand, knife in the other, Bracken entered.

"Who are you?" Bracken demanded.

"A friend," came the answer. Kendra knew that voice!

"I hope so," Bracken replied. "You have a much larger knife."

Kendra peered through the opening into Bracken's cell.

The spacious room was more cavelike than her cell, but equally bare.

The intruder was Warren, warily clutching the fancy sword he had claimed back at Lost Mesa.

She caught his eye. "Kendra!" he exclaimed.

"You know each other?" Bracken asked.

"This is my friend Warren," Kendra said. "Or I guess he could be a stingbulb."

"How did you get in here?" Bracken challenged.

"I understand you can protect those around you from outside scrutiny," Warren said. "Sort of a psychic shield."

"Yes," Bracken said. "How would you know that?"

"Are you doing it now?"

"I always do it. Nagi Luna is constantly trying to spy. The only scrying tool I can't thwart is the Oculus. I see that you have a charm that protects you from scrutiny."

Warren fingered the feathery, beaded amulet around his neck. "A recent gift. We need to talk."

Putting his knife away, Bracken approached Warren. "First, I need to confirm you are not an imposter."

"How?"

"Remove the amulet, and give me your hands."

Warren glanced at Kendra. "Do you trust this guy?"

She shrugged. "A little, I guess."

"I won't do anything hurtful," Bracken promised.

"He says he's a unicorn," Kendra inserted.

"So I've heard," Warren said. He removed the amulet and took Bracken's hands. They stared at one another.

"Just relax," Bracken said. "Think about what you hope

to accomplish by visiting me." Soon he released Warren's hands. "He's not a stingbulb. Nor is he an enemy. Good to meet you. I'm Bracken."

"Warren, how did you get down here?" Kendra asked.

"I wish I could say through my own brilliant innovation," Warren said. "I had help."

"From who?" Bracken wondered.

"The Sphinx."

"What?" Kendra exclaimed.

"I know how it sounds," Warren said. "Hear me out. It will make sense."

"We're listening," Bracken said skeptically.

"Tonight changed everything for the Sphinx," Warren explained. "He has lost control of the Society."

Bracken scowled doubtfully. "How?"

"Graulas is here."

"The demon who helped Seth back at Fablehaven?" Kendra asked. "Isn't he dying?"

"Not anymore," Warren said. "Apparently a demon called Nagi Luna here at Living Mirage had an agent slip Seth the Translocator and the Sands of Sanctity. Seth escaped the dungeon and went to heal Graulas. Once healed, the demon stole the artifacts, acquired the Chronometer, and came here."

"Seth healed Graulas!" Kendra cried.

"He must have thought he was being kind," Warren inferred.

"So now the Society has all five artifacts," Kendra said.

"And something the Sphinx never counted on," Warren said.

"A powerful demon vying for control," Bracken surmised. "The Sphinx always maintained he would open Zzyzx only on his terms."

"But his plans have fallen apart," Warren said. "Graulas has already won over most of the Society, including Mr. Lich. Many have long felt the Sphinx was too lenient and conservative. If the Sphinx doesn't play along, he'll end up a prisoner in his own dungeon. Blixes are mortal beings, and Mr. Lich has been with the Sphinx almost since the beginning, sipping from the same Font of Immortality. With or without the Sphinx, Mr. Lich can use the Translocator and the Chronometer to begin the process of opening Zzyzx."

"And the demons can finish it," Kendra said.

Bracken pounded a frustrated fist into his palm. "Deluded as the Sphinx was, we're all worse off than before."

"We have one ray of hope," Warren said. "If he can't do it on his terms, the Sphinx wants to abort the opening of Zzyzx. He wants to stop Graulas as badly as we do. He can't let the demons know his intentions. He wants to remain close to the center of things, in the hopes of bringing them down from the inside. But he provided me with some key information."

"How did you meet up with him?" Bracken inquired.

"Earlier in the night, I was part of a rescue attempt," Warren said. "Kendra came here as part of the same mission. I was dropped off separately from the rest of the strike force as a fail-safe. I began evasive maneuvers the instant the dwarf left my side, and good thing I did. Minutes later I was the target of a manhunt. Coulter, a friend of ours, had lent me his invisibility glove, which improved my chances. Even so, I barely managed to elude my pursuers.

"Not long after Graulas arrived at Living Mirage, the Sphinx decided to personally lead the hunt for me. Accompanied by a few wraiths under his control, the Sphinx tracked me down. But instead of bringing me in, he told me the situation, gave me some keys, and explained about a secret passage into the depths of his dungeon."

"You can lead us out of here?" Bracken exclaimed.

"By a pathway known only to the Sphinx," Warren confirmed.

"Then what?" Kendra said.

"He wants us to protect the Eternals," Warren said.

Bracken laughed bitterly. "The world is upside down."

"He said there are three Eternals left. He recently learned the location of one, a man called Roon Osricson, who has long occupied a heavily fortified stronghold in Finland."

"Okay," Bracken said uncertainly.

"The Sphinx feels certain Graulas will move against Roon immediately," Warren said. "The demon is already campaigning for support to remove Nagi Luna from her confinement in the dungeon. The Sphinx believes it will not be long before Nagi Luna holds the Oculus in her hands. Once she does, he believes she will speedily discover the remaining Eternals. Bracken, he wants you to leave one of your psychic communicators in your room. He will retrieve it and feed us information as it becomes available."

"This is a dangerous game," Bracken whispered. "You understand, our interests may temporarily align, but the Sphinx does not share our agenda. His end goal is not to stop the opening of Zzyzx, but to regain control of the situation and open it on his terms."

"I get it," Warren said. "But keep in mind, if Graulas is here and healthy, what are the odds of the Sphinx regaining control?"

"I see your point," Bracken said. "Nevertheless, we mustn't underestimate him. Or place full trust in him."

"Agreed," Warren said. "However, for the moment, I think it benefits everyone to use each other."

"How can we get out of here?" Bracken asked.

"It has to look like we escaped," Warren said. "The Sphinx said the main gate is heavily guarded. According to him, our best bet is to head to the fairy shrine."

"The shrine here is sealed," Bracken said resentfully.

"Right," Warren said. "By the Sphinx. He gave me the key."

Bracken cocked his head as if weighing the odds. "So we hope the Fairy Queen can conjure a way out of here."

"Seems like our best bet," Warren said.

"What do you mean, the shrine is sealed?" Kendra wondered.

"The Sphinx didn't want the Fairy Queen to be able to spy on him," Bracken said. "He lacked the power to destroy her shrine here, so he sealed it off, covering it with an ensorcelled iron dome."

"The dome has an access port," Warren said. "And I now have a copy of the key."

"Getting to the shrine will be no simple affair," Bracken warned. "This is not a mild preserve."

"Tell me about it," Warren said. "When the Sphinx showed up with his wraith squad, he had to rescue me from a manticore."

"Won't the wraiths share what is happening with the demons?" Kendra asked.

"The Sphinx is a mighty shadow charmer," Bracken said. "His wraiths and phantoms communicate only with him. They will not divulge his secrets, and he should be strong enough to shield his mind from Graulas and Nagi Luna."

"Let's hope so," Warren muttered.

"The Sphinx gave you that amulet?" Bracken asked.

"He did. And he promised to help divert the search for me away from the path to the shrine."

Bracken turned to Kendra. "What do you say? Your brother currently holds the record for quickest escape from the dungeons of the Great Ziggurat. You ready to dethrone him?"

"What about the others?" Kendra asked. "Can't we take my grandparents?"

Warren winced. "The passage out of the dungeon is down very deep. The Sphinx warned we should keep the escape small. In fact, the only people he specified were you two. He promised to try to aid the others."

Bracken patted Kendra's arm consolingly. "If the passage out is down here in the depths, we can't get to your parents or grandparents without passing numerous checkpoints. We might be able to collect Maddox and Mara. Of course, Mara is still recovering from injuries, Maddox has had trouble moving quickly ever since Rio Branco, and neither of them is nearby."

"Up to you guys," Warren said. "Speed will matter. As soon as Nagi Luna gets the Oculus, we won't be able to shield ourselves from her view."

"Then we should seize the moment and depart," Bracken decided. "Kendra?"

"Seems like the only choice."

"Either of you have a coin?" Bracken asked.

Warren dug in his pockets. "How about a quarter?"

"Perfect. I prefer coins to stones." Bracken cupped the coin in one hand and covered it with the other. For a moment, his hands shed a pearly radiance. Then he placed the quarter under a rock in a corner of the room.

"Did you just turn that into a communicator?" Warren asked.

"Correct. If the Sphinx wants to feed us intelligence, he now has the means." Bracken adjusted the position of the stone over the coin. "How did you get into my cell? There are three secret entrances."

"I came through the front door. The Sphinx gave me a key. The passage out of the ziggurat begins just around the corner."

Bracken smirked. "Right under my nose all these years. How could I have missed it?"

"It's perfectly disguised and heavily enchanted," Warren said. "Only opens for the password, which is in Akkadian. I had to memorize the syllables."

"I'm usually able to detect such things," Bracken said. "I suppose it didn't help that I spend most of my time skulking along forgotten passageways. I'm seldom out in the main corridors."

"We ready?" Warren asked.

"My possessions are few," Bracken said. "Lead on."

Warren opened the cell door. Kendra and Bracken shadowed him into the hallway and tiptoed around the corner.

Bracken nudged Kendra. "Nagi Luna resides around that next corner, at the end of the hall."

"Tough neighborhood," Warren whispered. He paused in front of a blank wall.

"Here?" Bracken asked, running a hand along the surface, eyes intent. "I must be losing my touch."

Warren spoke strange words, and the wall became semi-transparent. Warren stepped through it.

Bracken gave a low whistle. "I feel a little better. This was very well concealed, the work of a true master."

He and Kendra walked through the wall and started up a long stairway.

CHAPTER FIFTEEN

Message in a Bottle

His promise to Coulter helped pull Seth back from the brink of total emotional collapse. By degrees, he stopped looking inward at his guilt and became aware of the demolished room around him, of the golem waiting patiently at his side. He glanced at the steel safe crumpled in a corner like a crushed soda can. He heard timbers creak and crash as part of the burning barn collapsed outside. Outside. Did the house even have an inside or an outside anymore, now that so much of it had been torn down?

"I really blew it this time," Seth said to Hugo.

"Bad demon," the golem said.

"I just didn't see this coming," Seth moaned. "How could I be so blind?"

The golem said nothing. A big hand patted Seth on the shoulder consolingly.

Seth wiped his nose. He needed to get busy, to lose himself in a task. "I can't undo what happened. But I can't quit, either. Maybe Patton has an idea for a next move. We need to go to the old manor."

"Danger," Hugo warned.

"I know it isn't safe," Seth agreed. "With the treaty destroyed, we could run into bloodthirsty monsters anywhere. But that also means it isn't any safer here. Not anymore."

"Hugo keep safe," the golem rumbled.

"I believe it," Seth said.

"Hello?" called a timid voice. Seth whirled. It sounded like Kendra.

"Kendra?" he answered, confused.

"Sort of," came the reply. After a moment, his sister limped into the room, favoring her right leg.

"You're the stingbulb," Seth said. They had placed an injured duplicate of Kendra in the Quiet Box after Tanu had done all he could to heal her. "How did you get out of the Quiet Box?"

"They put Vanessa inside when they left on their mission, which meant I had to come out. My time is running short. I won't survive much beyond daybreak."

"Do you know what happened here?" Seth asked.

"Not really. Nobody brought me up to speed. I'm still hurt, so I can't help much. Being in the Quiet Box froze my healing. I'll expire before I become whole again. I wanted to listen to music, so they placed me in Vanessa's former cell. She has a terrific sound system."

"Would you be willing to go back into the Quiet Box?"

"Sure, if you want," she said. "It prolongs my existence. It isn't much different from back when I was just a fruit. Minus the connection to the tree, of course."

It was strange to be talking with his sister, knowing it was not his sister. "We got attacked by a demon."

"Sounded bad," the stingbulb said. "I was hesitant to come up, but curiosity got the better of me. You were captured, weren't you? They were talking about it after they got me out."

"They came to rescue me, and all of them got caught, but I got away. It's a long story."

She nodded, then glanced at the corpse on the floor. "The demon got Coulter?"

"Yeah," Seth said, voice getting husky. Her expression didn't change. "Does it make you sad?"

"Not in the same way it would make Kendra sad," the stingbulb said frankly. "I have memories of her feelings for him. But I'm aware they aren't my memories. Kendra gave me general instructions to help you guys, so I'm regretful that I couldn't prevent the mishap."

"Would you take orders from me?" Seth asked.

"Sure. The last standing orders I got from Kendra before entering the Quiet Box were to always help your family and never betray you. I could interpret that to mean I should follow your commands."

He wondered how he might make use of the stingbulb.

Nothing immediately came to mind. Her injured leg would limit his options. He could store her in the Quiet Box until a need arose, but that would mean freeing Vanessa. Did he want the narcoblix's help or not? Hard to say. He should probably visit Patton first.

"Is the dungeon in good shape?" Seth asked.

"The ceiling collapsed in part of the stairway up to the house," she replied. "A section of the ceiling in the first hall fell in as well. The main door in the hall was knocked askew, which let me get up here. The rest of the dungeon seems to be intact."

That was a relief. The last thing he needed was all those dangerous prisoners going free. He wondered how much the destruction of the treaty would weaken the dungeon.

"I think we'll leave Vanessa in the Quiet Box for now," Seth decided. "I might want her help later. Can we keep Coulter in Vanessa's cell with you?"

"Sure, I'll watch over his body."

"Hugo, would you mind?"

"Not mind," Hugo said, picking up Coulter.

"I'll wait here," Seth said. "Hugo, you might want to carry the stingbulb back down, too. Her leg is hurt."

Hugo picked up the stingbulb in his other hand and lumbered out of the room, rubble crunching underfoot. Seth plopped down on the remnants of a couch. Graulas must have used more than his physical strength to damage the house. He had destroyed too much too quickly. Magic must have been involved.

Seth considered his assets. The loyal golem topped the

list. He also had an expiring stingbulb, a semi-trustworthy narcoblix, and hopefully a message from Patton. And what about his emergency kit? Might Kendra have replaced it in his room? Knowing her, it would be in its place under his bed. Unless she had taken it to Living Mirage in order to return it to him.

He took the coin from his pocket. He could communicate with Bracken. The thought of talking to the unicorn made him shiver. How could he tell him that he had already lost the Translocator? No, he would reach out to Bracken later.

What about Dale? Might he have joined the rescue mission? Coulter hadn't specified. Seth had never known Dale to go abroad on a mission. He was probably around here someplace. If so, with the treaty undone, he might be in trouble. Seth would ask Hugo.

Before long, heralded by heavy footfalls, the golem returned. Seth rose from the damaged couch.

"Do you know where Dale is?" Seth asked.

The golem tilted his head back. Was he looking at the broken ceiling? Was he listening? Seth wasn't sure how the golem saw and heard, or if his senses worked some other way. "Stables," the golem said. "Safe room."

"Does the safe room still work?"

"Yes."

Seth regarded the golem. How could he know Dale was at the stables? "Do you see him, Hugo?"

The golem placed fingers into the empty hollows of his eyes. "Not here." Then Hugo tapped his temple. "See here."

"With your mind?"

"Yes."

"So Dale is safe for now?"

"Yes."

"Can you see Grandpa?"

Hugo raised his head searchingly, leaning first one way, then another. "Too far."

Seth hadn't expected it to work, but it had been worth a try. "I need to look for my emergency kit before we go." The staircase from the entry hall had collapsed, but the hall at the top partly remained. "Can you get me up to that hall?"

Hugo picked up Seth, walked over to where the stairs had once stood, and lightly tossed him up to the hallway. With Hugo's height and reach, the golem did not have to throw him far. In one direction, the hallway ended along with the rest of the house, leaving an open view of treetops and stars. The attic stairs were the other way.

Passing gaps in the walls, Seth hustled to the attic stairs, which he found mostly intact, although deep cracks ran through the stairwell. The playroom at the top was missing most of one wall, part of another, and a good portion of the ceiling. There were some holes in the floor. But the beds were in place. Peeking under his bed, Seth instantly spotted his emergency kit. He checked inside and found the contents in place, including the figurines of the leviathan and the tower he had brought from Wyrmroost.

Returning as he had come, Seth dropped into Hugo's reaching grasp. "I got it. Now we can head for the manor."

The golem exited the crumbling house through the

back. Glaring firelight brightened the night, the entirety of the barn now blazing. Another portion of the structure collapsed, sending a whirlwind of sparks above the towering flames. Even from a distance, Seth could feel the heat of the inferno.

As the golem started across the yard, a pair of figures emerged from the woods.

"Seth?" cried Doren.

"Seth!" shouted Newel.

The satyrs gamboled toward them across the lawn. Hugo slowed.

"You're all right!" Doren yelled. "I knew it!"

"What's happening?" Newel exclaimed.

"Put me down, Hugo," Seth said. The golem complied. "I escaped from the Society and healed Graulas."

"You healed Graulas?" Newel yelled. "Did the Society amputate your brain?"

"I thought it would ease his suffering as he died," Seth said. "Instead he stole the artifacts I had and went on a rampage. Coulter is dead. Graulas left not long ago. The Society now has all the artifacts to open Zzyzx."

"And the treaty is down," Doren added. "We felt the boundaries fall."

"Right," Seth confirmed.

"We came this way after we saw Viola crashing through the woods," Newel said. "This is going to be pandemonium. Where's Stan?"

"There's nobody around." Seth explained how the others had been captured when trying to rescue him.

"Quite a pickle," Newel lamented, hands on his woolly hips.

"What happens now?" Seth asked. "Will the creatures leave Fablehaven?"

Newel and Doren exchanged a glance. "Many of the satyrs are fleeing toward Grunhold," Doren said. "The domain of the centaurs will stand even with the treaty down. Of course, the centaurs will now be completely free to rove. Some creatures might depart. But most have their homes here now. It will be some time before many stray beyond the outer fence."

"Without a caretaker to calm things, the centaurs will probably try to take charge," Newel guessed. "They'll offer safe harbor to other creatures in exchange for land. They've always been sore they weren't running the place."

"What about the dark creatures?" Seth asked.

"Hard to say," Doren said. "The demons of Fablehaven are bound or gone. The swamp hag gets older and battier every day. The dark creatures will lack leadership. The minotaurs could cause trouble if they decide to leave their territory, but I doubt the centaurs would allow it. Without a leader, the goblins, hobgoblins, and imps will probably lie low. The fog giants love their swamp. The few trolls will skulk and look for advantages in the upheaval. Many of the darkest creatures hibernate except for on festival nights. You'll know better than anyone if the undead are on the move."

"I don't sense anything," Seth said.

"That's a relief," Doren said.

"What about you guys?" Seth asked.

"We wanted to get a grasp of the situation," Newel said.

"And now that you know . . . ?"

"It would be fun to catch a movie," Newel mused. "Do you know any theaters that allow goats inside?"

"No theaters will let goats in," Seth affirmed.

Newel frowned. "Maybe we could slip the ticket guy some of Viola's milk." He glanced at Doren. "We could wear boots and baggy pants."

"Or you could help me try to save the world," Seth said.

"You have a plan?" Doren asked.

"Best not to meddle in human affairs," Newel interrupted, grabbing Doren by the elbow. "I just remembered, we have some women and children to evacuate."

"The end of the world would mean an end to television," Seth reminded them.

Newel froze. It took him a few seconds to recover. "We'd have reruns."

"Not if people stopped running the TV stations," Seth said solemnly. "Your portable TV would be useless, even with the digital converter. On the other hand, if you helped me, there would be nothing to stop me from getting you guys a gas generator."

"A generator?" Newel said. "I'm listening."

"You'd need a reliable, long-lasting power source for your new flat-screen television and DVD player."

Newel licked his lips apprehensively. "What's the plan?"

"It's a work in progress," Seth explained. "First I need to get to the old manor. Patton left a message for me there."

Newel brightened. "So we get you to the manor, and you provide the gadgets?"

"I would need you guys to help me until this crisis is over," Seth said. "I'm not going to lie. It will be really dangerous."

"We can handle danger," Doren said stalwartly.

"Not so fast," Newel blurted. "We reserve the right to abandon you to your fate at any moment."

"In which case the deal would be off," Seth clarified.

The last major portion of the barn collapsed, a fiery wave breaking on a blazing shore. Newel folded his arms. "A gas generator needs a supply of gasoline."

"Two hundred gallons," Seth promised.

Newel was unreadable. His eyes shifted to Doren, who nodded. Newel sniffed. He swallowed. Then he spat in his palm and extended a hand. Seth shook it. Newel grinned. "You just acquired a crack commando backup unit."

"Who might abandon me at any time," Seth said, wiping his palm on his pants.

"In which case you won't have to spend your life savings on entertainment equipment," Doren added.

Newel rubbed his hands together. "I'm glad we've reached an accord. You know, it might be refreshing to embark on an actual adventure again."

"Adventures tend to be uncomfortable and deadly," Doren reminded his friend.

"Don't get me wrong," Newel said. "I've developed a keen preference for vicarious thrills. But nothing ventured, nothing gained."

Doren punched Seth playfully on the arm. "It saddened us to think we might have lost you. It will be good to help a friend."

"And to help yourselves," Seth stressed. "The end of the world sort of affects everybody."

"Hoping that these types of crises will somehow sort themselves out has served us well in the past," Newel muttered.

"Valid point," Doren seconded. He stared at Seth. "Are you sure you wouldn't rather find a place to hide and just see what happens?"

"I have to fix this," Seth said. "It's me or nobody. Sometimes I don't get you guys. You talk as if you don't have little adventures all the time!"

"*Little* is the operative word," Newel said. "Nipsie-sized. It's one thing to swipe a meal or filch some gold. That's just sport. It's easy to keep well within your limits. It's quite another decision to get involved in an actual cause. Causes have a way of tainting your reason until a person takes much bigger risks than sanity would otherwise allow."

"Which is why you reserved the right to bail," Seth said.

"Exactly," Newel said.

"Seth did save you from the influence of Ephira and Kurisock," Doren reminded him.

"I know," Newel snapped. "No need to dredge up the past. If I didn't like the boy, I wouldn't agree to this."

"Sounds like you're already investing in the cause," Doren teased.

"Enough chitchat," Newel spat, shaking a fist at Doren.

He turned to Seth. "I assume the dirtman can get you to the manor without our help. If this fiasco could snowball into a real quest, we should collect some gear."

"Not a bad idea," Seth agreed.

"We'll meet you at the manor," Doren said, turning away.

"Don't take it personally if we never show," Newel called over his shoulder.

"Let's go, Hugo," Seth said.

The golem lifted Seth and charged into the woods in a different direction from the satyrs. Seth wondered if Newel and Doren would return. If they showed up, should he really let them join him? He would love the company and the help, but hadn't he gotten enough people killed?

In the darkness beneath the trees, there was little to see. Seth could hear Hugo crashing through the undergrowth, snapping limbs and flattening shrubs. Occasionally Hugo vaulted an obstacle or climbed a steep slope. At times his route veered around unseen obstructions. Although vegetation congested the way, the golem did an expert job of shielding Seth as they plunged through dense foliage.

At one point, Hugo paused and crouched. Perhaps a minute later, Seth heard hoofed creatures galloping through the undergrowth, crossing their path ahead of them.

"Probably best to avoid being seen," Seth whispered after the sounds had faded.

"Yes," Hugo replied, as softly as he could manage, before resuming his loping gait through the trees.

At length they reached the edge of the yard that

surrounded the pillared manor. The stately building looked dark beneath the stars.

"Let's get this over with," Seth whispered, rummaging in his emergency kit for a flashlight.

"Wait," Hugo cautioned. "Troll inside. Looting. Two goblin guards."

"Can you take out the goblins?"

Hugo shook and let out an irregular exhalation. Seth realized he was laughing.

Seth patted Hugo's stony shoulder. "Let's get them."

With Seth cradled in one arm, the golem charged out into the yard. As they drew near to the manor's porch, one of the goblins called out, "Who goes there?"

Hugo didn't slow. He set Seth down before the porch steps and cleared them with a single leap. Seth glimpsed one goblin lunging with a spear. Hugo batted the weapon aside, seized the goblin by the ankles, and used him to swat the other guard. Armor clanged as they connected, and the second goblin went tumbling loudly along the porch. Still clutching the first goblin by the ankles, Hugo hurled him sidearm across the yard. The creature skimmed the grass for an incredible distance before skipping and rolling to a stop. Both goblins stumbled away at full speed, leaving their dropped weapons behind.

"Good job, Hugo," Seth said, coming up the steps.

With that same irregular exhalation, Hugo pantomimed how the goblin had bounced and spun across the yard. Seth found himself laughing as well.

"What's going on?" hissed a voice from inside the manor.

"Intruder!" Seth called in a commanding voice. "Cease your activities and come out this instant!"

A moment later, Nero appeared in the doorway, glaring until he saw Hugo. His eyes then fell on Seth. "Good evening to you," the troll said in his deep, silky voice.

Seth switched on his flashlight. The troll had a reptilian look about him, his glossy black scales highlighted by yellow markings. The nostrils of his snout flared, and his cunning eyes narrowed. His formidable muscles bunched as he coiled into a tense crouch.

"Why are you looting the manor?" Seth asked.

"Go ask your mentor," the troll replied, his tone reasonable despite his edgy posture. "Graulas ended the treaty. You can't blame an old trader for seizing an obvious opportunity."

"Graulas left me in charge," Seth said, inventing as he went. "He had to undo the treaty in order to leave Fablehaven. But he'll be back. And he wants the manor as his residence."

Baring rows of needle teeth, Nero glared at Seth suspiciously. "You openly serve him?"

Seth displayed no uncertainty. "My family abandoned Fablehaven. I stayed behind. I have much to learn. Graulas sent me to make sure his future home remained secure."

Nero became fidgety. "I had no way of knowing . . ."

"I don't blame you," Seth said. "You've helped me in the past. Help both of us tonight. Spread the word that nothing in or around the manor is to be touched. Same with the main house at Fablehaven, especially the dungeon. Graulas knows every item in both houses, and he will show no mercy to any who claim his prizes."

"Knew it was too good to be true," Nero mumbled.

"Excuse me?" Seth asked, a hint of warning in his voice.

"It will be as you say, young master Sorenson," the troll answered obsequiously, inclining his head. "Naturally, for your sake, these words had best be proven faithful when Graulas returns."

"Was that a threat?" Seth bristled. If he was going to bluff like this, he needed to play the role convincingly. "Maybe a conversation with a shade would relieve your doubts."

Raising his webbed hands, the cliff troll finally looked truly intimidated. "No need for unpleasantness."

"You're the one causing unpleasantness," Seth snapped. "I was going easy on you. I guess you vermin only speak one language. Hugo, let's see if trolls can fly as far as goblins."

The golem grasped Nero by his torso, turned, and flung him out into the yard like a football. Seth used the flashlight to follow the trajectory of the troll as he soared in a long arc. The cliff troll righted himself in the air, spreading his arms and legs like a flying squirrel. Extendable fins fanned out to help him glide. When he landed over fifty yards away, Nero rolled adroitly and ended up on his feet.

"Don't let me see you again," Seth barked, turning his back on the troll and entering the house. Not far from the door lay a bulging sack crammed with candlesticks, silverware, and other household treasures. Behind Seth, Hugo squeezed through the doorway.

"Is he leaving?" Seth whispered after a moment.

"Yes," Hugo confirmed quietly.

Seth sagged. "Good. I'm glad he landed all right. I didn't want to be mean. I wanted to protect our property and keep dark creatures away from us. Thanks for backing me up."

"Hugo help."

"You sure did." Seth shouldered the heavy sack and lugged it to the pantry, where it would be slightly more hidden. Regardless of the message he had shared with Nero, there would probably be more looters. No need to make their job easier. "Let's find the stairs to the cellar."

Hugo leaned his head back searchingly. "Come."

Flashlight brightening the way, Seth followed Hugo to a locked door. A nudge from Hugo broke it open, and they descended the stairway beyond. Barrels, crates, and boxes cluttered the webby basement. The flashlight beam revealed an iron door on a nearby wall. Seth wondered if it led to a dungeon.

They located the fireplace without much effort. Hugo swiftly brushed some large barrels aside to clear a path for Seth, stirring up dust and making sheets of cobweb flap and tear. Seth ducked into the fireplace and recited, "Everybody loves a show-off."

Immediately the back of the fireplace turned to dust. Seth walked through the insubstantial barrier, particles swirling in his wake, and passed into a tunnel with rock walls braced by wooden beams. The air in the man-made tunnel was noticeably cooler. Hugo followed on hands and knees.

They proceeded along the passage, the ground sloping constantly downward. After some distance, the tunnel widened into a spacious natural cavern. A gentle stream trickled across the lowest part of the room, appearing from under one wall and vanishing beneath another. The flashlight illuminated several chests, a bed, a desk, a safe, camping gear, stacked crates, a few barrels, and a large table covered with maps.

A green, corked bottle on the table caught Seth's eye due to the large white label on it with *SETH* written in bold letters. He crossed to the table and picked up the bottle, then unfolded the note he found underneath, scanning the succinct message.

The contents of this bottle are meant only for Seth Sorenson.

Seth worked at the cork with his thumbs but could not get it to budge. Digging into his emergency kit, he got out his pocketknife, selected the corkscrew attachment, and twisted it into the cork. After a good tug, the cork came unplugged with a hollow pop, and colored gas started gushing out of the bottle.

Seth set the bottle on the table and backed away, briefly concerned that a saboteur had turned the message from Patton into a poisonous trap. But a moment later, as the gas finished flowing from the mouth of the bottle, it gathered into the form of Patton—old, wrinkled, and semitransparent.

"Patton," Hugo rumbled.

"If this is Seth," the Patton cloud said, "try to touch me."

Seth strode forward and passed a hand through the

gaseous figure, creating a temporary disturbance in his midsection.

"Very good," Patton said. "I'm glad we managed to connect. Our friend Coulter delivered a most disturbing message earlier tonight. Based on the scant available evidence, we managed to deduce what had transpired. We assume the group sent to rescue you failed, losing the Translocator, which was then somehow entrusted to you along with the Sands of Sanctity. Meaning well, you went and healed Graulas, who stole your artifacts and then went on to steal the Chronometer. Forgive me if our deductions were incorrect, but it was the only way we could reconcile the sudden wellness and freedom of Graulas with your unexpected presence at the edge of the yard."

"Can you hear me?" Seth asked hopefully.

The gaseous Patton continued speaking as if no question had been asked. "Coulter expected to lose his life upon his return to your time. He took it like a man. I expect if you're listening to this message, you're dealing with his recent demise. You're feeling alone and desperate, and you could use some advice. I'm sorry there can't be any actual communication between us. I'm not much more than a talking letter. I could have simply written this message, but I figured you could use the company, even if it was just an illusion. In addition, candidly, I have too much time on my hands these days. Creating this gaseous monologue was an engaging proposition.

"Seth, against all odds, I've lived a longer life than most men. And like any thinking man, I've tried to figure out the meaning of my existence. Closest I've ever come is deciding that the purpose of life must be to learn to make wise choices. I believe that, and try to live by it.

"In my opinion, good choices are not always safe choices. Many worthy choices involve risk. Some require courage. You elected to heal Graulas. Seth, I believe that had I been in your shoes, with your knowledge, I would have done the same thing. I imagine you thought you were easing the departure of Graulas from this world. The demon had aided you in the past, and you were granting him what seemed a small favor. Had you known enough to anticipate what might happen, it would have been a poor choice indeed. But I've mulled it over, and I understand your decision. So did Coulter.

"Making mistakes is part of learning to choose well. No way around it. Choices are thrust upon us, and we don't always get things right. Even postponing or avoiding a decision can become a choice that carries heavy consequences. Mistakes can be painful—sometimes they cause irrevocable harm—but welcome to Earth. Poor choices are part of growing up, and part of life. You will make bad choices, and you will be affected by the poor choices of others. We must rise above such things.

"Although cataclysmic at a glance, your choice might have some benefits. Getting Graulas involved shuffles the deck for the Sphinx. Clever as he is, he would not have seen this coming. The Sphinx certainly was not the one who loaned you the artifacts. If he had the Translocator, all he had to do was bring a force to Fablehaven, recover the

Chronometer, and proceed with his plans to open Zzyzx. I expect your decision has disrupted his calculations. If that is the case, it could create opportunities.

"I knew you for only a short while, Seth, but I was impressed. You are my kind of person. When guys like us make mistakes, we clean up the mess. It will not be easy, it may not even be possible, but I'm going to make some drastic suggestions based on things I might attempt in your situation. Do with my ideas what you will."

The gaseous Patton gave a little smile. "Your family is trapped. Your enemies are on the move. The world is on the brink of destruction. I suggest that you save it."

A tingling thrill went through Seth. He liked where this was headed.

"If I were you, I would consider the artifacts gone and work under the assumption that my enemy will succeed in opening Zzyzx. When that prison opens, I would want to be on hand to oppose the demon horde."

Goose pimples rose on Seth's arms. Could he do something so bold? Wouldn't the demons trample him?

"You will need a weapon. In this case, I would think big. I would try to find Vasilis, the Sword of Light and Darkness, the most fabled blade of which I am aware. Remember the name: Vasilis. Say it to yourself." Seth whispered the word. "This storied blade reflects the heart of the wielder. In the hands of a virtuous shadow charmer, I expect it would be quite powerful.

"I once sought Vasilis, but since I had no pressing need for the weapon, I abandoned the quest. I do not know where

Vasilis lies, but I believe it is hidden in our region of the world. I imagine the Singing Sisters could send you in the right direction. Your grandparents would have my head for suggesting that, but you need a weapon of this magnitude, and you have no time to find it without assistance. The Sisters only help others for a price, and it is always steep, but I have visited their lair thrice, and here I stand.

"There is no way to prepare for a meeting with them. They will bargain with you. If you fail to reach an agreement, they will take your life, so be very careful. In an envelope in my desk drawer, you will find the latitude and longitude of their residence. The Singing Sisters dwell on an island in the Mississippi River, protected by a gentle distracter spell. They have resided there for a long time.

"You will also require passage to Shoreless Isle, where Zzyzx lies. Again, the latitude and longitude are included in the envelope, but they will do you little good. No ordinary ship can sail there. I have been to Zzyzx, aboard a ship I would rather forget. I required the help of a necromancer. You will not, if your mind is firm. The ship you must seek is crewed by the undead, and such will hearken to your instructions. To summon the *Lady Luck*, you must journey to Hatteras Island off the coast of North Carolina and follow the guidelines in the envelope. Before you can carry out those instructions, you will need to collect a bell, a whistle, and a music box from a certain leprechaun at Fablehaven. You'll find more details in the envelope.

"You may want companions on your adventure. Hugo should be able to leave Fablehaven. After he was granted a will by the fairies, he never covenanted to remain. Of course, Graulas may have overturned the treaty, in which case any of the creatures could come and go as they please. Choose your companions carefully. Based on my recent conversations with your grandparents, I believe Vanessa may be an asset worth using, but I will leave the ultimate decision in your hands.

"I also recommend you practice soliciting help from the undead. In the same drawer as the envelope, I left copies of keys to the Fablehaven dungeon and the Hall of Dread. If the treaty is broken, recruit a wraith to stand guard over the dungeon. Although help from phantoms is generally undesirable, in your case, it would be wise. You need the practice, and your cause is sufficiently desperate. There are certain entities in the dungeon that you do not want released. When dealing with the undead, make sure they vow loyal service, and make sure all of the particulars are settled. Appoint limits, establish rewards. They thirst for the living, so an obvious reward for standing guard is the right to claim any victims who come along. That sort of thing. If the dungeon is inaccessible, you could also conscript liches from the Grim Marsh. Hugo knows the way. Should you travel there, be sure to stay on the wooden walkway. Hopefully it has been kept in good repair.

"Should you require further aid, as I suspect you might, consider finding Agad, the wizard in charge of Wyrmroost. Unbeknownst to most, he is one of the five wizards who founded Zzyzx. He may be able to provide wisdom in dealing with this threat. None wish to see those demons remain in confinement more than he.

"You now have all the ideas I have managed to compile. Use whatever makes sense. No doubt you will devise other strategies on your own as the situation evolves. Ephira should effectively safeguard my communications to you until less than a year before your hour of need arises. I trust you will find my messages undisturbed.

"I wish I could do more for you. Please do not obsess over choices you cannot change. Mistakes happen. Learn from the past, but concentrate on the present and the future. Difficulties like I have never faced await you. I don't want to guide you toward harm, but when the world is about to end, the only real option is to save it. With a threat like the opening of Zzyzx impending, no safe choices remain. This message will repeat if you uncork the bottle again. It will play only for you. Good luck."

The gaseous form of Patton returned to the bottle in a rush. Once the gas was inside, Seth pressed the cork into the mouth.

So much to digest! Too much! Seth squeezed his head. For some reason, it was one thing to tell himself he was going to try to save the world, and quite another to receive that assignment from Patton, as if everything really did depend on him. Too much was at stake!

But Patton was right. All safe choices were gone. And trying to hide from the responsibility would be a choice as well. A bad one. At least Patton had shown him a path to follow. He would do his best, one step at a time.

Crossing to the desk, Seth found an envelope with his name on it in the second drawer he checked. Beside it he discovered the dungeon keys. Opening the envelope, Seth scanned the pages inside. He saw the promised latitudes and longitudes, along with accompanying explanations and descriptions. At the end he read about the Eternals and the final steps required to open Zzyzx.

Satisfied that he had everything Patton had promised, he folded the papers back into the envelope and tucked it in his pocket. "Come on, Hugo," Seth said. "Let's go see if those satyrs have shown up."

As the golem followed him out of the grotto, Seth reconsidered using the coin to contact Bracken. It would be painful and embarrassing to explain how he had lost the Translocator, but Bracken could possibly find ways to help. After all, he was at Living Mirage, and he seemed like a resourceful guy. Who knew when a well-timed prison revolt at the Sphinx's headquarters might provide an important diversion? At this stage, Seth could not afford to ignore any possible assets.

CHAPTER SIXTEEN

The Sealed Shrine

Near the top of the stairway, Bracken grabbed Kendra by her upper arm. "Your brother is contacting me," he whispered.

"Is he all right?" she asked.

Bracken paused, listening inwardly. "He's unharmed. He's devastated by how Nagi Luna used him to free Graulas. The sentiment comes through in more than his words. Your friend Coulter has perished."

"No," Warren said, reflexively rejecting the news.

"My condolences, but Seth seems certain," Bracken said. "He feels tremendous guilt, potentially enough to break him. I am telling him he was used, tricked, and that there is nothing to be done about it now."

Kendra tried to choke back her tears. How could Coulter

be gone? He was supposed to be safe back at Fablehaven! Warren watched Bracken expectantly.

"Seth says Graulas destroyed the foundational treaty of Fablehaven."

"He needs to get out of there," Warren said.

Bracken nodded, holding up a finger. "Seth says he will depart soon. Apparently he has received advice from an ancestor of yours, Patton Burgess, and Seth is now preparing to embark on a quest."

"Patton would have provided sound guidance," Warren said.

"I'm telling Seth that you two are with me. He's thrilled to hear it. I'm telling him we're in the middle of an emergency of our own, and am advising him to contact me again soon. I'm advising him not to fret about losing the Translocator. I can tell he appreciates the support, but he is still wrestling to come to terms with the crisis resulting from that loss. He longs for a way to make restitution. He has put away the coin."

"Will he be all right?" Kendra asked anxiously.

"I think so," Bracken said. "Evidently your ancestor gave him an ambitious assignment. We didn't go into specifics, but if Seth can channel his energy into an active endeavor, it should help him cope. He will hail us again soon. We must press on."

They continued upward. The stairway had been tunneled through smooth, dark stone. Warren ran a hand along the wall. "No digging into this stairway," he said.

"These walls are harder than steel," Bracken agreed.

The stairway ended at a blank wall. Warren recited an unintelligible phrase, and the wall faded, almost vanishing.

"Should I extinguish my light?" Bracken asked.

"Keep it shining," Warren said.

They passed through the ghostly wall into a cave composed of sharp, angular rocks. Bracken's light glared off the glossy black stone. Glancing back, Kendra noted that the wall appeared solid again.

Farther along the cave, a creature stood at the edge of the light. It had the body of a large bull and the head of a bearded man wearing a bronze crown. The creature spoke in a garbled language.

Bracken answered with equally strange speech.

"Don't worry," Warren whispered to Kendra.

The creature spoke again.

"What is it?" Kendra asked in hushed tones. "What is it saying?"

Bracken took her hand, and the garbled words became instantly untangled. The creature was still speaking.

" . . . many years it is a relief to have a shred of hope."

"We will do our best," Bracken promised. "You have met Warren. This is Kendra."

The creature bowed his head politely. "Greetings."

"Kendra, this is Halad," Bracken continued, "one of the proud lammasu enslaved by the Sphinx."

"He is no sphinx," Halad stated in his strong, calm voice. "Call him the Ethiopian."

"Halad stands guard over this secret entrance to the dungeons," Bracken explained. "He is not an evil being, but he would be bound by covenant to slay us if we trespassed here without permission from the Ethiopian."

"I take no pleasure in my assignment," Halad said stoically. "Nevertheless, a sworn sentinel must perform his duty."

"Any sense of what lies beyond the cave?" Bracken asked.

"My vision is restricted to my domain," Halad answered. "As you shall observe, my domain here is insulting. I am a prisoner guarding a prison."

"We thank you for safe passage through your domain," Bracken said.

"I lament the loss of your horns," Halad replied. "Go in peace."

Bracken released Kendra's hand. "Off we go."

"No trouble?" Warren asked.

"Just exchanging pleasantries," Bracken explained.

They advanced quickly. The lammasu stepped aside to let them pass. Halad was so large that Kendra doubted she could reach the bottom of his beard even if she jumped. Once beyond the lammasu, Bracken put his glowing stone away. Warren led the way out of the cave into the predawn light. They crouched behind some jagged boulders to survey the vicinity.

"Living Mirage contains a lot of land," Bracken whispered to Kendra. "In fact, the careful observer will find more land inside the surrounding fence than there should be."

"Several of the preserves are like that," Warren added. "Kind of like the knapsack but on a larger scale."

Bracken nodded. "A long, fertile valley runs north to south through Living Mirage. We're just barely in the northern half of that valley. The sealed shrine lies farther north where the valley narrows."

"The Sphinx suggested a course that should get us past most patrols and around the most dangerous areas," Warren said. "He has wraiths herding the undead away from our route."

"How do you know so much about Living Mirage?" Kendra asked Bracken.

"I first came here to investigate why the shrine had been sealed. I had some time to explore the area before I was captured. "

"What kind of dangerous creatures are here?" Kendra asked.

Bracken shrugged. "Beyond the ordinary I know of jinn, various demons, manticores, a chimera, steppe giants, sphinxes, river trolls, sirrushes, and of course the simurgh."

"He means the roc," Warren clarified. "Which is hunting a lot lately to feed three enormous hatchlings." He drew his sword. "The Sphinx warned that an actual sphinx guards the sealed shrine. It will pose riddles to us."

"Let me handle the riddles," Bracken said.

"The Sphinx seemed to think you'd have that covered."

"I've been around a long time," Bracken said. "I would almost prefer if the puzzles surprised me. I suppose we'll skirt the river, try to get cover from the trees."

"That was the route he described," Warren confirmed.

"We should walk, not run," Bracken said. "Haste draws attention."

"I'm with you," Warren agreed. He handed Kendra a glove. "That belonged to Coulter. It will make you invisible when you hold still."

"I remember it," Kendra said.

"Take the key as well," Warren said, handing her a short rod with a complicated shape at the end. "If the need arises, I'll draw off attention so you two can reach the shrine."

"We'll all escape together," Kendra insisted.

"Right," Warren said, trying to be patient. "We'll all try to make it. But if we have to choose, let's get the people to the shrine who can actually communicate with the Fairy Queen. Some of us would get blasted into sawdust if we dared to tread upon her sacred ground."

"We should move," Bracken said. "You lead, Warren."

For the first five minutes, Kendra expected enemies to descend on them with every step. As they proceeded without incident, and as the cover offered by the trees became better instead of worse, she started to unwind. She began to wonder how the Fairy Queen could help them escape. Could she admit them to her realm? Kendra was pretty sure that was forbidden under any circumstances. The realm where she ruled had to remain unspoiled or it could mean the end of all fairydom.

Kendra kept an eye out for fairies. If she could recruit a few of them to act as scouts, it would improve their chances.

At one point, where the trees became sparse, the roc

soared across the sky, outstretched wings temporarily blocking out the rising sun. A huge beast thrashed in its claws.

"Does it have a rhinoceros?" Kendra asked, shielding her eyes as the sun reappeared behind the gigantic bird.

"A karkadann," Bracken corrected. "Bigger than a rhino, with a sentient horn. Pray we don't cross paths with a karkadann out here unprotected."

"I have my sword," Warren objected.

"And I have my little knife," Bracken said. "Neither would avail us if a karkadann charged. What I need are my horns."

"How did you lose them?" Kendra asked.

Bracken hesitated, as if uncertain whether to respond. He broke his silence after a small shrug. "The Font of Immortality is fashioned from my third horn."

"One of the five artifacts?" Warren exclaimed.

"How old are you?" Kendra asked.

"From your point of view, ancient," Bracken said. "Among unicorns, I'm still considered young. I have walked many roads, and I have seen much, but I still feel young. Like fairies, unicorns are youthful beings."

"You surrendered your horn?" Warren asked.

"I was willing to do anything to help lock those demons away," Bracken asserted. "I gave my first horn as a gift years ago. Many of my kind do not retain their first horns once the third has grown. My second horn was taken when the Sphinx captured me. I have no idea what he did with it."

"He should return it to us," Kendra said.

"It would help," Bracken said. "I can feel my horns out

there. None have been destroyed. Without them I feel like a shadow of myself. They house much of my power."

"Your third horn is irretrievable?" Warren wondered.

"If the Font of Immortality is ever broken, it will disappear and re-form elsewhere, taking the horn with it. That horn would be retrievable only should Zzyzx open. Without my third horn I'm trapped in human form, but I would much rather live this way than see Zzyzx breached."

They continued in silence. Several times they crouched or fell flat or hid behind tree trunks as Bracken sensed creatures in the area. Kendra glimpsed lions with the heads of men and scorpion tails. She caught sight of vicious packs of scaly flying dogs. She observed burly, armored nomads half the height of the surrounding trees, laughing loudly and brawling without provocation. But all of these potential threats were viewed from a distance. Many of the hazards Bracken detected were never perceived by Warren or Kendra. Their little group would simply hide in silence until Bracken suggested they proceed.

After hours of fitful progress, Warren squatted behind a fallen log to confer with them. With the sun now high, the day was growing uncomfortably warm. Ahead, at the far side of a clearing, Kendra observed trees with foliage of remarkable colors. "The Beckoning Grove lies ahead," Warren said. "The Sphinx gave specific warnings about this stretch of our route. To go around to the left would take us along the riverbank through a community of river trolls."

"They would consider us extraordinary delicacies,"

Bracken said. "We would be devoured with much cere-
mony."

"To loop around to the right would take us into the
domain of the chimera," Warren said.

"Which would also mean certain death," Bracken said.

"And if we go through the grove?" Kendra asked.

"The fruit smells are unbearably tempting," Warren said.
"All have harmful effects. Most are lethal. The Sphinx said
one might liquefy your bones, another might make you a
lycanthrope, a third might cause you to burst into flames."

"I'll take fruit over trolls or a chimera," Bracken voted.

"We mustn't succumb," Warren warned.

"We'll help each other," Bracken said. "Make up your
minds now. No matter what happens while we are under
those trees, no matter what cravings strike us, no matter
what desperate urges arise, no matter what argument we
make with ourselves, we will sample no fruit."

"What if the fruit overpowers our common sense?"
Kendra asked. "What if we can't resist?"

"I might prefer the type of threat I can stab," Warren
muttered. "In the grove our enemies will be ourselves."

Kneeling, Bracken scraped together dirt. Spitting into
his palm, he mashed the dirt and worked it into pellets, then
slipped two into his nostrils. He held out his hand. Kendra
hesitantly took a pair of dirt balls and pressed them into
place. Warren did likewise.

"I have to believe our wills are stronger than the allure
of some fruit," Bracken said. "To be slain by a troll or a
chimera would be sad. But to destroy ourselves to scratch an

itch would be so pathetic I refuse to accept the possibility. The dirt will help you, and so will I."

"Good enough for me," Warren said, his voice a little different with his nose plugged. "Kendra?"

"Let's try the grove." She spoke like she had a cold.

"Promise me that you will not sample the fruit," Bracken said. His voice sounded no different with the dirt up his nose. "Promise me and promise yourself. Say the words."

"I promise," Kendra said.

"I swear," Warren offered.

"Link arms," Bracken instructed, rising. "Breathe through your mouths and ignore your senses. I suggest we jog."

Elbows linked, the three of them broke into a trot, breathing only through their mouths. Kendra wondered if her fairykind status would offer extra protection from the enchantment. After all, she was immune to most magical forms of mind control. But experience had shown that although her mind was protected, her emotions were vulnerable to manipulation, like from Tanu's potions or magical fear. She worried that the attraction of the fruit might attack emotion more than intellect.

Ahead of them, the trees looked like what autumn aspires to be but never quite attains. Kendra marveled at the variety and vibrancy of the leaf colors: fiery reds and oranges, deep blues and purples, electric yellows and greens. She also saw leaves of more peculiar shades, including bright pink, shiny turquoise, metallic silver, and radiant white. Some leaves featured stripes or other patterns. Even the trunks of the trees displayed unusual colors, ranging from lava red to sparkling gold to midnight black.

As they passed beneath the trees, the plump fruit came into view. Different from the leaves, the fruit tended to exhibit opalescent blends of color, smooth skin shimmering like mother-of-pearl. Other fruit possessed the rich shades of fine jewels: sapphire blues, emerald greens, and ruby reds. Kendra found herself fascinated, unable to help speculating what such beautiful fruit might taste like.

But it was not until the scents of the Beckoning Grove began to trickle past her clogged nostrils that Kendra felt a dangerous pull from the fruit. The fragrance awakened hunger like she had never known, a desperate starvation that she instinctively knew could be quickly cured by the fat fruit dangling within reach. With the hunger came a profound thirst, along with a certainty that the juices inside the fruit would satisfy the need as no thirst had been quenched before.

Kendra knew she could not be experiencing the full smell of the place. A carnal impulse screamed for her to tear the dirt balls from her nostrils so she could luxuriate in the undiluted aroma of the orchard. Her reason tried to support the urge, telling her that smelling was not eating. Why should she needlessly forgo the most stimulating smell of her life? The aroma alone would cause no harm!

Bracken released Kendra, swatting at Warren's hands as he reached to unplug his nostrils. If she exhaled sharply, Kendra felt certain she could blow out the dirt pellets. Why not? She was salivating almost painfully. The full scent of the grove might actually provide enough limited satisfaction to help distract her from the raging hunger.

"Remember!" Bracken shouted. "This orchard is a death trap! The pleasures it promises are garish wrappings over deadly gifts. Remember that we chose not to partake. Force your mind to control your base urges."

Kendra resisted.

Warren slapped himself and then bit down on his thumb.

Bracken linked arms with them again. "Take a deep breath, hold it, close your eyes, and let me lead you."

Kendra obeyed. With her breath held, the call of the fruit became less immediate. She tried to see the situation logically. What would those sumptuous fragrances do to her without the pellets in her nose? She had imagined the grove would smell good, but had ignored the desperation that smell might awaken in her appetite. If she removed the pellets, the smell would probably overwhelm her reason.

It was difficult to run while holding her breath. After a time she simply had to breathe, so she began gulping down air, trying to compensate for lost oxygen. With those deep breaths, the scents of the grove assaulted her as never before. The overpowering aroma promised more than a way to sate her appetite and slake her thirst. The smells promised ecstasy. They promised rest. They promised peace.

She kept her eyes squeezed shut and resisted. The smells were lies. False promises. Her instincts rejected the mental assertions. How could something so sublime be hazardous? But Kendra kept her mind in control. As her breathing began to stabilize, she held her breath again. The lack of air quickly made her feel light-headed, so she promptly returned to inhaling.

She could hear Warren gasping greedily on the other side of Bracken. Their progress slowed. Then Bracken released Kendra. She opened her eyes. Bracken and Warren were on the ground wrestling.

"Go," Bracken demanded. "You're almost there. Leave the grove!"

Looking ahead, Kendra could see where the exotic orchard ended. Focusing on the clearing beyond the final trees, she started running. She was acutely aware that Bracken was no longer there to help her. Her solitude increased the weight of the temptation. She tried to envision a bite of fruit blasting her to pieces, but her body would not believe the image. Maybe Warren had misunderstood the Sphinx. Maybe the grove would provide all the joy its aroma promised! Bracken and Warren might already have given up. They might be behind her right now, delicious juice dribbling down their chins, laughing at her for fleeing.

Kendra glanced back. Bracken was dragging a thrashing Warren by his feet.

Turning forward, Kendra saw that she was almost out of the grove. What if she removed the dirt pellets just for the last few steps? She wanted at least one unobstructed whiff of the grove before she exited.

No. She had promised herself, and her friends, that she would pass through the grove without trying the fruit. Even with the best intentions, to smell the fruit might lead to tasting the fruit. Lowering her head, she charged out of the orchard, raced across the clearing beyond, and took cover behind a bush.

Looking back, she saw Bracken staggering forward with Warren draped over his shoulder. They were not yet out from under the shadows of the dazzling trees. Should she return to help? Kendra wasn't sure she could trust herself.

With labored strides, Bracken carried Warren out of the grove. As Bracken crossed the clearing, Warren struggled less. Silver liquid flowed freely from one of Bracken's nostrils. Perspiration gleamed on his face. He dumped Warren on the ground beside Kendra.

"I'm so sorry," Warren panted. "I'm so sorry." He snorted out a dirt ball. Kendra cleared hers out as well.

Bracken produced a frayed handkerchief and held it to his nose. A wet silver stain spread across the threadbare material. "Don't mention it."

"Silver blood?" Kendra asked.

"I'm not quite human," Bracken said.

"If your nose is bleeding, did the dirt come out?" Warren asked.

"Of one nostril, yes," Bracken said.

"How did you resist?" Warren asked in genuine amazement.

"It wasn't easy," Bracken said. "I'm sure it helped that I have lived a long time. And it helped that this is not my true form."

"It helped that you rule," Warren said. "You have an iron will. I owe you my life. Please forgive me. One of my nostrils came unplugged as we were running. After that, my rational side went on vacation."

"Nothing to forgive," Bracken said. "I felt the draw of the fruit. It was almost too much. Had I been alone, without responsibility, I might have failed the test."

"Both of you really smelled it?" Kendra asked, a little jealous.

"My nostril cleared when Warren punched me," Bracken said. "The scent was intoxicating. It may have been fortunate that blood replaced the dirt."

"I'm so sorry," Warren said. "I was out of control. All I knew was that I needed that fruit at all cost!"

"You don't feel that way now?" Kendra asked.

"The memory is appealing," Warren said. "But the irresistible urge is gone."

"We should move on," Bracken said.

"I dropped my sword," Warren said.

"That was way back there," Bracken said. "The first time you started to stray."

"I really wanted to clear my nose and fully smell the grove," Kendra confessed.

"Me too," Warren said. "Be glad you didn't. The full smell was a hundred times more compelling. I take it we leave the sword?"

"I don't want to risk the grove again," Bracken said. "The sword provided more the illusion of security than any actual protection. Stealth is our real weapon today."

"A fairy," Kendra said, pointing.

The fairy glided toward them, gauzy wings flowing more

than flapping, as if she were underwater. She had dark skin and long dark hair, and wore lavender wrappings that matched her wings. Tiny golden trinkets adorned her arms and ankles.

The fairy alighted on Bracken's shoulder, and he moved the handkerchief away from his face. She caressed his cheek. From the look on her face to the expressive language of her movements, Kendra had never seen a fairy express such tender concern. The fairy placed her brown hand on the side of his nose. There was a brief glow, and then she used a diaphanous strip of material to clean the flecks of blood from the rim of his nostril.

"Can you guide us to the sealed shrine?" Bracken asked gently.

The fairy nodded eagerly. Kendra felt certain the fairy was in love. Apparently the persuasive influence of her fairykind status would not be needed today.

"Could you gather a few of your sisters to help us avoid trouble?" Bracken asked.

The fairy looked suspicious, as if the mention of other fairies had suddenly spoiled much of the fun.

"I would consider it a tremendous favor," Bracken said earnestly. Color rising in her cheeks, the fairy glided away.

"You have a way with fairies," Warren said.

"I may lack my horn," Bracken said, "but I'm still a unicorn. We're sort of the rock stars of the fairy world."

Sure enough, a few minutes later, the first fairy returned with several others. Most had dark skin and elaborate wings. Bracken was the obvious center of attention. The majority of the fairies whispered and tittered from afar. A couple of the boldest drifted close to gaze at him dreamily. One started mending a tear in his shirt.

Bracken laughed. "Do not concern yourselves with my attire. I need scouts. Who will keep us safe from harm?"

"I will," chirped a chorus of tiny voices. Miniature hands waved as fairies vied for selection.

"I would be forever grateful for help from all of you," Bracken said warmly. He made assignments regarding which fairies would rove far, which would stay close, and which direction they would cover. When the fairy who had first found them received the honor of serving as Bracken's personal escort, she beamed with pride.

With their fairy entourage scouting ahead, they made faster progress than before, advancing without hesitation. Occasionally warnings would be passed back to them by their escorts, and they would pause or alter their course accordingly. More fairies joined the group, bringing Bracken nuts and berries and sips of water or honey cupped in fragrant leaves. Bracken shared these offerings with his companions. Eventually the steady parade of minute portions filled them and he had to ask for no further food to be brought.

At length, with the sun past midday, fairies returned reporting a sphinx up ahead guarding the sealed shrine. Bracken assured the fairies that a confrontation with the sphinx was necessary and asked them to hang back. Part of Kendra hoped that he would invite her to hang back as well, but Bracken made no such offer.

The iron dome came into view through the trees. The size surprised her. It was several stories tall, and looked big enough for a circus to perform inside. Devoid of any signs of corrosion, the dull, black iron absorbed the afternoon sunlight, reflecting nothing.

As they drew nearer, Kendra spotted the sphinx lounging in front of the dome, tail swishing back and forth. The sphinx had the body of a golden lion, with feathery wings tucked at the sides, and the head of a woman. She had large, almond-shaped eyes the color of jade, and wore a self-satisfied expression.

Bracken approached her, flanked by Warren and Kendra. The sphinx made no movement aside from her languidly waving tail.

"We want access to the dome," Bracken said.

"Consider two sisters," the sphinx intoned in a sultry voice. Audible to the ears, the words also penetrated directly to the mind. Though she spoke in a subdued manner, each word somehow arrived with the force of a shout. "The first is born of the second, whereupon the second is born of the first."

Bracken glanced at Kendra and Warren. Kendra had no idea.

"The sisters born of each other are day and night," Bracken replied.

The sphinx gave a sage nod. "I surround the world, yet I dwell within a thimble. I am outside of—"

"You are space," Bracken interrupted.

The sphinx compressed her lips and gave him a hard stare. She spoke again. "In the morning I walk on four—"

"Stages of a man's life," Kendra blurted. All eyes turned to her. "It's a famous one," she apologized. "In the morning I walk on four legs, in the afternoon on two, in the evening on three—the more legs I have, the weaker I am. Something like that."

The sphinx was fuming.

"Knock, knock," Warren said. The sphinx glared at him.

"Don't take offense," Bracken placated, stepping in front of Warren diplomatically. "We have had a taxing day. There are three of us, we answered three riddles. May we pass?" He bowed politely.

"You may pass," the sphinx allowed, serenity returning.

"Say no more," Bracken whispered to Warren.

Warren struggled against a grin.

Kendra felt like the eyes of the sphinx were boring into her back as they passed her and walked to the dome. Bracken led them to a hatch in the side that had a large key-hole. As Kendra studied the hatch, she recalled that the Fairy Queen had recently destroyed three of her shrines. What if this was one of the shrines she had eliminated? It seemed a likely candidate since it was sealed.

Deciding she would have an answer to her concern soon enough, Kendra inserted her rod, jiggled it until it caught, and then twisted. The lock clicked, and Warren pulled the hatch open.

Fairies crowded toward the open portal from all directions. Bracken stepped through first, followed by Kendra, who felt fairies brushing past her as she entered. The dome cut out all daylight except what filtered in through the hatchway, but the inside of the dome was also lit by scores of glowing fairies and the steady radiance of a luminescent pond. Kendra gazed at the vibrant variety of fairies, wondering how many years they had been trapped in here. As Warren came through the hatchway, more fairies poured in, twittering at long-lost friends.

The oblong pond took up nearly a quarter of the room. Water trickled down from the top of a conical island in the center of the pond. Five terraced mounds surrounded the glassy water, blooming with exotic flowers despite the lack of sunlight. From one side of the pond, white stepping-stones created a somewhat precarious walkway from the shore to the island.

"This is where I sit on the sidelines," Warren said. "I'll stay back and guard the hatch."

"Fair enough," Bracken said. He led Kendra over to the stepping-stones, lightly leaping to the first, which Kendra thought had been placed a little too far from the shore. He stepped to the next stone and waited for Kendra. Not wanting to look scared, and trying not to think about what guardians might lurk beneath the surface of the glowing water, Kendra sprang to the first stone. It was slick, but she landed well. Bracken reached back to steady her. They proceeded along the rest of the stones without difficulty and reached the steep, grassy shore of the island.

Bracken led the way around to the back of the island. As they went, Kendra saw that water actually trickled down from the top of the island along three different routes. The drizzling flow of water on the far side of the island collected in a pool halfway up the back slope. Beside the pool stood a tiny figurine of a fairy beside a bronze bowl engraved with delicate patterns.

Kendra started toward the pool, then paused to look back at Bracken, who had halted farther down the slope. He met her eyes. "It has been a long time since I last spoke with the Fairy Queen." He clenched his jaw, fingers fidgeting, eyes shining. Was he nervous?

"I'm sure she'll be happy to see us," Kendra encouraged. "I feel really good about this."

"Of course," he said, striding forward, head erect.

They knelt together in front of the fairy figurine. The water in the pool next to the figurine did not glow, although it struck Kendra as abnormally reflective. A breeze stirred the still air, and Kendra smelled citrus fruit, sand, sap, jasmine, and honeysuckle.

Bracken spoke first, aloud, but seemingly also with his mind. "Greetings, your majesty. It is I, Bracken the hornless unicorn, also known by other titles. I am accompanied by Kendra Sorenson."

A feeling of pure joy flooded over Kendra, clearly emanating from the Fairy Queen. *How did you reach this shrine?* Kendra had never before sensed surprise from the Fairy Queen.

"We had aid from the Sphinx," Bracken replied. "The demon Graulas brought him the remaining artifacts, and is in the process of usurping his authority. First things first. Could you please vouch for my trustworthiness to Kendra?"

A potent emotion of heartbreaking love washed over Kendra. *Bracken is among the most trusted of all my servants. I have deeply missed his presence.* The feeling of love abruptly hardened into chastisement. Her next words were directed to Bracken. *I warned you not to travel to this preserve.*

"And I spent long years in a dungeon as payment for my disobedience," Bracken replied. "Forgive me, your majesty, I took the risk in your service."

You should come home, the Fairy Queen pressed. A powerful feeling of longing accompanied the statement. Suddenly Kendra felt like she was eavesdropping on something intensely private. Bracken shot her a glance, as if guessing her feelings.

"Necessity dictates otherwise," Bracken said. "I still have much work to do, your majesty. Nearly in a position to open Zzyzx, the Society is now run directly by demons. I must oppose them while there remains any chance to thwart their designs. Perhaps we can converse privately in a moment. First, Kendra has a favor to ask."

"Me?" Kendra exclaimed, glancing at Bracken uncomfortably. "Seems like you have this handled."

"Go ahead," he urged.

Kendra cleared her throat, feeling self-conscious. Her conversations with the Fairy Queen had always been unobserved. To make matters worse, it was clear that Bracken had a long, close relationship with her. Shouldn't he be the one making requests? "We are desperate for a way out of Living Mirage. Warren is with us too."

You have not transformed any of my astrids yet. I have tried to send them in your direction. I lost track of you when you came to this accursed preserve. No astrids are currently near. Yet even without my warriors, I believe I have a solution to your dilemma. It will require a little time.

"Thank you, your majesty," Kendra said.

Bracken winked at her. "Could you give me a few minutes alone with her? There are a few unicorn-type matters I would like to discuss."

"Sure," Kendra said, standing, the dismissal making her even more uncomfortable.

"I'm glad you were here for this much," Bracken assured her. "Hopefully you now have good reason to trust me. Stay here on the island. We'll walk back together."

Feeling a little better, Kendra strolled down the slope to the edge of the radiant water. She could not help wondering what Bracken and the Fairy Queen were discussing. Was she angry at him for getting captured? Did they simply need to catch up? What was their relationship? Did the Fairy Queen have as big a crush on him as the other fairies seemed to? Would the Fairy Queen put more pressure on him to come to her realm? Kendra figured if any creature belonged in an unspoiled realm of purity, it would be a unicorn.

But it was hard to think of Bracken as a unicorn. He seemed way too human. He just felt like a really cool friend. Kendra looked up the slope, watching him as he knelt beside the little pool, his back to her. What a relief to know she could trust him! He was right that an endorsement from the Fairy Queen allowed Kendra to lay aside her concerns about his legitimacy. After so many betrayals, it felt heavenly to know there was somebody she could truly count on.

After some time, Bracken came down the slope. He looked rejuvenated.

"You're all smiles," Kendra said.

"I missed that complete form of communication the Fairy Queen can provide," Bracken said. "Mind to mind, heart to heart. And I missed her. She is very important to me. Since her consort fell, she has borne a very heavy burden alone."

"What kind of help do you think she'll send?" Kendra asked.

"I'll be curious to see," he responded vaguely. "Let's go tell Warren help is on the way."

CHAPTER SEVENTEEN

Preparations

Newel and Doren arrived at the manor just as Seth was deciding they wouldn't show. Seth had waited on the porch for nearly an hour after contacting Bracken, his confidence steadily waning. He was on the verge of asking Hugo to take him back to the main house when the satyrs came scampering across the unkempt lawn. Each had a pack over his shoulder. Newel wore a dented helm. Doren had a bow.

"The word is abroad that Graulas has claimed this house," Newel said by way of greeting.

"We were hoping it was a hoax," Doren added.

"No trick," Seth said loudly. "I was asked to claim it on his behalf." He lowered his voice. "Please don't yell about my hoaxes where any imp can hear."

"Right," Newel said with a knowing wink. He cupped a

hand beside his mouth. "We had better clear out of here before the dark master of this haunted abode returns!"

"You don't have to oversell it, either," Seth whispered.

"We brought you some gear," Doren said, unshouldering his pack and rummaging through the contents. He pulled out an oval shield about a yard tall. "Heroes need proper equipment."

"Thanks," Seth said.

"Adamant," Doren said proudly, handing over the shield. "We fished it out of the same tar pit where we found the shirt of mail."

"Probably all belonged to the same careless adventurer," Newel speculated. "Too much money, not enough talent."

Seth hefted the shield. It felt light, almost like a toy or a prop, but he knew that if it was made of adamant, it was stronger than steel and absolutely priceless. "What a great gift."

"We were reserving it to trade for batteries," Newel explained. "But in light of our new arrangement—well, investors need to protect their interests."

"It would be a shame if I died before you got your generator," Seth said.

Doren nudged Newel. "The shield isn't all."

From his pack, Newel removed a sword in a battered leather scabbard. Jewels adorned the golden hilt. Newel presented it to Seth, who drew the sword. It felt too light. "This isn't adamant too?" Seth asked.

"Tempered adamant," Doren gushed. "We found just the

naked blade. The edge is keen. The nipsies crafted the hilt, and we salvaged the scabbard from an old scrap heap."

"The nipsies couldn't have made it just now?" Seth asked.

"No," Newel chuckled. "It took them six weeks. We were simply preparing another item for barter."

Seth belted on the scabbard and sheathed the sword. "Why don't you guys have armor?"

Newel snorted derisively. "Slows us down. We prefer to avoid injuries by not getting hit."

"What about the helmet?" Seth asked.

Newel rapped the helm with his knuckles. "This old thing? It's my good-luck charm."

"Tell him the story," Doren urged.

"Satyrs never wear armor, including helmets," Newel began, using his hands expressively. "But years ago I was in a play, and the helm was part of my costume. During the big battle scene, a few of us were assailing a castle. We had quite a set. The main tower must have been fifteen feet tall, fashioned from real stone. Anyhow, as we actors were laying siege, a big chunk of the battlement dislodged from atop the tower."

"Shoddy workmanship," Doren inserted.

"Definitely not part of the rehearsed scene," Newel emphasized.

"Newel was delivering a line," Doren laughed.

"*Behold, the enemy falters!*" Newel quoted in a bold voice, raising a finger skyward for dramatic effect. "I was facing the audience and focused on my diction, so the falling stone-work blindsided me."

"Biggest laugh of the night," Doren chuckled.

"Those might have been my last words if not for this helmet," Newel said. "Cumbersome or not, any object that lucky deserves to be worn in battle."

"Is that how the helmet got dented?" Seth asked.

"Exactly," Newel confirmed.

"Newel wouldn't let anyone repair it," Doren said.

"I'm surprised you weren't injured," Seth said.

"I was unconscious for almost two days," Newel clarified.

"His understudy was elated," Doren said.

Newel smirked. "The botched scene was such a success, I had to give up the theater. All everybody wanted from me thereafter was slapstick. And trust me, with satyrs involved, slapstick hurts a lot."

"He came home from rehearsals mottled with bruises," Doren remembered.

"I see Doren brought a bow," Seth pointed out.

"He's a handy archer," Newel said. "I prefer a sling."

Seth motioned for them to lean close and lowered his voice to a faint whisper. "I got our assignment from Patton. It will take us on quite a journey. I think we should probably get Vanessa out of the Quiet Box to help us. What do you guys say?"

"Absolutely," Newel affirmed. "Best idea I've heard all day."

"I'll second that," Doren said gladly.

Seth gave the satyrs a doubtful scowl. "Wait a minute. You guys just think she's pretty."

"I've been around a long time," Newel said. "Vanessa Santoro is not just pretty."

"He's right," Doren agreed. "She's walking dynamite. My pulse is rising just talking about her."

"She also might be a traitor," Seth stressed.

"The lethal temptress," Newel said with relish. "Even better."

"It will definitely spice up the adventure," Doren encouraged.

"I'm obviously talking to the wrong guys," Seth sighed.

"Believe me," Newel said cockily, "you're talking to the right guys. We've been chasing babes since the world was flat."

Seth rolled his eyes.

"The boy needs objectivity," Doren scolded. "He's leading this expedition. He needs valid opinions. Seth, considering all sides of this, I am deeply convinced that the right move to make would be to bring Vanessa. And any outfits she may require. And makeup. And perfume. And hair products. Whatever she needs."

Closing his eyes, Seth rubbed his face. Did the fate of the world really rest on these clowns? Should he even be involving them? At least he had Hugo.

Newel slugged him on the arm. "Seth? Lighten up! We're just kidding around. Keeping up morale!"

"We know you'll do the right thing," Doren said.

Seth opened his eyes. "I actually think Vanessa might be on our side. Plus, we may need her help to get where we need to go."

"If you bring her, we'll watch your back," Newel promised.

"A man would be a fool to trust a woman that gorgeous," Doren murmured shrewdly.

"That's a little more helpful," Seth said. "We have a lot to do. We should get back to the main house."

"Lead on," Newel said.

"Have either of you caught a leprechaun before?" Seth asked as Hugo lifted him.

Both satyrs perked up.

"We haven't," Newel said.

"We've tried," Doren added. "Did Patton have some advice on the subject?"

"He did," Seth said as they started across the yard. "It's part of our mission."

Newel rubbed his hands together. "This adventure keeps sounding better and better."

"You just have to get into the right spirit," Doren laughed.

Seth smiled weakly, quietly wondering if the satyrs would remain as eager once the undertaking stopped seeming fun. "Do you guys want Hugo to carry you?"

"How slow do you think we are?" Newel complained. "Go on, we'll keep up."

Hugo loped out of the yard. Seth thought the golem was going a little slower than he had before the satyrs had joined them, but they still made fast progress through the woods, and, true to their word, Newel and Doren kept pace, dashing along behind.

They had been charging through the dark forest for some time when Hugo stopped. Overhead, all but a few stars were blocked by the canopy of leaves.

Seth heard and saw nothing.

"Centaurs?" Doren asked.

"Behind us," Newel agreed. "Coming this way. Right this way. Sounds like they're tracking us."

"Can we outrun them?" Seth asked.

Newel chuckled. "I'm not sure anything at Fablehaven can outrun a centaur."

Hugo set Seth down and stood in front of him. A few seconds later, Seth could hear the approaching hoofbeats. As the drumming hooves got louder, he also heard leaves rustling and the occasional branch snapping. The satyrs were right. The centaurs were coming straight at them.

Seth shone his flashlight as the centaurs cantered into view. They quickly came to a halt. Cloudwing led the group of four, an arrow set to the string of his enormous bow. The flashlight beam rose from his silver fur to his extravagantly muscled human torso, then swept across the other centaurs.

"Greetings, Seth Sorenson," Cloudwing boomed. "I need to have words with you."

"In the middle of the woods?" Seth asked from behind Hugo. "In the middle of the night?" He was not anxious to converse with centaurs. He felt certain they still suspected him of stealing their unicorn horn, and even though it had been returned, he knew centaurs were the type to hold serious grudges.

"The treaty has fallen," Cloudwing replied, his voice

clear and strong. "The preserve is in disarray. We need to know what you humans propose to do."

"We're working on it," Seth assured him.

"We have had tidings that you claimed the manor house on behalf of the demon Graulas," Cloudwing accused sternly.

"Word spreads like wildfire around here," Newel said to Doren.

"Even the cavalry knows," Doren replied.

"I'm doing what I can to keep dark forces away from the houses while the defenses are down," Seth admitted. "Maybe you guys could help the rumor spread."

"So the tale is false?" Cloudwing pressed.

"Yes," Seth said. "But don't go telling everybody."

"A false rumor will not dissuade wrongdoers for long," Cloudwing said. "I understand your grandparents have abandoned the preserve."

"Not on purpose," Seth said. "But yes, they're gone right now."

"Let me suggest you place the houses under centaur protection," Cloudwing advised. "It appears to be our fate to rise up and serve as the true guardians of Fablehaven."

"That might not be a bad idea," Seth said. "Can you spare a few guards until my grandparents get back?"

Cloudwing shook his head. "You misunderstand. We only protect our own property."

"You want the houses!" Seth cried. "What would centaurs do with human houses?"

"We could find uses for them," Cloudwing said. "For instance, we would keep them free of humans."

The other centaurs chuckled.

"Then no, we don't want your protection," Seth said.

"Choose your words carefully," Cloudwing advised. "If you deny our protection, you may face our aggression."

"Now you're threatening me?" Seth asked.

"The artificial order of Fablehaven has been over-turned," Cloudwing declared. "It is the natural order for the strongest to take what they want. Be grateful that we extend the hand of mercy by offering our protection."

"Be grateful they let you grant your permission in order to firm up their claim," Newel muttered.

"This is none of your concern, goatman," Cloudwing warned.

Newel reddened, fists clenched, but held his tongue.

"You will have to claim the houses yourself," Seth said. "I surrender nothing. My grandparents will be back, and Fablehaven will be repaired."

Cloudwing exchanged amused glances with his fellow centaurs. "You believe the treaty will be reconstituted?"

"Probably," Seth said, hoping he correctly understood the meaning of *reconstituted*.

"Fablehaven as you knew it is finished," Cloudwing asserted boldly. "Be glad the centaurs are here to keep the sanctuary from degenerating into gated chaos."

"Don't you mean be glad the centaurs are here to bully and enslave the weaker creatures?" Doren asked.

Cloudwing drew his arrow to his cheek and aimed it at

Doren. Hugo stepped between them. Cloudwing relaxed. "Another word from either goatman and we duel," Cloudwing vowed. "Did you wastrels not hear that your people have already signed over their lands to us?"

Newel raised his hand like a student and pointed at his lips.

"You may speak," Cloudwing said.

"We weren't part of that arrangement," Newel said.

"Then I suggest you clear out," Cloudwing said. "Vacate the premises. We have already claimed the great cow Viola after finding her roaming the woods unattended. By sunrise, most of the former Fablehaven preserve will be part of Grunhold."

"We plan to clear out," Seth said. "There is a battle being fought elsewhere that we must join."

The centaurs laughed. "If the battle is important," Cloudwing said, "I hope you do not represent the reinforcements."

"You should wish us success," Seth said darkly. "We're trying to stop the opening of Zzyzx. I may not have really been claiming property for Graulas, but trust me, if the prison opens, he will be back to make claims for himself, and he will not come alone."

The centaurs no longer appeared quite as jovial. "Is this where Stan went?" Cloudwing asked.

"It is where everyone of any value is going," Seth said.

Cloudwing bristled. "Fortunately for you, I have little interest in the naive opinions of humans. Even so, I am surprised that previous lessons have not taught you to restrain your tongue."

"Previous lessons?" Seth asked. "Like when Patton beat up Broadhoof?" Newel and Doren whipped around. Their stares warned Seth to cut it out. He understood their concern, but he couldn't help himself.

Cloudwing stared grimly down at Seth, who made sure the flashlight beam was focused right in the centaur's eyes. "I do recall an occasion when an outsider intervened in a dispute any real man would have handled himself." His tone warned that Seth was treading on thin ice.

Seth wanted to brag about stealing the horn. He yearned to remind them about Broadhoof begging for mercy from a human. He knew those words would sting. But he had a mission to perform, and friends to protect. He could not risk enraging the centaurs to action.

"You're right," Seth said. "I provoked the fight, I should have handled it myself."

The faintest hint of a smile appeared on Cloudwing's lips. "You say you are preparing to abandon this preserve as well?"

"Not in those words," Seth said. "We are leaving to try to save Fablehaven and the world from certain destruction. You would be welcome to help us."

Cloudwing smirked. "We will not meddle in the petty affairs of lesser races. But we will grant you until sunrise to be gone."

"We have to gather some gear," Seth said. "How about you give us a free pass until next sundown?"

"Very well," Cloudwing allowed. "Let it be known that after the coming sundown, any of you found upon the property formerly known as Fablehaven will be trespassing on centaur holdings and will be dealt with accordingly."

"Just so we're clear," Seth said, "I don't recognize your claim, and I will be back."

"At your peril," Cloudwing said. He turned to the other centaurs. "We have squandered enough time here. Onward!"

The four centaurs pounded away into the woods. As the hoofbeats faded, Newel glanced back at Seth. "Are you starting to grasp why satyrs hate centaurs so much?"

"I kind of am," Seth replied. "At the same time, considering how messed up everything has become, it might be good to have them protecting Fablehaven."

"If you say so," Doren mumbled. "After that exchange, I would have joined your quest without a reward. This used to be a fun place. I suspect it will soon be unrecognizable."

"Things are tough all around," Seth said heavily. "Thanks for the support."

"We still want the generator," Newel hastened to add.

"I get it," Seth assured them. "We should hurry to the house."

❋ ❋ ❋

Seth found the stingbulb version of Kendra in Vanessa's cell listening to a love song. He tried to ignore the dead body under a blanket in the corner. Newel and Doren murmured to each other about how authentic the false Kendra looked. Hugo was standing guard up by the back porch.

"Have you been all right?" Seth asked.

"It's been quiet," Kendra confirmed. "Are you ready for me?"

"I think we'll need Vanessa's help," Seth said.

The stingbulb switched off the sound system and followed Seth out into the hallway. After the accommodations at Living Mirage, the Fablehaven dungeon seemed simple and cozy. Seth hurried to the tall cabinet that contained Vanessa. He opened the door, and the stingbulb stepped inside. He closed the door, the cabinet turned, and when the door reopened, Kendra was gone, replaced by Vanessa.

Vanessa exited the cabinet, regarding Seth and the satyrs curiously. "Why do I get the feeling that something has gone terribly wrong?"

"Because it has," Seth answered frankly.

"I know the others intended to rescue you," she said. "Start there."

Seth recapped all that had happened, openly taking his share of the blame. Vanessa listened quietly, asking a few clarifying questions. By the time he had sketched out the basics of what Patton had advised him to do, she began to look very tired.

"Why didn't you give *us* the full rundown?" Newel asked when Seth had finished.

"I figured I'd wait until we were all together," Seth said tactfully.

"So we need to set up some wraith guards, catch a leprechaun, and get off the preserve before sundown," Vanessa summarized.

"Those would be the first steps," Seth agreed.

"Have you any idea how perilous it will be to visit the Singing Sisters?" Vanessa said.

"Not entirely," Seth replied. "Do you have a better plan?"

She stared at him silently. "I wish I did. We're so close to utter defeat that the reckless schemes Patton proposed probably do represent our best hope for success. But that only holds true because we basically have no chance for victory. We are talking about pulling off multiple miracles before we earn even a small chance of slightly harassing these demons."

"You don't have to help," Seth said, a little crestfallen.

"I'll help," Vanessa said. "It would be criminal to let you attempt this alone. Any chance of saving the world is worth pursuing. I don't want to crush your faith in the plan. It does offer a glimmer of hope, which we would otherwise lack. Who knows? With luck, Kendra, Warren, and your hornless unicorn friend may find unforeseeable ways to be useful at Living Mirage. And if the new dynamics of the situation are forcing the Sphinx to work against the Society, we may have acquired a very powerful ally. That said, I want to make sure we're all clear that we're probably marching to our deaths."

Newel raised a finger. "Doren and I actually have an escape clause. We're free to withdraw our support and flee at any time."

Vanessa gave him an incredulous glance. "Keep in mind that by the time you know you should flee, it will probably be too late."

"Noted," Newel said.

"Seth will be doing the most dangerous work," Vanessa went on. "If he falls, we'll all cut and run."

"No more cheerful thoughts," Seth said. "All this optimism is giving me a headache. Now, I want to know if a wraith can beat up a bunch of centaurs."

"A wraith in the sunlight would fall to centaurs," Vanessa said. "But in the dark, or underground, or in a building, a hundred centaurs would retreat from a wraith."

"Then I need to go to the Hall of Dread," Seth said. "Can you help me figure out which ones are wraiths?"

"I can."

Seth led the way to the bloodred door. Although they had to walk some hallways and round a couple of corners, the Hall of Dread seemed much nearer to the Quiet Box than it had before his time at Living Mirage. The instructions from Patton explained that he had to say some words before turning the key to open the door to the Hall of Dread. Seth opened the letter and found the words. They were not in English.

"Can you read these?" he asked Vanessa.

She peered at the letter. "Yes. Give me the key." She inserted the key into the keyhole, placed a palm against the door, muttered a few incomprehensible words, turned the key, and pushed the door open. She handed Seth the key and the letter.

The air in the hall felt chilly.

"We'll stand guard out here," Newel said stoutly.

Vanessa gave him a knowing look. "Probably for the

best." Newel avoided eye contact. Seth and Vanessa entered the hall. "I feel strong presences here," Vanessa said.

"How can you tell the difference between the dark creatures?" Seth inquired. He could hear them whispering about hunger and thirst, pain and loneliness.

"Experience, mostly," she said. "There are two basic types of restless beings: corporeal and ethereal. The corporeal entities have a physical form, like wights and liches and zombies. The ethereal beings are more ghostly, like specters or phantoms or shades."

"I can hear them gibbering," Seth said. "I've spoken to one of these prisoners before. It offered to serve me."

"Might be a good place to start," Vanessa said.

Seth hurried down the hall, passing many doors on either side. Forlorn voices babbled in the darkness. He paused at the last door on the left. Ahead was the blank wall where a secret passage could take them farther.

"I've returned," Seth said, facing the door.

The other voices went silent.

"I have been waiting, Great One," came the attentive response. "How may I serve you?"

Seth turned to Vanessa. "Can you hear him?"

She shook her head. She looked pale.

"Can you tell me what he is?"

She edged stiffly forward and peeked through the peephole. Seth assumed she was feeling the effects of the magical fear to which he was immune. She backed away. "Jackpot," she said. "It's a wraith. A strong one. Be sure it is bound by oath to serve you or we will all perish together."

"I will be your greatest servant, Strong One," the wraith promised.

"I could use your help," Seth said. "I need a, um, servant to stand guard over this dungeon. Any who draw too near would be yours to claim."

"Let me perform this duty," the wraith asked fervently.

"You would have to leave those who belong to this house unharmed, like my grandparents or my sister."

"I sense your intent. I understand."

"You would have to return to this cell upon my command."

"Yes, yes, anything you ask. Release me and I am yours."

"Swear to do these tasks and to follow my orders in all things," Seth said.

"By solemn covenant, I swear fealty to you, Wise One. I vow to obey word and spirit of all your commands."

Seth glanced at Vanessa. "I think he swore. He seems really eager."

Her brow twitched. "Make sure he's alone in there."

"Are you alone in that cell?" Seth asked.

There came a pause. "I am not alone. Two of my lesser brethren accompany me in my confinement."

Chills tingled down Seth's back. It had been a trap! One wraith swearing loyalty while two others waited in ambush. In the end, with the "master" killed by the unsworn wraiths, they would all have gone free!

Seth had to seem in control. "Would the other wraiths care to serve me?"

"They would serve you," came the reply. The eagerness was gone.

"I would send one of them to protect the old manor. The other to protect the stables and the livestock. They would be under the same terms and conditions as the first."

"I pledge fealty, and to perform your commands," affirmed a new voice.

"I pledge fealty, and to embody your commands," promised another new voice.

"Swear to me that no ambush or deception will come from you or others of your kind," Seth said. "Promise to protect me and my friends and my cause from harm."

"We swear it," answered three voices in unison.

"This woman, Vanessa, and the satyrs, Newel and Doren, are with me, and under my protection. If centaurs should come anywhere near these properties, they are yours to claim."

"We understand," answered three voices. "Release us, Mighty One."

"You understand the places I want protected?"

"We can see them in your mind."

Seth turned to Vanessa. "I think we're ready."

"Is there a key?" she asked.

Seth fished out a separate key and the letter from Patton. "There are new words also."

Vanessa took the letter and approached the cell door. She inserted the key, placed her palm against the door, and mumbled unsteadily. Turning the key sharply, she backed away.

The cell door swung open. A wave of cold spilled out as

if the room were an industrial freezer. Three dark forms emerged, upright, gliding forward with shadowy grace. One stood a little taller than Seth, the two others almost a head shorter. It was hard to discern details. The flashlight did not illuminate them. Their whole beings seemed to swallow light, making them indistinct.

Seth glanced at Vanessa. She crouched, head down, utterly immobilized. "You three wait here for now," Seth said. "Let me clear out my friends before you take your positions."

"As you say," the tall wraith pronounced in a low voice as hard and cold as ice.

Seth took Vanessa by the hand, her fingers coming back to life at his touch. Straightening her posture, she stared at Seth in astonishment. He led her down the hall and out the door to where the satyrs awaited them.

"Something feels unnatural," Doren said.

"Whatever you released are no common wraiths," Newel agreed. "Took all we had to stand our ground."

"You three should go," Seth said. "Wait for me with Hugo."

Both satyrs offered Vanessa their arms. Back in full possession of herself, she shunned them both, striding briskly down the hall. The satyrs scampered to keep up.

Seth waited until they were out of sight. Then he counted to a hundred, forcing himself to keep it slow. "Okay!" Seth called. "You can come out now!"

The three wraiths glided to the doorway, arriving more quickly than Seth had expected. "Just a second," Seth said.

The tallest wraith drew close to him. "Do you feel nothing in my presence?" the wraith asked.

"A little cold," Seth said. "But the others have a hard time around you guys."

"Truly you are powerful," the wraith said, exuding almost worshipful esteem.

"I'm a social person," Seth replied, feeling awkward. "I don't discriminate. You seem pretty powerful yourself. What would your chances be against the Demon King?"

"None," the wraith answered, the harsh word cutting like frozen steel.

"Gotcha," Seth said. He closed the door to the Hall of Dread. "When you take your positions, try to avoid my friends."

"As you command," all three replied.

Silently as shadows, the wraiths started forward, simultaneously walking and sliding. Seth could not keep pace with their odd, gliding gait, and they soon drifted out of view. When Seth finally reached the stairs to exit the dungeon, he noticed the tall wraith standing guard. No words were exchanged.

Seth found Vanessa and the satyrs on the back porch near Hugo. "We felt the wraiths go by," Vanessa said.

"Did they seem to be going in the right direction?" Seth asked.

"Looked that way," Newel replied.

Seth stared out into the yard. A few glimmering fairies bobbed in the darkness. He had a feeling the night was nearly spent. "What if I assembled a huge army of wraiths and creepy things to fight the demons?" Seth mused.

"It would be like trying to fight sharks with seawater," Vanessa said. "Our best hope lies in walking the path Patton outlined."

Seth unfolded his letter from Patton and used the flashlight to read about the leprechaun. "The letter says the best time to catch the leprechaun is in the afternoon."

"You should get some sleep," Vanessa suggested. "You'll need your strength. Hugo and I can keep watch."

Seth did feel weary. "All right."

The satyrs started improvising beds out of ripped couch cushions. Using the flashlight, Seth went to the garage and retrieved a couple of sleeping bags.

"May I borrow your light?" Vanessa asked when he returned. "While you sleep, I want to forage."

Seth handed over the flashlight.

"Get some sleep," she said gently.

Hugo cleared a spot in the rubble. Seth unrolled the sleeping bag, unzipped it part of the way, and burrowed inside. He wished somehow sleep could make all of this go away.

Newel and Doren began to snore magnificently. At first Seth thought they were teasing him, but eventually he realized it was no joke. He tried to tune out the droning duet. For some time he lay there struggling to get comfortable, shifting and turning, striving not to obsess about the future, wondering if sleep would ever come. Eventually his exhaustion overpowered all other variables and he sank into a troubled slumber.

CHAPTER EIGHTEEN

Flight

Warren, Kendra, and Bracken sat with their backs against the iron wall of the dome, legs stretched out in front of them, feasting on pomegranates. Kendra plucked red arils until she had a small handful, then slapped them into her mouth, chewing lazily. The cool juice inside had a faintly sour aftertaste.

The fairies had once again provided them with an abundance of nuts and fruit. One industrious group of fairies had even gone back and retrieved Warren's sword from the Beckoning Grove. Bracken had heaped praise on them for their efforts, making the fatigued fairies blush with pleasure. After the display, a second team of fairies brought them a rust-cankered dagger, and a third fetched a moldy gauntlet. Bracken toned down his enthusiasm, but accepted the offerings graciously.

When the luminous pond began to churn and bubble, Bracken scrambled to his feet for a better view. Warren and Kendra did likewise.

"Will our help come out of the pond?" Warren asked.

They had expected the promised assistance to enter through the hatch. With the implication that help might arrive through the pond, Kendra had a sudden suspicion who the Fairy Queen might be sending. She had only heard of one being who could travel between fairy shrines.

A sleek, winged form burst out of the water surrounded by luminous spray. The undersized dragon wheeled through the air and landed in front of Bracken, silver-white scales reflecting a faint rainbow sheen.

"Raxtus!" Kendra exclaimed.

The dragon shook his head briskly, expelling water from his burnished snout. "Hello, Kendra," the dragon replied, panting. "Greetings, Bracken. You look well. And, wait a minute, small world! You're Warren, the guy who had the punctured lung." The dragon gave a nervous chuckle. "Glad you found a competent healer. And a barber. Sorry about the whiskers."

"This is our reinforcements?" Warren asked in concern.

"Think of me as your transportation," Raxtus said. "You'll feel less disappointed."

"We're very happy to see you," Bracken said.

The dragon dipped his head respectfully. "It's been too long. I'm glad you're out of confinement."

"You know Kendra and Warren?" Bracken asked.

"We met at Wyrmroost." Raxtus looked around. "I've

been here before. The sealed shrine. Is that little door the only way out?"

"I'm afraid so," Bracken said.

Warren considered the door, then glanced back at Raxtus. "You're small for a dragon, but not that small." Kendra tacitly agreed. Raxtus had a body the size of a large horse. Even with his wings fully tucked, it didn't look like his midsection could fit through the hatchway.

Raxtus sighed. "I'll figure it out. Once you get really acquainted with humiliation, the dread starts to fade."

"What humiliation?" Bracken inquired.

"Take your pick," Raxtus grumbled. "I was referring to my avatar."

"Your avatar is a unique wonder!" Bracken cried.

"My avatar is a wimpy little fairy boy," Raxtus corrected.

Kendra stifled a giggle.

"I didn't have time to learn your whole situation," Raxtus said. He seemed intent on changing the subject. "The Fairy Queen stressed that haste was paramount. What's the plan?"

"Our most urgent objective is to flee Living Mirage," Bracken said. "Then we need to make our way to Finland."

"Why Finland?" Raxtus asked.

Warren related what they knew concerning the Eternals, including the whereabouts of Roon Osricson.

"Finland is a big place," Raxtus pointed out.

"I have instructions," Warren said. "Have you ever heard of Shipbreaker Fjord?"

The dragon stamped his forelegs and flexed his wings. "I

adore Shipbreaker Fjord! It's one of the most scenic water-ways on the planet. Towering cliffs, raging tides, deep blue water. The area is magically concealed."

"I know the place too," Warren said. "The Sphinx said if we fly northeast from Shipbreaker Fjord, we can't miss Roon's hideout. A distracter spell shields his stronghold, but the camouflage should be no match for Kendra."

"Sounds easy enough," Raxtus said, swiveling his head to study the hatchway. "What awaits us outside?"

"Evidently our escape remains undetected," Bracken said. "None of us can say how long that will hold true. We should expect pursuit."

"Can you carry three of us?" Kendra asked.

Raxtus reared up and unfurled his wings. The dragon seemed much larger with his wings spread wide and his neck craned high. He fanned the area with a few trial flaps. After a moment, he folded his wings and dropped down on all fours. "I might be a runt, but I can carry three people."

"Are you sure?" Warren challenged. "A lot depends on this. I could stay behind."

"I can carry you three," Raxtus pledged. "Maybe not around the world, but I can get you away from this preserve."

"We're surrounded by desert," Warren reminded him. "Together the three of us must weigh around five hundred pounds. Have you carried three people before?"

"I've carried an elk," Raxtus replied. "It had to weigh more than five hundred pounds. Wasn't easy. Imagine run-ning uphill wearing a backpack crammed with bricks. Not ideal, but doable. With you three as passengers, I'll lose much of my maneuverability. But I can conceal myself. Unless we get unlucky, this should work."

"Luck has a way of evaporating when you lean on it," Warren muttered. "Maybe you should go on without me, lighten the load."

"You're determined to be a martyr," Bracken laughed.

"This needs to succeed," Warren maintained.

"We'll escape together," Kendra said adamantly. "We need each other for what lies ahead."

"I can do it," Raxtus asserted. "If dragons depended on pure physics to fly, none of us would do more than hop around. Magic is involved. I'll find a way. I have my weaknesses, but flying is my forte."

Warren folded his arms. "If things go bad, promise to drop me."

"Enough with the negativity!" Raxtus said. "You're freaking me out!"

"Show a little confidence," Kendra urged. "This is the dragon who destroyed Navarog!"

Raxtus swiveled his head left and right. "Not too loudly," the dragon murmured. "He might have a relative."

"Well done, by the way," Bracken said in a low voice.

Raxtus swung his head away shyly. "She makes it sound impressive. I snuck up behind him while he was in human form. I'm not a fighter. But I'll do my best. The Fairy Queen made it clear that the fate of the world depends on our mission. I want to do my part. After all, your current needs don't require a fighter. What you most need right now is to run away. I know a thing or two about that."

Bracken patted Raxtus affectionately on the neck. "You're too humble. I can't claim to like many dragons, but you're the cream of the crop."

"Of course the unicorn likes the fairy dragon," Raxtus grumbled. "If you want to boost my self-esteem, act scared of me."

"You could bite our heads off," Warren remarked. "That's scary."

"I couldn't," Raxtus sighed.

"You could!" Kendra insisted. "I saw you gobble up Gavin."

Raxtus showed his impressive teeth. "Physically, yes, I could eat you. Emotionally, no way. Maybe while under hypnosis. How can you consume somebody you just spoke with? I mean, once I've had a conversation with someone, that person is no longer food. Some dragons get a big thrill out of talking with their meals, playing cat and mouse. I don't get the allure. Knowing a creature can converse takes it off my menu."

"Unless it's evil and threatens your dad," Kendra amended.

"Touché," Raxtus replied.

"We should probably depart," Bracken said. "We don't want to lose the initiative."

"Translation?" Raxtus said glumly. "Time for me to become fairy boy."

"Wait," Warren said, fingering the hilt of his sword. "Can't you take us out the way you came in?"

"I can leap from shrine to shrine by cutting through the Fairy Queen's realm," Raxtus explained. "Although her realm connects to all of her shrines, the distance between shrines is much shorter where she resides. It's a great way to travel. Here's the problem: When she opens a portal to let anyone into or out of her realm, it leaves her kingdom vulnerable for a time. For some reason, I can slip through without opening a portal. But I can't carry passengers that way."

"Do you go to her realm a lot?" Kendra asked, intrigued.

"I never stay there," Raxtus said. "It would be . . . unhealthy. Emotionally. Psychologically. Look, I'm already not very dragonly. If I lived there, I'd lose all sense of what I am. I'd end up like a child who refused to leave the nest, never amounting to anything. But I love to visit her kingdom. As wonderful and diverse as Earth can be, no beauty quite compares."

Bracken cleared his throat uncomfortably. "I believe we were getting ready to depart."

"Right," Raxtus said. "Do you mind closing your eyes?"

"Not at all," Bracken said.

Kendra covered her eyes. Even with her hands in the way, she sensed the bright flash.

Several of the fairies in the area tittered. It was hard for Kendra to decide whether they were mocking or flirting. Perhaps a little of both.

"No peeking," Raxtus said, his voice pitched higher.

The comment tempted her. She slid her fingers apart just enough to see the back of a rather scrawny fairy with shaggy silver hair and an elaborate set of metallic wings fluttering toward the hatchway. The fairy was the largest Kendra had seen, about a foot tall. His head turned as if to glance back, and Kendra closed her fingers before he completed the motion.

"Okay, you can look," Raxtus called a moment later.

Kendra dropped her hands and opened her eyes. The spindly male fairy stood at the hatchway. His face was impishly handsome, with a sparkle of mischief in his bright eyes.

"Is that you?" Warren asked.

"I could tell Kendra wanted a look," Raxtus said. "I can't blame her." He spread his arms wide and turned around. "What do you think?"

"You're . . ." Kendra stopped herself.

"Spit it out," Raxtus said. "I can take it."

"Adorable," Kendra finished weakly, hoping he wasn't too insulted.

"Too big to be a fairy," Raxtus said. "Too small and much too winged to be a human. And the exact opposite of how any dragon would aspire to be seen."

"You're a marvel, Raxtus," Bracken said kindly. "Truly splendid."

"The sideshow's over," Raxtus said. "Let's get under way." He flitted out the hatch and out of sight.

Bracken turned to address the fairies. "I am going to close the hatch to help cover our tracks. If I left it open, others would come and close it shortly. If you would prefer the open air at the price of staying away from the shrine, come out with us."

Several groups of fairies darted out of the hatchway, followed by a few stragglers. Kendra was surprised to see more fairies opting to remain within the dome than had been trapped inside when they had first arrived.

"So many are staying?" Kendra asked.

"They love their queen," Bracken said simply. He led the way out of the enclosure. When Kendra and Warren had exited, Bracken gave the door a shove, and it clanged shut.

The sphinx remained sprawled on the ground, tail swishing. She did not condescend to look back at them. The day had grown quite hot. Raxtus had returned to dragon form. Beneath the bright sun, his scales really gleamed.

"Time to fly," Bracken said.

Raxtus sprang into the air and glided toward them like the world's most dazzling kite. The dragon snatched Kendra with one claw, Warren with another, and Bracken with a third. Jerking Kendra off the ground, Raxtus gripped her torso from behind, causing her to tilt forward once airborne. The ground became a blur beneath her dangling feet. Wings beating with the sound of heavy tarps in a windstorm, Raxtus gradually climbed, barely clearing the nearest treetops. The dragon went invisible, creating the illusion that Kendra was soaring through the air on her own.

"You all right?" Warren called.

Raxtus veered left and right, wings flapping furiously. "You're heavy," the dragon grunted, "but I'll make it." They continued to laboriously gain altitude.

Up ahead, the steep wall of the valley approached, a wide precipice of rock and dirt. Down below, the trees shrank, growing ever more distant. In a clearing, Kendra saw a pair of thickset giants hammering at each other with clubs.

As Raxtus reached the wall of the valley, he began to bank and circle, sometimes flapping his wings, sometimes gliding. They started to rise more swiftly. The air grew a little cooler, and the ground became shockingly distant. Soon Kendra had a view of the entire long valley, including the river, the woodlands, numerous cultivated fields, and the stepped pyramids with their garden terraces. Beyond the tops of the valley walls, Kendra beheld the tawny expanse of the surrounding desert.

A shrieking cry of tremendous volume shattered the sense of airborne solitude. Kendra twisted toward the source of the sound and saw the roc rising toward them, at least the size of an airliner.

"The roc spotted us," Warren warned.

"They have amazing eyesight," Raxtus said, wings working to lift them higher. They curved toward the roc, giving everyone a better view of the gargantuan wingspan.

"Isn't it time to run?" Kendra cried nervously.

"We need altitude," Raxtus said. "With all of this weight, my best maneuvers will involve diving."

The roc wheeled away from them, rising to a higher elevation with alarming ease. When the great raptor turned back toward them, it approached from above, gaining terrific speed.

Raxtus slipped into a straight, level glide, moving perpendicular to the path of the oncoming predator. As the roc closed, talons large enough to crush a school bus opened wide.

At the last possible moment, Raxtus turned toward the roc, tucked his wings, and dove. The rush of wind brought tears to Kendra's eyes. She could feel the enormous roc swoop past above them, outstretched talons grasping at empty air. The great bird let out an earsplitting shriek.

Raxtus pulled out of his dive, using the momentum to regain some altitude. Above, the roc circled around for another attack.

"Make yourself visible!" Bracken yelled. "Simurghs prefer light to darkness. As she approaches, roll so she can see me."

Raxtus became visible, scales resplendent in the sunlight. "Touch me, Kendra," Raxtus said. "I could use the extra energy."

Kendra laid a hand against the claw around her torso, and Raxtus began to shine with his own light. They seemed to gain altitude faster.

The roc closed again, wings shortened for greater speed. As the vast bird drew near, Raxtus banked, tilting his underside up to better display his passengers.

"Mighty simurgh," Bracken called in a magically magnified shout. "Like you, I am numbered among the Children of the Dawn. Lend us your skies, windkeeper, for our need is dire."

The roc swerved away, apparently giving up the pursuit. Raxtus righted himself and resumed climbing. The roc let out a screech that seemed less of a challenge than the previous cries.

"Good thing," Raxtus gasped. "I didn't want to frighten anyone, but that would have been only a matter of time."

"The simurgh here is well fed," Bracken said. "So are her young. She would willfully devour a unicorn only in a time of famine."

"Don't celebrate yet," Warren warned, pointing toward the largest ziggurat. "We have company."

"I see them," Raxtus said. "Just clearing the trees."

"Three harpies," Bracken reported. "The roc drew the attention of our enemies. How far to the edge of the preserve?"

"Too far," Raxtus puffed. "We need more altitude. They'll catch up and I'll have to evade."

At first, Kendra didn't see what the others meant. Then she spotted the three winged specks rising toward them. "How big are harpies?"

"Not huge," Warren said. "Our size. Horribly fierce, though. Picture winged hags."

"Can't you take them, Raxtus?" Kendra asked.

The dragon spoke in panting bursts. "Unburdened? Fresh? In an emergency? Yeah, I could probably handle them. Right now? I'll do my best."

As Raxtus circled higher, the harpies closed, becoming more distinct. The wiry women had wings instead of arms, and talons instead of legs. Their long hair fluttered wildly in the wind.

"Here we go," Raxtus said, veering away from the fertile valley toward the arid monotony of the desert. Though his wings flapped vigorously, they no longer rose as rapidly. "I hate to leave that updraft. If we'd had another couple of minutes to focus on climbing, I could have outrun them."

"Should all else fail," Bracken said, "swoop low and set us down."

"Or drop me now," Warren said.

Kendra looked down. They were thousands of feet above the desert. "Are you crazy?"

"If it means the rest of you make it out, it would be worth it."

"I won't drop anyone," Raxtus said.

"These harpies are only engaged in reconnaissance," Bracken said. "I see no other pursuers. If our enemies knew who we were, they would be throwing everything they have at us. It could be much worse."

"Can the harpies leave the preserve?" Kendra asked.

"Not over the wall," Bracken said.

"Unless," Raxtus gasped, "they don't belong . . . to Living Mirage."

"They belong here," Bracken assured them. "The Sphinx keeps Living Mirage locked down tightly. He wouldn't want any creatures coming and going."

"Won't the wall stop Raxtus from leaving?" Kendra asked.

"Nothing can enter over the wall," Raxtus wheezed. "But most of the defenses . . . are focused outward. I don't belong here. Finding a way in . . . is the trick. After that, I'm free to leave. Same with you three."

"They're gaining," Warren said.

Kendra was facing forward, so she really had to contort herself to look back at their pursuers. Two of the harpies had climbed higher than them. One was flying lower. Their gaunt, greenish faces glared with determination.

"Don't let them scratch you," Warren cautioned. "I'd rather get bitten by plague rats."

Kendra held her palm against Raxtus, hoping her energy would give him a boost. He had not reverted to his invisible state.

"The one below is trying to cut off a dive," Bracken warned.

"I see her," Raxtus said, sounding flustered. The two above them were quickly gaining. One bared her pointy teeth.

Warren spoke up. "If you drop me from here, could you catch me?"

"Probably," Raxtus said.

"Good enough," Warren said. "Wait for it. Wait for it."

"I'm not going to—"

"Don't argue!" Warren snapped. "Now!"

Raxtus let go of him, then curved into a steep dive. Kendra craned her neck to watch Warren. The harpy below was on a course to intercept him. Plummeting through the air, Warren drew his sword. The harpy tried to swerve away, but with a brutal downward stroke, Warren hacked off a wing as he plunged past her. The momentum from the blow made him spin awkwardly as he fell. The caterwauling harpy went into a spiraling plunge of her own. Shedding feathers, the severed wing descended more slowly.

The desert rushed up toward Kendra with alarming haste. Fully committed to a whistling dive, Raxtus neared Warren, who had righted himself and was now falling spread-eagle like a skydiver. The dragon grabbed Warren and then tried to pull out of the hurtling dive. G-forces tugged dizzyingly as Raxtus wrenched them back toward level flight.

Blackness encroached around the edges of Kendra's vision, and then they were skimming along the ground with her feet inches above parched dirt.

Raxtus slowed, dropping them gently. Beating his wings, the dragon gained altitude and veered off to one side, becoming invisible.

"I take it all back," Bracken said. "I'm glad you have the sword."

"Are you all right?" Kendra asked.

Warren grinned. "I'm surprised to be alive. That would have been a very big belly flop into a very dry pool. Here they come!"

The two remaining harpies were soaring toward them. One was looking over her shoulder, an extended finger tracing the flight path Raxtus had taken. Either she could see him or else she was estimating. The other harpy increased her speed, coming right at them.

"Care to lend me your sword?" Bracken asked.

"I've got her," Warren said, holding the weapon ready. "Watch Kendra."

Bracken took her hand and pulled Kendra back. The harpy who had been tracking Raxtus swerved to one side, wings flailing, talons raised, and was suddenly jostled roughly from the sky. Raxtus flickered into view after the impact. The headless harpy flopped to the arid ground.

The final harpy swooped at Warren, shrieking with rage. He sidestepped and slashed viciously, chopping off a claw, but the other claw raked him, and he spun to the dirt.

Howling furiously, the maimed harpy hopped twice on

her remaining leg, then leapt back into the air, flapping her
wings and coming toward Bracken and Kendra. Bracken
tossed a rock at her, which exploded with a blinding flash.
The harpy closed her eyes but kept coming, her remaining
claw outstretched. Bracken drew his little knife.

Just before the harpy reached them, she dropped hard to
the dirt, as if an unseen piano had landed on her. Raxtus
became visible again, standing on top of her, stamping and
raking with razor claws. Feathers fluffed into the air. Kendra
averted her eyes.

Warren staggered over to them, hand clutching his
shoulder, a sheen of sweat glistening on his haggard face.
"Rather . . . be mauled . . . by a pack of rabid dogs."

Raxtus stopped shredding his prey and flew off to inspect
the one-winged harpy.

"Let me see," Bracken said.

Warren removed his hand. Ugly stripes had been slashed
into his shoulder, the edges yellow, the blood almost black.
Warren bit his lower lip. "I can feel the poison spreading."

Bracken placed his palm on the wounds. Flinching
slightly, Warren gasped in pain. Bracken bowed his head and
closed his eyes. His nose and lips twitched. His hand gave off
a pearly glow. When he removed his hand, the edges of the
wounds were no longer yellow, and the blood looked less dark.

"Wow, that felt hot," Warren growled through clenched
teeth.

"I burnt away most of the poison," Bracken said, swaying. He shook his head as if to clear it. "Once upon a time
that would have been simple."

Raxtus came gliding back to them. "No more harpies," the dragon announced proudly, landing nearby.

"Good work," Warren said. "How do they taste?"

"Terrible!" Raxtus exclaimed, baring his teeth in disgust. "I bit the head off one of them. I couldn't spit it out fast enough!"

"Warren got hurt," Kendra said.

"I tried to hurry," Raxtus apologized. "They were so intent on you three, it made them easy prey."

"You did great," Warren said. "Those harpies barely knew what hit them. I'm impressed."

"Want to try to heal him?" Kendra asked the dragon.

Raxtus chuckled nervously. "Bracken might be more the expert."

"I've done what I can," Bracken said. "With my horns gone, I'm a ghost of my former self. Trace amounts of toxin remain. I can't close the wounds any more than I have."

"I can try," Raxtus said uncertainly. "Kendra, it might help if you keep a hand on me."

The dragon brought his chrome-bright head close to Warren, and Kendra rested her hand against the gleaming neck. Raxtus glowed brighter. Lowering his nostrils to the wound, the dragon exhaled a glittering, multihued spray. The wounds closed, leaving three angry welts.

"Well done," Bracken said.

"It helped to have Kendra steadying me," Raxtus replied.

Warren rubbed his shoulder. "Much better."

Bracken stepped forward and felt his forehead. "You still

have trace amounts of harpy venom in your system. We need to get you to a healer."

"How long do I have?" Warren asked solemnly.

Bracken frowned. "Maybe twelve hours. Maybe fourteen."

"What?" Kendra cried.

"He would have been dead within minutes without our intervention," Bracken said. "If I had a horn, curing him would be simple. But any decent healer should have the required antivenin."

Warren rubbed Kendra's shoulder affectionately. "I told you, it's better to get chewed up by plague rats. Harpies are foul."

"Try biting off one of their heads!" Raxtus griped, shuddering. "Sorry, I know, at least I didn't get poisoned."

"Do you know any healers in the area?" Bracken asked.

"The closest I know of would be in Istanbul," Warren apologized.

"Think you can carry us to Istanbul?" Bracken asked.

"I can make it," Raxtus said stoutly. "Might help if the attacks would slow down."

"Let's get back in the sky," Bracken urged.

Raxtus backed up, sprang into the air, snatched Kendra, Warren, and Bracken, and started climbing. Several minutes later, still gaining altitude, they passed over the border of Living Mirage with no signs of pursuit.

CHAPTER NINETEEN

Cormac

The sky had threatened rain all morning, but not a drop had fallen yet. Slow, gray clouds currently obscured the sun. Seth checked his watch. Almost 1:30. He hoped the leprechaun would make an appearance soon. Once the sun went down, the centaurs would certainly be after them.

Seth knelt behind a bush between Newel and Doren, watching a sack that hung from a limb over a sandy patch beside a stream. Not far upstream, the water tumbled over a series of ledges, sending up a fine mist around the rocky base of the final drop. According to Patton, the banks near the base of the waterfall were frequented by a leprechaun named Cormac.

"Do you really think this will work?" Doren asked.

Seth flicked the letter in his hand. "Patton seems convinced."

"Patton doesn't have a hefty sum of gold coins at risk," Newel grumbled. "I wish this design had been tested."

"No you don't," Seth said. "Patton made it clear in his letter that the same trap never works twice on the same leprechaun. He has caught Cormac five times with five different traps, and he feels like this new trap will do it again."

"If you keep talking, the leprechaun will never come," Vanessa hissed, making Seth jump. Since hazardous creatures were now free to wander Fablehaven, she and Hugo had been scouting the area. Seth still didn't see her, but apparently her prowling had brought her within earshot.

"Good point," Seth whispered back.

He surveyed the trap in silence. An irregular trail of gold coins led from the stream to a wide patch of sand ringed by rocks. Along the trail, a few of the coins were half-buried, a couple completely buried. In select places they had scattered multiple coins within a small area. Patton had explained that leprechauns couldn't resist unattended gold. Finding lost and hidden treasure was how the little men built their wealth.

In theory, the trail of gold would lead Cormac to a point where he would notice the hanging sack, which contained seventy gold coins. A small flask of whiskey, provided by the satyrs, awaited atop the coins inside the sack.

Minutes trickled by. Without the stimulation of conversation, Seth began to nod drowsily. He had not slept soundly the night before, and had awakened early. He was slipping into a colorful dream involving pie and llamas and water-slides when Doren elbowed him in the ribs.

Seth jerked his head up. A little man in a red frock coat was pulling a half-buried coin out of the sand. He stood not much taller than Seth's knees, wore an outdated hat, and had a bristly auburn beard. The leprechaun wiped the coin on his coat, sniffed it, and tucked it away into a pocket.

Cocking his head back, the little man studied the sack above him. "Foolish place to hide a treasure," he said in an Irish brogue. He spoke loudly, as if to a slightly deaf companion, although he appeared to be alone. "Might be the poor sap hoped to keep it out of the reach of animals. Might be he had no time to stash his savings properly. The fellow might be so rich he can afford to be careless. Might simply be an idiot—the world boasts an endless supply. Then again, might be a trap."

Glancing left and right, the leprechaun rubbed his knobby nose. Fortunately, Seth and the satyrs had chosen a thick bush a good distance from the bag.

Creeping forward, the leprechaun recovered another coin from under the sand. The little man flicked the coin, held it to his ear, then addressed it fondly. "Tell me about your brothers. Do you hail from a large family?" He squinted up at the sack. "I expect you do."

The coin disappeared into a pocket. The leprechaun stood with his hands on his hips, considering the bulging sack and the tree from which it hung. In his letter, Patton had explained that leprechauns tended to be clever, but that gold and whiskey had been known to cloud their judgment. Seth watched intently.

"Might be a trap," the little man repeated, peering furtively over his shoulder. "If so, what if old Cormac swipes the bait and leaves the rest? I see no evidence of sophistication. History has shown that few have the wits to get the better of me. That blighter Patton Burgess has been dead and buried for years. And what if it isn't a trap? I would be the prince of fools to leave a rich haul like this to another." He rubbed his hands together. "Very well, no use debating once my mind is made up."

The leprechaun scampered to the base of the tree and scaled the trunk. Newel and Doren crouched lower, and Seth mimicked them. The little man walked out along the limb to the spot where the bag was tied. There he paused, surveying the vicinity one last time. Satisfied, he shinnied down the cord to the mouth of the sack, loosened it, and squirmed inside.

The instant the leprechaun disappeared from view, Newel and Doren were up and running. Despite their haste, Seth didn't hear a single leaf rustle. He did hear the leprechaun talking to himself inside the sack. "Well, well, fancy meeting you here. Don't mind if I do."

Seth found it hard to hold still, but the satyrs had warned that the leprechaun would hear him if he tried to stay with them. He watched as Newel and Doren stepped softly onto the sandy patch beneath the sack. Newel used a knife lashed to a pole to reach up and sever the cord. Doren caught the sack and held the mouth closed.

Now that they had the leprechaun, silence no longer mattered. Heedless of the leaves he rustled or the twigs he snapped, Seth dashed to join the satyrs. Now all they had to do was prevent the leprechaun from outsmarting them. Once he was caught, as long as they kept hold of him, Cormac's magic was useless. Patton had provided an extensive list of warnings and advice.

Doren opened the mouth of the sack just enough for Seth to reach in. Seizing the little man by his feet, Seth pulled him out. The leprechaun clung to the flask of whiskey.

"Unhand me!" the leprechaun demanded, upside down, squirming doggedly.

"Hi, Cormac," Seth said. "Patton sends his regards." The letter had promised this would quickly get the leprechaun's attention.

The little man stopped struggling. He looked stricken. "Patton, you say? He gave you my name? Who are you? What is this?"

Seth set the leprechaun on the sand, but kept hold of one arm. The little man used his free arm to hug the whiskey flask.

"The bag's empty!" Doren said, feeling inside.

Cormac scowled up at him. "Of course it's empty. It was empty when I found it."

"It was full of gold coins," Newel corrected.

The little man glowered. "I may be a clumsy dullard for getting caught, but I'm not so slow that I would miss the chance to pocket a coin or two."

"Or seventy!" Doren said. "And thirty along the bank of the stream. How many pockets do you have?"

The leprechaun permitted himself a cunning smile. "More than a trio of gangly criminals might expect."

"Criminals?" Seth challenged. "We weren't the ones stealing."

"Who was stealing?" Cormac protested in a hurt tone. "I find a coin in the woods, I pick it up. Any honest chap would do the same. There were no potential owners in sight. I was salvaging."

"This could have been our camp," Newel argued. "We could have been off hunting."

"Aye, but you weren't off hunting," the leprechaun corrected with a wink. "You were skulking in the bushes, professional villains hoping to entrap an honest citizen of Fablehaven and extort his wealth. You're con men. You're extortionists. I demand to be released at once."

"Sorry, Cormac," Seth said. "We need you to take us to your lair and give us some items Patton left with you."

The leprechaun huffed and shook his head. "I'm not in the habit of storing items for friends, let alone archenemies. Do I look like a warehouse foreman to you? Do I look like a cargo handler? It's like I said, you're extortionists, and I won't stand for it."

"Call us whatever names you like," Seth said. "We caught you, and you're going to do what we want."

"You can start by returning our coins," Newel pressed.

Cormac gave him a blank stare. "Coins, you say? My memory is faulty of late. I'm sorry, lads. I'm afraid you apprehended the wrong fellow. I am custodian of no items, I've seen no gold, and I have no lair. I'm a humble cobbler by trade. I could repair a shoe or two, I suppose, if you require recompense to spare my life."

"We don't have a lot of time," Seth said. "Maybe we should just take your coat and call it even."

Cormac glared, lips pressed shut, cheeks reddening. Seth could feel him trembling. "Very well," he said cordially. "I can see you're no novices. What would you have me fetch for you?"

"You won't fetch anything," Seth said. "You'll take us to your lair, give us what we want, then escort us back out. I'm not taking my hands off of you until all of that happens."

Cormac tugged at his beard with his free hand. "Patton Burgess," he spat like profanity. "Will the scoundrel ever quit haunting me? Even from beyond the grave he reaches out to take what's mine."

"No," Seth said. "We just want the items Patton left with you."

"And our gold back," Newel reminded everyone.

The leprechaun hung his head, his body limp. Then he jerked hard against Seth, who maintained a firm hold of his arm. Cormac bit Seth's hand, but Seth held tight and flicked the leprechaun sharply on his ear. The little man howled as if he had lost a limb.

"Enough," Seth said angrily, shifting his grip to hold the leprechaun's legs. "Take his coat off."

"With pleasure," Newel said, going to work on the tiny gold buttons.

Doren snatched away the whiskey flask.

"No!" Cormac bellowed. "Please! I submit! You'll have the bell, the call, and the music box."

Newel kept working at the buttons, nimble fingers moving swiftly.

"And I'll return your gold!" the leprechaun promised glumly. "No more trouble."

"That's enough, Newel," Seth said. The satyr stopped unbuttoning the coat. Seth held up Cormac so they could stare eye to eye. "Any other trick, any other attempt to escape, the coat comes off, no questions asked. Then we'll shave your whiskers. And then I might go ahead and use you as a fishing lure. Don't test me. I've had a really bad week."

For the first time, the leprechaun seemed to stop acting. "You'll have no more trouble out of me, lad. You can't blame an old shyster for working a few angles? Tell me your name."

"Seth Sorenson."

"Well, Seth, for the first time since Patton Burgess, I seem to have met my match. I have not formally introduced myself. The name is Cormac."

"We're not doing this for fun," Seth said. "We really need those items. We don't mean to harass you."

"Which way to your lair?" Doren asked.

"Behind the waterfall," Cormac said.

"That one?" Newel asked, pointing upstream. "We've checked that waterfall for caves!"

The leprechaun gave him an exhausted stare.

"Right," Newel backpedaled. "Magic."

Seth carried the leprechaun upstream to where a curtain

of water spilled over a twelve-foot ledge. Cormac tugged Seth's sleeve. "This is the tricky part, youngster. I need my magic to open the way, but your keeping hold of me inhibits my powers. Would you consent to let me go momentarily? I'll give you my word as a leprechaun not to slip away."

"Patton warned me that your promises mean nothing," Seth said. "And I warned you not to try any more tricks. I'll hold you by your beard. Patton said that will free you to open your lair without enabling you to use magic against me." Seth set the little man down on a rock, pinching his chin whiskers between thumb and forefinger.

The leprechaun snapped his fingers and the waterfall stopped flowing. A tunnel, square with rounded corners, appeared in the rock face behind.

Seth picked up the leprechaun and pulled out a flash-light. Treading carefully over loose rocks, he ducked into the tunnel. The low ceiling forced him to walk in a crouch. Newel and Doren followed.

The earthy corridor reeked of pipe smoke. Large, uncut emeralds lay scattered on the floor and embedded in the walls.

"Look at those stones," Newel said. "I know a jeweler who could make them sparkle."

"Who, Benley?" Doren asked.

"No, Sarrok, the troll. No one at Fablehaven has a keener eye or a steadier hand." Newel crouched to study a dull emerald the size of a new bar of soap.

"The instructions warned us to touch nothing in here,"

Seth reminded them. "We must only take what Cormac gives us."

"Waste of resources," Newel grumbled.

The tunnel broadened into a rounded room with several wooden doors. Casks and barrels were stacked against one wall. A low table sat beside a still pool of water in the center of the room.

"The items," Seth prompted.

"Are you sure you wouldn't rather have a crock of gold?" Cormac asked. "Much more traditional."

"We want the items Patton left with you," Seth said. "The whistle, the bell, and the music box. And Newel and Doren want their gold back."

Cormac brushed a finger along the side of his nose and gave the satyrs a wily glance. "Fauns have no business consorting with human youths," the leprechaun scolded. "Tell you what—free me from the boy, and I have a crock of gold for each of you!"

"Take off the coat," Seth ordered.

Newel hesitated. After Doren nudged him, he started unbuttoning the frock coat.

Cormac twisted and hollered. "Side with the humans, will you? This won't be forgotten! Mercy! Leave me my coat!"

"No," Seth said. "You had fair warning."

Newel tugged off the coat. The leprechaun was left pouting in a dark yellow shirt with a patterned vest.

"You'll get it back if you cooperate," Seth said. "Next step is we shave your beard."

"You've bedeviled me enough!" Cormac spluttered. "Set me down by that door." He pointed at the one he meant.

Keeping hold of his beard, Seth placed the leprechaun beside the door. Cormac knocked three times and snapped.

"Is that all?" Seth asked.

"Open it," the leprechaun said.

Seth picked up Cormac and opened the door, revealing a closet cluttered mostly with empty bottles.

"Close it," Cormac instructed. "Then open it again."

Seth complied. When he reopened the door, the closet was gone. Instead he found himself looking down a long tunnel.

"One more time," Cormac sighed.

Seth closed the door again, then opened it to reveal a large room full of shelves, crates, and chests. Sundry treasures crowded the shelves, including fine porcelain figures, strands of pearls, enameled urns, ivory carvings, jeweled goblets, and an extensive collection of snuffboxes. Old paintings hung on the walls in gilded frames. Three heavily ornamented suits of plate mail stood together in a corner beside a rack of halberds.

"Where are Patton's items?" Seth asked.

"The case on the bottom shelf," Cormac said with a gesture. "Help yourself."

Keeping a hand on Cormac, Seth crouched and pulled the wooden case from the shelf. Unfastening the catches, he opened the case to reveal a handbell, a music box, and a slender whistle, each housed in a velvet-lined compartment contoured to match its respective shape. Satisfied, he closed the case and exited the room.

"Success?" Doren asked.

"Looks like it," Seth replied. He gave Cormac a squeeze. "If you cheated us, we'll be back."

"I never lie when I deliver on a captor's request," Cormac said. "That's what keeps my kind alive. Those are the items Patton left with me."

Seth pointed at the satyrs. "Return their gold and we'll leave you alone."

"I brought the sack," Doren said, shaking it open.

"I'll need my coat back," Cormac said. "The coins are inside."

"I couldn't find any," Newel said, handing the dapper coat back to the leprechaun.

Raising his eyebrows, Cormac slipped his arms into the sleeves. "Hold me by my feet and shake me over the sack."

Seth turned the leprechaun upside down and began bobbing him up and down above the open mouth of the bag. Cormac's deft little hands reached into the coat, and a cascade of gold coins began to pour into the sack with a musical shimmer of clinking. The cascade eventually slowed, a few final stragglers plunking onto the rest.

"Feels about right," Doren verified, hefting the sack.

"Tell you what," Newel said, extending the flask to the leprechaun. "Keep the whiskey."

Cormac brightened. "That is right neighborly of you." He accepted the flask. "I'm sure you three can find your way out."

"You need to escort us out," Seth said. "Patton warned us. Then we'll quit bothering you."

"Fine, let's get on with it," the leprechaun groused.

Seth went down the corridor toward the waterfall. At the end they reached a blank wall. Seth held Cormac's beard, the leprechaun snapped his fingers, and the wall folded open to reveal a light rainfall.

Seth stepped out and hurried to the side of the streambed. Newel and Doren paused at the mouth of the tunnel.

"What's the holdup?" Seth asked.

Newel eyed the sky. "This rain is going to mess up my hair."

"Your hair?" Seth cried incredulously.

"He wants to look good for Vanessa," Doren explained.

"So do you!" Newel shot back.

"I could provide a proven love tonic for a hundred gold coins," Cormac offered.

"You guys are starting to act like Verl," Seth said.

Newel and Doren shared a disgusted glance, then hurried out into the rain. Newel raked his fingers through his hair, messing it up. Doren rubbed some mud onto his arms.

"Are we finished?" Cormac asked, exasperated.

"Yes," Seth said, setting him down.

The leprechaun sprang like a toad to the mouth of the tunnel and snapped his fingers. The waterfall began to spill over the ledge again, masking the disappearance of the tunnel.

A sudden flurry of hoofbeats made Seth whirl. Six

centaurs cantered toward them, led by Cloudwing and Stormbrow. Cloudwing held an arrow nocked to his bowstring. Stormbrow clutched a huge mace. The other centaurs carried weapons as well.

The centaurs had evidently been waiting for them. Where were Vanessa and Hugo? Seth had a sword at his waist and a shield over his shoulder, but he did not want to test them against centaurs. Cloudwing had given them until nightfall. Hopefully he could talk his way out of this.

"You lied to us," Cloudwing accused without introduction. "You are in league with darkness."

"Did you have trouble trying to claim our property?" Seth asked innocently.

"You have unleashed unnatural fiends on centaur lands," Cloudwing said. "Surrender as our prisoner or die. Same goes for your mangy entourage." His tone called for immediate compliance.

"You gave us until sundown," Seth protested. "Are centaurs liars?"

"We gave you until sundown to depart," Cloudwing said sternly, "not to make preparations for war against us. Your aggression nullifies our concession."

"My aggression?" Seth blurted, getting mad. "Did I send wraiths against you? Or did you run into wraiths when you tried to steal our property?"

"The locations in question were abandoned," Cloudwing said. "You loosed evil on territory under our protection. We will not risk the possibility of more mischief."

"But you are risking the possibility of more mischief,"

Seth said, unsure what to do besides bluff. "Do you really want to deal with an undead army?"

"We do not," Cloudwing said. "Which explains our presence. As our prisoner, you will order the wraiths to depart. At the first sign of undead aggression, you will die."

"Enough empty words," Stormbrow snarled. "Fleetfoot, Edgerunner, seize them."

Two of the centaurs began to trot forward. Cloudwing slapped his neck as if bitten by an insect. He swayed unsteadily, dropped his bow, and flopped to the ground.

"Hold," Stormbrow ordered, raising a fist, eyes scanning the surrounding trees. A centaur with bluish fur stooped to examine Cloudwing, while the other three turned defensively to survey the area. The light rain pattered down, making leaves wag. Stormbrow flinched and cursed. Inspecting his meaty shoulder, he plucked out a small, feathered dart. He held out his mace in the direction the dart had come from. All eyes raised to Vanessa, well concealed high in a tree, reloading her blowgun.

"Ambush!" Stormbrow roared, forelegs buckling. Mud splattered as he slapped the ground.

Hugo came charging out from among the trees. Three of the centaurs wheeled to face him, brandishing their weapons. The bluish centaur threw a javelin at Vanessa, who dropped gracefully to a lower branch to evade the projectile. Producing his sling, Newel crouched, grabbed a smooth stone, and sent it hissing into the back of a blond centaur's skull, making him stagger.

Two of the centaurs galloped to meet Hugo's charge, one

holding a spear as if jousting, the other brandishing a longsword. Hugo batted the spearhead aside and then lunged forward, his extended arms brutally clotheslining the oncoming centaurs. The longsword ended up buried in the top of the golem's shoulder. Hugo pulled the weapon free and tossed it aside.

While the bluish centaur prepared to hurl a second javelin, a blowdart lodged in his chest, dropping him within seconds. The centaur Newel had tagged with the stone fixed his eyes on Seth and charged, holding aloft a double-bitted battle-ax. Doren launched an arrow, but, turning his ax like a shield, the centaur deflected the shot.

Dropping the case with Patton's items, Seth drew his sword and held up his shield. Hugo was coming his way, but was not close enough to stop the centaur. Vanessa was reloading. Newel grasped for another rock. Doren reached for a second arrow.

There was no time. Seth would face this charge alone.

Bending his knees, Seth angled his shield and held his sword high, hoping the centaur would believe he meant to meet the charge head-on. As the furious centaur bore down on him, Seth dove and rolled. The ax swished through the air above him.

The centaur turned to come at him again, but was suddenly moving sluggishly. Seth saw the small, feathered dart protruding from his cheek. A moment later, the golden-haired centaur collapsed.

Vanessa used another pair of darts to silence the centaurs Hugo had injured. Descending from the tree, she ordered the golem to keep watch. Then she approached Seth. "Are you all right?"

"Better now," Seth replied. "Those darts really knocked them out."

"You know how I love putting people to sleep," Vanessa said. "While foraging last night, I came across a sleeping toxin Tanu derived from Glommus, the dragon I killed at Wyrmroost. It's the most potent I've ever encountered."

"You slew a dragon?" Newel said in awe.

"What a woman," Doren mouthed.

"You got Patton's items?" Vanessa asked.

"Yes," Seth said, picking up the case and brushing it off.

"Excellent," Vanessa said. "We need to get away from Fablehaven. We bested those centaurs thanks to surprise. Sorry to use you as bait, by the way. Once they had tracked you to the leprechaun's cave, it seemed the most prudent strategy."

"It worked," Seth approved. "How long will these jerks sleep?"

Vanessa walked over to Cloudwing and prodded him with her toe. "It was a small dose, and they are powerful creatures. Still, they should be out at least a day. The substance Tanu derived is truly amazing. Our problem is that other centaurs undoubtedly knew of this mission and will come snooping. Next time the centaurs will attack us in much greater numbers."

"But we'll be gone," Doren said.

"That's the hope." Vanessa knelt beside Cloudwing,

opened her mouth, and latched on to his neck. After holding the pose for a few seconds, she pulled back, wiping her lips.

"Are you going to control him?" Seth asked.

"In a minute." One by one, she bit the other centaurs. "The penalty for claiming six will be the same as claiming one. You never know when a muscle-bound brute might come in handy."

Vanessa stretched out on the rain-dampened ground and closed her eyes. Cloudwing stirred and then rose to his feet. Newel and Doren scampered away several paces.

"Wow," Cloudwing said, flexing his arms, biceps clenching into swollen mounds. "I've never inhabited a centaur before." Cloudwing reared, lashing the air with his front hooves. "I could get used to this."

"Don't we need to hurry?" Seth reminded her.

"Right," Vanessa said through Cloudwing. "Drape my body over the back of the centaur. I'll need someone to ride with me and steady me."

Newel and Doren immediately raised their hands.

"I'll keep you steady," Doren assured her.

"I could lash you in place," Newel said, taking a length of rope from his pack.

Stooping, Cloudwing retrieved his bow. "Newel, I like the idea of using rope." Cloudwing raised his voice. "Hugo! Come! We must depart."

Hugo placed Vanessa's unconscious body on the centaur, and Newel bound her to the back of the human torso as well as to the horse. "I'll ride with you to be certain," the satyr added, attempting a casual air.

Hugo picked up Seth and Doren. Seth looked down at the five sleeping centaurs. "I wish we had saddles," he said. "I'd love for them to wake up wearing saddles."

Newel and Doren cackled.

"We should give them embarrassing tattoos!" Doren cried. "Maybe kittens. Or mustaches!"

"Cut off their tails," Newel suggested.

"Trust me, guys," Cloudwing said, not even cracking a smile, "they'll be mad enough."

"I think Vanessa is becoming a centaur," Doren laughed.

"Their sense of humor is rubbing off on her," Newel teased.

"I'm simply aware that by biting them, I've made myself their mortal enemy. In the eyes of all centaurs, I signed my death warrant."

"Way to bring a joke to a screeching halt," Newel said.

"We don't have time for merriment," Cloudwing said. "I'll run ahead. Hugo, keep up as best you can. We'll meet at the garage." Cloudwing broke into a furious gallop. Hugo followed with his long, loping gait.

CHAPTER TWENTY

Roon

K endra stared down at the mouth of Shipbreaker Fjord, shivering despite the heavy coat she had picked up before leaving Istanbul. Turbulent water gushed into the fjord through a foamy stretch of tidal rapids, complete with a number of violent whirlpools. Beyond the rapids, snow-clad cliffs bordered the pristine inlet.

"Didn't I tell you it was amazing?" Raxtus commented.

"It's beautiful," Kendra agreed, teeth chattering.

"She's cold," Bracken said. "We should have foraged for better winter gear."

"You did great," Kendra insisted. "I'm all bundled. We already wasted enough time trying to keep me warm."

"I'll find a ledge where we can land," Raxtus said.

The sun was high and bright, the temperature above

freezing, but the wind of their flight had gradually siphoned away Kendra's warmth no matter how she positioned her stocking cap or scarf. "I don't want to hold us up," Kendra said.

"We could all use a quick break," Bracken insisted.

Raxtus soared into the gorge and alighted on a broad ledge halfway up a cliff. Large enough to support several trees, the ledge also currently benefitted from direct sunlight. Icy patches of snow survived only in the shade of the trees.

Taking off her gloves, Kendra stamped around, rubbing her hands together vigorously. The smell of the sea wafted up to her, cool and fresh with a salty tang. She enjoyed the stunning vista of deep blue water overshadowed by towering escarpments, although she stayed a couple of paces back from the edge.

"Shall I build a fire?" Bracken asked.

"No, I'm warming up," Kendra replied.

Bracken wore Warren's sword over his shoulder. By the time they had found the healer in Istanbul, Warren had been feverish. Warren had insisted they leave him behind rather than await his recovery. Given their urgent need to warn Roon Osricson, they had reluctantly accepted his demand. Bracken had left Warren with a communicator. Word had come while they were resting on a hilltop in Latvia that Warren was making a steady recovery.

Bracken had offered to spare Kendra from danger by having her stay behind with Warren. Although Raxtus assured her he could often see through distracter spells, Kendra knew they might need her to find Roon's hidden fortress. Besides, even if she had no pivotal role to play, Kendra felt she needed to help. Perilous or not, too much depended on protecting the Eternals to relax on the sidelines.

"What do you think we'll find there?" Kendra asked.

"Let's just hope we beat our enemies to Roon's stronghold," Bracken said, twisting and stretching. "If not, we'll have to assess the situation on the spot. I wish the Sphinx would get in touch and give us a better idea of what we're dealing with."

"You keep trying to contact him?" Kendra asked.

"I don't think he's retrieved the communicator from my cell yet. I'm sure he's trying to juggle a number of concerns. For all we know, Graulas may have already imprisoned him."

"I never thought any part of me would be rooting for the Sphinx," Kendra said.

"A calamity like the opening of Zzyzx can forge peculiar alliances." Bracken walked over to Raxtus and patted the dragon on the neck. "How are you holding up?"

"You don't need to keep asking. I'm fine. The two of you are light. I could go like this for days."

Bracken nodded thoughtfully. "You fought valiantly against the harpies. How would you feel about joining another fight, if it comes to that?"

Raxtus scratched at the ground. "I've always quietly wanted to be a hero. Putting that desire into practice has always been . . . complicated. When opportunities to prove myself come along, I have this tendency to run or hide. But my confidence is better than ever after those harpies, and having you two along should boost my motivation. After all, we're trying to prevent the end of the world. Hard to argue against that. It ends up amounting to option A, risk death now, or option B, die for sure later. I'm well aware that the demons will want to lynch me for killing Navarog. If we have any chance of winning, I'll join the fight."

"Fair enough," Bracken said.

Kendra looked out toward the sea. She had long imagined touring Europe, but had never pictured doing it by dragon. They had made good time. Raxtus flew much faster with only two passengers. It was just yesterday that the Sphinx had helped them escape Living Mirage. With luck, they would soon convince Roon to come away with them to a safe hideout, and Zzyzx would be a little safer. She knew they should hurry.

"I've thawed," Kendra said.

"You sure?" Bracken asked, coming to stand beside her.

She glanced up at him. He looked so young! He could be in high school. She could almost picture them studying together for a science test. But of course, he was really older than her grandparents. Much older. And a unicorn besides.

He definitely didn't seem like a unicorn. His perfect skin, those keen eyes looking at her, fringed by long lashes . . .

She fought to derail her train of thought. "I'm sure. We should hurry."

Raxtus swooped over and snatched them, and they glided off the ledge. Banking to take advantage of air currents, Raxtus followed the winding course of the deep, narrow fjord. Kendra wished she had a camera. Instead, she tried to imprint the spectacular scenery on her memory.

After growing somewhat narrower and shallower, the fjord came to an abrupt end. Raxtus veered to the northeast. The dragon's shadow rose and fell against rugged terrain. They flew over craggy hills, sheer ravines, stony ridges, ice-rimmed lakes, and scattered copses of fir trees.

"Up ahead," Kendra said, as a squat keep of gray stone came into view, situated on a flat rise between two rocky hills. Reaching well beyond the hills, a tall stone wall ringed a vast tract of wilderness. A heavy wooden gate in the wall had been smashed open and now hung askew from a single huge hinge.

"I see it now," Raxtus said. "My eyes kept straying away from there."

"I see it as well," Bracken said darkly. "The splintered gate is an ominous sign. Raxtus, take us down onto that ridge." He indicated a jutting spine of rock outside the breached wall.

Raxtus circled down. Kendra looked for movement inside the wall or around the keep, but saw none. The dragon landed gently.

"Would you like me to check it out?" Raxtus asked.

"Do you mind investigating?" Bracken asked.

Raxtus turned invisible. "It's a specialty. I'll be right back."

Kendra felt and heard Raxtus fly away. Bracken stared after him, seemingly following his flight path. "Can you see him?" Kendra asked.

"Barely," Bracken said. "You were wise to befriend him. There is a profound goodness to Raxtus that few dragons possess."

"Are we too late?" Kendra asked, eyes straying to the quiet keep.

"Almost certainly. I see no evidence of an ongoing struggle. The gate was destroyed recently. You can tell by the unweathered portions of the broken wood."

"You can see that from here?"

"Yes."

Kendra frowned. "Then what now?"

Bracken looked at Kendra, disappointment in his eyes. "Once Raxtus finishes his preliminary reconnaissance, we'll go see what we can learn, hope for some useful hints or clues. If all else fails, perhaps we'll rejoin Warren." Bracken sat down.

Kendra sat beside him. A chilly breeze ruffled her hair. "What's it like, being a unicorn?"

Bracken scrunched his brow. "Funny, I've never been asked that. Let's see. It's very different from inhabiting a human form. Peaceful. Almost passionless by comparison. We love, but from a distance. We experience extraordinary clarity. We wander, we heal, we serve. We're the guardians of the fairy world."

"So you feel different as a human?"

"I'm still the same being deep down. But my experiences as a human have changed me. Unicorns are generally solitary creatures. Spending all this time in a human form has helped me learn to socialize. At times I even enjoy it! I'm still trying to improve. Old habits die hard. But I would have liked you even in my former state. My kind have always had a weakness for virtuous maidens."

Looking down, Kendra willed herself not to blush. "Even in human form, you're not really mortal."

"No, I retain a connection to my horns. They would have to be destroyed for me to really age. I could be killed, but not by sickness or time."

"How exactly did you lose all of your horns? Is that too personal? You've told me the basics."

He grinned. "It's very personal. A unicorn's horn is his glory. But I'll tell you. It's almost impossible to take a horn from a unicorn. We normally have to give them. I gave my first horn as a gift to a man who saved my life. It has passed through many hands. I can still sense it out there.

"The next horn I gave away was my third horn. This was highly unusual. I'm not sure if any other unicorns have given theirs away, save perhaps Ronodin, the dark unicorn, who willfully corrupted his horns. To part with my third horn meant parting with my form as a unicorn, but it also meant sealing away the demon horde, so I surrendered it to Agad the wizard."

"Agad? The same Agad who lives at Wyrmroost?"

Bracken nodded.

"He helped seal the demons away?"

Bracken grabbed a pebble and tossed it off the ridge. "He was one of the five wizards who created Zzyzx."

"And you helped him?"

"Only by allowing my horn to be crafted into the Font of Immortality."

Kendra stretched her legs out. "And you've been stuck as a human ever since?"

"That was the price."

"Why did you care so much?"

He regarded her pensively. "Gorgrog, the Demon King, destroyed my father."

Kendra felt she had pried too deeply. "I'm sorry."

"It wasn't your fault. All of this happened long ago."

"No wonder you want to keep the demons inside of Zzyzx."

"Little matters more to me."

"What about your second horn?" Kendra wondered.

"The Sphinx took it when he captured me. I mentioned that it is almost impossible to steal the horn of a unicorn. The protections on our horns attack the emotions, but the Sphinx is a shadow charmer, and he was immune to the effects. He took my horn with impunity and cast me in a dungeon." His eyes were far away. "I tried to make the best of it, tried to bond with other prisoners, tried to find life down in the darkness. But my lifelong love is what now surrounds us: a fresh breeze, wild plants thriving, rushing rivers, the sun and moon and stars."

"It must have been hard being locked up," Kendra said, crossing her ankles. "Especially for a unicorn."

"Any creature hates a cage," he said. "And any creature can cope if he tries. The hardest part has been adapting to my human form. I had taken human shape before, but never for a prolonged period. After becoming human, for years—centuries, really—I lived alone, wandering. The solitude was a hard habit to break. As the seasons changed and the years slipped by, my identity began to feel diluted. Over time I experimented with human society. I dabbled with friendship and duty. There are aspects of humanity that I have grown to cherish. I have worn many masks, filled many roles. It is difficult living as an unchanging being in a temporal world."

"I bet," Kendra said.

"Don't waste any sorrow on me. I'm at peace with my choices. I feel sorry for you, so young, yet forced to confront so much."

"I'm all right."

"You cope, but you're not all right. I understand your worries and your pain. Kendra, I promise you that I will do everything in my power to protect you and your family."

Feeling tears threatening, Kendra turned her head away. "Thanks."

"These are dark times, but every generation has its challenges." Bracken stood. "Raxtus returns. I was starting to worry."

Kendra scanned high and low but could discern no sign of the dragon until she felt the whoosh of his wings as he landed nearby. Once on the ground, he flickered back into view. "It was a bloodbath," Raxtus reported.

"Do any foes remain?" Bracken asked.

"None," Raxtus said. "I searched carefully."

"Roon?" Bracken asked.

"There was a throne in the main hall. A big, charred man now sits on it. If it was Roon, he's very dead."

"He had guards?" Bracken asked.

"At least two dozen," Raxtus confirmed. "It must have been quite a skirmish. Severe losses on both sides. A boar the size of a hippopotamus was savaging some of the corpses, but I drove it away."

"Any women or children?" Bracken inquired.

"No."

Bracken gave a quick nod. "Let's have a look."

They glided down to the gate first. Inside the wall, a few armored men lay where they had fallen, surrounded by a dozen goblin corpses. Kendra allowed herself only brief glances at the deceased warriors. Bracken paced around the area, crouching, fingering footprints, rolling bodies, moving aside battered shields.

"Anything between here and the keep?" he finally asked.

"Not really," Raxtus said. "You'll see. It looks like everyone retreated to the main hall to make a last stand."

Raxtus flew them up to the keep. The heavy doors had been blasted to splinters.

"There was magic at work here," Bracken said.

Kendra instantly pictured Mirav.

"You can wait out here with Raxtus," Bracken offered.

"I'll come with you," Kendra said.

The cavernous hall was built around a long hearth where embers still smoldered. Huge trophy heads of exotic magical creatures stared down from the walls—triclopses, wyverns, trolls, and strange horned beasts. Kendra regretted

joining Bracken the moment she entered the room. She had never imagined such carnage.

A score of armored men lay butchered among a host of fallen foes. Kendra saw dead minotaurs and cyclopses, as well as a grisly variety of goblins and hobgoblins. Arrows or spears protruded from many of the bodies. Some limbs were missing.

Seated in a throne on a raised dais at the far side of the room, a carbonized cadaver presided over the massacre. A slain tiger lay beside the throne, fur matted with gore. Kendra tried to pretend she was looking at a phony scene on a gruesome carnival ride, but the smell kept persuading her otherwise.

"Quite a fight," Bracken murmured.

"Yes, it was," answered a masculine voice.

Kendra jumped. For a moment, she had a horrible certainty that the charred corpse on the throne had spoken. But then the tiger arose.

Bracken drew his sword and strode forward. "Who are you?"

"Peace, unicorn," the tiger said in a slow, tired voice. "I assume you are no friend of the raiders."

Bracken kept his sword out. "We came to warn Roon."

The tiger sighed. "Would that you had arrived last night."

"They attacked at dawn?"

"Two hours before sunrise."

"Who?"

"A wizard. Several skilled warriors. Some lycanthropes.

And the rabble you see strewn around the room. Minus the wizard and a couple of the more skilled warriors, we would have won the day. Roon always loved a brawl."

Bracken stepped closer. "Who are you?"

"I am Roon's guardian. He called me Niko."

"May I approach you?"

"You wish to verify my identity? Considering the circumstances, I will take no offense."

Bracken crossed to the tiger. Despite the deep, rational voice, it was still a tiger, and Kendra reflexively clenched with fear as Bracken knelt and placed his hands on the large paws.

After staring the tiger in the eye, Bracken backed away. "You're a shape-shifter."

"Correct," Niko said. "Which is how I survived. I had retained this form throughout the skirmish. Once Roon fell, I pretended to succumb to my injuries."

"Healing yourself internally while leaving some external damage," Bracken said.

"You have the idea."

"Tell me about the battle," Bracken invited.

"First tell me more about your purpose here."

"A demon called Graulas has taken control of the Society of the Evening Star," Bracken said.

"I remember Graulas. Shouldn't he be dead?"

"It's a long story. The short version is that he's healed. The Society now possesses all five artifacts. They're using the Oculus to track down the Eternals."

Niko arose, shaking his fur as if shedding water. His

wounds disappeared. "I have been waiting here to see who might come. I honestly did not expect allies."

"You wanted a bite of whoever planned this," Bracken said.

"Something like that. You desire knowledge of the battle?"

"Please."

The tiger stretched, claws extending. "As a glance at the walls will reveal, Roon son of Osric was a master hunter—a giant of a man, with a magnificent beard and a taste for mead. For centuries, this stronghold has served as his private hunting ground. He maintained two other secret hunting arenas not far from here. On all of his properties, he bred extremely dangerous game. The men who served him came here as apprentice huntsmen. To serve Roon meant to renounce the outside world. He never shared his secret, but they knew he had an unusual arrangement with Death. He drew the best to him. One to three perished every year on the hunts, but still they came.

"Blindsided, outnumbered, his men stood with him in the end. Old and young fought fiercely and died bravely. We all tried to save him. Roon felled more foes than any of us, first with bow, then with spear, then with mace, then with sword. His silver knife slew the pair of lycanthropes on the steps of his dais. But magic made the fight unfair. In the end, the woman whose arrows were fletched with phoenix feathers found her mark. In crimson flames Roon fought on, until alone, finally beaten, he staggered to his throne to die."

Kendra had never pictured a tiger shedding tears.

"Tragic," Bracken said solemnly.

"Hunting alongside Roon was the joy of my existence," Niko said. "In the end, I failed him. There were too many foes, several of them powerful. This is a dark hour. Putting my personal bereavement aside, the loss of another Eternal is the real tragedy today."

"Two left?" Bracken asked.

"Two left."

"You don't happen to know where we might find them?"

"To what end?"

"They must be warned," Bracken said. "They still imagine concealment to be a protection. Instead, I will encourage them to travel to Wyrmroost, where Agad now resides. Walls that strong might protect them."

The tiger began to pace. "Perhaps fortune smiles amid calamity. I am the single being in the world who might be able to help you. You see, I am the chief guardian of the Eternals, appointed by Agad eons ago. As such, I can sense the positions of the other guardians. Our lives are bound to those we have sworn to protect. When they die, we die. Except for me. I live on as long as any of the Eternals remain."

"Can you be killed?" Kendra asked, speaking up for the first time.

"I can," Niko replied, "although none of my opponents have proven clever enough to succeed yet." The tiger regarded Bracken coolly. "Tell me about your fairy princess."

"Her name is Kendra," Bracken said. "She's fairykind, and here to help."

"I can see. Does she know who you are?"

"She knows enough."

"And the dragon who was nosing around earlier?"

"Our ride."

"I've never seen a dragon like him."

"He's one of a kind."

The tiger growled. "Our enemies have struck a crippling blow. Roon was the mightiest of the Eternals. We must hurry before our cause is lost."

"Tell me about the other Eternals."

"I know of them," Niko said. "I lack specifics. The wizards kept the details secret. But I can sense the location of their guardians. One of them was in South America for years, until recently fleeing to North America. That one is now in Texas, near Dallas. The other is an inveterate wanderer. That guardian has been around the globe dozens of times, but is currently in the Los Angeles area."

"Both in the United States," Bracken said. "That could be fortunate. They could be much farther from Wyrmroost."

"But not much farther from here," Niko said dryly.

"Can you assume human form?" Bracken asked.

"I lack that ability," Niko said. "No humanoids. Closest I can get is an ape. But I can do a variety of animals approximately my size. I can fly. I can swim."

"We don't have paperwork to travel," Bracken said. "We may have to cross the Atlantic using old-fashioned means."

"How long will it take our adversaries to find the others with the Oculus?" Niko asked.

"I don't know. We have an inside man at the Society,

but he has been out of touch. Our problem is that Graulas may place the Oculus into the hands of Nagi Luna."

The tiger roared. The outburst made Kendra jump, awakening a primal fear. She felt like her heart must have paused. Raxtus poked his head in. "Everything okay?"

"It will not take Nagi Luna long," Niko snarled. "We must depart at once."

"Who's the tiger?" Raxtus asked.

"He helps guard the Eternals," Kendra explained.

"Can you fly us across the Atlantic?" Bracken asked Raxtus.

"Like to America? Sure. We'll want to follow shipping lanes so we can rest as needed."

"How quickly?"

"What's the destination?"

"Texas or California."

"Carrying you two, if we go hard, maybe three days."

Bracken turned to Niko. "Could you keep up?"

"No. But I'll follow as fast as I can."

"We'll want to keep in touch. I'll leave you with a communication node."

"Very well."

"Roon must have an impressive armory," Bracken said. "Mind if we comb through it to better equip ourselves? We recently escaped from a dungeon."

"Help yourself," Niko said. "I'll show you the way. Have you a name, dragon?"

"Raxtus."

"Dragon fire would be a suitable way to consume these fallen warriors."

"I'd be honored, but I have no fire," Raxtus said awkwardly. "I'm something of a disaster as a dragon. My breath makes plants grow."

"I see," the tiger said. Transforming into a hulking gorilla, Niko walked over to the throne and retrieved an iron key ring. "Follow me."

The gorilla led them out of a door in the rear corner of the hall, then underground by way of a winding stairwell. In the gloomy hall at the bottom, the gorilla used a key to open an iron door, then changed back into a tiger. Bracken conjured up a light.

Beyond the door they found a room stocked with weapons and armor. Kendra gawked at the racks of halberds, spears, javelins, tridents, axes, cudgels, maces, mauls, and an endless supply of arrows and quarrels. The armor ranged from heavy plate mail that would transform the wearer into a human tank to light leather pieces that would hardly hinder movement. Shields of countless shapes and sizes hung on two walls.

"Who is in here?" the tiger snarled. "I could smell you from the corridor. Come out at once!"

A pile of shields in a far corner of the room shifted and clattered as a shamefaced man stood up. He wore black leather armor studded with iron. His thick black hair fell in a braid to his waist. A long mustache drooped around his mouth.

"Jonas," Niko accused sharply. "How could you?"

"I fear no beast," he said, rough voice quavering, his English heavily accented, "but sorcery dissolves my courage."

"You were his sworn man!" Niko bellowed.

Jonas hung his head. "I am an oathbreaker."

"You are an undertaker," Niko said. "I task you with disposal of the remains of the fallen, friend and foe. The cairn for Roon had best be a monument to outlast the ages. After that, go where you will, but take nothing with you. May you never forget the shame of this day. Pray we never meet again."

"As you say." The man bowed stiffly and exited the armory, avoiding any eye contact.

"I suppose there had to be one coward in the bunch," Niko grumbled. "Jonas was never the most eager man on a hunt. He tended to hang back when things got dicey. He should at least have enough sense to erect a proper cairn."

"Are any of the arms off-limits?" Bracken asked.

"Take what you need and more," Niko offered. "I can envision no more fitting use for these armaments than to wreak vengeance upon our destroyers."

Bracken turned to Kendra. "Let's get you fitted into leather armor. We have work to do."

CHAPTER TWENTY-ONE

The Singing Sisters

Before embarking on this trip, Seth had forgotten how fast Vanessa drove. Now she was zooming along Missouri back roads near the Mississippi River. As they careened around corners, he swayed back and forth, held in place only by his seat belt. Several times he had felt certain that the enormous pickup would flip over, but the tires had remained flat on the road, seldom even squealing.

After leaving Fablehaven in an SUV with the satyrs in the back and Hugo sprawled on the roof, Vanessa had driven nearly an hour to reach an old contact who dealt in high-end automobiles. A few minutes on a computer informed Vanessa that four of her seven false identities had been compromised, but she assured Seth that the remaining three personas had valid passports and licenses, as well as access to millions of dollars.

Transferring the funds electronically, Vanessa had purchased a powerful black pickup with an extended cab and burly tires. Seth had felt like he needed a stepladder to climb into the passenger seat. The satyrs enjoyed plenty of room in the backseat, and the presence of Hugo in the bed did not seem to strain the formidable engine. At first Seth had felt exposed with the golem in the back, until Vanessa reminded him that to most people, Hugo looked like a pile of dirt.

So far, they had slept only in the truck. Seth and the satyrs dozed whenever they wanted. Vanessa caught a few hours here and there when they stopped for fuel or meals.

Finally slowing her aggressive pace, Vanessa pulled off to the side of the road. They had come south from St. Louis on I-55 for some distance before leaving the highway. Now she consulted her GPS, the letter from Patton, and a detailed map of the area.

The letter from Patton had plenty of details about finding the Singing Sisters, but lacked much information about what to do once they got there. After the many specifics Patton had shared about handling Cormac, Seth felt disappointed to have considerably less advice for the bigger challenge. All he knew for sure was that he needed to strike a bargain with the Sisters or they would take his life.

"Want me to drive?" Newel offered. "Then you can concentrate on navigating."

"Not in this lifetime," Vanessa replied calmly.

"I can't be a crazier driver than you," Newel pouted.

"It's more complicated than it looks," she replied. "I think we're almost there." Shifting the truck into drive, she set the map aside, accelerated, and turned onto a rutted dirt road.

"Can we get more fast food?" Doren asked.

"After," she answered tersely.

"I want burritos," Newel said.

"No way," Doren disagreed. "Cheeseburgers and curly fries."

"Toasted ravioli," Newel countered.

"Those were interesting," Doren conceded.

Thanks to Vanessa's illegal speeding and indefatigable driving, they had only been on the road two days since leaving Fablehaven. Every time the satyrs had spotted a fast food joint that they recognized from a commercial, they had hollered for a meal break. Vanessa had not always conceded, but whenever an opportunity was presented, Newel and Doren had inexhaustibly consumed milkshakes, burgers, sandwiches, tacos, nachos, pretzels, nuts, beef jerky, trail mix, soda, doughnuts, candy bars, cookies, crackers, and aerosol cheese. Of the fifty most impressive belches Seth had witnessed in his life, all had occurred on this road trip.

"I hate to interrupt the feasting," Vanessa said, "but we did come here for a purpose. Let's try to focus on something besides sweet fat and salty fat for the next little while."

"Some of us have fast metabolisms," Doren mumbled.

"We just want fuel in the tank before we risk our necks," Newel complained.

"You want nutrition?" Seth asked. "Remind me to teach you guys about the food pyramid."

"A pyramid made of food?" Doren said reverently.

"We are your humble pupils," Newel pledged.

Up ahead, the Mississippi River came into view again. Perhaps twenty yards across the water, a long island paralleled the shore. The dirt road ended at a sprawling, ramshackle shack roofed with aluminum siding. A rusted, antique truck sat on blocks off in the weeds. Beyond a dusty tire swing, Seth spotted a run-down dock and a weathered raft.

Several dogs ran up to the pickup, yapping and snarling. Vanessa brought the truck to a stop. When Hugo climbed out of the back, the dogs ran away yelping. Apparently they didn't require magic milk to sense that the golem meant trouble.

The door to the shack swung open, and an old man emerged, bald on top with white stubble around the sides of his head. He wore fading black trousers with suspenders and no shirt. Gray hair curled on his wrinkled chest. He stood on the sagging porch, a carved walking stick in one hand.

"He's the sentinel," Vanessa said.

In the letter, Patton had warned that to get to the island, they would have to pass a sentinel. He explained there was no sure way to do this, but the goal involved convincing him that the Singing Sisters should grant Seth an audience.

Vanessa rolled down the window.

"Private property," the man said abruptly.

"We need to cross to the island," Vanessa explained.

"There's nothing on that island you'd care to see," the man replied grumpily. "This ain't a public road. You're on my land. Order the golem back in the truck and go."

Seth leaned toward the open window. "I need to see the Singing Sisters."

"You'd best turn around before I call the police," the man said, retreating into his shack.

"Should we hijack the raft?" Newel asked.

"We need to settle this with him," Vanessa said. "Newel, Doren, wait in the truck. Seth and I are going inside."

"Should I bring my sword?" Seth asked.

"I have a feeling it would provoke him without being much use against him. This old guy is more than he appears. Leave it."

As Seth climbed down from the truck, he felt nervous. But he supposed if his end goal was to talk with the Singing Sisters, he had better at least have the courage to confront their guardian. No doubt they would be creepier than the old man and his dingy shack.

Hugo stayed near while they approached the house. Flies buzzed around them as Seth and Vanessa climbed the porch steps. Hugo paused at the bottom step, stamping and leaning forward as if trying to proceed.

"Wait here," Vanessa instructed. The golem stopped testing the unseen barrier.

Seth glanced down at a shabby tin washtub full of rotten apples. Vanessa tugged open the dirty screen and rapped on the flimsy door.

Nobody answered.

knocked again. The third time she pounded loudly.
door shuddered as if a little more force would bust it
open. Still nobody answered.

Vanessa turned the knob and opened the door. The old
man stood facing them in the middle of the room, his walking stick clutched in both hands like a baseball bat.

"You ought not come here," the man warned, showing
his grimy teeth.

"This young man desires an audience with the Sisters,"
Vanessa said, stepping cautiously into the shack, as if entering the cage of a lion. Seth moved forward with her.

"Shadow charmer, is he?"

"Yes," Vanessa said.

"And you're a narcoblix. And a couple of satyrs in the
truck. And a sentient golem. I'll grant that you're the odd-
est group to come my way since time out of mind."

"You're the sentinel for the Singing Sisters?" Seth asked.

He turned and spat on the floor. "You could say that.
Not many folk choose this road anymore. From that island,
not more than one in five return."

"How'd you get this job?" Seth asked.

The old man's lips twitched. "I had a need long ago. The
Sisters helped. Might be you can take over my watch."

"How do I get to the island?" Seth asked.

"You're the one who wants to go?" the old man asked.

"I'm the one," Seth said.

The old man held Seth's gaze. "Why not ask the little
lady to step outside?"

"I want to go with him to the island," Vanessa said.

"Have you business with the Sisters as well?" the old man asked, eyes never leaving Seth.

"I mean to accompany Seth to their door," Vanessa replied.

The old man compressed his lips. "Tell you what. Leave me with the petitioner. If he earns passage to the island, you can join him. But not the golem."

"Go," Seth said. "I'll have to face worse than this before we're done. It'll be good practice."

Vanessa touched Seth's shoulder, then exited. Seth refused to watch her, keeping his eyes on the old man. The screen banged shut.

"Close the door," the old man said.

Seth obeyed, shutting it softly. He and the old man stared at one another.

"What now?" Seth asked.

"You eat sandwiches?"

The question surprised him. "Um, yes."

"How about peanut butter and marshmallow fluff?"

Unlike the satyrs, Seth had been eating sensibly. He had room for a sandwich. "Is there a catch?"

"You mean will the sandwich bind you to me as my eternal slave? No, just a sandwich. Want one?"

"Sure."

"Come inside."

Seth followed the sentinel into the humble kitchen. Looking down, he saw gaps between the floorboards. Chips and scratches scarred the round table.

"Need help?" Seth asked.

"____ a seat," the old man said, leaning his elaborate walking stick against the wall.

Seth sat down by the table on a three-legged stool that wobbled when he shifted his weight. A battered old door on a pair of sawhorses served as the counter. The old man produced a jar of peanut butter and a container of marshmallow fluff, laid down a paper towel, and took two slices of white bread from a bag.

"Tell me why you want to visit the Singing Sisters," the old man said, carefully spreading peanut butter onto a slice.

"Some demons are about to open Zzyzx," Seth said. "I want the Singing Sisters to help me find the Sword of Light and Darkness."

The old man paused, blunt knife held motionless. "That sword has a name."

"Vasilis."

The old man resumed spreading. "Brother, sounds to me like you have a need."

"The demons are holding my parents hostage. Others in my family, too."

The old man wiped the knife clean on the paper towel, then started spreading marshmallow fluff on the other slice. "The Singing Sisters do not offer guidance lightly. They will require much of you. If you fail to strike a bargain to their liking, they'll destroy you."

"I have no other choice."

The old man set the paper towel in front of Seth and cut the sandwich in half diagonally. Folding his arms, he stared down at Seth broodingly. "Those are the magic words."

"Magic words?"

"I'm here to prevent people from going to the island who have no business there. I try to run folks off, scare them, talk them out of it. Having no other choice is the only appropriate reason for visiting the Sisters. I've been doing this a long time. I believe you. Try the sandwich."

"Aren't you having anything?"

"I just ate."

Seth took a bite. It tasted really good. "Yum," Seth said, mouth gummy with peanut butter.

"My specialty," the old man said, sitting down on the other stool.

Seth swallowed. "So I can go to the island?"

"Even if you can cajole the Sisters into pointing you in the right direction, retrieving Vasilis won't be easy. I can tell you're coping with a gigantic problem. You sure you want to bet the farm on Vasilis? Sure you're going to the Sisters with the right question to fix your problem?"

Seth held up a finger as he chewed and swallowed. "Unless you can tell me a better one."

The old man sat in silence as Seth finished his sandwich. Seth wiped his lips on the back of his hand.

"You can use the napkin," the old man said.

"It has crumbs from the sandwich. I didn't want to spread them all over."

The old man almost smiled. "This old place has much bigger problems than a few crumbs. But I appreciate the courtesy."

"What now?"

pole you over to the island. There is one condition."

"What?"

"You must never tell anyone what you did in here to gain permission."

"I hardly did anything, except eat a sandwich and explain my problem."

"Exactly. I don't want word getting out, or I'll have to change my approach."

Suddenly Seth understood why Patton had been vague in his letter about how to convince the sentinel. "I promise."

"I'll hold you to it." The old man stood, wadded up the paper towel, and threw it in the trash. "Care for a root beer?"

"Sure."

The old man retrieved a bottle and uncapped it. Seth took a sip. It was room temperature, but sweet and good. The old man waited while Seth drank. When Seth was finished, the old man dropped the bottle in the trash and retrieved his delicately carved walking stick. Seth followed the sentinel to the door.

The old man hesitated before exiting. "I don't normally give out hints."

"Okay," Seth said.

"I might be convinced if asked politely."

"Do you have any advice for me?"

The old man rubbed his chin. "That's a good question. You know, I've parleyed with the Sisters before. And I've talked to others who have returned from the island, posing questions now and again. I can't get too specific, but over time I've noticed a pattern. The Sisters ask for a lot, and won't accept much less. You'll have to give up ~~all it~~ and then some. My advice would be to stall after the first. Given time, they will each extend an offer. In the end, you can accept one of their propositions, or make a counteroffer. I've never heard of anyone returning from that island who has not accepted one of the initial offers or had their first counteroffer accepted. You follow?"

"I think so."

"Just a word to the wise. Do what you will with my observations. Once again, let's keep this conversation between ourselves."

"You got it."

The old man opened the door and led Seth outside. The satyrs had exited the truck. Newel, Doren, Vanessa, and Hugo waited together expectantly.

The old man noisily cleared his throat. "Well, it doesn't happen once in a month of Wednesdays, but the blasted boy bested me, so it seems I'll be poling whoever wants to come over to the island. With the exception of the golem."

Hugo hung his head.

"It's okay, Hugo," Seth said. "We need somebody to guard the truck."

"It's for the best," the old man said. "First off, he would swamp the raft, and second, his kind wouldn't be able to set foot on that island any more than he could enter my domicile."

They all followed the old man down to the swaybacked dock, where he retrieved a long pole at the edge of the water. He paused when they reached the raft. "At this point

⸻e to ask you to relieve yourselves of all weapons. It's ⸻e best. Don't try to get cute. I'll know."

Newel set down his sling. Doren tossed a knife onto the planks. Vanessa removed a hidden knife strapped to her leg, a blowgun from inside her sleeve, and several darts from various locations on her person.

The old man gestured for them to climb aboard, then knelt to untie the raft from the iron cleats at the edge of the dock. A moment later, he sprang aboard and started poling them out onto the water. His appearance belied his strength. With seemingly casual shoves of the pole, he held against the current and propelled them swiftly to the sandy shore of the island.

"The island is narrow," the old man said as the raft ran aground. "What you're looking for is that way." He waved his hand along a line diagonal to the shore. "Up against the highest bluff that runs across the island you'll find the door. Can't miss it. I'll be here to take you back, Seth, or just your companions, depending on the outcome."

"Thanks," Seth said, hopping off the raft.

Pushing her way through thick foliage, Vanessa led the way in the direction the old sentinel had recommended. Seth followed, mind racing as he tried to anticipate what requests the Singing Sisters might make of him in exchange for their services. He wondered what the old man had asked of them to end up serving as their sentinel.

They did not travel far before finding a door in the side of a rocky bluff. Despite the faded red paint peeling like a nasty sunburn, the door appeared solid. To one side of the

island Seth could see the broad expanse of the Mis...
placid as a lake, to the other the much narrower...
water separating them from the western shore.

"Do I knock?" Seth asked.

"It's traditional etiquette," Newel said.

Seth rolled his eyes. "I meant do you have any final advice?"

"Don't let your guard down," Vanessa advised. "You know they'll ask a lot of you. Come out of there with a bargain you can live with. We'll be waiting."

"You can do this," Doren said.

"If all else fails," Newel counseled, "throw sand in their eyes and run."

Chuckling, Seth strode to the door and knocked three times. It opened right after the third knock landed. Vanessa had brought walrus butter from the house, so Seth was able to properly recognize the scaly green troll with gill slits in his neck. Broad and heavily muscled, the troll stood a head taller than Seth.

"What business have you here?" the troll inquired in a low, slobbery voice.

"I want to talk to the Singing Sisters."

"I can make no promises that you will come out alive."

"I get it."

The troll smacked his thick lips. "I need you to declare that you willingly enter as an uninvited visitor."

Seth glanced over at Vanessa, who gave a nod. "I willingly enter as an uninvited visitor."

ide," the troll said, pivoting to allow Seth

Seth squeezed by and the troll closed the door. Carved stone stairs descended in an irregular series of curves. The troll walked in a slouch behind Seth, flat feet slapping the steps. He carried a clay lamp.

"What sort of troll are you?" Seth asked to end the silence.

"River troll," came the answer from behind. "Western variety. We're not as lanky as our eastern cousins, nor as afraid of the sun as the northern breed. How'd you learn Duggish?"

"Picked it up along the way," Seth said vaguely, not wanting to reveal more about himself than necessary. "Do many trolls live here?"

"Many. Only trolls serve the Sisters. Goblins are too stupid. It is a high honor."

At the bottom of the long stairwell, several short trolls with puffy builds and oversized heads greeted Seth. They had wide mouths with thick lips, gaping nostrils, and large ears. Huddling around Seth, the trolls ushered him along a hall. Thick lime coated the walls, giving the corridor the appearance of a pale gray throat. The river troll did not join them.

The hall opened to a damp room with multiple puddles on the floor. Each puddle contained a huge, white maggot, glistening segments flexing grotesquely. Around one of the largest puddles, three women stood in a ring, hands joined. The tallest was also the thinnest, the shortest had lost most of her hair, and the other was excessively flabby. All three looked to be approaching the end of middle age.

Another troll with a bloated head stood on a stool feeding leeches to the tallest woman off of a platter. The short trolls guided Seth toward the women. A closer look showed Seth that the women were not holding hands—they had no hands. Their wrists were fused together, creating a conjoined ring of three.

"Seth Sorenson," said the flabby woman. "We expected you. Draw closer."

Seth edged forward. The trolls fell back. The three women stared at him. The tallest had to look over her shoulder.

"He's nervous," cackled the short one.

"Are you the Singing Sisters?" Seth asked.

"We are known that way collectively," said the tallest. "I'm Berna."

"I'm Orna," said the shortest.

"And I am Wilna," said the flabby one. "Tell us why you have come."

"I need to find Vasilis, the Sword of Light and Darkness."

Orna cackled. "He has his bravado!"

"He looks like him," Berna said.

"Vaguely," Wilna sighed. "Takes a little wishing."

"Like who?" Seth asked.

"Patton, of course," Orna said.

"You know we're related?" Seth asked.

"We know whatever we choose to know," Wilna said importantly.

"Do you know I'm trying to save the world?" Seth asked.

"Told you," Orna snickered. "Patton Burgess all over again."

"We have no interest in your motives," Wilna said. "Like all of our other supplicants, we take for granted that you have your reasons. We care only about what you can offer us."

"What did Patton offer you?" Seth asked.

"Every negotiation is different," Berna said. "Patton came to us more than once, and the cost of our aid was never the same."

"Patton was our favorite," Orna whispered, blushing.

"He was a splendid specimen," Wilna said aloofly. "Come closer."

Seth stepped close enough to touch the ring of women. He looked down at the puddle over the conjoined arms of Wilna and Orna. The maggot in the puddle slowly reared up and twisted. It was as long as his leg and as thick as his forearm.

"Vasilis is no trivial prize," Wilna said, speaking with sudden vehemence. "It is one of the six great swords, a shining remnant from an age of wonders, its present location heavily shielded from prying minds. You ask much, Seth, and must give us much in return."

"Three lives," Berna hissed. "We want three lives. A friend, an enemy, and a relative. Give us three lives and we will share the location of Vasilis."

"You mean kill three people?" Seth asked. "Kill a relative?"

"Yes," Berna said.

He tried to think of a relative he would be willing to sacrifice in order to save the others. Nobody came to mind. "Why do you care if I kill a relative? Why not have me kill three enemies?"

"Our needs are simple," Berna said. "We principally care about the price you pay. We only aid those who are willing to prove how highly they value our assistance."

"Don't explain so much," Wilna snapped.

"He's so young," Berna said.

He remembered that the old sentinel had suggested they would each make a proposal. "Is there any other choice?" Seth asked.

"We can give you three trials," Wilna said ominously. "If you succeed and survive, we will grant your request."

"What are the trials?" Seth asked.

"You must agree in order to know," Wilna replied.

"The trials are rigged," Orna blurted. "Nobody ever survives. They're just for our entertainment."

"Orna!" Wilna shrieked.

"They are!" Orna protested.

"Orna, really," Berna chastised.

"I'd take trials over killing a friend," Seth said. "Any other offers?"

Wilna gave him a hard stare. "Did somebody tell you to expect multiple offers?"

"You'd know," Seth said.

crunched her nose. "The sentinel. He should know better."

"The boy is disarming," Orna said.

"Enough out of you, sister!" Wilna spat. "This negotiation is on sandy ground. Seth, you do not get to pick and choose. Do you accept the bargain offered by Berna? Yes or no."

"No."

"Do you want the trials?"

"No."

Wilna nodded at Orna.

"What?" Orna asked, still hurt from being reprimanded. "Now I can speak? Are you sure?"

"Go ahead," Wilna said.

Orna cleared her throat. "In return for information on how to retrieve Vasilis, one year after you acquire the sword, you will return to us as our lifelong servant."

"Too generous," Berna scoffed.

"I like him," Orna said.

Seth considered the offer. Would a lifetime of slavery to these sorceresses be worth saving the world? Probably. But what if he could get a better deal?

"Can I make an offer?" Seth asked.

"We will hear a proposition from you only if you turn down Orna," Wilna said.

"Take the offer," Orna said. "You look too much like him to become maggot food."

Seth pondered. Even if he succeeded in recovering Vasilis, he would probably be killed when Zzyzx opened. The chances were that he would not live to carry out the sentence of servitude. Accepting the deal would guarantee access to the sword.

But what if he somehow survived the opening of Zzyzx? The goal was not to fail. Patton had dealt with the Singing Sisters without becoming their lifelong slave. He must have worked out his own bargains.

"I turn down the offer," Seth said, going with his deepest instincts.

Orna pouted.

Wilna glowered. "If you do not have a better alternative, then we will have to terminate this interview."

"Let me get something straight," Seth said. "Part of the reason you're asking for so much from me is because Vasilis is so valuable."

"Yes," Berna said. "The worth of the prize influences the price."

"How would you like Vasilis?" Seth asked.

"Is that your offer?" Wilna questioned.

"I'm just curious," Seth said.

"It would be quite a trophy," Orna said, "but you want it much more than we do."

"No hints," Wilna hushed.

"It would cost me a lot to give up a powerful magic sword," Seth said. "That's part of the point, right?"

"Partly," Orna said.

Seth could tell that the sword alone would not be enough. He tried to think what else would be hard to give

ed to imagine what might please them. What
ey use?

"An offer," Wilna stated flatly.

"Okay," Seth said, rubbing his hands. "Let's mix some ideas. Within a year after finding Vasilis, I will bring it here to you. And I'll bring you a wraith, to use however you like." Orna nodded, quietly urging him to offer more. "And, um, at your request, using the sword, I will serve as your champion, to retrieve whatever item you desire."

"What say you, sisters?" Orna asked briskly.

"This is Patton all over again," Berna muttered.

"The offer is meager," Wilna said. "He denied our proposals. Only one option remains. The boy must die."

"Yours is not the only voice here," Orna carped. "Being the pushiest does not make your opinion matter more. You demanded the death of our last petitioner. How entertaining was that? What say you, Berna?"

Seth held his breath as Berna studied him. "He makes a reasonable bargain," she assessed. "Three gifts: the sword, a wraith, and one of our choosing. Consider the possibilities."

"I am inclined to accept as well," Orna said. "Is it unanimous, sister, or shall we outvote you?"

"Very well," Wilna declared bitterly, casting a venomous glare at Orna. She turned to Seth. "We will accept your dubious proposition, upon one condition. You must not divulge the terms of our proposal to anyone, or share the particulars of our other offers."

"Agreed," Seth said.

"Gromlet," Wilna cried. "Bring us a covenant knife."

A stubby troll waddled over, an embroidered cushion in his hands. A sleek dagger with a black hilt rested on the cushion.

"Let the knife taste your blood," the three women sang in unison, eyes focused on the puddle.

Seth picked up the knife and pricked the side of his thumb. The blade was so keen that he hardly felt the incision, but when he pulled the knife away, blood oozed from the tiny slit.

"We vow to show you how to find Vasilis," the sisters chanted in an eerie harmony. "Knife in hand, make your vow!"

Seth kept hold of the knife. "I promise to bring you Vasilis within a year after I find it, to bring you a wraith bound to serve you, and to retrieve an additional item for you upon your request."

"Once we perform our obligation, you will be bound," the women sang. "If you fail to perform your duties, or if you divulge the particulars of our arrangement, this knife will take your life. So be it."

The women relaxed, seeming to awaken from a trance. Seth replaced the knife on the cushion, and the top-heavy little troll toddled away, overlarge head tilting from side to side.

"What now?" Seth asked.

"You'll see," Orna answered.

"Concentrate," Wilna commanded.

The conjoined sisters raised their inseparable arms above their heads and began to hum. At first they held a single note in unison, but soon the humming became a tangle of discordant harmonies. The humming grew to singing, although Seth comprehended none of the words. The harmonies became beautiful for certain stretches, but most of the time the chords they sang were unsettling.

The puddle at the center of their attention started to glow, and the maggot inside began to writhe. Droplets splashed as the maggot thrashed with increasing vigor. The singing grew more urgent. During a long, minor chord, the maggot burst. An inky cloud of deep purple roiled in the luminous puddle. The light in the puddle began to pulse unevenly. Amid the agitation, Seth glimpsed a ravine and several emaciated faces.

The sisters finished their song abruptly, and the puddle went dark, the water almost black. Berna began to cough violently, and the other sisters were breathing raggedly.

"We should have called for a steeper price," Orna wheezed, drool seeping from the corner of her mouth.

Wilna scowled, blood leaking from one nostril. "Had you forgotten what it required to seize such guarded knowledge?"

"It has been so long," Orna apologized.

"Quit wasting words," Berna panted. "The bargain is made." Her eyes had become badly bloodshot.

"Seth Sorenson," Wilna intoned. "You will find Vasilis behind the legendary Totem Wall."

"What's the Totem Wall?" Seth asked.

"The Wall serves an oracular purpose similar to ours," Orna said. "We never knew it also hid Vasilis."

"The Totem Wall awaits you in Canada," Wilna continued. "Our servants will produce a map of British Columbia."

"Tibbut!" Berna called.

A troll with a bulging forehead tottered forward. Berna closed her eyes, and he closed his. A moment later he bowed and hastened away.

"How do I get past the Totem Wall?" Seth asked.

"The Totem Wall demands sacrifices in exchange for favors," Berna said. "Everything depends on which totems you involve."

"The Wall can be more finicky than we are," Orna tittered. "Chance plays a major role."

"Without our help," Wilna corrected. "Insights gained through our vision can eliminate much of the chance. We will provide guidance. After all, it is in our interest to see you succeed."

"Unless we would rather watch you fail and die than collect on your promises," Berna mused.

"We have already expended much effort to view the way to Vasilis," Wilna asserted, jowls flapping. "We will impart what knowledge we can."

"The Totem Wall has many heads," Orna said.

"You will have to select four totems to treat with," Berna added.

Wilna stared at Seth purposefully. "In order to open the hidden door, speak with Anyu the Hunter, Tootega the Crone, Yuralria the Dancer, and Chu the Beaver."

"Addressing them by name should surprise them," Orna said.

Seth practiced the names.

"They will require an offering to open the hidden door,"

Wilna said. "Tell them you will eradicate the evil entombed within."

"Even if they doubt you," said Berna, "they may enjoy the sport of the attempt."

"What evil?" Seth asked.

"Only you will be permitted to pass through the door," Wilna said. "You are uniquely suited to accomplish the task. Beyond the door is a room full of the Standing Dead. Only one without fear may pass. If they sense fear, they will seize you, and you will join them."

"In the chamber of the sword awaits a greater threat," Berna murmured.

"An entity of terrible power," Wilna agreed solemnly. "You must slay that entity to gain Vasilis. Therefore, your promise to the Wall will not increase your burden. Those particular totems should accept the offer."

"So much depends on what heads you address for any given issue," Orna said. "We really are removing most of the guesswork."

"What if the totems deny my offer?" Seth asked.

"Then it will be time to improvise," Berna said. "Tibbut! The map!"

The troll hustled over to Seth, a scroll in his hand. Seth accepted the rolled parchment.

"He just drew this?" Seth asked.

"Tibbut works fast," Orna said.

"Do you have any other advice to share?" Seth asked.

"None," Wilna said.

"Hold true to your end of the bargain," Orna advised.

"I would never lie to a magical knife," Seth said. "I think."

The short trolls escorted Seth back the way he had entered. The river troll awaited at the foot of the carved stairs.

"You survived," the brawny troll said.

"For now," Seth replied.

"You did better than most," the troll approved, leading the way up the serpentine steps.

At the top, the troll opened the door, and Seth stepped out into the late afternoon sunlight. The troll closed the door unceremoniously behind him.

"Told you," Doren trumpeted. He gave Newel a shove. "You owe me five gold coins!"

"You bet against me?" Seth asked Newel.

"We were bored," Newel apologized.

"He wouldn't let me join in," Vanessa said, "or he would have lost another ten."

"With your record, I didn't expect to win," Newel explained. "I figured I could get five coins back from Doren without much trouble."

"We'll see about that," Doren huffed.

Newel folded his arms. "How about, double or nothing, we see who can eat the most tacos at dinner?"

"No way," Doren said. "I've learned never to bet against your stomach."

"I'll take on all three of you," Newel challenged.

Doren paused. "Maybe. Assuming we go someplace with tacos."

"I see you have a scroll," Vanessa said.

"It's a map to a place called the Totem Wall," Seth said.

"The Totem Wall?" Vanessa exclaimed. "Couldn't the Sisters see the location of the sword?"

"They saw it," Seth said. "The sword is hidden behind the Totem Wall. They gave us a map that should lead us there, and advice on how I can get inside." He handed the scroll to Vanessa.

"What did you have to do?" Newel wondered.

"They made me promise not to tell," Seth said.

"I just hope you didn't promise to assassinate a couple of handsome satyrs," Newel said.

"I don't have to kill anybody," Seth said. "I think I can say that much."

Vanessa studied the map. "The road trip continues. We should get under way."

They returned to the raft to find the old sentinel leaning on his pole. While the others boarded the raft, the shirtless old man pulled Seth aside.

"I know you can't say too much," the old man said. "But you made it back alive. I don't need to know particulars. Did they make more than three offers?"

"No."

"Did you make more than one?"

"No. I think they could tell you coached me."

The old man scratched his shoulder. "There was risk involved for both of us. But if my hints were open violations, you would not have succeeded. I'm glad you survived. I hope the knowledge you gained will take you places."

Seth regarded his friends on the raft. "The first place it will take us is Canada."

CHAPTER TWENTY-TWO

Mark

Kendra and Bracken earned plenty of stares as they strolled along the Third Street Promenade in Santa Monica. She had carefully draped her wolf-hide cloak to conceal her sword and crossbow, just as Bracken had hidden his weapons beneath his bearskin cape, but even with a number of odd dressers in the crowd and an unusual assortment of street performers pandering to the pedestrians, they stood out in their rugged clothes and armor.

A guy with dark eyeliner and a ring in his lip came up to Bracken. "What are you supposed to be?" the skinny stranger asked.

"The Santa Monica Seaside Players are putting on *Henry V* next weekend," Bracken replied warmly. "Sorry, I'm out of flyers."

weet outfits," the guy muttered as Bracken and Kendra moved away.

Bracken had already employed a similar story several times. He had even sidestepped the suspicions of a police officer.

Up ahead, a ring of onlookers watched a man balance a chair on his chin while juggling rubber balls. A young woman kneeling beside him added live accompaniment to the spectacle on a small keyboard. Eyes roving high and low, Kendra and Bracken wandered through the crowd.

They were looking for a cat. Bracken had maintained contact with Niko, who had pinpointed the shape-shifter among these trendy blocks of shops and eateries near the Southern California coastline. Niko had no communication with his fellow shape-shifters, but his sense of their location remained precise, even though he had only just reached the East Coast. Niko could also discern that their current quarry was at the moment inhabiting the form of a black cat with white markings.

Kendra passed a triceratops with a metal head and hedge body. She studied the street and glanced up at the surrounding rooftops, expecting to glimpse the cat at any moment. The descending sun gave everything a pink glow, and a gentle sea breeze kept the warm evening fresh. In an effort to suppress her raging hunger, Kendra tried to ignore the diners eating on a patio at small, round tables. Raxtus had recently dropped them off after three days of relentless flying, with irregular breaks for meals. They had left Europe with provisions, pausing on cargo ships and ocean liners to eat and rest. Kendra would have never imagined that she could fall asleep in the claws of a dragon while soaring over the ocean, but she had succeeded. Raxtus had kept up a grueling pace, with Kendra sharing energy with him through touch.

The dragon was currently circling above them, invisibly keeping watch. A day ago, Bracken had received a brief message from the Sphinx warning that an Eternal named Mark living in California would be the next target. The Sphinx had further cautioned Bracken that Nagi Luna had seen him, Kendra, and Raxtus in the Oculus. They had been constantly on edge since receiving that unwelcome news.

Warren had also contacted them. The healer had reluctantly released him early, and he was on a plane over the Atlantic headed to New York. The plan was for him to contact Bracken once he landed for guidance on where to fly next.

Seth had been in touch as well. He was working on an assignment Patton had laid out for him, along with Vanessa, Newel, Doren, and Hugo. Bracken had advised him to keep the particulars vague unless a time came when their paths needed to converge.

A striking redhead in her early twenties sauntered toward them, wearing tall sandals and a snug, stylish outfit. Her eyes lingered on Bracken, who ignored her attention as he scanned the rooftops. The girl shot Kendra a catty glare before she passed them. Kendra had already observed several women interested in Bracken for more than his outlandish apparel.

ere," Bracken murmured, nudging Kendra.

She followed his gaze to a narrow balcony above a restaurant. A cat stared down at them, black with a partly white face and a white chest. Bracken curled a beckoning finger at the animal. Looking away, the feline started licking a paw.

Bracken walked closer to the restaurant, eyes glued to the balcony. The cat continued licking obliviously. Bracken crouched to grab a pebble and tossed it. The little rock missed the cat but clanged against the wrought-iron railing.

The cat looked up, and Bracken waved it down. After a languid stretch and a toothy yawn, the cat sprang from the balcony to an awning, from there to a planter, and then took off along the street. Bracken ran after the darting feline, with Kendra close behind.

The cat raced into a narrow alley between some shops. Jostling through a group of boisterous high school kids, Bracken tried to keep up. Kendra followed less forcefully, overhearing comments like "Take it easy, Robin Hood," and "I think that dude had a sword."

Shouldering through the amused group, Kendra stumbled and fell. A pair of hands helped her up. It was a husky boy with red hair. "What's with the outfit?" he asked.

"I'm helping advertise for some play," Kendra said. "Seven bucks an hour. Worst job ever."

Several of the high school kids were listening. "Is that a real crossbow?" the redhead asked.

After the fall, Kendra had failed to keep it hidden. "I wish," she said. "I'd shoot my boss. I have to go."

Kendra hurried to the alleyway. When she arrived, she found Bracken edging toward the cat with his palms up. "I really am a friend," Bracken was saying. The cat watched him warily, coiled, ready to bolt. "I've been talking to your leader, who goes by the name Niko. Three of the Eternals have perished. We need to talk."

"What about the girl?" the cat asked suspiciously. "She's no unicorn."

"She's fairykind," Bracken explained. "We're on your side. But bad people are heading this way. We need to find Mark."

"Follow me," the cat sighed.

Kendra and Bracken walked down the alley with the cat, and then along a different street, until they reached a parking lot. The cat led them to a corner of the lot, where they found a bench beside a low hedge. The cat leapt up to the bench. Kendra and Bracken sat down.

"Is Mark nearby?" Bracken asked, looking around.

"Not too far," the cat replied. "A few blocks. I've learned to give him some space. We don't really get along anymore."

"But you're sworn to protect him," Bracken said.

"I do my job," the cat replied. "It's become a little complicated. Look, I can tell you're a unicorn, and the girl has a peculiar aura, but before I take you to him, I need to hear your whole story."

Bracken told the shape-shifter about Graulas, the Sphinx, and the Oculus. He recounted what they had found when they had tried to warn Roon Osricson. He explained about the recent warning from the Sphinx, and told how a dragon sanctuary might offer protection.

"So we have assassins closing in as we speak?" the cat asked.

"We don't know exactly when," Bracken said. "Could be now, could be tomorrow, but soon."

"Mark is fine at the moment," the cat said. "I can clearly sense his location and his mood, but I have no way of anticipating trouble. I'll know only when it arrives. I should have stayed closer to him. Come with me. I'll explain our problem on the way. Don't say more than necessary. Wearing armor makes you conspicuous enough. Talking to a cat on top of that might be too much, even for Santa Monica."

The cat led them down a street toward the beach. "You can call me Tux, by the way. This is my favorite shape. The name started as a joke, but now it's all he calls me. He thinks I hate it, but I actually don't mind. He's called me much worse things.

"Marcus began his journey as an Eternal with a clear sense of purpose and commitment. Despite all that has happened since, I still look back on those early years fondly. We enjoyed many good decades. But the centuries gradually eroded his character. He began to regret his long life and the commitments he had made. His dedication wavered. Then it floundered.

"Mark has tried to kill himself many times. To tell you the truth, I don't know how much he really wants to end his life. He might just like pretending to die. He has never sought out anything that could actually kill him. Instead he jumps off bridges or drives motorcycles into oncoming traffic. He ends up injured, but he heals rapidly, and I watch over him. I've had to fish him out of the sea more than once. He has come to blame me for his immortal state, even though I'm just doing my job. Wouldn't you rather be miserable on dry land than miserable bobbing around in the ocean?"

"So he might not listen to us," Kendra said.

"I'm not sure," Tux replied. "Maybe the prospect of assassins who truly know how to kill his kind will snap him out of his depression. Or maybe he'll run to them with open arms. If we're lucky, a couple of new faces and voices might help rekindle a sense of duty."

"The danger is real," Bracken said. "We could all lose our lives. Dozens of men defended Roon, and high walls, and he wanted to live, but they got him."

Tux sped up. They crossed Ocean Avenue to a narrow park with paved paths, green lawns, and lots of palm trees. The cat approached a long-limbed man sleeping on the lawn in a filthy green army jacket and frayed jeans. He had long hair and an unkempt beard. His odor made it clear that he had not bathed in many days.

"Wake up, Mark," Tux ordered.

The man shifted his position and smacked his lips. "Lay off, Tux. What's the idea?"

"We have visitors."

The man sat up, eyes flicking between Kendra and Bracken. "What is this? Circus come to town?"

"We know who you are," Bracken said gently.

have no idea," the man replied. "You want me to move along? I'll move along. Leave me alone."

"You're Mark, one of the Eternals," Kendra said.

He started, naked surprise flashing across his face, then took a swipe at Tux, who avoided the swat smoothly. "What've you been blabbing?" he accused the cat.

"Tux told us nothing," Bracken said. "Only two Eternals remain alive. Your enemies have the Oculus. They're coming."

Mark grunted. "About time."

"Don't be a fool," Tux said.

Mark brushed greasy hair away from his eyes. "You think we can do anything if somebody with the Oculus wants to find me? Catching me here will be the same as catching me down the street, or a couple of towns over."

"We need to move," Bracken said. "If we stay in motion, changing course unpredictably, we can shuttle you to a safe haven, like Wyrmroost."

"A dragon sanctuary?" Mark scoffed. "You want me to hide out in a dragon sanctuary? Isn't my life pathetic enough?"

"This is bigger than you," Bracken said, trying to stay patient. "We are two Eternals away from seeing Zzyzx opened."

"Had to happen eventually," Mark said, rising. He stood half a head taller than Bracken. "I can see where this is heading. Listen, I'm tired, guys, really tired. Weary in every way. Mind, body, soul—everything that can wear out wore out long ago. You don't spend years getting mugged by hoboes and chased off park benches until you're pr[...] [...] to gone. Might be wiser to go focus on that last Eternal."

"We may not make it to the last one in time," Kendra said.

"Look, Mark," Bracken said, starting to lose his cool. "I've been around a long while myself. Longer than you. Quitting is not an option. The commitment you undertook doesn't fade away once you're no longer in the mood. You need to man up. The struggle between light and darkness hinges on this. Billions of lives are at stake. If you want to rest, live simple, why not do it at a dragon sanctuary?"

"He's stubborn," Tux warned in a singsong tone.

"Stay out of this," Mark spat.

"And touchy," Tux added.

Mark kicked at the cat. Tux scampered back to a safer distance.

"We have a dragon with us," Bracken said. "A little one. He can fly you to Wyrmroost. He can take a circuitous route, alter his heading a lot. It's your best chance."

Mark put his hands in his pockets. "What's your name, stranger?"

"Bracken."

"I'm Marcus. Mark to most people. How about the girl?"

"Kendra."

"Is she a person?" Mark asked. "A human?"

"Yes." Bracken said.

"You're not."

"I'm a unicorn."

Mark chuckled. "Perfect," he muttered, wiping his lips

with the back of his hand. "How am I supposed to know whether I'm insane? My only friend is a talking cat, and here I've got a unicorn dressed like a Viking who wants me to come live with the dragons?"

"You're not insane," Bracken said evenly. "Take my hand."

Mark stepped away. "No, no. So sorry. All I have left is my free will."

"I wasn't—"

"Don't try to convince me you don't want to manipulate my emotions," Mark said. "I know what you're after. Same thing the cat wants. You want me to pay for my mistake forever."

"What mistake?" Kendra asked.

"The mistake of agreeing to become a lock!" Mark snarled. He closed his eyes and took a breath, regaining his composure. "It was for a good cause, I know. You two have honorable intentions. I take no issue with the cause. Nobody lied to me. I simply didn't understand the cost. Not really, not fully. The exacting toll of existing, and existing, and existing, long after you want to stop, long after all meaning has died. That price is much too high. My intentions were pure. I remember why I volunteered. I simply lacked the vision to see myself ending up this way. I'm just not cut out for this much living. Becoming an Eternal was a mistake, and nobody will let me off the hook."

"I can sympathize with you," Bracken said. "Life can wear a man down. Especially a long life on the run. Still, mistake or not, you have to fulfill your duty. The stakes are too high. This is not the time to let your existential crisis come to a head."

"This is exactly the time," Mark argued, eyes intense. "Do you know how long I've been waiting for this? I've toyed with death, sure, mostly to sample the illusion of an end. To pretend I had some control over my fate. But I've never sought out a dragon or a phoenix to conclude my life prematurely. If I had put my mind to it, I could have. Now a natural end is coming. Not suicide. Just the inevitable finally catching up. After all of these centuries, I have a right to stop fighting."

"You don't have that right," Bracken said. "If this was just you, I'd agree. But you can't let the rest of the world pay for your mistake. This became about more than just yourself the day you agreed to help keep Zzyzx closed."

Mark clapped his hands over his ears. "You need that to be true. I get it. Here's the problem. I am still a person. Like it or not, I have a will. All the guilt and all the accusations and all the compulsion in the universe can't fully take that away. Is it wrong of me to have accepted this responsibility and then not follow through? Yes. Tux tells me, my heart tells me, a few others like you have told me. Wrong or not, it remains my promise to break. I'm not the one trying to end the world. If you want to blame somebody, blame them. I'm just a guy trying to finally move beyond a mistake I made centuries ago. You can try to force me to live. But since we're talking about vows, let me make a new vow. First oath I've taken in a long time. If you drag me to a dragon sanctuary by force, I will immediately and without hesitation seek out a dragon to end my life. You'll be putting me in a place with limitless opportunities. I'll probably last longer if you leave me be."

"Please," Kendra said. "Think of all the lives that will be destroyed."

"I have," Mark said. "Believe me, darling, I grasp all aspects of this, I really do. But how much has the public I'm protecting worried about me? My sanity, my happiness, my right to find peace?"

"They made no promises," Bracken said. "They are not preventing the end of the world. Those who know about your sacrifice appreciate you immeasurably. Your life may not be fair, but it is absolutely necessary."

"Leave me alone," Mark growled. "I don't need to justify myself to you. This conversation is over. Trust me, I have no feelings left to manipulate. You'd have better luck tickling a corpse. At least there's one other Eternal. Hopefully somebody as tough as you, Mr. Unicorn. Take the other sucker, I mean hero, to your sanctuary. Leave me be."

Mark turned and ran. Bracken and Kendra watched him in silence. "Raxtus is following him," Bracken said. He crouched beside the cat. "What do you make of this?"

"I'm unsurprised," Tux said wearily. "This was the most likely response, but I quietly hoped the confrontation might go differently. I'm so familiar to Mark, like a nagging sibling; I hoped he might put on a bolder face for noble strangers. I was also hoping the prospect of actual impending death might shake him up. After this display, I'm convinced that

Mark really is as hollow as he claims to be. He was a good man, once."

"What now?" Kendra asked.

"We abduct him," Bracken said. "Raxtus will carry him to Wyrmroost. Agad will have to lock him up. Meanwhile, we'll get a car and track down the last Eternal."

"I have to stay with him," Tux said. "If he gets too distant, I start to feel like a chain is dragging me toward him. I agree with you, by the way. Incarcerating us has become the only option."

"I don't reach that verdict lightly," Bracken said, walking in the direction Mark had run. "I've spent time in prison. It's inhumane. But prisons serve a necessary purpose. Prisons protect the freedom of the masses from those who abuse their freedom. On my scale, the freedom of the world outweighs Mark's personal rights. He may have made a mistake in becoming an Eternal, but the rest of the world shouldn't pay for his error. Like it or not, it remains his chore to pay for his decision."

"Amen," the cat approved.

"Are you in touch with Raxtus?" Kendra asked.

"I just told him to grab Mark," Bracken replied. "Okay, Raxtus has him. We'll meet up on the beach so Tux can join him."

"This way," Tux said, hurrying. Bracken and Kendra broke into a jog.

Tux led them along a path to a footbridge that spanned the Pacific Coast Highway. They hurried onto the bridge. Cars zoomed beneath them, most with their headlights on.

MARK

The sun had dipped below the horizon, leaving the hazy sky above the ocean streaked pink and orange. The footbridge led down to a deserted parking lot where pulverized glass glimmered in the fading light. A barren expanse of sand separated the lot from the foamy breakers. Unmanned lifeguard stations stood guard along the beach at regular intervals. Off to the left, a larger parking lot alongside the Santa Monica Pier contained dozens of cars and several people.

Mark lay sprawled on the sand not far from the water. Seagulls wheeled and cried in the air above.

Kendra, Bracken, and Tux crossed the parking lot and a jogging path and started across the sand. The way the sand absorbed each step made walking a little awkward. Kendra glanced over at the roller coaster on the pier. Between the beach, the pier, the shops, the weather, and the restaurants, this could be a really fun place under different circumstances.

They reached Mark. He glared up spitefully. From his posture, Kendra could tell that Raxtus was holding him down. "You're thugs," he accused.

"And you're a sorry joke of a man," Bracken said. "I'm out of patience. We're going to save your life, so you had better get used to the idea."

Mark glowered at Tux. "What have you got to say for yourself?"

"Meow," the cat replied, pronouncing the word the way a human would.

"Raxtus, take Mark and Tux to Wyrmroost. Explain the situation to Agad. Give him this stone, so we can communicate."

[425]

Bracken held out a small pouch, and the invisible dragon took it. "Take an unpredictable route."

Raxtus flickered into view, his neck craning up. "We have company."

Kendra's gaze went to the sky. A pair of large winged creatures were quickly approaching. "Wyverns," Bracken muttered.

Mark started laughing.

A Hummer screeched to a halt in the parking lot near the footbridge. "Fly!" Bracken urged, drawing his sword. "Take Kendra!"

"Wait," Kendra protested, reaching for her sword. Without hesitation, Raxtus turned invisible and seized her around the waist. Kendra, Mark, and Tux rose into the air, the unseen dragon's fierce wingbeats stirring up gritty clouds of sand.

As they soared out over the water, Kendra looked over her shoulder at the people exiting the Hummer, at Bracken striding across the sand, and then up to the oncoming wyverns.

"More wyverns," Raxtus warned, veering up the coast.

Scanning the horizon, Kendra saw a wyvern approaching from out to sea. Another was coming toward the pier from the south. Yet another was streaking down the coast from the north. As Raxtus fought to gain altitude, the wyverns closed in from all directions. They had wolfish heads, batlike wings, and long black claws.

"Wyverns are quick," Raxtus panted. "They're built like me. I'm not sure I can lose five, not with visible passengers."

"Over here!" Mark yelled, waving his arms. "Come and get me!"

"Shut it," Kendra snapped, readying her crossbow.

As the nearest wyverns swooped at them, Raxtus rolled and dove. Kendra fired her crossbow, but the evasive maneuver made her quarrel go astray. Claws clashed against dragon scales and Kendra felt Raxtus shudder; then the ocean came rushing up at them with alarming speed. Raxtus pulled out of his dive and skimmed the wave tops, paralleling the shore. Wyverns descended from both sides, keeping pace. With a triumphant howl, one crashed down onto Raxtus, and all of them plunged into the brine.

After recovering from the shock of the impact and of the cold water, Kendra found herself blinded by bubbles. Tearing free from her wolf-hide cloak, she stroked to the surface, the weight of her leather armor and sword slowing her ascent. She found herself beside Mark, fighting to keep her nose and mouth above water. Huge bodies surged and lashed nearby, snarling and splashing, sending up fountains of spray.

A wyvern who had not yet joined the fray swooped at them. Mark raised his arms invitingly, and the wyvern seized him. Kendra grabbed Mark's leg and was yanked up out of the water, heading toward the beach.

"Leave me alone," Mark growled, kicking at her arms with his free leg.

Kendra clung desperately for a few seconds, then lost her hold and dropped into the foamy surf. The water helped break her fall, but she still hit the seafloor hard, and then a curling wave sent her tumbling forward. Regaining her feet,

Kendra staggered through the shallows toward the shore, throat burning as she coughed up salt water.

On the beach, an arrow thunked into Bracken's shield as a pair of swordsmen descended on him. Blocking one sword with his shield, Bracken deflected the second sword with his blade, then dispatched one of his assailants with a vicious counterstroke. The other swordsman backed away, weapon ready, waiting for Bracken to make the next move.

The wyvern had dumped Mark on the far side of the beach, near the parking lot and the Hummer. Beside the Hummer, bow in hand, Kendra recognized Torina. Sand clung to Mark's clothes as he knelt on the sand facing his executioners. He shed his army jacket and tore open the shirt underneath, baring his chest in an unmistakable token of surrender. Torina nocked an arrow, and a man robed in gray from head to foot strode forward, a slightly curved sword in each hand. Kendra recognized him as the Gray Assassin from Obsidian Waste.

"No!" Kendra shouted, running across the damp sand, fumbling with the hilt of her sword, much too far away to reach Mark in time.

Swords clashed as Bracken engaged his foe. Their blades met several times before Bracken skewered the other man. Wrenching his sword free, Bracken raced toward Mark, kicking up sand with every stride.

Kendra reached drier sand and it slowed her. Her water-logged clothing clung heavily. The parking lot remained hopelessly distant. A falcon dove at the warrior in gray but he slashed it out of the air with a casual sweep of his sword.

Bracken shouted in frustration as the Gray Assassin stood before Mark and issued the killing stroke. Instantly, Mark dissolved into dust, wet clothes flopping emptily to the sand.

Torina switched arrows and took aim at Bracken, who lifted his shield as he charged. She released the arrow, and he caught it on the very bottom of his shield.

"Kendra!" Raxtus called from somewhere behind her.

Turning, she saw a wyvern diving at her. With rage and frustration, she swung her sword above her head. Ringing against razor claws, the sword flew from her grasp. Kendra fell to the sand, hands stinging, the wyvern's swiping claws missing her by inches. The wyvern banked to come back around, then abruptly crumpled to the sand, head askew. A moment later, with a rush of wind, Raxtus alighted beside her, becoming visible.

Tires squealing, the Hummer roared out of the parking lot. Kendra and Raxtus joined Bracken beside the wet army jacket and jeans. Bracken smoldered impotently. His eyes softened when he saw Kendra. "Are you all right?"

"I'm fine," Kendra said.

Sheathing his sword, Bracken plucked an arrow from his shield. "We were so close!" He glanced at the sky, then at Raxtus. "How many wyverns did you get?"

"All five. Two in the water, three in the air. Hardly a fair fight. Their claws couldn't penetrate my scales, and I was invisible. They have this really fragile spot, right where the neck joins the back of the head. My dad taught me that."

"What happened to Tux?" Kendra asked.

"He changed into a falcon and tried to help," Raxtus said. "The shape-shifter turned to dust along with Mark."

Bracken kicked the army jacket. "Blasted craven! If only I'd been a little quicker."

"They were watching," Raxtus said. "They knew just how to thwart us. If we'd been a little faster, they might have still tracked me and gotten Mark."

"How did that sword kill him?" Kendra asked. "I thought it had to be phoenix or dragon fire or unicorn horns."

"He had magic swords," Bracken said bitterly. "The hilts were made of dragon teeth, and the blades were enchanted. The magic must have been equivalent to dragon breath."

"Torina was with them," Kendra noted.

"She had a few arrows fletched with phoenix feathers," Bracken said. "Magical as well. They would have done the job too." He pulled the other arrow from his shield and held it up. "She didn't bother to use the special ones on me."

"They ran from you," Raxtus encouraged.

"I expect they were running from you," Bracken said. "As well they should. You're becoming quite formidable. I'd give chase, but it could be a trap, and our only priority now is the Eternal in Texas. We could waste time pursuing these clowns while another hit squad moves in on our last hope."

Raxtus exercised his wings. "After our last trip, Texas is just around the corner. Hmmm. Might be time to make an exit."

"The police are coming," Bracken said.

After the comments, Kendra noticed the distant whine

of sirens. She looked over to the pier. "People must have seen us."

"I'm not sure what I look like to bystanders," said Raxtus. "Not sure about the wyverns either. But onlookers certainly could have glimpsed people flying around and firing arrows and stabbing each other. Bracken left a couple of bodies on the beach. The police probably received multiple calls. It's time to flee."

"You're right," Bracken said. "I'll try to contact the Sphinx. Meanwhile, get us out of here."

CHAPTER TWENTY-THREE

Vasilis

Seth sat on the rocky hillside while Vanessa consulted the hand-drawn map he had received from the Singing Sisters. She compared it to a second map, consulted her compass, and checked the GPS reading. Up ahead, Newel and Doren were fencing with their walking sticks, wood clacking sharply as they slashed and blocked and stabbed. Hugo loomed over Seth, waiting silently as Vanessa got her bearings.

After leaving the paved roads of British Columbia, Vanessa had driven almost tentatively. Seth supposed isolated dirt roads that skirted sheer drops of hundreds of feet would make anyone a little cautious. Vanessa had piloted them along obscure, pitted roads for hours, winding among rugged mountains and picturesque bodies of water until, with dawn approaching, the latest road had ended at a small camping area, where she had proclaimed they would proceed on foot.

"We're close," Vanessa said. "If I'm correlating these maps correctly, around this hill, we should find a long valley that narrows into a ravine. The Totem Wall awaits at the end of the ravine. Let's make this a real break and have a snack."

"Foo-ood!" Seth called. The satyrs quit their duel and trotted over, opening their packs.

"Would you care for a sandwich, Mike?" Newel asked, referring to the false passport Vanessa had used when bringing Seth over the Canadian border. It was the same passport he had used when traveling to Obsidian Waste. Elise had held their documents, so his passport had made it home to Fablehaven with her. Vanessa had recovered it during her foraging at Fablehaven, and had added forged documents establishing her guardianship. Her extensive experience with international travel had come in handy.

"Pretzels, Mr. McDonald?" Doren asked, using the last name from Seth's passport. He held out an open bag and shook it enticingly.

"Sure," Seth said, accepting a pretzel. "At least I didn't have to walk over the border and then get picked up on the far side."

"Best to assume the Canadians would have objected to foreign goats," Newel said, handing Seth a deli sandwich.

"Or a huge dirt pile in the back of the truck," Doren added. "Or weapons. We did you guys a service, kept all the possible contraband out of your vehicle."

Newel flung his arms wide, stretching. Appraising the

nearest mountaintops, he filled his lungs with the cool morning air. "I'm surprised more people don't live up here. This is some of the prettiest country I've seen, and it's also the least populated."

"Harsh winters," Vanessa said. "We're lucky they seem to be having a gentle spring. At higher altitudes or farther north I bet we could still find deep snow."

Seth compressed the tall deli sandwich with his hands and bit into it, crisp lettuce crunching. The satyrs had kept the sandwiches in a cooler, so it was chilled. The sandwich had more mustard and pickles than he liked, but helped satisfy his hunger nonetheless.

Doren tossed pretzels at Newel, who caught them in his mouth. Vanessa ate half her sandwich, then leaned back and closed her eyes. After all the driving she had done, she had to be exhausted.

Seth tried not to obsess about the upcoming task. He wished they could reach the Totem Wall and get started. The anticipation was driving him crazy.

The satyrs returned to fencing with their walking sticks. Vanessa didn't stir. Seth supposed she had earned a brief rest. To distract himself, he pulled out the coin Bracken had given him.

"You hear me?" Seth mouthed.

I hear you. I should have tried to reach you earlier. We failed to protect another Eternal. Only one left. We're on our way to Texas. How are you?

"I'm about to carry out one of the hard parts of my

mission. If I succeed, maybe we can meet up before long. Is Kendra all right?"

We're all fine. Uninjured, I mean. Just a little discouraged. Hopefully we'll both have more success in the near future.

"I'll be in touch," Seth whispered.

Keep that coin handy.

"Talking to Bracken?" Vanessa asked, sitting up.

"They lost another Eternal," Seth said. "Only one left."

"Which makes our role in this ever more important." Vanessa arose. "You shouldn't communicate too much with the coin. With our enemies in possession of the Oculus, everything we say and do can give away our purposes."

"I've been keeping my language vague," Seth assured her. "For all we know, they've been watching us all along."

"Not so," Vanessa said. "I expect their gaze has been directed elsewhere. To the Eternals, mostly, and to Zzyzx itself. If they knew what we were after, we would have encountered opposition long before now. Thanks to all they're dealing with, our little road trip seems to have escaped their notice thus far. Of course, that could change at any moment."

Newel's walking stick broke. Doren started chasing him around the hillside, poking him in the back.

"No fair!" Newel cried. "I'm unarmed!"

"Touché!" Doren exclaimed with each new stab.

"We need to move on," Vanessa said.

"This game was just getting interesting," Doren complained, halting the pursuit.

Newel pointed at Doren. "I'll remember this."

"You'd do better to forget it," Doren advised. "It looked humiliating."

Hugo scooped up Seth and Vanessa. She gave the golem directions, and the satyrs fell into step behind them.

They found the valley where Vanessa had expected, and, as predicted, it narrowed to a steep, dry ravine. When Hugo reached an invisible barrier that prevented him from proceeding, they knew they had almost reached their destination. Hugo set down Seth and Vanessa.

"I guess this is where I go forward alone," Seth said.

"We have only one favor to ask the Totem Wall," Vanessa said. "We mustn't risk the rest of us encountering it."

"I have my instructions from the Sisters," Seth said. "Can't be too bad, right?"

Vanessa arched an eyebrow. "It might be pretty bad. But I've developed faith in you. Bring back the sword."

"Should I take my sword?" Seth asked. He had buckled on his adamant sword and brought his adamant shield when they had left the truck.

"I don't know much about the Totem Wall," Vanessa said. "It's old magic. Considering what the Sisters shared with you about what lies beyond the wall, I'd guess you might want a sword. Just don't use it to make any powerful entities unnecessarily angry."

"Take the sword," Newel seconded. "Chop up anybody who gives you trouble."

"I've heard it's easier if you break their weapon first," Doren added, earning a punch in the shoulder from Newel.

"Okay," Seth said. "See you soon. You might as well take naps, let Hugo stand guard."

Seth turned and started walking along the ravine, treading carefully due to the many loose rocks. He looked back once and caught the others watching him somberly. They immediately cheered up and waved, but his initial glance had revealed a level of concern that his companions had been hiding. He wished he hadn't looked back.

The meandering ravine grew shallower and steeper as he proceeded. Back where the others waited, Seth thought he could have scaled the walls. Now an attempt to climb would be impossible.

Up ahead, a totem pole came into view, brightly painted, as if created recently, standing straight and tall in the middle of the ravine. The stacked images included a squat, chubby warrior on the bottom, three fierce faces above him, and a winged eagle at the top. The grotesque caricatures leered at him, wooden teeth bared, and on some instinctive level, Seth realized the elaborate pole was a warning.

Passing the pole, Seth grew more anxious. The ravine seemed unnaturally silent. He heard no buzzing of insects, no birdcalls, no rustling leaves. The air felt still and heavy. He sensed eyes spying, but could detect nothing to confirm the suspicion. He kept one hand on the hilt of his sword.

Around the next curve, the ravine abruptly ended, and Seth beheld the Totem Wall. Six times his height, built into the rear wall, the Totem Wall spanned the entire ravine like a dam. Hundreds of faces made up the seamless wooden monument, weatherworn, timeworn, but well crafted, each face still very recognizable. A wide variety of animals were represented—bears, wolves, deer, moose, elk, lynxes, beavers, otters, seals, walruses, eagles, owls, and many others. People were depicted in even greater diversity—male and female, old and young, fat and thin, fair and hideous. Some looked friendly, others furious, others wise, others ridiculous, others crafty, others ill, others smug, others frightened, others serene.

Seth had never seen anything like it. He could imagine the Totem Wall as the featured exhibit in the world's finest museum. It was that impressive, that detailed, that unique.

A low stump dominated the ravine in front of the Totem Wall. Seth approached it curiously. No higher than his chest, the stump was at least eight paces across. Seth tried to imagine how tall the tree might have been before it was cut. Judging from the countless visible rings, it must have been thousands of years old.

His intuition told Seth that he should address the wall from atop the stump, using it like a stage or platform. As he climbed up, he noticed that some of the exposed rings were spaced wider than others. He walked to the center, standing on the cluster of concentric circles that formed the inner-most rings.

With a cacophony of muttering, grunting, barking, growling, shrieking, and coughing, the Totem Wall came to life. The wooden faces blinked and sniffed and yawned. Tongues wagged. Expressions shifted. The jumbled words spoken by the human faces came out in a language that Seth didn't comprehend.

"I'm Seth Sorenson," Seth said. "I've come to speak with the Totem Wall."

The heads fell silent. A broad male head, old and proud, near the bottom center of the wall, spoke in a profound, resonant voice. "We are many. Choose four to treat with."

"Do all of you speak English?" Seth asked.

"You will hear your language," the head replied. "Choose." He sounded somewhat impatient.

"Very well," Seth said, trying to keep his manner official. "I will speak with Anyu the Hunter, Tootega the Crone, Yuralria the Dancer, and Chu the Beaver."

A surprised murmur rippled across the wall, ending as quickly as it began.

"I hear you," said a rough-hewn male face halfway up the left side of the wall. A knot in the wood disfigured one cheek like a scar.

"I hear you," said a shrewd, hooded face near the bottom right. Intricately carved, she had the most wrinkles of any totem.

"I hear you," said a young, beautiful face with high cheekbones near the top of the wall. The polished smoothness of her features betrayed little evidence of damage from the elements.

"I hear you," said the furry, bucktoothed face of a beaver just below the young woman. His voice sounded adolescent.

After this acknowledgment, the Totem Wall waited, all eyes on Seth. Shifting his weight from side to side, he clasped his hands behind his back. "I seek Vasilis, the Sword of Light and Darkness. I know you guard it. I want to enter and retrieve it."

Another outburst of muttered exclamations fluttered across the wall.

"Silence," demanded the Crone. "How do you know the location of Vasilis?"

"I paid a price," Seth said.

The Hunter spoke in a gruff tone. "Then you should understand that we grant favors only upon receiving an acceptable sacrifice."

"I understand," Seth said respectfully.

"Yet you have little of value," said the Beaver, "save perhaps the sword and the shield. They are unworthy shadows of the treasure we guard."

"Do not press him so hard," the Dancer fussed. "He is young." Her voice softened. "What have you to offer?"

"Along with the sword, you house great evil," Seth said. "Permit me to retrieve the sword, and I will purge the evil inside of you before I exit."

"Others have come to us in search of Vasilis," the Crone mused. "Rarely have they already suspected the location. We have admitted some. None have returned."

"The youth speaks with confidence," the Hunter approved.

"Any simpleton can speak with confidence," the Dancer said. "Sometimes the greatest fools have the most bravado. The boy is young and naïve. He will come to harm, and he will not deliver on his promise."

"The wise do nothing," the Beaver complained. "The

wise sit and advise. Their understanding prevents action. Do not underestimate the young."

"What deeds have you accomplished?" the Hunter asked.

Seth hadn't planned on turning in a resume. He tried to recall his highlights from the past couple of years. "I pulled a dark talisman from the neck of a revenant. I caught a leprechaun. I awoke Olloch the Glutton and put him back to sleep. I found the Chronometer, one of the keys to Zzyzx. I stole the horn of a unicorn from the centaurs at Grunhold. I have bargained with the giant Thronis and left him satisfied. I killed the dragon Siletta in order to retrieve an item from the dragons of Wyrmroost. I survived the Dreamstone at Obsidian Waste and helped retrieve the Translocator, another key to Zzyzx. And I've bargained with the Singing Sisters."

"He speaks true," the Crone said.

"And I'm telling you the truth now," Seth said. "I don't feel fear. I can get this sword and rid you of the evil hiding near it. And then I'll use the sword to save the world."

"He means what he says," the Crone said.

"Tootega knows truth," the Dancer admitted.

"He has accomplished much," the Hunter granted.

"We should not measure him by age or appearance," the Beaver said.

"He seeks no knowledge," the Crone murmured. "No divination is required. What say you, Kattituyok?"

The proud face who had spoken first answered in a booming voice. "The evil behind the Alder Door has plagued us for many summers. The youth has named the four who control the Alder Door. This seems a good omen."

"He may not return," the Dancer said. "He should leave us tokens."

"The sword and the shield," the Hunter said.

"And the magical items from his bag," the Crone added. "The tower and the fish."

"Won't I need my sword to fight?" Seth asked.

"Your sword and shield are well crafted from fine material, but they will avail you nothing beyond the Alder Door," Kattituyok said. "Leave behind the requested items to seal the pact."

"And I can reclaim my things if I succeed?" Seth verified.

"Purge the evil lurking beyond the Alder Door," the Crone said, "and you may depart in peace with Vasilis and the rest of your items."

"I say the same," the Hunter stated.

"I say the same," the Beaver echoed.

"I say the same," the Dancer sighed.

"Do you accept?" Kattituyok asked.

"I accept," Seth said, unbuckling his sword belt.

"The pact is made and sealed," Kattituyok thundered. His resounding words made the stump vibrate.

Seth set down his sword and shield. Then he fished out the onyx tower and the agate leviathan. He set the items down. A previously unseen door swung open near the bottom right of the wall. The Crone's withered face filled the center of the door.

"Can I go?" Seth asked.

"Away," Kattituyok said. "Good hunting."

Seth climbed down from the stump and walked to the doorway, conscious of the many eyes of the Totem Wall scrutinizing his movements. Cold air wafted from the dark corridor beyond. A primitive torch on the wall ignited spontaneously. Stepping through the door, Seth pocketed his flashlight and picked up the torch. Behind him, the door swung shut with the finality of a coffin lid.

The crude, rounded corridor sloped gradually downward. No beams or stonework supported the crumbly walls and ceiling. The air grew colder as Seth progressed, and he held the torch close for warmth.

The Singing Sisters had warned him about the Standing Dead. He was unsure what exactly to expect, but he imagined they might be like the revenant. He lacked a sword, but perhaps the fiery torch would serve him better. The Sisters had told him that he could pass the Standing Dead only if he remained without fear. He knew that magical fear would fail against him, and tried to prepare his mind to resist the more natural variety.

The corridor stretched onward, deeper and colder. He walked briskly, partly to stay warm, partly hoping that haste might help keep him from freaking himself out.

At last the corridor opened into a rectangular room where the top of his head almost reached the ceiling. Despite the great width and length of the room, the low ceiling gave it a claustrophobic feel, like a sprawling basement.

The frigid air suggested the presence of magical fear, although, as expected, he felt no paralysis.

As the light from his torch revealed the scene, the hair stood up on Seth's arms, and goose pimples erupted on his skin. Row after row of standing corpses filled the expansive room. And not just any corpses. They were bony and dry, as if their ancient remains had been mummified. What meat remained on their discolored bones looked like black jerky. What skin survived looked brown and stretched and utterly dehydrated. Evenly spaced, the cadavers stood upright, arms at their sides, like an army at attention. Rank upon rank of empty eye sockets stared vacantly.

Seth had been prepping himself not to react with fear. He had told himself that no matter what he saw, or heard, or smelled, he would shrug and continue onward. After all, if the Standing Dead only preyed on fear, he didn't need to fret about them. He just needed to maintain control of his emotions.

But despite his intentions, Seth felt his control slipping. The sight of the torchlit bodies surprised him. It was creepier than he had imagined. This was how corpses looked when they had been buried in the desert for centuries. They should not be standing in orderly rows and columns, deep underground.

Some of the nearest corpses began to twitch. The move- ment made Seth gasp, and a few of them took steps forward. Rustling movements rippled through the entire assemblage. Doubt fully awakened inside of Seth. He became scared that he was becoming scared. Dry bones scuffed against the dirt floor. Desiccated arms reached toward him.

His mind scrambled. What was his problem? Why was he losing his grip? Was it being alone? Was it self-doubt? Was it the thought of walking through the undead crowd? Was it the cold? Was it the low ceiling? The quantity of corpses? The inhumanity of their appearance? The way their joints creaked when they moved? The fact that he had lost control enough to start them moving? Some snowballing combination of all these factors?

Perhaps he had been too overconfident, too assured that his immunity to magical fear would prevent natural fear. Like anyone, he still got scared.

He realized that he couldn't hear their minds. He had gotten used to hearing the undead. For some reason, these were silent. That had helped them surprise him and made them feel more foreign.

Entire rows of mummified bodies shuffled toward him. The nearest had almost reached him. He could see stringy ligaments and tendons working. Was he about to die? What about his family? Who would save them? Would they ever learn he had perished because he was afraid?

Shame blossomed in his breast. He could almost hear Kendra disbelieving that cowardice had killed him. Courage was supposed to be his best attribute!

How could he change his feelings? When he had nightmares, the experience was always worst when he was alone. If there was ever a friend in his dream, somebody to protect, the fear lost potency. At this moment, as fleshless fingers grasped for him, he needed somebody to be brave for, some-body to not let down. He struggled to summon images of his family—his parents, his grandparents.

What came was the memory of Coulter. He saw his friend pinned under a beam, heard him gasping his last breaths. Coulter, who had saved him in the grove with the revenant, when magical fear had frozen them. Suddenly Seth no longer felt alone. There was no way he was going to let Coulter down. He had promised.

"Stop!" Seth yelled, swinging his torch angrily. The corpses paused. "I'm not afraid anymore! You just startled me." As he said the words, he realized they were true. Apparently the Standing Dead could sense it as well. None of them stirred.

"You guys have got to be the shabbiest dead people I've ever seen," Seth accused. He strode forward, passing between the unmoving corpses. "You're what's left after the vultures give up. You make zombies look healthy. If you want to scare people, you better pool your funds and rent a wraith or something."

Making fun of them helped his spirits, and the Standing Dead didn't seem to mind. He saw them with new eyes, pathetic puppets without wills of their own. Slaves to his mood, unable to harm him if he simply refused. Decrepit, frail, pathetic. He hurried past them, too full of purpose and new confidence to leave room for doubt.

A black door stood at the back of the room. It had no knob, no keyhole. When he pressed on it with his free hand, the door swung inward.

The torch went out immediately. One instant it was blazing, the next not a spark remained, leaving behind impenetrable darkness. Trying to keep his courage steady, Seth stepped into the room and closed the door, relieved to have a barrier between himself and the Standing Dead. He dropped the torch and pulled the flashlight from his pocket. He switched it on, but no light came out.

"Why have you intruded on my privacy?" a weary, male voice rasped from further in the room.

"Who's there?" Seth asked.

"It took courage to pass the Standing Dead," the voice said. "Especially after you initially lost your composure. Yet they are nothing compared to me. I could slay you with a word."

"Who are you?" Seth asked again.

"I am one of the undead," the voice answered. "Aren't you supposed to be a shadow charmer, Seth? Can't you probe my thoughts?"

"How do you know my name?"

"Your mind was open to me the moment you entered the Alder Door. More open than most would be. What do you suppose your parents are doing right now? Dying, perchance, like your friend Coulter?"

Seth squeezed his flashlight. "I don't care what you are, you better shut up."

"Careful," the voice warned. "Down here, I am judge, jury, and executioner. Why do you want Vasilis?"

"Well," Seth said, gathering his thoughts, wondering what the voice wanted to hear.

"Don't bother with words," the voice said. "I just needed to get you thinking along the right track. Zzyzx is really so close to falling? And Graulas is running the Society?"

"Yes. You know about Zzyzx?"

"Perhaps I should introduce myself." A sword appeared toward the back of the room, standing vertically, blade in the ground, visible only as a black silhouette, but surrounded by a corona of pristine white light that illuminated the entire chamber. It was not a large room, round with a domed ceiling. One other person inhabited the room, off to one side, a strange, decaying zombie. Every part of his body except his head and one arm had turned to stone.

"What happened to you?" Seth asked, aghast.

"I am Morisant," the zombie answered. His voice seemed very lucid considering how corroded his head and arm appeared. "I can tell the name means nothing to you."

"Sorry," Seth said. "Should it?"

"I was the chief architect of Zzyzx."

"What? I thought wizards made Zzyzx."

"Precisely," the semipetrified zombie answered.

"You're a wizard?" Seth asked.

"I am all that remains of a once powerful wizard. Ages ago, some might have considered me the most influential wizard in the world. I see you know Agad. I am glad to know he is well. He assisted me with Zzyzx."

"How did you end up here?" Seth asked.

"There is more than one answer to that question. I am here because Agad put me here. That is an accurate response. I am here because I was master of Vasilis. Also accurate. Best answer? I am here because of hubris."

"Hubris?"

"That unhealthy variety of pride which leads a man to destroy himself. You see, sometimes, when a person gains too much power, he believes he is above the rules that apply to others. You're aware that wizards live a long time."

"Right."

"I was the eldest of the wizards who created Zzyzx. The eldest by far. Wizards age slowly, but nevertheless we age. To a human, we may seem immortal, but death still awaits us in the end. Even enormous quantities of time inevitably pass. When my end drew near, in defiance of the wisdom my long life should have granted, I opted to cheat death."

"What happened?" Seth asked, fascinated.

"I turned myself into one of the undead," Morisant said with regret. "I wove a complicated spell of my own design, a spell so complex and potent that I believed I could fully preserve my mental faculties and continue my life in an undead body."

"Sounds like it failed."

"Something was lost," Morisant said. "I did manage to sustain most of my intellect. But certain sensitivities abandoned me, unforeseen appetites wakened, and my sword, Vasilis, began to lose its luster. I found ways to ignore the changes. I refused to admit my mistake, particularly to myself. Over time, I became a different person. Indeed, I became a threat to the safety of the world. My most trusted colleagues were forced to capture me and bind me here in this prison, changing most of my body to stone in the process. I vowed they would never take my sword, and, as they lacked the power to do so, they chose to hide me away with Vasilis, making me the guardian of the blade I had wielded in life."

"Wow," Seth said. "You seem to be back in control of yourself."

"Do I? Centuries trapped in this cell have provided ample opportunity for reflection. I have recognized my mistakes and mastered my inability to slake my appetites. But don't be fooled. I am no longer the same man I used to be. My nature is fundamentally corrupted. I fought against darkness my whole life, only to become everything I despised. My only hope for atonement is to undo the perversions I sired and submit to the inevitable."

Seth glanced at the sword. "So what now? Do I have to pass a test?"

"I have waited a long time for the arrival of one worthy to wield Vasilis. Some candidates have been slain by the Standing Dead. The rest were slain by me, after I examined their minds. Your need is just, as are your intentions. Should you fail, Vasilis will have been honorably employed. Should you succeed, the Singing Sisters will serve as suitable guardians. They will certainly never wield it. The sword is yours under one condition."

"What?"

"You use it to dispatch me, then put to rest the Standing Dead."

Seth stared at the pathetic zombie. He had almost

forgotten that part of his mission was to rid this area of evil. "But you're nice."

"Many would disagree. I prolonged my life unnaturally. Please remedy this mistake, or I will have to slay you and wait for another. Believe me, Seth, you will be killing me in self-defense. My death is the only way for both of us to get what we need."

"What about the Standing Dead?" Seth asked.

"I created them," Morisant said. "A mindless undead legion, loyal only to me. After my capture, I turned them into effective guardians. It will be a mercy to unmake them. Not to mention, you must keep your promise to the Totem Wall, or you will never escape with your life. Will you do as I ask? Don't lie, I will know."

"I'll do it," Seth said, thinking of Coulter, and of his family.

"Thank you," Morisant said with great relief.

"Do you have any advice? Can you help me? If Zzyzx falls, I'm not sure what to do."

"You're on the proper course, in ways you may not yet understand. I tried to design Zzyzx intelligently. I am glad that Bracken is with you. Try to get word to Agad. He could be useful. Ancient magic bound the demons; ancient magic might save you. Not to minimize the threat. This horde of demons is stronger than any force you could possibly muster. Should the chance arise, give Bracken and Agad my regards. Thank them for me, and please convey that I hold no grudges."

"Is there any trick to the sword?" Seth asked.

"None. Vasilis reflects and reinforces the heart and mind of the wielder. As a young, loyal, courageous, well-intentioned shadow charmer, you should find the sword formidable in your grasp. I see you have a sister. Fairykind. That could prove interesting." Morisant paused as if lost to internal musings.

"You were saying?" Seth prompted.

Morisant snapped out of his stupor. "The sheath rests beside the door. Do not unsheathe the blade more often than necessary. Should you fall, no enemy can claim Vasilis, only a friend. In life, the sword can only be given away voluntarily. A single caution? Vasilis is powerful, and power can have an adverse effect on the heart and mind, which can in turn alter the sword. Many have acquired the sword while walking in the light, only to lose it in darkness."

"I'll do my best," Seth promised.

"Coulter would be proud. Now, Seth Sorenson, I hereby transfer Vasilis into your care, on condition that you release me and my fellow abominations from our necrotic prisons. Take up the sword and keep your promise."

Seth crossed the room to where the sword stuck out of the ground. He could hardly believe he had made it this far. Maybe he really would keep his promise to Coulter! Maybe he would find a way to stop the demons and save his family.

When he grabbed the hilt, warmth flooded through him. The dark blade burst into red flames, and the white radiance became scarlet. The blade came out of the ground easily. The sword felt less like something in his grasp and more like an extension of his arm. His emotions were magnified—his fury at Graulas keener, his sense of purpose clearer, the concern for his family more poignant. The courage he had struggled to find when facing the Standing Dead now seemed to spring from an unending well.

Seth whirled to face Morisant. The undead wizard looked even more wretched by the blazing red light.

"Yes," the wizard said, obviously delighted. "You will be most formidable."

Seth strode forward and raised the sword. He knew what he had to do, yet he hesitated.

"You promised, Seth," the wizard reminded him. "It is a true act of mercy." The wizard raised his voice. "Let it be known that Morisant the Magnificent died in possession of himself! Better late than never."

The pathetic ruin of a man closed his eyes, and Seth brought the sword down with a fiery whoosh. Morisant instantly burst into flames. Within seconds his corrupted flesh had been entirely consumed.

Seth walked out of the room to where the Standing Dead waited in their columns and rows. Was it his imagination, or did Vasilis feel eager in his hands, tugging him forward? As he stalked through the room cutting down the Standing Dead, setting those tinder-dry corpses ablaze, he found himself wondering if he was wielding the sword, or if the sword was wielding him. The weapon felt alive in his hands, seemingly rejoicing at the massacre. Or was he the one rejoicing? Minutes ago, these burning figures had tried to kill him. Now he was mowing through them like the Grim Reaper during a manic phase. Every swing of the sword felt so natural, so perfect, it was as if he were performing some violent, predestined dance. Without screams, without blood, without any evidence of pain, the Standing Dead crumbled to ash around him, until he stood alone, surveying the empty room by the flaming glare of his sword.

Only then did he realize that he had forgotten the sheath.

Seth returned to the room where Morisant had perished and picked up the sheath. Without his torch, he would need the light from his blade to guide him out, so he held the sheath in one hand and Vasilis in the other. The coldness of this subterranean lair forgotten, Seth marched out radiating fervent heat.

The Alder Door opened as he approached, and he stepped out into the noonday sunlight. The door closed behind him. For a pregnant moment, the Totem Wall watched him in silence.

"Now, that is a sword!" the Hunter exclaimed.

Seth sheathed it, and experienced an immediate sense of loss. He suddenly felt tired, and clammy, and much smaller. The faces of the Totem Wall chattered and cheered as Seth crossed to the stump, scrambled up, and retrieved his things. He paused, studying the animated wall. The jubilant clamor was unintelligible. He heard no English.

Satisfied that the Totem Wall seemed content, he climbed down from the stump. Without a backward glance, Seth hurried to rejoin his friends.

Civia

With an overcast sky hiding the sun, Raxtus landed silently on a side street near the grocery store parking lot. Remaining invisible, the dragon took off again, leaving Kendra and Bracken behind. Bracken raced along the sidewalk, bearskin cape flapping, Kendra at his heels. Jumping over the low bushes bordering the sidewalk, they dashed across the parking lot and hurried into the back of an SUV.

Warren waited in the driver's seat. "Nice outfit, Bracken. You really blend."

"Is she still in the store?" Bracken asked.

Warren checked his wristwatch. "Almost eight minutes. I've been tailing her for about two hours. The info you relayed from Niko took me right to her apartment."

"Good," Bracken said. "No sign of our adversaries?"

"Not yet. Without an evident threat, I didn't want to approach her solo. I'm not a unicorn, I'm not fairykind—I have no way to prove I'm an ally."

"Probably wise," Bracken agreed. "Besides, there wasn't much you could do to help her escape until Raxtus arrived. Our inside source at the Society told me a new assassin was dispatched to help bring down the last Eternal. He said the others have orders to wait for the newcomer before moving in. It should buy us some time. Apparently they tried to take her out a couple of weeks ago in South America but blew the chance. She's supposed to be slippery."

"Her name is Civia?" Warren asked.

"So I hear from our source," Bracken said. "The source also hinted that the new assassin they sent out might somehow work in our favor."

"Let's hope your source is reliable," Warren said doubtfully.

"I'd rather not bet the fate of the world on it," Bracken said.

"Don't you have armor?" Warren asked Kendra.

"Everything I had got soaked," Kendra explained. "We had to stop and get dry clothes. I'm actually glad. Armor isn't my thing. I felt clunky."

"Armor gets much more convenient once people start trying to cut you open," Warren said.

"At least I look normal," Kendra said.

"I see you wrapped your sword in a sheet," Warren observed.

Kendra held it up. "Best disguise we could manage on short notice."

"I think we should let Kendra approach Civia," Bracken suggested. "We don't want to spook her."

"Approaching her could be dangerous," Warren cautioned.

"True," Bracken agreed. "Civia will be on the defensive and may react desperately. But Kendra will feel much less threatening than either of us, and you can go in with her to keep an eye on the discussion."

"Since I'm not dressed in animal hides," Warren said.

"I'm expecting a fight," Bracken said. "I'll wait out here. Sorry it took us longer than I had hoped to meet up with you. Raxtus had to rest for a couple of hours in Arizona. He has flown a lot of miles in very few days."

"No problem," Warren said. "I barely got to Texas ahead of you. My plane only landed three hours ago."

"Should I bring the sword?" Kendra asked.

"Leave it," Bracken said. "We don't want to make her even more nervous. Niko said her guardian is female, and is currently shaped like a bichon frise."

"A bichon frise?" Kendra asked.

"A *female* shape-shifter?" Warren wondered.

"A bichon frise is a lapdog with curly white fur," Bracken said. "I'm not sure how gender works with shape-shifters. But Niko called her female."

"Is Niko getting close?" Warren asked.

"He's not far," Bracken said. "Should catch up within the hour."

"We should probably get in there," Kendra said. "I'm scared the bad guys will show up again."

Bracken nodded. "What was Civia driving?"

"The little compact over there," Warren said, pointing. "Nondescript. She knows how to blend."

"Try to bring her back here," Bracken said. "Keep in touch with the stone."

"You got it," Warren said. "Kendra, follow me after about thirty seconds."

Warren got out of the SUV. Kendra counted to thirty in her mind and then exited the vehicle. She walked to the front of the store, chose a cart, and wheeled it past the checkout counters, in case a girl with a bichon frise was on her way out. She saw several women checking out, but none had a dog.

Kendra doubled back across the front of the store, looking down the aisles. When she saw Warren selecting cereal, he jerked his head toward the produce section.

In the produce section, Kendra immediately spotted a young woman with dark, straight hair examining apples. She wore jeans, running shoes, and a TCU sweatshirt. Her brown skin suggested she might be Indian or Middle Eastern. A fluffy white dog sat patiently in the infant seat of a well-laden shopping cart.

The dog took an interest in Kendra, so she looked away. She wheeled her cart over to the oranges and started handling them. The woman pushed her cart over to the broccoli. The dog caught Kendra staring again. Deciding to be direct, Kendra steered her cart toward the woman.

The dog seemed to mumble something, and the young woman studied Kendra as she approached. Kendra maintained eye contact with the woman.

"Can I help you?" the woman asked with a relaxed smile.

"Please believe me," Kendra began, glancing at the dog. "I'm here to help. The Society is moving in on you again."

"What society?" the woman chuckled, slipping a hand into her purse. "You must have mistaken me for someone else."

"No, Civia, I'm serious."

The woman's eyes widened. She quickly surveyed the area. They were currently the only shoppers in the produce section. "What are you doing?" she whispered uncomfortably.

"They have the Oculus," Kendra said in a quiet voice. "I'm here with a unicorn, a dragon, and a friend, to try to save your life."

"The girl has an uncanny glow," the dog murmured in a female voice.

Civia stepped toward Kendra, resting a hand on her shoulder. Her other hand covertly held a switchblade at her side. "Listen, sweetheart, I don't know who you are, but I've been doing just fine on my own for a long, long time. I work alone."

The knife at her side had Kendra's full attention. She realized that the wrong words or action might get her stabbed. "You're the last Eternal," she whispered.

Civia faltered for a moment; then her gaze hardened. The tip of the switchblade pricked Kendra. "Leave your cart," Civia ordered. "Walk out of here with me."

"I'm not alone," Kendra said.

Warren stepped into view, hands on his shopping cart, eyes on Civia. Kendra had never seen him look quite so serious. Civia glanced at him.

"Presumably your friends don't want you killed," Civia hissed. "I believe you're trying to help, or I'd have already gutted you. But I don't work with partners. No exceptions. I've obviously been identified here. I'll move on."

"Your enemies can follow you with the Oculus," Kendra argued. "And we can track you with help from the leader of your shape-shifters. He'll be here soon."

"I've killed many people over the years," Civia whispered. "I could end you right now, then take care of your glaring friend."

"You won't defeat the people who are coming for you," Kendra warned, braced for the switchblade to rip into her at any moment. "They have a big team, and all the right weapons. You need to change your strategy and flee to Wyrmroost. Agad is there. He may be able to protect you."

Warren trundled his cart toward them.

"That's close enough," Civia told him.

Warren stopped. "I don't care who you are," he said. "You harm Kendra and I'll break your neck."

Civia frowned, the knife moving slightly away from Kendra's side. "Okay, you win," she sighed, shoulders sagging. Then she shoved Kendra at Warren and sprinted for the back of the store.

As Warren steadied Kendra, the bichon frise sprang at Warren from the shopping cart, transforming into a small wolverine in midair. Warren batted the wolverine with the back of his fist, sending it flying into a bin of potatoes. "Go back to the parking lot," he told Kendra as he took off after Civia.

"Don't fight us," Kendra scolded the snarling wolverine. The wolverine changed into an owl and flew after Warren. From the back of the store, an unseen woman screamed. Kendra retreated out the front of the store in time to see the SUV screeching out of view toward the rear of the building. Apparently Warren was in communication with Bracken.

Running to the side of the store, Kendra sprinted along the asphalt toward the back. Upon arrival, she found the SUV parked crookedly, and saw Warren using a mop to fend off a furious owl. Civia was pinned to the ground as if by an unseen force. Raxtus.

"We've caused a scene," Bracken warned Civia. He stood over her, holding her switchblade. "Whatever our future arrangement, we need to get away from here."

"Fine," Civia spat.

"Into the car," Bracken said.

Suddenly able to rise, Civia hurried into the SUV. Warren claimed the driver's seat. Kendra took shotgun. Civia, Bracken, and the owl settled in the back. Warren started driving toward the street.

"A dragon?" Civia sputtered. "Really? Who are you people?"

Bracken took her hand. The act seemed to calm her.

"We're here to help," he said. "I can see that you've been running for a long time."

She jerked her hand away. "Get out of my head."

"Leave her alone!" the owl shrieked.

"Quiet the owl," Bracken said.

"Janan, be still," Civia said.

The owl turned back into a lapdog.

"I didn't mean to intrude," Bracken said. "It's just quicker if I examine your mind."

"I prefer words," Civia insisted. "You say the Society is after me. How do I know you aren't an enemy?"

"He really is a unicorn," Janan said. "They have distinctive auras."

"If we wanted you dead, we had you," Bracken reminded her.

Civia closed her eyes and leaned her head back. "Involving others in my life leads to failure and heartache. Most of my near misses have resulted from relationships. I've gotten good people killed. I've done much better on my own."

"Until recently," Bracken prompted.

She opened her eyes. "I was in a small village in Ecuador just a couple of weeks ago. Way off the map. I ran a modest bakery. I had a few casual friends. Nobody knew my secret. I had been there three years. And I was ambushed. No warning. Until you mentioned the Oculus, I had no idea how they found me. I killed a couple of my assailants and escaped into the jungle. Had I not been well prepared, they would have had me. But I'm careful. I hide weapons in convenient locations. I hide motorcycles and watercraft. Even helicopters. I set traps. My job is to stay alive, and I take it very seriously."

"The rules have changed," Bracken advised. "Your enemies now have the Oculus. They possess vast resources, and they know what it takes to kill you."

"I have identities all over the world," Civia protested. "I'm fluent in over thirty languages, passable in thirty more. I have access to huge sums of money. I'm an expert at altering my look."

"Even if you stay in constant motion, they'll catch you," Bracken said. "You have to change tactics and get behind unassailable walls."

"No walls are unassailable," Civia muttered.

"But many afford better protection than a grocery store," Warren commented. "Do we have a destination?"

"Do you have an opinion?" Bracken asked Civia.

"I have a storage locker loaded with equipment. Hand me the GPS."

Kendra took the GPS off the dashboard and handed it to Civia. She began punching in a destination.

"Our dragon can fly you to Wyrmroost," Bracken said. "Agad will grant you safe haven once he knows the particulars."

"Who is wielding the Oculus?" Civia asked.

"A demon named Graulas has wrested control of the Society from the Sphinx," Bracken explained. "Another demon, Nagi Luna, has proven to be most adept at employing the Oculus. Two Eternals have died in the last week. An inside operative has confirmed that assassins are presently moving to eliminate you."

"The last one," Civia sighed. "Calling us Eternals was never very accurate. We are not immune to death. Anyone who can die, will eventually die. I always assumed I would be the last. I don't know how anyone else could have been more cautious than I. I've studied endless fighting techniques, I keep my body well conditioned, I avoid suspicious behavior, I eschew vices, I shun close relationships, I'm always on guard, always preparing for the worst. Still, I can hardly believe the others are truly gone. There was an added sense of security knowing they were out there. The Society has all of the artifacts?"

"All of them," Bracken said. "And they know how to get to Zzyzx. You're their final obstacle."

She turned and stared out the window. "It had to happen eventually. For so long, I've lived like I was the last impediment to the opening of Zzyzx. And now I am. It isn't much of a life, the way I live. I'm detached. An outsider. My only companionship comes from Janan, for which I will be forever grateful. But my life is unpleasant. Funny, for a long while now, I have quietly relished the thought of an end, looked forward to the day my enemies would finally outmaneuver me. That day has finally arrived."

"You're not dead yet," Warren assured her.

"We'll get you to Wyrmroost," Bracken pledged.

Civia shook her head sadly. "We'll try. Based on the scenario you described, I won't make it."

"The dragon—" Bracken began.

"The dragon felt small," Civia said. "Valiant, no doubt, but small. If this demon is as adept with the Oculus as you say, we will be intercepted and I will be destroyed. With the Oculus to guide them, if all of their attention is now focused on me, and they have the kind of resources you described, we have no realistic defense."

"We have to try," Kendra said.

"Of course we'll try," Civia said. "I'm sorry if I sound fatalistic. I try to assess my circumstances honestly. Experience and effort have made my judgment reliable. But maybe we'll get lucky. You're right that hiding at Wyrmroost could provide a temporary solution. At least we know Agad will be sympathetic to my plight. Having the dragon transport me there probably represents my best chance for survival."

"But you don't think it's much of a chance," Warren said.

"Not really," Civia said simply.

"You're right," Bracken said reluctantly. "They used wyverns against us in Santa Monica. Raxtus managed to slay them, but had trouble protecting his passengers in the process. Of course, the Eternal in Santa Monica had a death wish. Even so, our enemies are too close to their goal. They'll throw everything they have at us before they let you reach Wyrmroost. But what else can we do?"

"I'm not properly established here yet," Civia said. "I spent the last ten days on the move. I suppose we could try to find a spot to make a stand."

"Which creates the same problem as running with the

dragon," Warren said. "They'll throw too much at us. But, unlike with the dragon, you'll be cornered."

Civia furrowed her brow. "I suppose if the dragon takes an erratic route, we might have a small chance."

"I'll come with you," Bracken offered. "I can help defend you if Raxtus ever needs to set us down. I'm handy with a sword. And Niko, the leader of the shape-shifters, will catch up before long."

"Don't forget me," Janan said.

Civia gave a nod. "The storage locker isn't far. Let's gather the appropriate gear." Her expression softened. She leaned forward and patted Kendra on the shoulder. "I'm sorry I reacted so harshly when you tried to approach me. You collided with centuries of habit. I see now that your intrusion into my affairs was warranted."

"Wow," Janan said. "Civia never apologizes."

"I do so," Civia replied defensively.

"Not when I'm around," the dog murmured.

"Thanks, Civia," Kendra said. "We understand how shocking all of this must seem."

"We were just happy to find you alive," Bracken said. "We'll do all we can to keep you that way."

"Lonestar Lockers?" Warren asked.

"That's the place," Civia said.

Warren pulled up to a keypad in front of an electronic gate. Beyond the gate awaited rows of squat, cinder-block structures. The evenly spaced blue doors made the storage complex look like a crowded neighborhood composed entirely of adjoining garages.

"Code?" Warren asked.

"Nine, seven, zero, one, pound," Civia recited.

Warren punched in the numbers and the gate slowly opened. Warren pulled into the complex. A wall topped with barbed wire surrounded the facility.

"Turn left," Civia directed. Following her instructions, after the first turn, he cut down the third aisle, then stopped the SUV about halfway down.

"Let's make it quick," Warren said. "We're on borrowed time."

Civia exited the SUV, and Janan hopped down after her. Bracken and Kendra got out as well. Warren remained in the vehicle with the engine running.

Producing a key chain from her purse, Civia opened the heavy padlock on her storage locker, then lifted up the door. The locker contained several trunks and tall cabinets. Kendra also noticed a pair of motorcycles, one big and heavy, the other small and sleek.

Moving around the locker purposefully, Civia opened a trunk and strapped a short sword around her waist, then added a dagger. Next she removed a compound bow from a cabinet and snatched a quiver of arrows. "What do you need?" she asked.

"Do you have swords?" Bracken wondered.

She opened a metal cabinet. "Take your pick."

Bracken removed a sheathed sword and pulled it from the scabbard. "You really are prepared," he admired.

"It's what I do. Kendra, would you like a shirt of mail?"

Raxtus landed heavily in front of the storage locker. "They're here," he said urgently.

"Explain," Bracken said.

"Four black vans speeding toward this storage area. Three wyverns closing in by air, along with a firedrake. They all showed up together."

"Can you outrun them?" Bracken asked.

"I can try," Raxtus said without confidence. "The wyverns are coming from all directions."

"Can you take out the firedrake?" Bracken asked.

"I think so," Raxtus said.

"Go up alone, invisible," Bracken said. "Take care of the airborne threats, then return for Civia. We'll hold off the others."

Raxtus took flight, becoming invisible soon after leaving the ground. They heard the gate being smashed, followed by the sounds of tires squealing.

"Wait in here," Bracken told Civia and Kendra.

Sword in hand, he stepped out of the locker. Civia shrugged into a leather biker jacket and put on a motorcycle helmet. Kendra grabbed a second bow from a cabinet and a quiver of arrows. She nocked an arrow, her hand shaking. Outside, Bracken conversed with Warren.

"Is this it?" Janan asked candidly.

"I sincerely hope not," Civia replied, voice muffled by her helmet.

"Our fight is not with you," declared a magically magnified voice. "Give us the Eternal and you may depart in peace."

Kendra knew the voice! She peeked out of the storage locker. Black vans blocked both ends of the aisle, two at each end. In front of the vans to the left stood Mirav the wizard, wearing a richly embroidered robe that descended to his ankles. Behind him, Torina pulled an arrow from her quiver, flanked by a quartet of minotaurs wielding hefty axes.

At the other end of the aisle, the Gray Assassin drew his swords. Trask got out of a van, carrying his heavy crossbow. By his demeanor, Kendra could tell he must be under the influence of a narcoblix. Armored goblins clambered out of the vans as well.

Kendra glanced at the overcast sky. Apparently Mirav could withstand daylight with sufficient cloud cover. She wondered if he had summoned the clouds.

"Let's talk about this," Bracken soothed, now holding his shield as well as his sword. Still inside the SUV, Warren clutched a sword as well.

Overhead, a wyvern shrieked and fell from the sky, neck kinked disgustingly. Mirav glared upward. Mouthing strange words, he waved a hand upward, and Raxtus became visible as he swooped to engage what looked like a flying snake about the length of a telephone pole. Upon seeing Raxtus, fire bloomed from its fanged jaws, and the firedrake took evasive maneuvers, wriggling like a ribbon in a windstorm.

"You have chosen destruction," the wizard pronounced, yanking the horn of a unicorn from within his robes. The pearly horn was much larger than the horn Kendra had used at Wyrmroost, perhaps three feet in length. From either side of the wizard, minotaurs charged, armed with axes and maces. The Gray Assassin dashed toward them from the other direction, followed by goblins carrying swords and spears. The wizard pointed a long-nailed finger at Bracken and commenced chanting.

Laughing, Bracken threw his sword aside and extended a hand toward the wizard. "To me," he said. Although Kendra understood the meaning of his words, she felt certain he was not speaking English.

The unicorn horn leapt from the wizard's hand and streaked to Bracken, who caught it effortlessly. In his grasp, the horn immediately transformed into a sword with an opalescent hilt and a gleaming silver blade. Despite the cloudy sky, with the weapon in his hand, Bracken suddenly appeared as if standing in sunlight. A new glow suffused his countenance, and a sudden fire flashed in his eyes.

"The fool brought him his second horn," Janan murmured beside Kendra.

Mirav looked stricken, but continued his spell. As the wizard finished his incantation, sizzling darts of energy began to leap from his extended finger. They blazed through the air, only to reverse their course as Bracken held out his sword. Every dart Mirav launched returned to burst against him, knocking him backward and setting his robe on fire.

As Bracken rushed forward to confront the oncoming minotaurs, Warren stepped on the gas, driving the SUV in the other direction. Trask shattered the windshield with a pair of quarrels from his crossbow, but the SUV kept gaining speed. The Gray Assassin maneuvered left and right, but Warren kept the vehicle on a line to run him down. At the last instant, the Gray Assassin flipped to one side, narrowly avoiding the SUV. The vehicle then plowed through a group of goblins, running some over and bashing others brutally to the ground. As the SUV neared the vans at the end of the aisle, Warren opened the door and dove out, rolling on the asphalt. The SUV crashed into the vans at a high speed, sending all the vehicles tumbling with a spray of shattered glass.

Kendra drew back her arrow, aimed, and fired it at the Gray Assassin. She had practiced archery a little, and the arrow was on target, but the Gray Assassin slashed it from the air with an almost casual swing of one sword.

In the other direction, Bracken dodged and spun to avoid minotaurs, cutting them down with efficient regularity. Robes ablaze, Mirav shuffled forward, a knife glinting in his hand. Bracken thrust his sword through a minotaur, ducked to avoid a mace swung with tremendous force, then yanked his sword free and sliced open his next assailant with a single spinning motion. Though strong and fierce, the minotaurs seemed slow and clumsy as Bracken danced among them, slaying one after another.

Kendra nocked another arrow, and Civia stepped out in the aisle with her, an arrow set to the string of her bow as well. The Gray Assassin drew nearer with a small group of goblins. Behind them, farther down the aisle, Warren battled three goblins with his sword. Kendra and Civia fired at the Gray Assassin together, but even at short range, he intercepted both of their arrows, one with each sword.

"Civia!" Janan shouted. Springing higher than any

ordinary lapdog could, the tiny canine leapt into the path of a phoenix-feathered arrow coming from the other end of the aisle. The arrow that would have hit Civia in the back impaled the little dog. Crimson flames promptly consumed the shape-shifter, leaving no remains.

Face contorted with grief, Civia retreated out of the aisle back into the storage locker. Kendra drew back as well, pulling the door to the storage locker shut, then fumbled to get another arrow ready. Behind her, Civia kick-started the smaller motorcycle.

A pair of goblins heaved the door to the locker up. Kendra released her arrow and hit one of them in the chest, sending him staggering backwards. As the Gray Assassin moved forward, swords ready, a growling grizzly bear slammed into him from the side, sending him somersaulting across the asphalt. When the other goblin turned to confront the threat, the bear transformed into a tiger and pounced on him, teeth tearing at his throat. Niko had finally arrived.

Another goblin attacked the tiger from behind, slashing him with a scimitar, but before Kendra could fire an arrow to help, the tiger had turned and dispatched the attacker. The wound the scimitar had opened knitted itself closed and disappeared.

As the Gray Assassin rose from the pavement, Niko changed back into a bear and reared up on his hind legs. The Gray Assassin backed away, moving toward the end of the aisle where Torina awaited with her bow, so Kendra stepped forward into the aisle to help cover Niko.

On the end of the aisle where the SUV had crumpled the vans, goblins littered the ground, several killed by Warren, a few nearer ones slain by Niko. No goblins remained standing in that direction, but Warren was currently wrestling with Trask.

The Gray Assassin continued to retreat in the other direction. Behind him, dead and dying minotaurs lay sprawled along the aisle. Near the vans, Mirav held up both hands, creating a shimmer in the air. Bracken chopped at the invisible shield, each stroke sending up a flurry of brilliant sparks and causing the badly burned wizard to flinch. Currently, the bulk of the bear prevented Kendra from having a shot at the Gray Assassin.

Wheeling the motorcycle forward, Civia peeked out into the aisle, checking left and right, then gunned the engine, heading toward Warren and the totaled vehicles. In the other direction, Kendra saw Torina climb atop one of the vans. She drew an arrow back to her cheek.

"No!" Kendra shouted, aiming briefly and releasing her own arrow, which streaked harmlessly past the distant viviblix, missing by a good five feet.

Torina let her arrow fly. Niko jumped, trying to intercept it, but could not quite reach it, and the Gray Assassin seized the opportunity to dart forward and start hacking the bear.

Kendra turned and watched in horror as the arrow curved down toward the fleeing motorcycle. The considerable distance combined with the rapid acceleration of the motorcycle made the shot difficult—nevertheless, the arrow pierced Civia through the center of her back. Crimson flames spread across her shoulders as the motorcycle tipped and she bounced, tumbled, and skidded across the asphalt.

Roaring, Niko became a tiger and raced toward Civia, blood gushing from his multiple wounds. Civia pushed herself up to her hands and knees, the hungry flames spreading, then fell flat.

Mirav called for help, and the Gray Assassin answered, running toward Bracken from behind. Kendra screamed to alert Bracken, who turned and engaged the attacker, blades ringing sharply as they clashed.

Atop the van, a triumphant Torina nocked another arrow, but Raxtus swooped down from the sky and sent her flying with a vicious swipe of his claws. She had drawn the arrow back, but the impact sent it wildly astray. Wings flapping, Raxtus rose to engage the final wyvern.

Kendra watched in agonized suspense as the Gray Assassin battled Bracken. She could not risk helping with an arrow for fear of hitting the wrong person. Bracken seemed on the defensive, barely able to hold off the two swords with his single blade. Whenever he attempted a counterstroke, the attack was blocked and he had to duck or spring back to avoid a deadly blow.

Kendra rushed to a cabinet in the storage locker, retrieved a sword, and ran to help. The thought of challenging a warrior like the Gray Assassin terrified her, but if she could provide a distraction, perhaps Bracken could finish him quickly.

As she returned to the aisle, Bracken held up a hand and produced a blinding burst of light. Lowering his sword,

Bracken narrowly dodged two hasty slashes without parrying, and then, blade flashing like lightning, cut down the Gray Assassin with a single stroke. Bracken turned and stalked toward Mirav, who was lying on his back, hands held up to maintain the shimmer of his magical shield.

"I'll break you if I must," Bracken said.

Eyes brimming with malice, Mirav spat at him.

Bracken held up a fist, his whole arm trembling. The shimmer in the air seemed to fold, then shattered. Mirav screamed. Kendra looked away as Bracken used his sword to finish the wizard.

After facing the other way, less worried about Bracken, Kendra ran to Civia and Niko. The flames had gone out. Niko lay beside her charred body. Beyond them, Warren continued to grapple with Trask.

Kendra reached the tiger, who had a glassy look in his eyes. His head turned as she crouched beside him. "She's gone," Niko mourned, voice groggy. "I'm going. The final Eternal has fallen. I failed."

"You saved me," Kendra said, patting his thick fur.

"My pleasure," Niko mumbled, the words slurred. "Perhaps it will be enough. When Roon fell, I worried all was lost. I always expected he would be the last. Close enough. I go to him."

The tiger went slack, and he and Civia dissolved into fine black dust.

Bracken ran past Kendra toward Warren and Trask.

"He's a friend," Warren grunted. "I think a narcoblix has him."

Setting down his sword, Bracken promptly helped Warren pin Trask on the ground. While Warren held Trask down, Bracken retrieved his sword. The weapon reverted to the shape of a horn, and Bracken held the tip against Trask, who continued to struggle. "Begone," Bracken commanded. Once again, Kendra knew he was not speaking English.

There was a harsh flash of light, and Trask no longer resisted. "Warren?" Trask asked, sounding befuddled. "Oh, no. Where are we? What have I done?"

As Warren explained the situation, Bracken hurried over to Kendra.

"Are you all right?" he asked, extending a hand and helping her to her feet.

"She's dead," Kendra said numbly.

"I know," Bracken replied.

Kendra gritted her teeth, fighting back tears. "We blew it."

"It's a terrible blow," Bracken admitted.

"What are we going to—"

Bracken thrust Kendra aside and held up his shield. An arrow thumped against it. Down the aisle, Torina knelt with her bow in hand. She had deep gouges in her side where the dragon had swiped her, and road rash on one arm and leg from her fall off the van. Raxtus landed on a van behind her, the vehicle wobbling beneath his weight. After a hasty glance over her shoulder, Torina tossed her bow aside and ran toward Bracken, hands in the air. "I surrender!"

"On your knees," Bracken ordered, striding toward her.

She complied immediately, wide eyes frightened and

innocent. Even injured and with her hair disheveled, she looked strikingly attractive. Bracken kept walking toward her.

"Careful, Bracken," Kendra warned. "She bites! She can drain your life."

Reaching her, he turned and looked back. "I've got it covered. She can't possibly—"

Torina lunged forward, wrapping her arms around Bracken's torso and sinking her teeth into his neck. Bracken went limp in her arms.

"No!" Kendra shrieked.

Torina latched on a second time. Her skin shone with an inner glow. The brilliance intensified, making her veins and bones temporarily visible. And then she burst apart in a stunning surge of white flame.

Tears falling, Kendra ran to Bracken, who rose to his feet and caught her in an embrace. She squeezed him as hard as she could, burying her face in his shoulder.

"Are you all right?" she gushed, confused.

He pulled back and smiled down at her. "Not many viviblixes get the chance to drain a unicorn. Those who do never get to warn the others. They can sense the immense supply of vitality, and they ardently crave it, but none have ever been able to handle it."

"Kind of like filling a water balloon with a fire hose?" Warren remarked, approaching with Trask.

"That's the idea," Bracken agreed.

"Did you cure him?" Warren asked, jerking a thumb at Trask.

Bracken gave a nod. "With my horn back, I can undo most curses, heal most injuries." Bracken placed a hand on Trask's shoulder. "The narcoblix no longer has any hold on you."

"You have my gratitude," Trask said. "Sorry for any part I played in your troubles."

Warren looked up and down the aisle. "We're leaving a trail of destruction wherever we go."

"All in a day's work," Trask mumbled.

"We came so close," Warren grumbled in frustration. "What do we do now? This was our last chance." Warren had always been resilient. Kendra had never seen him so defeated. She felt the same way, but was striving to hold herself together.

"Our last chance to prevent Zzyzx from opening," Bracken clarified. "Unpleasant as our prospects may be, this still isn't over." He turned to Raxtus. "You get the firedrake?"

"Got him," the dragon replied. "My scales are tougher than I ever knew. I'd never really tested them. The fire barely tickled. And even though the wizard jinxed my invisibility, I managed to handle the wyverns."

"You're a chip off the old block," Kendra said.

"Hardly," Raxtus huffed. "At least I'm learning to stand my ground and fight. Small as I am, I must have inherited my dad's scales. His armor is almost impenetrable."

"What now?" Kendra asked.

"Your role in this is over, Kendra," Bracken said. "Our paths part here. I'll be going to Zzyzx. I have to make a last stand."

"You're not leaving me behind," Kendra argued. "The end of the world is coming. I'd rather help prevent it than be another random victim."

Warren folded his arms. "Just because missiles are flying doesn't mean you have to run to ground zero."

"You should go to a stronghold like Wyrmroost," Trask said. "There are a few places that might stand even against the demon horde."

Bracken took Kendra's hand in his. "I'll be sending Raxtus to Wyrmroost. You can ride with him. We'll need him to recruit whatever help Agad might offer."

"No way," Kendra said. "You need me. You need warriors, and I can restore the astrids. I'm not hiding. I'm coming."

"Not long ago, the astrids left Wyrmroost," Raxtus said. "I'm not sure where they went."

"She has a point about the astrids," Warren said. "She's as likely to find them with us as anywhere."

"Perhaps more likely," Bracken murmured, pinching his lower lip.

"And she's been incredibly helpful during past emergencies," Warren added.

Trask nodded. "It's true that she's a full-fledged Knight of the Dawn."

"Very well," Bracken relented. "If we fail to stem the tide when Zzyzx opens, nobody will be safe anywhere. On top of that, Kendra will surely be an early target. She may as well stay with us."

"Good choice," Kendra said, quietly hoping that she would not regret her insistence.

Bracken turned to Raxtus. "Could you keep an eye out for police? You should now be able to go invisible again."

Taking to the sky, Raxtus disappeared from view.

"Wait," Kendra realized, "does anyone even know how we get to Zzyzx?"

"I haven't gotten into details with your brother yet," Bracken said. "I hoped his labors might prove unnecessary, at least for a time. But from what I've glimpsed, I believe Seth knows a way to Zzyzx. The hour has arrived to coordinate our efforts."

CHAPTER TWENTY-FIVE

Lady Luck

Seth walked barefoot on the beach, enjoying the coarse sand and smooth shell fragments under his soles. Black-headed gulls hung suspended in the air, gliding against a breeze. Nearby, water hissed softly as it spread flat against the sand, millions of tiny bubbles bursting. As the water retreated, sandpipers darted on quick feet, stabbing for food with needle beaks.

Not far behind him, Vanessa lounged on a towel, wearing large sunglasses, a loose T-shirt, and fashionable sandals. He could see nobody else on the seashore. The only signs of civilization were some lifeless beach houses in the distance.

Seth had never been to the Outer Banks. Bridges and ferries linked a series of long, narrow barrier islands off the coast of North Carolina. He and Vanessa were on Hatteras

Island. With the Atlantic on one side and the Pamlico Sound on the other, spending time on the island made him feel far out at sea, even though he could walk to the mainland.

They had arrived two days ago, flying into Norfolk, Virginia, then driving the rest of the way in a rented sedan, through towns with names like Kill Devil Hills and Nags Head. While Seth and Vanessa had eaten crab cakes at a roadside grill, locals had informed them that the tourist season hadn't really started yet. Reportedly the summer would bring heavy traffic and abundant crowds, but currently none of the restaurants seemed busy, and many of the beaches looked desolate.

At the moment, a cool breeze prevented the afternoon from feeling warm. After wading in the cold water, Seth had decided not to swim. Instead he was content to roam the edge of the dying waves, searching through the infinite shells along the shore for the very best. Almost all of the shells were small, many bleached white or broken, but some featured alluring colors. He had most appreciated several glossy, colorful bits of shell shaped vaguely like guitar picks, and rattled his favorites in one hand.

Tonight he would try to summon transportation to Shoreless Isle. The question remained who else would join him.

Bracken had continued in touch telepathically. He had learned from the Sphinx that, as expected, Zzyzx would be opened the morning following the next full moon. Which was less than four days away.

According to the letter from Patton, the voyage from Hatteras Island to Shoreless Isle would take almost exactly three days. The ship could only be called at midnight, and picked up passengers about two hours later. Tonight was the last night they could depart if they hoped to arrive before Zzyzx opened.

From the communication Seth had received, it sounded as though Bracken, Warren, Trask, and Kendra would reach Hatteras this evening. After losing the last Eternal and contacting Seth, they had rented a car and set out to join him on the Outer Banks.

Somewhere, Hugo, Newel, and Doren were trying to catch up as well. Seth and Vanessa had flown out of Seattle, leaving the satyrs and the golem with the truck, a credit card, and the challenge to reach the embarkation point on Hatteras before the *Lady Luck* came for them. The satyrs had been thrilled at the chance to finally drive. Vanessa had helped them plan which roads to travel. If they speeded, stopped only for gas, and avoided getting involved in a police chase, they had a chance of making it.

Seth flung the bits of shell in his hand into the ocean. He had enjoyed his time on Hatteras with Vanessa. She had slept a lot, catching up from consecutive days of relentless driving. He had done his best to forget his abducted parents and grandparents, ignore the opening of Zzyzx, and pretend he was here on vacation. But the time for pretending had almost ended.

He plopped down on the sand. No matter how much Bracken assured him that they were on schedule, he wouldn't rest easy until they arrived. What if they had car trouble? Worse, the Society could ambush them!

Seth removed the letter from Patton from his pocket and unfolded it. He skipped to the section about hailing the *Lady Luck*.

> *To summon the* Lady Luck, *you will need the bell, the whistle, and the music box from Cormac the leprechaun (see previous). On Hatteras Island, at midnight, climb to the top of the Cape Hatteras Lighthouse and ring the bell. The ship will respond only if the bell is rung at midnight from this vicinity.*

Seth paused his reading. Upon arriving at Hatteras Island, he and Vanessa had learned that the Cape Hatteras Lighthouse had been moved in 1999 to protect it from the encroaching ocean. The lighthouse had not been moved very far, but Seth worried it could mess up the bell's ability to call the ship. He wondered if it might be better to ring the bell on the ground where the lighthouse used to stand.

> *After you ring the bell, proceed to the embarkation area circled on the map below. A hundred minutes after ringing the bell, blow the whistle three times every few minutes until a rowboat arrives to bring you to the* Lady Luck. *Once aboard, head aft to the captain's cabin. Regardless of who you may bring on the voyage, go alone to the cabin. A Presence inhabits it. Play the music box inside, and then secure passage to*

Shoreless Isle. I am not sure of everything this will entail. But the voyage will consume three days, down to the hour, so time it right.

Remember, passage on the Lady Luck *is one-way. You will have to prepare some alternative method of return. Flying creatures will find it considerably easier to depart Shoreless Isle than to arrive there.*

This concludes my advice. Counsel with your allies to plan how best to mount a defense on Shoreless Isle. It will not be easy. It may not even be possible. Again, do what you will with these ideas. I am simply suggesting desperate actions I might try. Good luck.

Yours always,
Patton Burgess

Seth folded the letter and tucked it away. He leaned back, stretching out on the sand, and listened to the waves. Closing his eyes and breathing the salty air, he grabbed fistfuls of sand and let it sift through his fingers.

From down the beach, a voice called his name. He sat up and saw Kendra running toward him. The sight of her brought such relief that the emotion escaped in a burst of laughter as he charged to greet her. They met near where Vanessa sat on her towel.

"We made it with hours to spare," Kendra declared. "Bracken said you were worried."

"Well, it would have been hard for you guys to catch the next boat," Seth said. Behind his sister, Bracken, Warren, and Trask approached. "I'm so happy to see you."

"Me too," Kendra said. "Although I wish we could have saved one of the Eternals."

Vanessa stood up as Bracken drew near, hand on his sword. They stared at each other with open distrust. "Hello, Seth," Bracken said, eyes still on Vanessa. "So this is your blix?"

"I'm Vanessa," she said.

"Bracken," he replied stiffly. He held out his hand. "Nice to meet you."

Vanessa scowled at the offered hand. "You want inside my mind?"

"Seems appropriate," Bracken said.

"She's been really great," Seth affirmed. "A big help."

"Then it should be no issue to shake my hand," Bracken maintained.

Vanessa made no move to comply. "Who's scrutinizing *your* secret intentions?"

"My kind enjoy a more reliable reputation," Bracken said evenly.

"Your kind hunt blixes," Vanessa replied.

Bracken shrugged. "From time to time. Frankly, I wish blixes had more predators. Most of them deserve to be hunted."

Vanessa measured him with her eyes. "Debatable. But you do not deny that enmity exists between your kind and mine."

"I do not deny it."

"Then perhaps you can grasp why I don't want a unicorn as spokesman for my intentions."

Bracken lowered his offered hand. "Are you suggesting I might lie about what I see in your mind?"

"It would be the quickest way to justify my destruction."

Bracken smirked. "So here you stand trying to insulate yourself against what I might discover. If you have nothing to hide, you have no need to object. I will tell the truth, and they know that."

"But I don't," Vanessa said.

"Vanessa could have tried to take the sword," Kendra said.

Seth glanced at Kendra. "Who told you about the sword?"

Bracken turned to Seth. "I did. We can start conversing more openly. I've learned to sense when Nagi Luna has directed the Oculus toward us. It required some practice. I'm accustomed to her mind reaching out to spy on me, but the extra subtlety and power granted by the Oculus confused me for a time. Regaining my horn helped. I only mastered what to look for as we undertook our recent road trip. Ever since Civia was murdered by a blix," he shot Vanessa a meaningful glance, "Nagi Luna has essentially lost interest in us. She has only peered at us twice today, briefly, and without concern."

"So we're free to speak right now?" Seth asked.

"As long as I'm with you," Bracken said. "I'll warn you otherwise. By the way, where is Vasilis?"

"In the trunk of our rental car," Seth said.

Bracken frowned. "Maybe not the ideal place for one of the most powerful weapons in the history of the world, but I suppose it would be conspicuous on the beach."

"Vanessa could have tried to steal Vasilis," Kendra repeated.

"She could have tried," Bracken agreed, "but I'll assume she is clever enough to know she couldn't have succeeded. The sword can only be given to a friend, never taken by an enemy, even in death."

"I had no idea," Vanessa asserted sarcastically. "I'm very naïve."

Bracken extended his hand again. "For good or ill, let's get this over with."

Vanessa raised her eyebrows. "First, why don't we judge you based on your success in protecting the Eternals. How many of them survived your assistance?"

"None," Bracken said, his tone hard, his extended hand closing into a fist.

"How do we know you're not some rogue unicorn the Sphinx turned?" Vanessa accused. "We sure don't have any rescued Eternals as evidence. What assurances can you provide?"

"Bracken is no traitor," Kendra said. "The Fairy Queen vouched for him."

"To you, personally?" Vanessa asked.

"Yes," Kendra affirmed.

"Enough with the animosity," Warren interrupted. "Isn't tonight going to be long enough already? Please, Vanessa, just let him make sure. Think about your past. We'll all sleep easier."

Vanessa took Bracken's hand. He stared into her eyes for a long moment. "Just relax," Bracken said. "Think about your relationship with the Sorensons. Think about your current goals as they relate to our present mission." He released his grip.

"Well?" Vanessa asked.

"She used to love the Sphinx," Bracken reported.

Vanessa's expression hardened. "Did I hear the past tense?"

"After he betrayed her, she became a true ally to us," Bracken confirmed. "She still worries about the Sphinx. She cares about his welfare now that Graulas has taken over the Society, but not in any way that would harm our cause. Her affection is now directed elsewhere."

"Careful," Vanessa warned.

Bracken glanced at Warren. "Blix or not, we can trust her."

"Did you look at Warren?" Seth blurted. "Does Vanessa like Warren?"

Warren coughed uncomfortably.

Vanessa glared at Bracken. "Very tactful. Warren and I have some history from when I served as a Knight of the Dawn. I'm glad that's out in the open for everybody to whisper about. By the way, Bracken clearly has strong feelings for Kendra. Sometimes it doesn't take a mind reader."

Bracken opened his mouth, paused, and then closed it.

"Don't be shy," Vanessa teased, prodding his chest with her finger. "It really is the end of the world. Time to unbottle those hidden feelings. People make such a fuss about age discrepancies. Your attraction to Kendra is kind of like me having a crush on a newborn infant. Perfectly natural."

Bracken reddened. "I think your imagination is running away with you. I'm very fond of Kendra, but not in the way you're describing."

"You're right," Vanessa chuckled. "My mistake. It isn't quite like I described. After all, Kendra looks much more mature than an infant."

Trask cleared his throat noisily. "Enough with the blix-unicorn rivalry. I'm afraid we have larger concerns."

"Seth has a letter from Patton Burgess outlining our present objectives," Vanessa said. "I already have the key to the lighthouse. We blixes have our uses."

"There isn't much to do until tonight," Seth agreed.

Warren rubbed his hands together. "Anybody know where we can score some quality crab cakes?"

※ ※ ※

Less than a mile from the Cape Hatteras Lighthouse, Kendra sat in a rented SUV with Trask. Overhead, twinkling stars passed in and out of view as patchy clouds shifted. She unrolled the top of a bag of pretzels and popped one in her mouth, chewing without relish. After a shrimp quesadilla for dinner complemented by half a crab cake sandwich, she wasn't hungry, just fidgety. She checked her watch: twenty minutes to midnight.

Awkwardness had plagued Kendra the entire evening. Vanessa's accusations on the beach had left her profoundly embarrassed. Not only had Vanessa put Bracken on the spot about his feelings, she had publicly pointed out the age gap that separated him from Kendra. What made everything so much worse was that Kendra was developing a genuine attachment to Bracken. He was cute, brave, protective, smart, sweet, and, maybe best of all, she knew he was for real.

All night she hadn't known what to say to him, how to look at him. In the end, she had ignored Bracken, concentrating on Seth. Her brother had been through a lot since she had last seen him. He seemed sadder, more brooding.

Kendra rolled up the pretzel bag. What if Vanessa was right? What if Bracken liked her? It was one thing to harbor a crush on an unattainable guy, but quite another to consider him actually returning her affection. Even without Vanessa stressing the point, she knew he was a unicorn, and centuries old. But most things about him seemed so human! So normal! Well, handsomer than normal. Despite the reality of his true identity, in practice, Bracken seemed like a good-looking guy only a couple of years her senior.

Of course, in those moments after Bracken had reclaimed his second horn, he had come across as other-worldly. But once the crisis was behind them, he had quickly reverted to his old self. He still couldn't assume his horse shape without his third horn. For all practical purposes he was human. And even if he was a little otherworldly, Kendra sometimes wondered whether she were entirely human herself anymore. After becoming fairykind, she could hardly view herself as a regular teenage girl.

Kendra leaned her head against the window. Was she really sitting here worrying about how Bracken felt about her when the world was about to end? How simple was she? What if he read her mind? She would be mortified!

"Can I have a pretzel?" Trask asked.

The question made Kendra jump a little. "Sure," she said, handing him the bag. "Are we just going to abandon the rental car?"

"They'll figure it out," Trask said. "We'll compensate them financially. The Knights of the Dawn always pay their debts, and a little extra. We do it anonymously because too often we'd get arrested otherwise, but we do it. Naturally, if the world ends, I think everyone will have more pressing issues to complain about."

"True," Kendra said.

She had grilled Trask about her parents and grand-parents, but he had been kept in isolation at Living Mirage. She had asked Vanessa as well. The narcoblix had traveled into Tanu's body along with some of the others, but they were kept in separate cells, locked up day and night, so she had learned nothing except that they remained in the dungeon.

Having parked where they could observe the main road, Kendra and Trask sat up as a huge pickup truck approached at high speed. The truck zoomed past their SUV; then the taillights flashed brighter and the truck turned around. Headlights glaring, the truck came to a stop facing them, and Hugo vaulted out of the back.

Kendra and Trask got out of the SUV as Newel and Doren hopped down from the truck. "Told you!" Doren said, swatting Newel with the back of his hand. "Trust the golem."

Newel cracked his knuckles. "We were heading to the rendezvous when Hugo started to sense you guys. He led us here."

"We're two hours early," Doren said proudly.

"Seth," Hugo rumbled, pointing toward the lighthouse.

"He's fine," Kendra said. "He's just calling our ride. Warren, Bracken, and Vanessa are with him."

"You boys must have disregarded some speed limits to get here," Trask said.

Newel laughed. "That truck can move! We rarely went less than twice the speed limit."

"It was exhilarating," Doren gushed.

"Did you hit any speed traps?" Kendra asked.

"Twice," Newel said. "We pulled over politely. Both times the officer looked shocked to find a goat at the wheel without a human in sight."

"They searched the car both times," Doren said. "It was easy to prick them with one of the darts Vanessa left us. They went to sleep, we put them back in their car, and no trouble ever caught up with us."

"I'm sure other officers responded when they stopped calling in," Trask said. "But they probably dismissed the report of a truck driven by goats as a hallucination."

"Vanessa had five spare sets of plates with corresponding registrations," Newel explained. "We swapped them after any trouble."

Trask chuckled. "That may have helped as well. We did

some speeding to get here ourselves, but had better luck with speed traps."

Kendra regarded the satyrs. "You guys are really going to come to Zzyzx with us?"

"We've come this far," Doren said.

"Seth promised us our own flat-screen TV with a generator," Newel explained. "Besides, having front-row seats to the end of the world beats waiting for the disaster back at Fablehaven with the centaurs in charge."

"Seth told me about the centaurs," Kendra said.

"There will be a reckoning if we can survive the demons," Trask vowed.

"We have a chance," Doren said. "Seth has Vasilis. There are poems and songs about that sword."

"Not to mention a unicorn on our side!" Newel exclaimed. "They are the superheroes of the fairy world. They're not very outgoing, but when they decide to help, it can make all the difference."

"Don't join us buoyed by false expectations," Trask said. "Consider the enemy. We're talking about Gorgrog and his horde. We almost certainly will not be coming back."

"We get it," Newel said cheerfully. "If it's the end, so it goes. We had a good run. But can't we hope for the best?"

Trask shrugged. "I suppose we can hope."

❧ ❧ ❧

Above the red brick base, visible in the cloud-muted moonlight, white and black stripes spiraled to the top of the lighthouse, making it look like a giant barbershop pole.

Vanessa led Seth to the door at the base and opened it quickly. He followed her inside.

They climbed the curving stairs, a small flashlight helping them see. Roughly thirty at a time, the stairs ascended to semicircular landings. Periodic windows granted higher and higher views. By the time they reached the top, Seth was panting.

An observation platform surrounded the top of the lighthouse. Vanessa and Seth stepped outside. The gibbous moon came out from behind a cloud, throwing silver highlights on the corrugated ocean and the vegetated coastline. The salty breeze and great height made Seth feel like he was in the crow's nest of some enormous ship.

"Is it time?" Seth asked.

"Close enough," Vanessa replied, checking her watch.

Seth took out the handbell and removed the leather muffle from the clapper. He shook the bell over his head vigorously. The bell rang loudly, but nothing about it seemed supernatural. Seth clanged the bell constantly until Vanessa told him to stop. Then he stepped forward to the railing and looked down.

Far below, Bracken flashed a light at him. After muffling the clapper, Seth tossed the bell over the edge. As planned, Bracken and Warren would now run the bell to the former site of the lighthouse and ring it again. Hopefully, ringing the bell at both locations, they could be more sure the ship would respond as desired.

Seth followed Vanessa down the long flights of steps and out of the lighthouse. She locked up, and they trotted back to where they had parked. Before they reached their vehicle, a huge humanoid shape came stomping toward them out of the darkness. After a brief fright, Seth recognized Hugo. He ran to the golem, who scooped him up in a rocky embrace.

"You made it!" Seth said.

"Drove fast," Hugo replied.

"Did the truck arrive in one piece?" Vanessa wondered.

"Truck fine," Hugo assured her.

Newel and Doren gamboled over to them. Hugo set Seth down.

"I can't believe you guys made it," Seth said. "I expected you'd take your time, running up the credit card at fast food joints."

"Not a bad way to confront the end of civilization," Newel conceded. "But after enough fast food, it starts to all taste the same."

"Good, but greasy," Doren said. "Besides, driving fast is another new pleasure we both enjoy."

"We may not come back from this," Seth said seriously.

"We know," Newel said. "Everyone keeps warning us. If I didn't know better, I'd suspect you guys were trying to ditch us. Here's the thing—if we succeed, we don't just save the world. We save television. We save fast food. We save soft drinks and doughnuts and candy bars and ice cream."

"We save Frito-Lay," Doren said solemnly.

"You've enjoyed a lifetime of these marvelous conveniences," Newel accused. "You take them for granted. Doren and I are just getting introduced."

"Nobody is going to mess with Hostess," Doren said. "Not on my watch."

"We'll be honored to have you," Seth said.

"Hugo could pose a problem," Vanessa observed. "If the ship is sending just one launch to shuttle us aboard, the golem might swamp it."

"I don't want to go without Hugo," Doren said. "Did you see him beat up those centaurs with his bare hands?"

"Do we need to hijack a watercraft?" Newel asked.

"You'll have to be careful," Vanessa said. "These waters are famously treacherous. This area is called the Graveyard of the Atlantic for a reason. The shifting shoals off this coast have claimed hundreds of ships."

"Which explains the lighthouse," Newel said. "We'll figure it out. The golem should be able to discern your location. Come on, Hugo. We'd better hurry."

"See you on the water," Doren said.

The satyrs climbed into the truck, and Hugo settled into the back. Vanessa explained to Trask what the satyrs intended to do, and he agreed with the idea.

Kendra walked over to Seth. "How did it go?" she asked.

"I rang the bell. We'll see if it works."

"Want a pretzel?"

"I'm stuffed. I overdid it on the crab cakes."

They stood in silence for a moment.

"Do you get the sense that this is our last adventure?" Kendra asked.

Seth rubbed the hilt of Vasilis. "Yeah. You too?"

She nodded. "It's sort of obvious since we haven't even

prepared a way back. We couldn't stop any of this when we had a chance. And we had lots of chances. The artifacts. The Eternals. Now we're out of chances. I guess going to Zzyzx is better than nothing. It will be better to die bravely among friends than to die in hiding."

"You don't have to go," Seth said.

"Neither do you."

"I'm going. That was the whole point of getting Vasilis. If I'm going to die, I'll die fighting demons, not running from them. It helps to imagine what Patton would do. It helps to think about Coulter."

"I'm going too," Kendra said. Her lip trembled. "I wish I could say good-bye to Mom and Dad."

"Don't think like that," Seth said. "Think about winning. Think about protecting the world."

His sister managed a faint smile. "I'll try."

When Bracken and Warren returned, everyone got into the SUV and the sedan and drove to the location marked on Patton's map. After checking their gear, they walked down to the edge of the water and waited for the proper time to start blowing the whistle.

Seth noticed Bracken sitting down beside Kendra. He couldn't resist casually eavesdropping.

"I'm sorry about Vanessa earlier," Bracken said. "She was trying to lash out at me for embarrassing her."

"Don't worry," Kendra said. "I get it."

Bracken took Kendra's hand, regarding her intently. "Vanessa wasn't wrong."

Seth knew it was time to stop listening. Thrusting his

hands in his pockets, he strolled up the beach. He could not help dwelling upon what Kendra had said about this being their last adventure. Alone in the dark, he had to admit she was right. Vasilis was cool, and Hugo was tough, and Bracken probably had some tricks up his sleeve, but then he considered the raw power of Bahumat, pictured Olloch the Glutton tearing off Hugo's arm, and recalled Graulas demolishing the house at Fablehaven. Demons were nightmarishly powerful, and Zzyzx held the worst of them in huge numbers.

What if Raxtus succeeded in getting Agad involved? A wizard could be useful. Especially if he brought some dragons. But supposedly the horde inside of Zzyzx was even more powerful than dragons.

"Strange time to roam this beach," a conversational voice said behind Seth.

He whirled to see a grayish man with a bristly beard wearing a hooded slicker and sturdy boots. He had not heard the man approach. "I'm here with some friends."

"So I noticed," the man said, staring out to sea. "Word to the wise: This beach may be getting some unsavory visitors shortly."

This was no ordinary man. When Seth stared hard, the stranger seemed slightly translucent. "I know," Seth said. "I called them."

"Sure you want to be doing that?"

"I need to get somewhere."

The man turned his head and looked at Seth. "There are plenty of ways to get around."

"Not where we're going," Seth explained. "We have to reach Shoreless Isle. Some demons are going to open Zzyzx."

The man looked back out at the water. "Can't say I know much about that. Sounds like you have your reasons. Watch yourself when negotiating passage. She can be unreasonable."

"You have any advice?" Seth asked.

The man looked at him again. "I don't mean to intrude."

"Please."

"You have quite a sword there. Don't forget it, if she gets temperamental. Some people only respect those who might do them harm. Myself, I would steer clear of the *Lady Luck* altogether."

Bracken came jogging down the beach. Seth took a step toward him, waving him over. When Seth turned back, the gray man was gone. There was no place he could have hidden. Chills tingled across Seth's shoulders.

"Did you see him?" Seth asked as Bracken came near.

"An apparition," Bracken said. "He's what brought me this way. Benevolent, by the feel of him. Some sort of guardian spirit."

"He talked to me about the *Lady Luck*," Seth said.

"I hope you listened," Bracken said. "You all right?"

"Good enough. I saw you chatting with my sister."

"Vanessa made things uncomfortable. Some words had to be exchanged."

Seth grinned. They walked back to the others together. Once there, Seth kept his eyes on the water, hoping to see Hugo, Newel, and Doren show up in a stolen boat. The six of them sat in silence. Kendra leaned her head against Bracken's shoulder. Trask and Vanessa dozed.

Eventually Bracken eased away from Kendra and nudged Seth. "Time for the bosun's whistle."

Seth removed the whistle from the case, stood, and gave three long calls. Two minutes later, he repeated the calls. And again two minutes later.

The moon went behind heavy clouds, dimming their view of the sea. Seth continued to toot the whistle every couple of minutes. When the moon came out again, a large rowboat was approaching, still some distance out.

The whistling had awakened Vanessa and Trask. Seth stowed the whistle, and everyone gathered their gear. The rowboat ran aground, and a pair of seamen splashed out into the water. Seth had seen zombies, and he had seen wraiths. These figures appeared to be somewhere in between. Not as dark or graceful as wraiths, they moved with much more agility and competence than zombies. Their brown, knotted flesh looked lean and tough.

After scanning the murky ocean a final time for any sign of Hugo or the satyrs, Seth waded into the cold water with the others, accepting help from an undead seaman to climb into the rowboat. A second pair of undead sailors awaited inside, manning the large oars. Once everyone was aboard, the pair of seamen on the beach pushed the boat back into the water, then scrambled inside.

The boat accommodated all of them comfortably, but would have barely fit the satyrs. Hugo would certainly have been too big. Seth consoled himself that they had not left Hugo behind needlessly.

The sailors at the oars managed the craft with efficient competence. If there were dangerous shoals nearby, Seth saw no sign of them. The rowboat progressed quickly away from the shore, bobbing up and down on the swells.

Seth listened carefully to the undead sailors, but, as with the Standing Dead, he detected no thoughts. He tried to start conversations mentally, but sensed no response.

The moon hid behind the clouds again. Rowing across the black, undulating water felt creepy. Everything was surreal: the rolling motion of the vessel, the salty tang in the air, the undead mariner sitting beside him, an oxidized ring dangling from his shriveled earlobe. Seth noticed that Bracken had an arm around Kendra.

They had been rowing for a long time when Bracken arose. He held up a hand, and a bright ball of white light rose from his fingers, casting a ghostly light over the wooden ship looming beside them.

"Whoa," Seth mouthed, impressed by the size.

The ship had three tall masts, hung with complex rigging, but no sails. Far above the water awaited decks of different heights, bordered by ornate railings. The wood looked old and weathered but not rotten. Seth could see the name of the ship engraved in metal. An elaborately carved mermaid figurehead hung at the front, face panicked, arms chained to her sides.

Paying no heed to the added radiance, the undead sailors maneuvered the rowboat alongside the *Lady Luck*. Seth heard the buzz of a motor. Turning, he saw a motorboat approaching over the water.

"They found us," Trask said.

"Up the ladder," Bracken instructed.

Seth waited while the others climbed, until only he and Bracken remained in the rowboat with the four undead seafarers. One of the sailors motioned for them to scale the ladder.

"We have friends coming," Seth explained.

Showing no evidence of comprehension, the sailor gestured once again for them to climb. Taking his time, Seth shuffled over to the ladder. The motorboat was drawing near. He adjusted his sword belt and fiddled with the case Cormac had given him.

"Wait," Newel called. "We're here. Sorry it took so long. I think we damaged the boat. Hugo had to rescue us from a few sandbars."

The engine died, and the motorboat drifted forward to thump against the rowboat, jostling the occupants. Newel and Doren sprang into the rowboat.

"These are our friends," Bracken said. "They travel with us."

The undead sailors made no move to stop them. Seth started up the ladder, followed by Bracken. Looking down, Seth saw Hugo transfer gingerly into the rowboat, the vessel wobbling beneath his weight. A moment later, the golem was following Doren up the side of the ship.

When Seth reached the top, he found the others huddled together, confronted by a crowd of twenty undead deckhands. Although the raggedly dressed sailors made no aggressive movements, a threat was implied by their grouping and their posture. Bracken, Newel, Doren, and Hugo joined Seth and the others.

"The captain's cabin will be at the stern," Bracken said, pointing. "I imagine they'll want us to wait here while you secure our passage. We need this to work. Whether or not we could stand against these cursed seamen, we can't make the ship ferry us to our destination."

"No problem," Seth said, gritting his teeth. He walked away from his friends, passing among the undead sailors. He kept one hand on the hilt of Vasilis and tried to betray no fear. None of the sailors impeded his way, and, as he left them behind, some of his concerns faded.

He walked to the door of the captain's cabin, considered knocking, then just opened it. The shadowy room looked richly furnished. A fine rug covered much of the floor. Detailed maps and charts hung on the walls. The desk was small but ornate, and the generous bunk had silky sheets.

The room appeared to be empty.

Kneeling, Seth opened the case, removed the music box, wound it, and placed it on the floor. Nothing happened. He opened the lid to the music box, and it began to chime.

Immediately the air started to swirl, and the temperature plunged. The door banged shut, and the shadows suddenly became much deeper. Maps and charts fluttered on the walls, and papers took flight from the desk. He saw no personage, but Seth knew that he was no longer alone. An inexplicable Presence had joined him.

Why have you imposed upon me? inquired a girlish voice in his mind. Although she sounded childlike, Seth intuited that the speaker was ancient.

"I have to reach Shoreless Isle," Seth said. "This is the only way I know to get there."

You did not come alone. What is the meaning of the unicorn? The golem? The girl was clearly displeased.

"I am traveling with friends to prevent a catastrophe," Seth said. "Will you take us?"

Will I take you? The words stung his mind, and he flinched. *I will not. I hate that island. You and your companions will join my crew. Except for the unicorn and the golem, who will go into the deep.*

"That's not acceptable," Seth said, worried, hand straying to the pommel of his sword.

Not acceptable! Have you any idea who you are dealing with? I heeded the summons, as promised. After you come aboard, I do as I will. You do not belong here. I will not bargain with you. Away! Deliver my verdict to your companions.

Seth drew Vasilis, and the warm comfort of rage awakened inside of him. Confidence crowded out his doubts and fears, and he felt shame for how he had been cowering. His friends were counting on him! The sword flared red, brightening the room and revealing a faint form in the corner. It looked like a sparse cloud of dust motes in the shape of a woman with long hair. Vasilis tugged him toward the hazy entity.

"Enough nonsense," Seth commanded, resisting the eager pull of his sword. "I've been through too much to argue with a thousand-year-old child. My friends and I go to our deaths. You are merely the ride. I summoned you politely. You will provide us with safe passage, or your existence will end as I carve your ship into matchsticks and your crew into fish bait."

Silence.

My apologies, came the timid response, all menace gone. *You carried yourself like a fraud at first. You are cruel to tease us so. Cause us no harm, and I hereby grant you and your companions passage to Shoreless Isle.*

"You have three days," Seth said. "We need to be ashore well before sunrise."

As you say, Great One.

Seth turned to go. "I'd prefer if this were the last time we have to speak."

With no disrespect intended, I would prefer the same.

Shoreless Isle

Kendra leaned against the railing near the front of the *Lady Luck*, gazing out over the gloomy water. Although clouds currently obscured the full moon, she could see for a good distance. The ship advanced smoothly and steadily. Even during the storm the day before, the *Lady Luck* had remained miraculously level, cutting through the heaving water with unnatural haste.

During their three days at sea, the undead sailors had never raised a single sail. In fact, once the sailors had dispersed after Seth returned from the captain's cabin, Kendra had not seen much of her undead shipmates. They mainly stayed down in the hold, never venturing into the forecastle where she and her friends were sleeping.

Bracken had wakened her a few minutes ago. Their

voyage almost over, her friends were readying their equipment. Kendra had come up here to peek at Shoreless Isle, but she had not yet glimpsed land.

"See anything?" Seth asked, startling her.

"Not yet."

"How far can you see?" he asked.

"I don't know. A few hundred yards, I guess."

Her brother chuckled. "I can't even see the water."

"We'll all see land soon enough."

They stood together in silence.

"Have you smooched Bracken yet?" Seth asked.

"No, sicko," Kendra replied with annoyance. "That's none of your business!"

"You've been pretty cuddly," Seth observed.

"He's just keeping me warm," Kendra said. "He's trying to comfort me. And he might need a little comfort."

"I know what might give him some extra courage," Seth said, puckering his lips.

Kendra shoved him. "Don't be an idiot."

Seth laughed. "Just for the record, you may not have many more chances."

Kendra scowled. "I know. Hey, I see something."

"What?"

"Mist."

Seth rolled his eyes. "Mist doesn't count as news."

"No, lots of mist. A wall of mist. You'll see, we're getting closer to it."

"See anything in the mist?" Seth asked after a moment.

"No. It's too thick."

Kendra watched as the bowsprit pierced the vaporous wall. A moment later, she felt the dampness on her face and hands, and tasted it when she inhaled.

"You're right," Seth said. "That was sudden."

Bracken came up from behind. "All our gear is ready."

"Any word on reinforcements?" Seth asked.

"Agad is on his way," Bracken said. "I can't get into specifics. Nagi Luna has been watching us a lot lately. We caught her eye once we boarded this ship. She's watching us right now."

Kendra shivered. "Can you tell where she is?"

"She's nearby, on the island," Bracken said. "Inside the dome. I can't discern much else. She's not really worried about us, just interested."

"Can you brighten up the mist?" Seth asked.

"I'm not sure you'd like what you saw," Bracken said. "Undead guardians on jagged teeth of rock."

"I'm starting to hear them," Seth said. "Most of them are moaning. A few sound thirsty. Some are inviting us to join them."

"You can see them?" Kendra asked Bracken.

"I can sense them," Bracken said. "Huge beasts in the water as well. They keep away from our ship, though."

As the ship continued forward, Kendra heard a churning, sucking sound up ahead and a little to the right. "Do you hear that?"

"The whirlpool?" Bracken asked. "It will get louder."

The *Lady Luck* passed right by the gurgling vortex, never

swerving or rocking. As the ominous sucking of the whirlpool receded, the mist began to thin.

"I see the island," Kendra said. "It's big. I can't see the whole thing. There are lots of sharp rocks in the water. I don't see any beach, just waves pounding rugged stone."

A moment later, the *Lady Luck* slowed to a halt.

"This must be our stop," Bracken said.

They descended to the main deck, where a pair of undead mariners ushered them over to the side. Down below, two rowboats awaited them, crewed by more undead sailors.

"They even brought Hugo a boat," Seth said.

"These zombie pirates think of everything," Warren said. "I'm going to recommend the *Lady Luck* to my friends."

Kendra climbed down the side of the ship between Bracken and Seth. All of them went in one boat, except for Doren and Hugo. Once the passengers were situated, the rowers began maneuvering away from the ship.

As the launches glided toward the island, the moon broke through the clouds, brightening the scene. Everywhere Kendra looked, water sprayed against treacherous rocks, the frothy foam reflecting the moonlight. She could not envision how they would reach the shore without drowning.

In the volatile water, the smaller boat did not enjoy the same supernatural stillness as the *Lady Luck*. Kendra clung to the gunwale as the boat pitched and rocked, cold spray slopping over the sides. Fighting hard, the rowers guided the craft through a turbulent slalom course of menacing boulders. Three times Kendra closed her eyes as a crash seemed imminent, but each time the undead seamen managed to dodge the obstacle.

The forbidding shore drew near, fountains of brine exploding over angular rocks and blasting up through blowholes. The rowboat surged forward with the breaking waves, and Kendra braced for the inevitable collision, ready for the craft to shatter against unforgiving stone. At the last moment, oars thrashing, the rowboat veered left, lurching sideways under a stone arch into a small, hidden cove.

Although mostly sheltered from the breakers, the water in the cove rose and fell erratically. The boat containing Hugo entered after them. Steep rock faces surrounded the cove on all sides. The rowers piloted the boats over to the most climbable face.

Hugo lunged out of his boat, finding purchase on the steep slope. The golem reached out, and, as the water level in the cove rose high, Bracken guided Kendra into his hand. Holding Kendra in one earthen hand, Hugo quickly scaled the face. From the top, Kendra peered down as the others disembarked and scrambled up the steep slope. Bracken created a floating ball of light to help illuminate the climb.

By the time everyone reached the top, the rowboats had exited the cove to return to the ship. Kendra could hardly imagine how the launches could row against the incoming barrage of breakers, but as far as she could see, the undead sailors made a smooth escape.

Bracken increased the size and brightness of his light ball and left it hovering about twenty feet above his head. Not far from the craggy shore, the island became vegetated, with tall trees draped with vines overshadowing exotic ferns. Nearby lay a timeworn statue of a lion, webbed with cracks and missing three legs. Standing, it would have been almost as tall as Hugo.

Bracken took the lead, guiding them along the coast until they reached a sandy lagoon. A barricade of dark rocks, jutting like rows of fangs, shielded the far side of the placid lagoon from the fury of the sea. Huge stone slabs and broken pillars littered the beach, as if graceful structures had once stood here. Kendra ran a hand over the crooked base of a broken column, examining the remnants of intricate carvings.

"This looks like a good spot for a picnic," Seth said, sitting down on the edge of a half-buried foundation. "These are sort of like benches."

"I could eat," Warren said.

"This might represent our best chance for a meal," Bracken agreed.

Kendra sat down, digging into her backpack for water. The voyage on the *Lady Luck* had used up much of their food and water, but enough remained for one last decent snack. At this point, it would consist mostly of jerky, nuts, crackers, and dried fruit. As everyone took inventory, Kendra realized they had packed their provisions on the assumption that after today they would need no more food. If they somehow survived, she supposed they could fish.

Nobody spoke as they ate. The dangerous trip to shore had left Kendra shaken, and the mysterious atmosphere of the dismal beach did little to brighten her spirits. The knowledge that they were all about to die hung over the meal. None of them discussed their impending doom, but Kendra felt certain they were all pondering it. She ate mechanically, the nuts and jerky tasteless in her mouth.

As the eating slowed, Bracken stood. "I can sense the shrine to the Fairy Queen farther along this coast. The shrine lies near the east side of the dome encasing the door to Zzyzx. If I understand the lore correctly, the dome should open to face the rising sun, so the shrine might be a good place to make our final preparations."

"Lead on," Trask said.

"You realize we have to live through this," Warren said, shouldering his pack. "There's no way my last meal is going to be hiker food."

Newel and Doren laughed. Nobody else could muster the effort. They started walking, Bracken in the lead.

"Come on, people!" Newel chided. "Warren made a joke. He has a point! We don't have to trudge to Zzyzx like mourners at our own funerals! We came on this mission knowing the outcome would be our demise. Doesn't that remove most of the stress? I'd be a lot more nervous if I thought I had a chance."

"It's like Bodwin the Bold," Doren agreed cheerfully. "He faced his executioners with a smile on his face and tipped the headsman. We may be doomed, but why not enjoy ourselves? It will lessen the victory of our adversaries."

"I like that," Seth said. "I'm going to smile at the demons. I really am. You guys watch me."

"I'm glad to be off that ship," Kendra said. "At least we'll die on a tropical island."

"I kind of like Warren's plan to not die," Vanessa said. "Any of you have last messages you want me to deliver?"

"You're all nuts," Trask chuckled.

"This beats letting it gnaw at us," Warren said. "I bet I'll be the last one standing."

"You wish," Seth said. "That will be Bracken. I bet he takes some demons with him."

"And I won't?" Warren exclaimed.

"Maybe a little one," Seth laughed.

"Not many weapons can harm a greater demon," Bracken said. "Seth's blade is our best by far. My horn can do it. Warren has the adamant sword, and it should pierce most demonic hides. The swords we took from the Gray Assassin will cut demon flesh. Trask has both at the moment, but he should give one to Vanessa. I saw her mind. She's very talented with a blade. The rest of you should hang back and take up our arms when we fall. And, for the record, if you want to place bets on the last of us standing, my money goes on Hugo."

"No," the golem rumbled. "Not last. Hugo save Seth. Hugo save Kendra."

Tears stung Kendra's eyes.

Newel raised a hand. "How do I get added to that list?"

This time everyone laughed, even the golem, stony shoulders shaking.

The banter continued for a time, fueled mostly by Warren, Seth, and the satyrs. Eventually the conversation died. Kendra felt glad they had acknowledged the danger and tried to laugh at it. The peril remained the same, but the camaraderie had helped lighten her mood.

Walking behind Bracken, Kendra tried to imagine how she could help in the final battle. If they didn't find any astrids to transform, she doubted she could contribute much. Everyone else was better than she was with weapons. Besides, Torina had used all of her phoenix-feather arrows, leaving none to appropriate. Based on what Bracken had said, regular arrows like Kendra had brought would only annoy the demons. Maybe the Fairy Queen could grant her some sort of weapon. She would definitely ask.

They reached a second lagoon, this one sheltered by spiny reefs. A jumble of fallen walls, arches, and columns cluttered the crescent-shaped beach. Scattered architectural remnants continued inland among the trees. Farther inland loomed the bulk of an immense stone dome.

"The first hints of dawn remain an hour away," Bracken said. "The shrine is not far off."

Bracken led them inland from the beach through a grove of tall palm trees. They passed a headless statue of a horse. Up ahead, Kendra saw a large ring of pillars connected by arches. In contrast to the other stonework they had found, the impressive circle of archways appeared perfectly intact.

"Is that the shrine?" Kendra asked.

Bracken nodded. "The rest of you may want to wait here." He took Kendra's hand.

"You don't need me," Kendra said.

"I need all the help I can get," Bracken said, coaxing her forward. "We have a lot to ask."

Hand in hand, Bracken and Kendra approached the wide ring of connected pillars. Passing beneath an engraved arch, Kendra found the ground paved with stone. Shallow steps led down to a circular pond with a small island in the center. A single delicate arch spanned the water to the island. They walked to the near end of the fragile bridge, where Kendra hesitated.

"What are we going to ask the Fairy Queen?" she asked.

"You'll see," Bracken replied. "Let's wait until her majesty can help shield our words. Nagi Luna keeps prying."

"Can the Fairy Queen block the Oculus?" Kendra asked.

"Not really, but she has ways of encouraging Nagi Luna to gaze elsewhere. Come."

He led her onto the narrow arch. Without his hand to hold, Kendra would have worried about her balance, but he felt so stable that she crossed without difficulty. The moment she set foot on the island, Kendra sensed electricity in the air, as if lightning were about to strike. The fine hairs on her arm stood up.

"Do you feel that?" she asked.

"Yes." Bracken led her to the tiny statue of a fairy beside a golden bowl. They knelt together, and powerful aromas washed over them. The desert during a rainstorm. The inside of a decaying log. Honeycombs dripping with sweetness.

So it has come to this. The words arrived with a flood of

conflicting emotions. Profound sadness. Deep exhaustion. Simmering wrath. Tender concern.

"We both saw it coming," Bracken said simply. "I did everything in my power to prevent this."

Try as we might to postpone them, days of reckoning inevitably arrive.

"Is this going to be the end of the world?" Kendra asked.

It could be.

"I've been in touch with Agad," Bracken said. "He will arrive as planned. You have received my messages?"

Yes. I agree with your assessments.

"You can talk to her away from the shrines?" Kendra asked.

"Not really," Bracken said. "Without my third horn I can't hear her. But she can hear me. I counted on that."

Kendra stared at the little fairy statue. "Can you help us?"

I must help you. The realm where I rule is connected to your world. For all its splendor and beauty, my kingdom is an extension of your reality. Without the terrestrial influence of the shrines, my unspoiled realm of light would eventually fade.

"Are you prepared to go all the way?" Bracken asked.

Emotions warred inside the Fairy Queen, and Kendra momentarily experienced them as if they were her own. Hesitation. Doubt. Concern for her realm. Concern for her subjects. Concern for the world. Concern for Bracken, specific and desperate. A desire to hide. A desire to rest. And an old hatred, a yearning for vengeance that had quietly smoldered for years.

Only as a last resort. It would be a desperate gambit.

"It's our only choice," Bracken said. "It's why this shrine was placed here. Their final obstacle."

What if I open my realm to you and your friends? Kendra, Seth, even the golem. We could find a way to shield ourselves.

"Open your realm to us?" Kendra asked. "Wouldn't that make your realm vulnerable?"

It might be safer than open battle.

"This is unbecoming," Bracken said. "Do not give utterance to these fears. My presence makes you weak."

You cannot imagine how you strengthen me. Kendra felt such a surge of love that she gasped and clutched her chest, tears spilling from her eyes.

"We can't win this battle," Bracken said. "There is no point in deluding ourselves otherwise. But even without winning the battle, we might earn a chance to win the war. Hours of crisis often call for sacrifice. In matters of consequence, when have doubt and fear given the best advice? Why not heed faith, courage, duty, and honor? Kendra has, her friends have, and without reason for hope."

Sound counsel, as usual. I will obey your plan. Kendra felt a wave of reluctant resignation.

"Not my plan," Bracken said. "I'm proposing we implement it, but I did not design it. This stratagem was authored by the wizards who arranged to locate a shrine here."

"What plan?" Kendra asked.

"Only the Fairy Queen and I know all the particulars," Bracken said. "It needs to remain that way. Agad has probably deciphered our strategy, but that was unavoidable.

Should the enemy anticipate our intentions, our final hope will unravel."

"We have a chance?" Kendra asked.

"A small one," Bracken said. "I would never have allowed you or your friends to come here if there wasn't a chance."

You have an important role to play, Kendra.

"How many have you gathered?" Bracken asked.

Ninety. Three of the six rebels returned. And of course three have perished.

"Are you talking about astrids?" Kendra asked.

The pool around the island erupted with the flutter of golden wings as astrids emerged from the water. Within moments, ninety owls perched atop the linked pillars, human faces staring down at Kendra and Bracken.

"No wonder I couldn't find any of them!" Kendra complained.

"They were out searching for you," Bracken said. "But as events unfolded, I decided it might be best for the Fairy Queen to gather them home in preparation for this day."

Kendra frowned at the little fairy statue. "Didn't all that travel weaken the protections to your realm? All the astrids coming and going?"

Yes. But do not fret, I repaired most of the damage by closing all other shrines besides this one. I have marshaled all of my energy for this confrontation. Follow Bracken. His leadership is now our best hope.

"Can you give us a clear morning?" Bracken asked.

The weather is the simplest part.

"You're ready to do the rest?" Bracken asked.

I am ready.

Bracken became sober. "If the right conditions do not unfold, we'll have to abandon the effort."

I understand. Make your preparations. Onward to victory.

Kendra felt a surge of hope so strong she almost believed it. Then she was left with her natural emotions. The presence of the Fairy Queen had departed.

Bracken took Kendra's hand and guided her back over the arch. "Gilgarol, you first!"

A golden owl fluttered down and alighted in front of Kendra.

"This is the captain of the astrids," Bracken said. "Give him a kiss on the forehead."

Kendra crouched in front of the owl. The solemn face stared up at her with an unreadable expression. At least she didn't have to touch her lips to his feathers. She leaned down and gave his waxy forehead a quick peck.

Golden light flared, and, after a scintillating whirlwind of sparks, Kendra found herself crouched before a tall warrior. Gilded armor protected his muscular frame, and an owlish helmet guarded his head. His facial features appeared much more masculine than before. He clutched a spear in one hand, a sword in the other. Broad, gleaming wings fanned out from his back.

The splendid soldier turned and knelt before Bracken, head bowed. "Forgive our failure, my liege," he implored, his strong voice thick with emotion.

"Rise, Gilgarol," Bracken said. "All is forgiven. We have work to do."

The strapping warrior stood up. "We prayed this day would come. At long last, a chance for redemption."

Kendra confronted Bracken. "Okay, seriously, who are you? The Fairy Queen treats you like her favorite. The astrids kneel to you. Are you the only unicorn left or something?"

"No, there are others," Bracken said.

Gilgarol harrumphed. "Are you not aware of—"

A hard glance from Bracken silenced him.

"What?" Kendra pressed. "Come on, you have to tell me."

Bracken sighed. "The Fairy Queen has five children—four daughters, one son. I'm the son."

"The Fairy Queen is your mother?"

"Yes."

Kendra rubbed her forehead. "No wonder she seemed so worried about you. But how could your mother be a fairy?"

"Did I say she was a fairy?"

"She's not?"

"Unicorns were the founders of fairydom. My mother was the first."

"The Fairy Queen is a unicorn?"

"Very few beyond our inner circle share this knowledge," Bracken said. "The fairies honor her as the first of their kind. Gorgrog destroyed my father, which is part of the reason I want to defeat him. Time is running out. We have eighty-nine astrids to go."

Kendra felt stunned. She had been cuddling and flirting with the son of the Fairy Queen? There was no time to sort through the implications. "Let's get going."

"All but the unfaithful," Bracken called.

Kendra knelt, and one by one the astrids came forward to have their true forms restored. It took longer than she expected. Soon she started closing her eyes with each kiss to avoid the blinding blizzard of sparks that accompanied each transformation. All of the astrids looked more or less like the first. The weapons varied, as did some elements of the armor, but each had golden wings, and each looked intimidating.

At last, with eighty-seven astrids restored, three darker astrids remained. These lacked the shining golden feathers of the others, and they wore remorseful expressions.

"You turned on the Fairy Queen after she chastised you for your failure," Bracken reprimanded. "But you came when she called. You will hereafter be considered the lowest rank of all those present. May you reclaim your honor through outstanding valor." He nodded at Kendra.

When she kissed the final three, they grew into shining warriors indistinguishable from the others. The three knelt before Bracken. They spoke in unison. "We apologize for our disloyalty. Our rebelliousness will forever shame us. Thank you for this opportunity to prove our penitence. We will not fail you."

"You picked the right day to prove yourselves," Bracken said. "Behold, dawn approaches."

Looking to the east, Kendra saw color in the sky. Overhead, the clouds were thinning. Accompanied by several astrids, Kendra and Bracken returned to where their companions waited, a short distance from the shrine.

"Looks like you recruited some help," Trask said, sounding heartier than he had in days.

"These are astrids?" Seth said, giddy with excitement.

"This is only the beginning," Bracken promised. "Agad is on his way with a group of dragons. Additional reinforcements may issue from the shrine. We may not have the strength to defeat our opponents, but we'll give these demons a welcome to remember."

"What's the plan?" Warren asked.

"We'll form up on the far side of the shrine," Bracken said. "A large clearing separates the shrine from Zzyzx. Since the Fairy Queen is using the shrine as a portal, our sacred homeland will be somewhat vulnerable. We'll try to lure the combat to other locations, and twelve astrids will hang back specifically to protect the shrine."

"Should I build a tower?" Seth asked. "I have a little tower that will grow into a real one if I plant it in the ground."

Bracken shook his head. "Mobility will be too crucial. These are beings of immense power. The strongest of them tear down walls and towers for sport. Save your tower for another day. The demons will try to paralyze us with fear, but the astrids and I can counter their dark auras. None of you will feel the effects of magical fear unless the rest of us fall. Kendra and Seth will each have two astrids assigned as bodyguards; the rest of us will each have one."

"This will be an unstoppable horde," Vanessa reminded.

"We can harass their vanguard, but more will keep coming, too many to handle. We need concrete objectives."

"I have specific maneuvers in mind," Bracken said. "But Nagi Luna is watching. The restoration of the astrids really caught her attention. Much of our hope depends on surprise. I'll share the specific assignments as our adversaries emerge."

Vanessa chuckled. "You require a lot of trust."

"He's the one who brought the army," Warren said. "We don't have much choice but to hope his plan is a good one."

"Our situation is ridiculously perilous," Bracken said. "Yet I'm confident that, under the circumstances, my plan grants us the only possible opportunity to win the day."

"Don't start saying we might win," Newel complained. "You're making me nervous."

"We won't defeat them," Bracken clarified. "But we could survive."

"I think he's lost it," Doren whispered, twirling a finger beside his ear.

"This way," Bracken said. "When the sun rises, the prison will open."

Kendra fell into step behind Newel and Doren.

"Think they remember?" Newel asked Doren, eyeing the astrids.

"Remember what?" Kendra inquired.

Doren placed a hand beside his mouth and whispered, "Newel used to sling rocks at the astrids for sport."

"Hush," Newel hissed urgently, clamping a hand over Doren's mouth. "Doren and his stories."

Up ahead, Kendra saw human-sized fairies rising from

the pond around the shrine. Kendra had not seen fairies like them since she had helped to rescue Fablehaven from Bahumat. Tall and graceful, they carried slender spears and swords, and gave haughty looks to the astrids.

A group of the oversized fairies gathered around Hugo and started chanting. The ground rippled, and Hugo began to swell as earth and stone flowed up into his body, giving him new mass. Huge thorns sprouted on his arms and legs. By the time they finished chanting, Hugo stood at almost twice his former height, larger than when the fairies had prepared him for battle during the shadow plague. A group of fairies brought the golem an enormous sword, longer than Trask was tall, with a broad, sharp blade.

Seth ran up to Kendra. "Did you see that? They beefed up Hugo! Maybe we have a chance!"

"Bracken thinks we might," Kendra said.

"I'm freaking out," Seth said, stamping his feet anxiously. "I'll be better once the battle starts. My sword really helps my nerves."

"Just obey Bracken," Kendra implored. "He's our general today. Do what he says and we might make it."

"I'm with Newel," Seth said. "I thought we were dead, so hearing we might beat them is messing with my mind."

"Stay calm," Bracken said. He and Gilgarol fell into step alongside them. "When the demons first emerge, it may look overwhelming. Remember, we don't have to fight them all head-on. We'll have specific objectives."

"Where are those dragons?" Seth asked.

"All in due time," Bracken assured him.

The sky had grown brighter. They reached the far side of the shrine. Ahead of them, a wide field separated them from a tremendous dome of rock, its entire surface etched with cryptic runes. Here and there on the field lay the eroding ruins of ancient structures.

Surveying their newly assembled army, Kendra counted at least a hundred oversized fairies. The heavily armed astrids looked grim and competent, some on the ground, some hovering in the air. And Hugo had become absolutely gigantic. Whatever the outcome, this was much better than facing Gorgrog and his horde with a team of nine.

Bracken trotted ahead of everyone and turned to speak, waving both arms to summon attention. "Our foes will emerge at any moment. Look to me for orders! Take heart— we have the support of the Fairy Queen and other powerful allies. And after centuries of exile, the astrids have returned to their true form!"

This earned a cheer.

"For ages," Bracken went on, "you astrids served as the honor guard for my family. This regiment had a name. Would any of our human companions care to guess what they were called?"

Nobody answered.

"The Knights of the Dawn," Bracken said. "The same name taken by the brotherhood that stands in opposition to the Society of the Evening Star. I believe this name is no accident. I believe this name makes reference to this moment. No star can abide the light of the dawn, nor has evil ever loved light. After their long incarceration in darkness, let our enemies come against us with the sunrise at our backs!"

Kendra had chills. She had no idea Bracken possessed such dramatic flair for leadership. His words had kindled real hope. All around her, fairies and astrids clapped and whistled. Many applauded by clashing their weapons against their shields, producing a soldierly ruckus.

The sun peeked over the horizon, flooding the world with golden rays. And then the dome began to quake. A thunderous rumbling arose as if from the bones of the planet, drowning out all other sound. Tremors radiated through the ground, making trees sway. Kendra stumbled against an astrid, who prevented her from falling. The quaking intensified, and a vertical crack appeared in the lower portion of the dome, growing wider by the second. As the sun cleared the horizon, the demon prison opened.

CHAPTER TWENTY-SEVEN

Knights of the Dawn

When the quaking subsided, the breach in the dome had become as wide as a basketball court. Seth stared at the gaping rift, waiting for a demon to appear. Around him, astrids and fairies milled anxiously.

"Steady," Bracken called. "Await my commands."

"Are you my bodyguard?" Seth asked an astrid who had taken up position beside him.

"Yes," the brawny astrid replied. "I am Peredor. Denwin is assigned to you as well."

The second astrid stood a little taller than the first. He carried a pair of short spears. Peredor wielded a war hammer, and a brace of long knives crossed at his waist.

"How did you get your assignment?" Seth asked.

"Bracken issues most of our orders mind to mind,"

Denwin said. "He is only using his voice for the benefit of you humans."

"He talks to me telepathically sometimes," Seth said. "He gave me a magic coin."

"Keep your fine sword ready," Peredor advised, glancing down at Vasilis. "We will try to shield you, but this will be a host of demons such as the world has never known."

"I'll do my best," Seth said, fingering the hilt of his sword. The waiting was agony. How long before a demon would appear? Would Graulas be the first one out?

A murmur ran through the assembled astrids and fairies as the first demons emerged from the rift in the dome. Seth pulled binoculars from his emergency kit for a closer look.

In the lead slithered a muscular woman with four arms and the body of a serpent. Near her limped a pale man, considerably taller than a regular person, his body pocked with sores. His long, spindly arms and legs gave him spidery proportions, slaver dripped from his slack mouth, and buttery goo clotted around his red eyes. On the other side of the snake woman padded an enormous wolf, with crooked fangs that protruded like tusks and fur as dark as ink.

"You recognize these guys?" Seth asked.

"The tall skinny one is Zorat the Plagueman," Peredor said. "Without unicorns on our side, he could wipe us out himself with disease."

"Bracken will hold his influence in check," Denwin said. "The woman is a greater demon called Ixyria, a mentor to witches and hags. The wolf is called Din Bidor. Darkness and fear increase his size."

Behind these three demons came a figure who nearly filled the gap, a shirtless mountain of a man with an iron collar around his neck and a steel mask over his face. In one hand he clutched a gigantic flanged mace, in the other a tremendous morning star. Beneath gray, elephantine skin and thick layers of blubber, rotund muscles swelled with every movement.

"Brogo," Peredor murmured with intimidated respect. "One of the three sons of Gorgrog. He used to attack castles unaided. The oaf has single-handedly felled forests, smashed monuments, crushed armies, and destroyed cities."

"Arguably the strongest demon in history," Denwin said. "He was one of the first locked up in Zzyzx."

More demons poured out alongside and behind Brogo. Some walked on two legs, some on four, some on six. Others slithered. Others jumped. Others rolled. Others had wings. Some had horns, or tentacles, or shells, or scales, or quills, or fur. Many wore armor and bore weapons. Some had heads like dragons, others like jackals, panthers, humans, or insects. Several stood larger than Hugo. A few lounged on litters borne by underlings.

As the nightmarish procession continued to flow out of the rift, an idea struck Seth, and he hurriedly approached Bracken, his bodyguards half a step behind. Bracken was addressing Trask, Vanessa, Warren, and Kendra.

"This is good," Bracken said, eyes on the growing mass of demons. "Impatient after years in prison, many of the demonic leaders have emerged early. Among them I already see several notorious cowards. Although they love destruction and mayhem, many demons are hesitant to risk their own necks. They prefer bullying."

"How do we use this?" Trask asked.

"We need to spread the fight as wide as possible. We harass and scare the weakest leaders. And we fall back before them, hoping Gorgrog will emerge with his vanguard to celebrate his freedom and observe our demise."

"This is just the vanguard?" Warren asked.

"What you see is but a small delegation of the many demons entrapped in Zzyzx," Bracken confirmed.

Across the field, demons continued to emerge from the rift. Groups of human-sized fairies and astrids began to attack in small groups from multiple directions, darting in, striking a few blows, then soaring away. When flying demons gave chase, astrids converged, outmaneuvering the winged attackers and cutting them from the sky.

"Bracken," Seth said, "I have an idea."

"Let's have it," Bracken replied, eyes on the battle.

Seth began unbuckling his sword belt. "Why don't you take Vasilis? I'm sure you could make better use of it than I could."

"A noble gesture," Bracken said, temporarily taking his eyes off the scattered skirmishes. "But you're wrong, Seth. A sword like Vasilis does not always connect to a new master as it has connected to you. You and the Sword of Light and Darkness complement each other. I can sense that in my hands it would be a fine weapon, but it would fail to draw power from my mind and heart as it does from yours. I will fare just as well using my horn. Keep your blade."

"What should we do?" Vanessa asked.

"We wait," Bracken said. "Without wings, we can't harass the enemy like the astrids or the fairies. Our weapons will be needed as the battle unfolds."

On the field between the shrine and the prison, the harassing raids had enraged the demons, and the battle was growing fiercer. Seth saw a couple of fairies torn from the air, and an injured astrid had to be rescued by companions. The demons spread ever wider to confront the multidirectional sorties. For the moment, Bracken had succeeded in preventing the demons from concentrating their efforts on the shrine.

Without warning, the Sphinx appeared near Bracken. Dusty and winded, he held the Translocator in his hands and supported the Chronometer in the crook of his arm. The Font of Immortality protruded from his belt.

"The other two artifacts?" Bracken asked the Sphinx, evidently unsurprised by his appearance.

"Nagi Luna will not let the Oculus out of her grasp," the Sphinx said. "Graulas is the same with the Sands of Sanctity. This was the first moment when I had a chance to snatch any of the artifacts. Gorgrog has just emerged from confinement, and all attention was on him. As it was, I had to garrote Mr. Lich."

"You killed your friend?" Seth asked.

"He sided with the demons against me," the Sphinx said. "His willful treachery helped create this disaster. I thanked him appropriately."

"Will the artifacts do us any good at this point?" Kendra asked.

"My plan depends on recovering them," Bracken said, taking the Sphinx by the hand and fixing him with a level stare. "Will you shuttle in a strike force to recover the other artifacts?"

"It would be my honor," the Sphinx said.

"Fair enough," Bracken said, releasing his hand. "Targoron, Silvestrus, go with the Sphinx and retrieve the remaining artifacts."

"I need a better weapon," the Sphinx said.

"Take mine," Trask offered.

The Sphinx handed the Chronometer and the Font of Immortality to a nearby astrid, and then accepted the sword from Trask. "This belonged to the Gray Assassin," the Sphinx recognized, hardness entering his eyes. "It should do the job."

"You will engage the enemy only as a last resort," Bracken said. "Your priority must be to transport the artifacts back to us."

"And try to return my sword," Trask added.

"Graulas and Nagi Luna will not relinquish the remaining artifacts lightly," the Sphinx affirmed, swishing his sword through the air.

"Let me come," Seth blurted. "I'll take care of Graulas."

Bracken looked at Seth's sheathed sword. He hesitated, glancing at Kendra, who shook her head. Bracken rubbed his temple. "The Sphinx will take Targoron and Silvestrus first, then return for Seth and Peredor." Kendra gave Seth a worried frown. He tried to reassure her with a small smile. Bracken rested a hand on the Sphinx's shoulder. "After retrieving the artifacts, your priority will be to protect Seth and his sword."

There came a tremendous roar from the rift in the dome, a bellow of rage and triumph, easily overpowering the clamor of battle. An enormous figure came striding from the rift, a humanoid with a tremendous rack of contorted antlers. Body covered in thick fur, the personage stood taller than Hugo but shorter than the colossal Brogo. In defiance of the direct glare from the rising sun, darkness rippled around him. One fist held a huge, elaborate sword, edges bristling with spikes and serrations. Several corpses dragged on the ground behind him, affixed to his wide belt by black chains. An iron crown hugged the base of the antlers, atop a bullish head.

"Gorgrog," Bracken said.

"The time to move is now," the Sphinx insisted.

"Go," Bracken ordered.

The Sphinx twisted the Translocator and disappeared with Targoron and Silvestrus. A moment later he reappeared alone. Seth stepped forward with Peredor. They each laid a hand on the Translocator. When the Sphinx twisted the device, they were suddenly inside the dome.

Enough sunlight gleamed through the gaping crack in one wall to light the dome, but persistent shadows remained off to the sides. The ceiling seemed to curve impossibly high. At the center of the room, demons continued to emerge from a circular void in the floor, the real gateway of Zzyzx.

From this closer vantage, the demons appeared much more terrifying. Targoron was already locked in combat with a six-armed foe, and Silvestrus put a spear through a two-headed brute with teeth like knives. Peredor brought his war hammer down on the head of a stocky, bearded foe with blue skin and bright yellow eyes.

Graulas stood not far off, near the wall, away from the throng of demons parading toward the fissure in the wall of the dome. His face broke into an eager, evil smile when he met eyes with Seth. In one hand he held the Sands of Sanctity. The other hand gripped a heavy spear.

"You came looking for me after all," Graulas said, boisterous voice penetrating the tumult. "I should have known. You have collected quite a sword. Again, you astonish me, Seth Sorenson. Sadly, my final lesson will be that any blade is only as mighty as the wielder. Come. We have unfinished business, you and I."

Several demons had beset the Sphinx and the three astrids, but the other demons ignored Seth. Maybe he didn't look threatening enough to worry about. Maybe they were leaving him for Graulas. Whatever the case, Seth found himself walking forward, closing the gap between himself and the demon who had tricked and betrayed him.

Seth gazed up at the ram head framed by a set of curled horns. Broadly built, thickly muscled, clad in a breastplate and greaves, Graulas did not appear sickly in any way. Seth kept his hand on the pommel of his sword, instinct telling him not to draw it yet. Graulas seemed to assume that Seth was an unworthy wielder of Vasilis, and Seth saw no reason to persuade him otherwise.

"I can sense your confidence in your weapon," Graulas said. "Vasilis is a celebrated talisman. I almost claimed it once. Much better men than you have lost it. Your cause is hopeless. No help can avail you today. Stop delaying. The sword will function better unsheathed."

If Graulas lunged forward, he could now reach Seth with his spear. Seth's mouth felt dry. The wild ruckus of the cavorting demons faded from his attention. How had he imagined he could defeat Graulas? The demon had torn down a house with his bare hands! He had usurped the power of the Sphinx!

Seth clenched his jaw. There was no turning back now, nowhere to run. His only allies were fighting for their lives. And Graulas had the Sands of Sanctity.

Seth no longer advanced. "I healed you and you killed my friend."

Graulas sneered. "Don't stop there. By healing me, you essentially opened Zzyzx."

"Yeah, well, I'm here to unheal you." As Seth pulled out Vasilis, the blade sang in his hand, glaring with a scarlet intensity he had not yet seen. The sparks of defiance inside of Seth flamed into fury and confidence.

Graulas grimaced, uncertainty flickering in his eyes. The demon glanced away, and Seth followed his gaze to Nagi Luna, who perched on a rocky outcrop cackling wildly. Grunting, Graulas jabbed the spear at Seth. The thrust seemed slow and clumsy, and Seth hacked the head off the spear with a quick sweep of his blade.

"You claimed the sword had not taken to him!" Graulas growled vehemently. Seth could tell that the demon was no longer speaking English, but he could still comprehend the meaning. Scarlet flames spread down the shaft of his spear.

"Try to claim authority over me, will you?" Nagi Luna jeered at Graulas. "Try to steal the glory of my conquest?"

Graulas threw the shaft of his spear at Seth, who dodged aside without trouble. "Curse you for this, hag," Graulas rumbled. "You'll pay. If I fall, I'll summon a curse that will—"

"Kill him, boy," Nagi Luna snapped.

Graulas and Seth sprang toward each other simultaneously. Vasilis blazed, slicing through fur and breastplate almost without slowing. Angry flames erupted over Graulas as his claws raked down Seth's sides and his teeth clamped shut on his shoulder.

Seth fell flat on his back, Vasilis still in his hand, the crushing weight of the flaming demon pressing down on him. Stripes of pain seared his sides, and the demon's teeth remained embedded in his shoulder. The stench of burning meat and fur filled his nostrils. Seth could not move. As the fire spread over Graulas, Seth realized he would be cooked along with his blazing enemy. At least he would not die alone! Coulter would be proud.

Strong hands started prying the teeth apart at his shoulder, and the weight of the fiery demon rolled off of him. The Sphinx helped Seth to his feet. Peredor stood at his side. Targoron and Silvestrus continued to fight valiantly nearby. Beside Seth, raging flames consumed the lifeless corpse of the old demon.

"You really can use that sword," the Sphinx said, impressed.

"The Sands of Sanctity?" Seth asked, feeling light-headed. Refreshing energy flowed into his arm through Vasilis. Without the sword, Seth doubted whether he would be standing.

"Nagi Luna grabbed the artifact the instant Graulas fell," the Sphinx said darkly.

Turning, Seth saw her grinning on her rocky perch, the Sands of Sanctity in one hand, the Oculus in the other. Other demons had gathered around her in a defensive formation.

"Return the artifacts," the Sphinx demanded.

Nagi Luna gave a strangled cackle. "I am no longer your prisoner! I am the liberator of demonkind!"

More demons surged to protect her. Hunched and shriveled as she was, Nagi Luna would soon get away. Seth charged forward, Vasilis held high. Strength flooded into him from the sword, and the blade blazed like the hottest coals in a forge. Demons howled and wailed as Vasilis cleaved them, often striking two or three with a single swipe. As when he had dispatched the undead behind the Totem Wall, the sword seemed to subtly guide Seth, as if they were partners working together.

Alongside Seth, the Sphinx, Targoron, Silvestrus, and Peredor joined the fray. The demons gave way before them, particularly cowering from the fiery blade that effortlessly carved through armor and shield, shell and scales, setting ablaze all who came near.

Nagi Luna began to scramble away. Across the room, a

hulking, shaggy demon with antlers like a moose moved toward them, holding an enormous battle-ax.

"Orogoro approaches," the Sphinx panted beside Seth. "The eldest son of Gorgrog. If he intervenes, all is lost."

Seth experienced a heightened sense of awareness, absorbing all the details of the scene in an instant. Despite the ferocious attack he and the others had mounted, too many demons separated them from Nagi Luna. Orogoro would reach her first. And the artifacts would be gone, the artifacts Bracken had said were central to his plan. Without those artifacts the world would end.

The decision was made in an instant. Mustering all his strength, Seth hauled back Vasilis and flung it at Nagi Luna. The sword leapt from his hand with more force than the throw warranted, as if determined to reach the target, shedding flames and sparks as it spun through the air. The blade pierced the wizened demon through the back, and flames engulfed her shriveled form.

Seth crashed to the ground. Without Vasilis, all vitality had fled. The agony of his wounds reached new intensity, as if acid had been poured on his injuries. Dimly, Seth was aware of Peredor, Targoron, and Silvestrus springing into the air. Cheek against the ground, he foggily watched heavy boots shuffle near. Succumbing to pain and exhaustion, he did nothing to protect himself as jostling demons began to trample him. As his consciousness faded, the pain diminished.

The bite and scratches from Graulas had been poisonous. He could feel the toxins flowing in his veins. He had cheated death several times. Now he would finally die. He had done his best. Hopefully one of the others would recover the artifacts from Nagi Luna.

Then Peredor knelt at his side and slid the hilt of Vasilis into his hand. The blade glowed, and awareness returned.

"The artifacts," Seth mumbled, sitting up.

"The Sphinx and Targoron got them," Peredor said. "They were being swarmed, so they teleported away with them. Silvestrus has fallen."

Cradling Seth in his strong arms, the astrid took flight. Seth looked down at the mass of demons continuing to flood from the round void in the floor, and watched the crowd marching out through the rift in the side of the dome.

"I feel . . . weak," Seth mumbled.

"Vasilis strengthens you, but it doesn't heal you," Peredor said, evading a winged demon. "Hang on. There is poison in you. Stay awake. Keep talking."

"Who got the artifacts?" Seth asked sluggishly.

Peredor dove through the rift in the dome, and a moment later they were gliding over the battlefield toward the shrine. With Seth in his arms, rather than fight, Peredor spent his whole energy dodging adversaries. Above the army of demons, Peredor employed dizzying acrobatics to keep away from enemies, but Seth experienced the maneuvers numbly, as if from a great distance.

"You still with me?" Peredor asked. They were nearing the shrine.

"Still with you," Seth slurred. In his hand, the glow of Vasilis had grown faint.

"Silvestrus got to the artifacts, and he passed them to

Targoron as he fell," Peredor explained. "Targoron brought them to the Sphinx. They tried to get to you, but too many demons were attacking. Our mission succeeded. Hopefully this will help restore some of our honor."

"Your honor?"

"Targoron, Silvestrus, and I rebelled against the Fairy Queen after she transformed us into weaklings and banished us. Her consort had fallen to Gorgrog, and yes, as a body, the Knights of the Dawn had failed, but some of us found her punishment excessive. No betrayal was committed. Certain knights relaxed their vigilance, and Gorgrog got to our king in a surprise attack. Some of us felt she was assigning the blame deserved by some to all. To our everlasting shame, six of us renounced her. Three of us only recently returned, answering her call. We have much to prove. Bracken generously offered us an opportunity."

"You did well," Seth said. "Thanks."

"Save your gratitude! We succeeded because of you. Seth, I have never seen a sword thrown with such ability. For that matter, who would dare to throw such a sword? I am still in disbelief."

Seth smiled. He looked down at the shrine. The fighting looked fierce in front of it. "Is the shrine falling?"

"Our foes are hitting it hard," Peredor said grimly. "Without intervention, it will fall shortly. Our ranks have grown disorderly. Bracken has taken to the battlefield."

"Kendra?"

"We'll find her. And we'll find you a unicorn."

CHAPTER TWENTY-EIGHT

The Demon King

Kendra hated watching her brother vanish with the Sphinx into the unseen heart of the demon horde. She felt angry at Bracken for allowing Seth to endanger himself. But she did not directly intervene to prevent Seth's departure. After all, their situation was desperate, and she had a feeling none of them would see the end of the day without facing extreme hardship. Assuming any of them reached the end of the day alive.

As the demons had fanned outward from the rift, the skirmishes had grown fiercer and closer. A small team of astrids lured Brogo away toward the far side of the island, taunting the gigantic demon while he swatted at them like pesky insects. Others managed to injure some of the demons who had been reclining on litters. When Gorgrog moved aggressively forward, guiding a large portion of his host toward the shrine, Bracken departed to join the fight, along with Vanessa, Warren, and several astrids.

Bracken warned Kendra to stay near the shrine until the obvious moment, and then to flee. He did not explain what would make the moment obvious.

Currently, Kendra stood between Trask and Hugo as the demons pressed back the astrids and fairies guarding the shrine. Any moment the demons could break through, and Kendra would join the fight. Or perhaps when the demons broke through, it would be time to run away.

"This could be it," Newel said from behind Kendra.

"What a way to go," Doren said with relish. "Look at them. Sure, we've got plenty of lesser demons milling about, but I see many greater demons among them, including most of the demonic nobility."

"We'll go out in style," Newel agreed. "Killed by the best."

"I wish I had a decent sword," Doren sighed.

"I know the feeling," Trask added.

"At least we each have a guardian astrid," Newel said optimistically.

"I think my astrid could take yours," Doren muttered to Newel.

"Keep dreaming," Newel chuckled. "Mine looks like he could break yours in half with his bare hands."

"He'd have to catch him first," Doren countered. "Mine looks quick and wiry."

"Neither of us should get too cocky," Newel replied. "I'll wager Kendra has the best ones."

"No doubt," Doren huffed. "She has connections."

Kendra glanced back at the two astrids assigned to her. Surly warriors heavily armed, Crelang and Rostimus looked impatient to join the combat. By the appearance of the battle, they and the other astrid bodyguards would not have long to wait. The massive press of demons relentlessly forced back the defending lines of fairies and astrids.

A tall, burly demon with bulky claws like a lobster rammed through the defenders, allowing several other demons to trail through the gap. Hugo rushed forward, hacking the crustaceous demon to pieces with his hefty sword. The astrid bodyguards entered the fray and drove back the other demons who had broken through.

The small victory was short-lived.

An astrid and a stunning orange fairy fell to a trio of four-armed women with spider bodies. The demonic women held a sword or knife in each hand, and turned to widen the gap they had created as other demons rushed through. Another fairy fell, and suddenly the line of defenders collapsed into disarray.

Hugo came stomping back to protect Kendra, motioning for her to retreat to the edge of the shrine. She obeyed. And then the Sphinx appeared alongside Targoron. The Sphinx tossed his sword to Trask, who waded into battle, face grim, blade flashing. Blood flowed from a gash in the Sphinx's neck, but Targoron promptly dusted it with the Sands of Sanctity and the wound closed.

"Get the artifacts to safety," the Sphinx gasped.

"I'll carry them to the fallback position," Targoron replied, taking flight with the Oculus, the Sands of Sanctity, and the Translocator.

Kendra knew nothing about a fallback position. She felt like an outsider in this battle where so many plans were conveyed telepathically. "Where's Seth?" she asked the Sphinx.

"Injured," he replied. "He was heroic. Your brother made all the difference. He single-handedly slew Graulas and Nagi Luna. Peredor is flying him back here."

Kendra was glad they had regained the artifacts, since Bracken had claimed they were essential, but she felt horribly worried about Seth. How badly had he been injured? Would she ever see him again?

Rostimus landed beside Kendra, purplish slime dripping from his sword. "I may have to fly you out of here."

After giving up a lot of ground, the astrids and fairies were making a final stand in front of the shrine. But the frenzied demons only fought harder, and the defensive formation began to buckle.

"What about the shrine?" Kendra asked. If the demons broke through into the sacred kingdom beyond the shrine, it would be the end for creatures of light.

"My duty is to protect you," Rostimus replied.

Newel patted Rostimus on the arm. "Could you lend us a couple of weapons?"

"My arrows aren't causing harm," Doren complained. "We're tired of feeling like spectators."

Rostimus drew a pair of long knives, handing one to each satyr. "Use them well," he admonished.

"For endless television!" Newel cried, charging into battle.

"Frito-Lay!" Doren yelled, waving his knife overhead.

Behind her, Kendra heard multiple splashes. Turning, she saw more warrior fairies emerging from the pool around the shrine. With them came a number of unicorns, magnificent horses with pure white fur and gleaming horns. Many of the unicorns changed to human shape, men and women wielding glorious swords.

As the reinforcements charged forward, the demons fell back before the fresh onslaught, several falling to sword and spear. Other creatures continued to emerge from the pool: the tallest dryads Kendra had ever beheld, armed with bows and spears and halberds; a group of lammasu, huge and proud; a fiery flock of phoenixes; and dripping naiads, clutching daggers. As each wave of newcomers joined the fight, the demons surrendered more ground.

Countless small fairies began to fountain up from the pool. A few bore weapons and flew to help. Most did not join the battle, but zipped off in the opposite direction. Other creatures emerged and fled as well. Many more unicorns, tiny folk like brownies and elves, white stags with golden antlers, and other strange beasts exited the pond only to run away. Kendra could hardly believe the quantity of life escaping from the shrine.

An earsplitting roar drew Kendra's attention away from the pond. The bellow came from Gorgrog. Astrids and phoenixes had flown out to confront him, and many of the tall dryads and lammasu were bullying their way through the demon army to reach him. The astrids and others had formed a ring around the Demon King, holding back his allies while a small number of them engaged him in combat. Although the combat was not nearby, the shrine occupied higher ground, and Kendra could see Bracken leading the attack. Warren and Vanessa fought alongside him.

As Kendra watched, Gorgrog hacked an astrid from the air with his serrated sword. The Demon King towered over his opponents, stomping and slashing as they tried to surround him. The attackers looked like chipmunks assailing a gorilla.

A woman stepped up beside Kendra. Tall and graceful, wreathed in light, the woman shone with ethereal beauty. Kendra immediately recognized her from a vision she had experienced while using the Oculus.

Rostimus dropped to one knee, head bowed. "Your majesty."

"Rise," the Fairy Queen said, her voice rich and serene amid the cacophony of battle.

"It's you!" Kendra exclaimed, entranced by her presence. "It's really you! Why did you come out?" Worry filled her voice. The advance of the wave of reinforcements had already begun to slow.

"I am acting in accordance with our plan," the Fairy Queen replied. Her eyes regarded the fight with Gorgrog. "But I may have to deviate. Brave and capable as my son may be, Gorgrog is too much for him. I will not stand aside and lose my son as I lost my husband."

"Why is he fighting Gorgrog?" Kendra asked.

"We must at least injure the Demon King for our plan to have a chance," she replied. "Kendra, when my people retreat, go with them. This shrine will shortly be overrun."

"I will see her to safety," Rostimus pledged.

The Fairy Queen gave a nod. She turned to a slender, beautiful fairy warrior. "Ilyana, oversee the retreat if I am unable."

"Yes, your majesty," the fairy replied firmly.

The Fairy Queen drew a shining sword and took to the sky, flying without wings. Gorgrog, noticing her approach, sent Bracken tumbling with a vicious kick. The Fairy Queen swooped at the Demon King, and her sword clashed with his. Her bright blade looked tiny against his monstrous weapon, but the great force of his blow did not overpower her. Their swords connected again and again, each clash resounding loudly. There came a lull across the rest of the battlefield as many of the participants turned to watch.

At that moment, Peredor landed beside Kendra with her brother in his arms. The astrid placed him gently on the ground.

"Seth," Kendra gasped, kneeling beside him. Her brother was a mess, his face pale, his shirt tattered, his shoulder and sides drenched in blood. Vasilis glowed dimly in his grasp.

"I need a unicorn!" Peredor shouted.

"Hey, Kendra," Seth murmured weakly through chapped lips. "I got Graulas. We got the artifacts."

A handsome warrior came and knelt beside them, touching the tip of his sword to Seth's forehead. Then he

placed a palm against his chest. Some color returned to Seth's face.

"The poison had almost taken him," the unknown unicorn said. "I've purged the venom, but considerable internal damage remains. I have stalled the bleeding and tried to stabilize him. You need to get him to the Sands of Sanctity."

"Thank you," Kendra said as the man hastened to rejoin the battle. The forces that had rallied from the pond were now being pushed back. The Fairy Queen had lost the initiative with Gorgrog and was struggling to survive his incessant blows. As Bracken sought to aid his mother, Gorgrog struck his sword from his hands. Kendra watched in horror as a follow-up swing whistled toward Bracken. The Fairy Queen partly deflected the huge sword, but the stroke still sent Bracken reeling to the ground with a gaping wound across his chest.

"No!" Kendra cried, feeling useless.

Warren and Vanessa frantically helped the astrids, fairies, dryads, and lammasu hold back the encroaching demons vying to come to the defense of their king. The Fairy Queen stood over her fallen son, desperately deflecting mighty blows from Gorgrog.

Kendra had no way to help! She was about to witness the demise of the Fairy Queen, Bracken, and the rest of her friends. If only there were something she could do!

Her eyes fell on Vasilis. The weapon held her gaze, and the sounds of battle receded. She had a peculiar feeling that the weapon was calling to her. She made up her mind in an instant. "Seth, can I borrow your sword?"

"Vasilis?" he asked.

"Bracken and the Fairy Queen are about to die," she urged.

"It may not work the same for you as for me," Seth warned, sweat beading on his forehead. "But sure, take it. I'm in no shape to use it."

Kendra glanced at Peredor. "Get my brother to the Sands of Sanctity."

Seth held out Vasilis, and Kendra accepted the weapon. The dim blade flashed to life, shedding a brilliant white radiance. Kendra immediately felt galvanized, her senses sharpened, as if her whole life had been spent half asleep, and only now had she truly awakened. As blinding light beamed from her sword, the demons nearest to the shrine faltered, turning their heads away and trying to shield their eyes. Astrids, dryads, unicorns, and fairies once again drove them back.

But Kendra was focused beyond the nearby demons at the contest between the Fairy Queen and the Demon King. All her most desperate hopes and desires—to see her parents again, to rescue her grandparents, to protect her friends, to save the world from this demonic invasion—converged on the antlered form of Gorgrog. He was trying to kill Bracken and the Fairy Queen. He was the leader of the demons. He embodied the threat they had to overcome.

Vasilis towed her forward with such violence that her feet hardly touched the ground. She skipped ahead in huge bounds, much faster than any mortal could possibly run. Demons parted before the intense fervor of her blade, and, as Gorgrog drew nearer, rather than fear, she felt elation. All of the energy others claimed to perceive inside of her seemed to have suddenly surfaced. She felt no hesitation, no worry, only an overwhelming euphoria at finally being able to help the people she loved.

Sensing her approach, Gorgrog backed away from the Fairy Queen and turned to confront the newcomer. Kendra rushed at him, demons blurring by at either side, Vasilis shining like a white sun. The demon stood many times taller than Kendra, but she jumped before reaching him, gliding up so that she was almost level with his head as their swords clashed explosively.

The impact sent Gorgrog staggering backwards amid a coruscating shower of sparks, a white-edged notch in his monstrous sword. Kendra landed lightly, Vasilis humming in her hand. Behind the Demon King, Kendra noticed the Fairy Queen chopping at one of the black chains dangling from his belt, attempting to free a dehydrated corpse from its tether.

The Demon King was entirely focused on Kendra, eyes squinted against the brightness of Vasilis. The surrounding demons cowered back. Kendra stood her ground, and the Demon King charged her. Guided by an impulse from Vasilis, rather than try to meet his blade with hers, Kendra stepped aside as he swung his sword in an enormous overhand sweep. The blade plunged deep into the ground beside her. Springing forward, Kendra hacked at his leg. Flashing brilliantly, her shining blade sliced through fur and flesh like light through shadow.

With pure white flames running wildly up his leg and side, Gorgrog collapsed heavily. Kendra leapt forward, and

Vasilis glared like lightning as she slashed him with a fatal stroke.

As she backed away from the blazing form of Gorgrog, Kendra realized that the demon horde had grown tranquil. The astrids and fairies around her began to fly away. From the mass of stunned demons came a dark warrior who looked like a slightly smaller version of Gorgrog. His antlers branched more like those of a moose, and he wielded a great battle-ax.

"Orogoro," the Fairy Queen said, now standing beside Kendra, a withered brown corpse cradled in her arms.

The huge demon rushed forward to claim the crown from the burning form of his father. While Orogoro reached for the crown, face contorted in pain from the searing white flames, the astrid captain Gilgarol landed behind him and, with a mighty stroke of his longsword, slashed off one of his huge feet. Orogoro wailed in anguish.

"Away," the Fairy Queen cried, flying skyward, the corpse still in her arms.

Crelang and Rostimus alighted beside Kendra.

"Well done," Crelang said.

"We have orders to take you away," Rostimus added respectfully.

"Let's go," Kendra said. With the fall of the Demon King, and with Bracken out of danger, her euphoria had abated. She saw Bracken, Warren, and Vanessa being carried away by other astrids.

Rostimus picked her up and took to the skies. Crelang glided at their side. A flying demon belched fire at them,

and Crelang pierced its neck with a javelin. No other enemies harassed them. The entire demon army seemed confused. Kendra began to hear voices crying, "Dragons!
Dragons are coming! Dragons from the west!"

Rostimus brought Kendra to the top of a wide ridge
behind and to one side of the shrine. Many of the other
creatures of light already awaited them. From the high vantage point, Kendra looked out to sea, where at least twenty
dragons were speeding toward Shoreless Isle. Kendra
watched for a long moment, wondering if the dragons might
make the difference. She had slain the Demon King, but a
vast host of demons remained.

"Do you need healing?" Rostimus asked.

Kendra patted herself. "I don't think so." She studied the
crowd around her, searching for familiar faces. "Have you
noticed any of my friends?"

Rostimus and Crelang guided Kendra to Trask, Newel,
and Doren. She asked if they had seen Seth, and Doren
pointed her in the right direction.

Kendra found her brother seated beside Bracken. Both
had already been revived by the Sands of Sanctity. Seth rose
excitedly when she approached.

"I watched you with the binoculars," he gushed. "I think
Vasilis may like you even more than me! After you took the
sword, I remembered that Morisant hinted the sword might
take to you. I couldn't believe you did it!"

Kendra hugged her brother tightly, relieved that he
seemed all right. Then she turned to Bracken, and they
embraced desperately.

"None have ever seen a blade shine so brightly," Bracken said into her ear, making no attempt to hide his awe. "What you did was impossible. Not in our most far-fetched fantasies did we hope to slay Gorgrog."

Kendra released the embrace, feeling pleased and embarrassed. "What happens now?"

"Now we pray our plan works," Bracken said, brow furrowed.

Behind Seth and Bracken, Kendra saw the Fairy Queen seated beside an older gentleman with a frail build. She held his hand and spoke softly to him, but he sat motionless, wearing a vacant expression.

"Who is that with the Fairy Queen?" Kendra asked.

"My father," Bracken said softly.

"What?" Kendra exclaimed. "I thought he was dead!"

"None of us actually saw him die," Bracken explained. "We assumed he had been destroyed. As we fought Gorgrog, Mother sensed his presence, but she hardly recognized him. When Mother and I recovered him, at first we thought he had been changed into one of the undead. But then we realized that he was cocooned in powerful demonic spells that kept him alive, conscious and feeling, but on the brink of death. Gorgrog had been wearing him as a trophy, dragging him around Zzyzx for centuries. I can't imagine my father's suffering. The Sands of Sanctity brought him back physically, though he has not aged well, and there is no sign of his horns. He's catatonic."

"How terrible," Kendra said. "Is there hope he'll recover?"

"There is always hope," Bracken said. "Unicorns are among the most skilled healers, and Father had a resilient spirit. Time will tell. Mother swears he seemed to smile when Gorgrog fell."

Kendra, Seth, and Bracken watched from the ridge as a multitude of flying demons rose up to engage the oncoming dragons. The dragons attacked without reservation, lightning flashing from their jaws, or glaring bursts of flame, or seething streams of acid. At their lead flew Celebrant, scales gleaming like platinum. He looked to be everything Raxtus had described—enormous, agile, powerful. Whenever his teeth or claws struck, demons plunged from the sky.

A trio of dragons skimmed low across the mass of earthbound demons, drenching them with fire. From the midst of the demons, the gigantic Brogo threw his morning star, knocking one of the dragons from the sky.

Celebrant and three other dragons—the smallest of the foursome had to be Raxtus—swooped to the rescue. While the other three dragons defended their fallen comrade and helped him get back into the air, Celebrant opened his mouth and released a blinding blast of white energy at Brogo. The energy split open his mask and knocked the colossal brute to the ground. Tucking his wings, Celebrant rammed the titanic demon, raking and biting ferociously. When Celebrant returned to the sky, Brogo lay crisscrossed with deep lacerations and had lost an arm.

Elsewhere, the final team of astrids defending the shrine turned and fled, wings flashing. Orogoro hobbled near the front of the demonic host, using his battle-ax as a crutch.

Following his lead, the demon horde began pouring into the pool and vanishing.

"Oh, no!" Kendra exclaimed.

"This is part of the plan," Bracken said, watching in grim silence. "I ordered our forces to withdraw."

The Fairy Queen came up beside them. "The demons have always dreamed of conquering my realm. It is a kingdom of light and purity. Nothing will please them more than to ravage it."

"Wait," Seth said. "You hoped this would happen?"

"Mother destroyed all of her other shrines," Bracken said. "She has evacuated all of her people along with what talismans and energy she could bring. Her kingdom is now empty and has a single gateway."

Kendra watched the demons flood into the shrine. "Out of one prison and into another," she realized.

"If all goes as planned," Bracken confirmed.

"We have good reason to hope," the Fairy Queen said. "Their leaders are going. The others will follow. It will take some time for them to discover how completely I have sealed off my realm."

The dragons stopped attacking, content to circle over the demonic exodus, casting menacing shadows. As she regarded the dragons, once again Kendra picked out the smaller form of Raxtus darting among the larger creatures. Even without further violence, the threat of the many dragons overhead seemed to hurry the demons along.

For more than three hours, Kendra and her friends anxiously observed the procession of demons exiting the rift in the dome and entering a new realm through the shrine. The sheer quantity of demons left Kendra astonished. The others had been right. There was no way they could have defeated these demons in combat. For every demon they killed, a thousand more would have emerged.

"Don't they know it's a trap?" Kendra finally asked Bracken.

"They must know something is wrong," Bracken said. "They march into a realm they have dreamed of possessing since the dawn of time. But the realm is empty, undefended. It was handed to them with only token resistance. As we speak, they are tearing it apart. The smart ones know it's too good to be true. But their king has fallen, and his heir is injured. The sun is high. They don't want to face Vasilis. They don't want to face the dragons, especially Celebrant. They don't want to fight the unicorns, or the astrids, or the other fairy folk. And they probably are bewildered by the increased atmosphere of unbelief in the world. When many of these demons departed this world, they were universally feared. Now, most of humanity considers their existence a joke."

"They could have overcome all of this," the Fairy Queen said. "They could easily have destroyed this world. But providing access to my realm offered them a tempting, effortless option. They seem to have taken the bait."

"So you will lose your realm," Kendra said.

"It is no longer my realm," the Fairy Queen asserted. "It will become the new demon prison."

As the last demonic stragglers arrived at the shrine, a long gold and red dragon came gliding toward the ridge on two sets of wings. Seeing his lion's head, complete with a crimson mane, Kendra recognized the dragon as Camarat from Wyrmroost. At his side flew Raxtus. Kendra took Seth's hand as the dragons landed near them, and she saw that Agad sat astride Camarat in an elaborate saddle. Camarat crouched low as the wizard dismounted.

"Raxtus!" Kendra shouted as the dragon came near. "You brought reinforcements!"

"I did!" the dragon replied. "I even helped in the combat!"

Seth nodded toward Agad, who was walking away from Camarat. "I thought dragons didn't allow riders!" he said. Camarat spread his wings and returned to the sky.

"We make exceptions on occasion," Raxtus said. "Camarat and Agad are brothers."

"How did you convince the dragons to help?" Kendra asked.

"Agad promised to make Celebrant caretaker of Wyrmroost after all of this is over. The dragons of Wyrmroost have dreamed of governing themselves for centuries. Plus, I told my father how Navarog had vowed that the demon horde would slay him. I think that helped. He let me fly to battle with him for the first time!"

Agad came forward and knelt before the Fairy Queen. All eyes watched the wizard. "You have made an enormous sacrifice," he uttered reverently.

"It was necessary," the Fairy Queen replied. "My realm would have withered and died if the demons had claimed this world. Can you lock them inside?"

"If I may have use of the five artifacts, these noble dragons who accompany me have agreed to help me bind your last shrine much more securely than Zzyzx. I have had centuries to consider all that I wish I had done long ago. Now I can implement those improvements."

"What say you?" the Fairy Queen asked, turning to Bracken.

"You mean my horn?" Bracken asked. "By all means, use it as you used it before. I'm accustomed to this mortal shape. Seal those fiends away for as long as you are able."

Agad nodded pensively. "The former prison lasted for millennia. This new prison will endure far longer."

"What will you do?" Kendra asked the Fairy Queen. "Where will you go?"

"We will inherit a new home," the Fairy Queen said, regarding Agad.

"I will remove the bindings placed on Zzyzx," Agad said. "There is actually three times the space inside of Zzyzx as you had in your former kingdom."

"You'll live in the demon prison!" Seth exclaimed.

The Fairy Queen smiled. "Creators have many advantages over destroyers. It takes much more talent to build something beautiful than it does to tear it down. Before long, the demons will render my former realm as ugly as Zzyzx. But they will never re-create what they have spoiled. Conversely, with time and effort, one day Zzyzx will become as lovely as my former realm."

"More beautiful," Bracken promised. "We'll have more space to work with. And we'll have an eager force of workers. Considering the peril, our casualties are minimal. Two dozen fairies, eight astrids, two unicorns, a few others. The Sands of Sanctity are quickly restoring the wounded."

"You'll join me?" the Fairy Queen asked her son hopefully, tears in her eyes.

"Of course," Bracken said. "I love a challenge. I'll help supervise the rebuilding."

Kendra felt a heavy weight on her heart. Did that mean she would never see Bracken again? It sure sounded like it.

Agad bowed to the Fairy Queen. "You are most wise, your majesty. Some imagine the difference between heaven and hell to be a matter of geography. Not so. The difference is much more evident in the individuals who dwell there."

"We have much yet to accomplish," the Fairy Queen said. "Grant Agad his artifacts and let us be about our respective duties."

"I have a problem," Kendra said quietly.

"Speak, Kendra," the Fairy Queen invited. "We are all forever in your debt. If our aid is desired, it will ever be yours."

"My parents and grandparents and many of my friends remain imprisoned at the Living Mirage preserve. Can any of you help us rescue them?"

"It would be my honor," Agad said. "Dragons can be very persuasive."

"As can astrids," Bracken promised.

"I expect the Sphinx himself would help convince his minions to stand down," the Fairy Queen suggested.

"Fablehaven is kind of a mess too," Seth reminded everyone.

"I will personally make sure all is set right at Fablehaven and Living Mirage," Agad pledged.

"And I second the promise," Bracken added.

Kendra felt relieved, mostly because her family would be safe and have Fablehaven restored to them, and partly because it sounded like she would get to see more of Bracken before he went away.

"There will be other odds and ends to tidy up," Agad said. "For example, Bracken mentioned to me that you received advice from your ancestor Patton Burgess. I would like to travel back toward the end of his life and tell him how everything worked out, for his peace of mind. He was a good man."

"Could that change the information he sends to us?" Seth asked. "Could it change how all of this turns out?"

"You already know what he told you," Agad said. "Your visits to Patton are already part of the past, even the visits you haven't made yet. The information he left for you is a consequence of all those visits. I'm sure he made tough choices regarding what information to share and what to withhold. I will make sure he knows that the information he shared was exactly what you needed. Everyone involved walked a delicate path to reach this victory."

"Could we have Patton let Coulter know we win?" Seth asked. "Coulter visited him right before he died."

The wizard winked. "I think we can help make sure that happened, although I can make no certain promises. Time travel is strange. When we try to alter the past, we inevitably find our involvement was already part of the past. The few wizards I have known who actively chased time paradoxes have all gone into the past without returning, so I strive to keep my interactions with history simple."

"A wise policy," the Fairy Queen said.

Seth cleared his throat uncomfortably. "While I have your attention, I have one more question." He began to rummage in his emergency kit. "We had a wooden servant named Mendigo who helped us survive Wyrmroost, but got destroyed in the process. I have the hooks that held him together." He showed Agad his palm, which held several hooks.

Agad picked up a hook and held it up to one eye, squinting. "Yes, I recall Camarat telling me about your automaton. The hooks are a good start. You said he was wooden. Did any of the wood happen to survive?"

Seth frowned. "It all got dissolved by Siletta's poison."

Agad scowled thoughtfully. "Then I'm not sure I can—"

"Wait," Kendra said. "Some wood did survive. At Wyrmroost, when Mendigo jumped into that canyon to escape the griffins, a long piece of him snapped off. I remember finding it when I went out to scout. It should still be in the knapsack."

"And we can get to the knapsack room with the Translocator," Seth added excitedly.

"In that case, I believe I can restore your automaton without much trouble," Agad assured them.

"And I can perhaps add a spark of free will," the Fairy Queen said. "It would help the servant learn and grow."

"Thanks," Seth beamed. "You guys are the best! Oh, Agad, Bracken, I almost forgot. Morisant sends his regards. He told me to thank you, and to convey that he bears you no grudges. He seemed sorry for what he became."

"This is wonderful news, Seth," Agad said, eyes shining. "It gladdens me to hear that my mentor has finally found rest. Morisant was once a great wizard, perhaps the greatest of our order. It was his wisdom that allowed for a shrine to the Fairy Queen so near to Zzyzx. It is truly miraculous that he entrusted Vasilis to your care."

"Loaning it to Kendra worked out pretty good too," Seth said.

The old wizard laughed, placing one hand on Kendra's shoulder, the other on Seth's. "You two have been through a grueling ordeal. Your names will go down in history. We are all so very proud of you. I wish there were a way to fully express our gratitude. For the present, this will have to suffice: You can finally rest."

Prisoners

"I bet you thought you'd never have to pay up," Newel said, munching on a piece of fruit.

"Let's just say I'm relieved you'll get your reward," Seth replied.

"You'll confirm with Stan about the new technology?" Newel verified, tossing a grape into the air and catching it in his mouth.

"You really think we should tell him?" Seth asked.

"We had a legitimate pact," Newel said. "I don't want to risk Stan taking away our generator or our flat screen. Our claim is just. We need him on board at the outset."

"What if Stan prohibits the deal?" Doren asked. "What if he tries to change the terms? What if he gives us a certificate?"

"We stand up for ourselves," Newel replied. "The terms were set. We followed Seth to the ends of the earth and confronted some incredibly ugly demons."

"They were unsightly," Doren agreed with a wince. "And tough. Without our astrids we would have been goners."

"Nonsense," Newel spat. "Those astrids barely survived thanks to our heroics. Don't you forget it."

"I'll do my best with Grandpa," Seth said. "I have to go. My parents are waiting. You should slow down on the grapes, you'll spoil your appetite."

"Spoil my appetite?" Newel exclaimed. "On fruit? Seth, I thought you knew us!"

"Newel's right," Doren conceded. "We could each down a meatloaf without wrecking our appetites."

"I'll talk to you later," Seth said. "Kendra and Warren are waiting."

Seth and Kendra had only recently arrived at Living Mirage. A few days ago, the Sphinx had used the Translocator to travel to his secret preserve with Trask and Warren to prepare his minions for surrender. Warren had promptly returned with news that their friends and family were safe. But he also brought news that Seth's parents and grandparents had insisted Kendra and Seth wait until Agad was in control of Living Mirage before they journeyed there.

After the dragons obliterated the insufficient rear guard left behind by the demons on Shoreless Isle, it had not taken long for Agad to seal off the fairy shrine. Combining their efforts, the wizard and the dragons had employed an impressive spell to transport the enormous dome that had sheltered the gateway of Zzyzx over to cover the shrine. Once conditions on Shoreless Isle had been stabilized, Agad and most of his accompanying dragons had departed for the fifth secret preserve.

Now that Agad had been established as the new caretaker of Living Mirage, Kendra and Seth had finally been permitted to use the Translocator to visit. Hugo, the satyrs, Vanessa, and Bracken had come along. The Fairy Queen remained on Shoreless Isle with her people, preparing to inherit the former demon prison as their new home.

"What was that about?" Kendra asked.

"I made some promises to the satyrs," Seth said. "They want to make sure I deliver."

"What did you promise?" Warren asked.

"A real television of their own," Seth said. "I think they've earned it."

"Does your grandfather know?" Warren asked.

Seth shook his head.

"Good luck with that," Warren said.

Warren led Kendra and Seth down a lavishly decorated hall to an ornamented door. The upper floors of the great ziggurat all featured luxurious furnishings. Warren knocked. Seth felt suddenly nervous. It had been a long time since he had seen his parents. He wondered how they were dealing with being forcibly inserted into the world of magical creatures he and Kendra had discovered two summers ago.

His dad answered the door. He looked good, maybe a little slimmer. "It's the kids," he called, face breaking into a huge smile. As he stared at Kendra, tears gathered in his eyes. He wrapped her up in a huge hug, rocking her from side to side.

"Hi, Daddy," Kendra said, resting her head on his shoulder.

Seth put his hands on his hips. "Of course Kendra gets all the attention because you thought she was dead. I had a bunch of near misses, you know. Probably more than her!"

"We love you, too, son," Dad said, still holding Kendra.

Mom came to the door in a rush and clung to Kendra, shedding hysterical tears. After she stole Kendra away, his dad finally put an arm around Seth. "I hear you were quite the hero," his dad said.

"I'm sure things got exaggerated," Seth said. "I did manage to kill two of the most powerful demons who ever lived. I pretty much got revenge for all humanity on the villains who opened Zzyzx. I wish you could have been there with the video camera."

"I heard Kendra played a role as well," Dad said.

"Yeah, she has this habit of trying to top me. I had a really good day, but guess what I didn't do? I didn't kill the Demon King. Kendra upstaged me again."

"I heard she did it with the sword you found," Dad said.

"That's what I keep trying to tell everyone! Finally, somebody gets it! I think Mom is going to choke Kendra to death."

The comment brought his mom over to him. She embraced him tightly.

"Hey, Mom," Seth grunted. "I thought I was kidding about the strangulation."

"Come inside," Dad invited, shaking hands with Warren.

Seth could not believe the opulent room his parents were occupying. From the art on the walls to the rich drapes, from masterful tapestries to bejeweled furnishings, the room seemed designed to flaunt limitless wealth.

"You guys know we've been staying in a tent?" Seth complained.

"We weren't in quite so nice a room until a few days ago when the Sphinx returned," Dad reminded him.

Grandma and Grandpa Larsen came out of an adjoining room. "I thought I heard voices," Grandpa Larsen said.

Suddenly Seth understood why his parents had gotten so emotional when they saw Kendra. Intellectually, he had known that his Grandma and Grandpa Larsen were not actually dead. But on some level, that knowledge had not been real until now.

He raced to Grandma Larsen and hugged her.

"What happened to my little Seth?" she exclaimed. "I can't believe how tall you are."

"I can't believe how alive you are," he replied, nose stuffy with tears.

Kendra was hugging Grandpa Larsen.

"You were so brave to be here all that time," Kendra said. "It must have been horrible."

"All for nothing," he chuckled. "I set you up for disaster. I may have blown it as a spy, but I hear you two are carrying on the Sorenson family tradition."

"You risked your life for us," Seth said, hugging his Grandpa Larsen. "I have the best family ever."

"I'll second that," Grandpa Sorenson said, entering the room with his wife. "My grandkids will be happy to know that their parents were brave and stalwart throughout their captivity."

"The Sphinx never mistreated us," Mom said. "Our room wasn't terrific, but it wasn't in a dungeon like I've heard others describe."

"The food was actually pretty good," Dad said. "If this had been voluntary, it could almost have been a vacation."

"What's happening with the Sphinx?" Seth asked.

"Agad said he will report about that at dinner," Grandpa Sorenson said. "Apparently they've organized quite a feast."

"Shall we catch up over the meal?" Dad asked.

Mom poked him. "Can't we finish saying hello?"

"I'm with Dad," Seth said. "I'm starving."

Warren led them all to a magnificent dining hall. Seth had never seen a table so burdened with food. As it was long enough to accommodate all of them, the Sorensons found seats with plenty of room for friends. Agad sat at the head of the table. Seth noticed that Warren sat by Vanessa, and Bracken by Kendra. Tanu joined them, and Maddox, and Berrigan, and Elise, and Mara, all fully healed by the Sands of Sanctity.

Newel and Doren rushed into the room after most of the others had claimed seats. Doren wore a dapper vest. They sat as close to Seth as they could—across from him and down a little, beside his mom.

"Mom, these guys are Newel and Doren, my best friends at Fablehaven," Seth said.

"Very good to meet you," his mom said politely, with a couple of uneasy glances at their legs. "I'm Marla."

"You've had milk, right?" Seth asked.

"Yes, I can see them," his mom assured him with a brittle smile.

"Don't worry," Newel said with a casual wave of his hand. "Babes always get shy around us."

Doren swatted Newel. "Stop! That's his mother!" He turned to Marla, spreading a napkin on his lap. "Seth is such an exemplary young man. He has been a terrific influence on me. He's not a shirtless ruffian like others I know."

"Ruffian?" Newel spluttered. "How about *hypocrite?* Know who you look like in that vest? Verl!"

"I told you," Doren murmured out the side of his mouth, "I'm trying to make a good impression."

"Well, I'm trying to make an honest impression," Newel complained. "Who wants to have a gravy-drinking contest?"

Once the meal got rolling, Seth discovered that the food already on the table had only been appetizers. Course after course brought endless dishes both familiar and exotic. Miniature hamburgers and chicken wings sat alongside stuffed pheasant and bizarre shellfish. Seth tried to pace himself, sampling a wide variety, enjoying the unique sauces and seasonings.

Mom and Dad warmed up to the satyrs, who entertained everyone by telling loud jokes and consuming enormous quantities of food while Seth timed them. The atmosphere so closely mimicked a joyous holiday that before long, Seth almost felt like nobody in his family had ever been abducted or presumed dead. By the time the dessert carts were wheeled in, he felt stuffed and relaxed and less worried than he had for as long as he could remember.

At the head of the table, Agad tapped a crystal goblet with the side of his fork. The diners grew quiet as the aging wizard prepared to speak.

"Thank you all for joining me for dinner. This is the most spirited feast I have enjoyed since before most of you were born. That includes Stan and Hank."

Everyone laughed.

"Together, we have won a miraculous victory. Having narrowly avoided disaster, I suspect we can all look on the simplest of pleasures with renewed appreciation. We now have an opportunity to help define a new future, to safeguard it against some of the perils we have endured, and to recover from the losses we have sustained. Let us take a moment to remember those who made the ultimate sacrifice to help bring us this victory."

Seth stared at his lap, trying not to think about Coulter, willing his eyes to stay dry. He pushed away mental images of brave astrids and fairies falling. Jaw clenched, he fought to ignore memories of Lena, Dougan, and Mendigo. He thought of them often, and would think of them again in a more private setting, but at the moment he wished Agad had not brought such strong emotions so close to the surface.

"We will all be dealing with change in the coming weeks, and months, and years," Agad went on. "For most of us this will be welcome, even if it entails new challenges. Preserves will be restored and reorganized. Where appropriate, new leadership will be appointed. Much of what has been broken will be mended, in most cases, to be stronger than ever. We will rebuild, and a new era of peace and security will dawn."

This earned spontaneous applause.

Agad stroked his beard. "I will bear many responsibilities as I seek to establish further protections for the new demon prison. In the end, once the artifacts are stowed away, along with a variety of new protocols and precautions, I believe the prison will be much closer to impregnable than ever. As the new caretaker of Living Mirage, I will base my activities from here, and some of you may be involved from time to time. I don't want to drown this merry occasion with tedious words, but there is one matter I feel we must resolve as a group before I can proceed with my duties. This matter involves the punishment of the Sphinx."

The room was dead silent.

"After the battle on the Shoreless Isle, I pondered on how to deal with the Sphinx. He offered us pivotal assistance at the end, but it was aid for a catastrophe that he had worked tirelessly to manufacture through deceit, sabotage, and even murder. My inclination was to let nature take its course. The Sphinx had been prolonging his life using the Font of Immortality, and I decided an appropriate punishment would be to forbid him use of that artifact—in essence, a death sentence.

"When I delivered this verdict to the Sphinx, a long

conversation ensued. The Sphinx accepted the justice of the proposed punishment, and then proposed another solution. Personally, I would be willing to accept the alternative he offered. He submitted to scrutiny from both Bracken and the Fairy Queen, who believe he is sincere.

"We all know the Sphinx is a master of persuasion. I decided to lay the matter before you, without the Sphinx here to exercise his powers of influence. I avow beforehand that, regardless of my own opinions, I will abide by whatever decision we make as a body right now."

Seth was on the edge of his seat. He glanced at Newel, who was gnawing on his fabric napkin, eyes wide with interest.

"As I lock the new demon prison tighter than the old, I will need new Eternals," Agad explained. "By now, all of you know the role the Eternals played in keeping Zzyzx closed. The Sphinx would like to be one of those Eternals."

An uproar of muttered exclamations followed. Agad held up his hands, and the murmuring quieted.

"Allow me to set forth the details for your consideration. Essentially, the Sphinx is attempting to exchange an execution for life in prison. Consider these points. As an Eternal, the Sphinx would not be able to open the demon prison unless he was dead. He has never believed anyone but himself should open the demon prison, which he proved on Shoreless Isle, so he would almost certainly be loyal to our cause. He has a knack for longevity, and for protecting himself. He knows how to keep a secret, and how to hide. He is remarkably cunning and patient. He has successfully coped with the challenges of a long life, and craves more. As a volunteer who would fulfill the requirements of an Eternal, I do not believe we could find a more ideal candidate.

"Keep in mind, being an Eternal is more punishment than prize. Ask Bracken or Kendra—most of our past Eternals had difficulty coping and considered their fate a weighty ordeal. An unnaturally long life, hunted, on the run, is no paradise.

"Considering the Sphinx's history, I would take extra precautions, personally monitoring him and installing a multitude of magical and practical safeguards. I would give him some latitude to choose a hideout and to implement whatever defenses he deemed most effective, but he would be on a leash.

"By giving into this request, would we be rewarding his crimes? Under other circumstances, I do not believe the Sphinx would want to be an Eternal. But as an alternative to death, he seems willing. Let's have Bracken testify to his motives."

Agad extended a hand and Bracken stood up. "The Sphinx has a strong will. He has much practice in shielding his thoughts from external scrutiny. But as I extensively probed his mind, I came to believe he wants to become an Eternal for acceptable reasons. First, he wants to persist. He has a profound fear of death, coupled with a powerful enjoyment of existence. Second, he wants a shot at redemption. He knows he spawned a catastrophe, which was never his intention. He wants to do everything in his power to ensure that a similar crisis never happens again. And last, he feels guilty and sees this as a fitting punishment. I have no love for the Sphinx, and I studied him long and hard. This is all I found."

Nodding at Agad, Bracken sat down.

"If you want my opinion," Agad said, "letting the Sphinx die would be a punishment quickly served from which we would derive no benefit apart from the satisfaction of his demise. On the other hand, making him an Eternal would cause him to pay for his crimes by providing a lasting and difficult service to humankind. But perhaps I am not seeing this clearly. I would gladly hear any objections."

Nobody spoke. People at the table eyed one another. Seth met eyes with Kendra. She gave a nod, he gave one back, and she stood.

"I hate the Sphinx," Kendra said. "I despise him for his lies and for what he did to us. If what he most wants is a long life, I desperately want to take that from him, to hurt him like he hurt us. I dread the thought of him feeling like he wormed out of the consequences of his treachery. But I think this punishment makes sense."

She sat down. Seth stood up. "Me too."

Bracken stood. "My horn has kept him alive. The influence of my horn will continue to keep him alive. I can live with letting the Sphinx survive under these conditions. I agree that he will fill the role well."

Vanessa rose. "I have known the Sphinx for a long time. I have worked for him. As Agad mentioned at the outset, he is a deceiver, a master manipulator. Making him an Eternal seems appropriate, but he's an expert at making his interests make sense. He may not be here to speak, but Agad is delivering his rhetoric. The Sphinx has a sinister history of working mischief while wearing a friendly face. The only way to be safe from the Sphinx is if he ceases to exist."

Doren leapt to his feet. "Vanessa is a beautiful woman, and should be taken very seriously. For her mind. And her charming personality. Thank you."

Mara stood. "I understand Vanessa's concerns. His agents killed my mother. I will never forgive him, but I think making him an Eternal is a better punishment than killing him. The long life of an Eternal will force him to provide much more payment for his crimes than a quick death could possibly offer. And those same qualities that made him so dangerous will hold the new Zzyzx shut."

Others began adding their endorsements. A few others expressed hesitations. Grandpa had questions for Agad about how the Sphinx would be monitored, and the wizard provided satisfactory responses. In the end, the vote to make the Sphinx an Eternal was unanimous, except for Vanessa and the satyrs.

"I did not want to try to make this decision alone," Agad said after the votes had been cast. "Nor did I feel it would be fair to the many he has wronged. I feel good about the decision we have reached. I think it will make the new demon prison more secure. And I believe time will demonstrate that, while having an element of mercy, the punishment we resolved on is exacting and severe. Now, how about some dessert?"

CHAPTER THIRTY

A New Shrine

On a hot summer day, Kendra strolled through the garden at Fablehaven. The humidity made her shirt feel sticky, but she loved the fragrances of the blooming flowers and the sight of blissful fairies bobbing from blossom to blossom. Perhaps later she would change into her bathing suit and go for a swim.

A new barn loomed over the yard, larger than the former structure, leaving Viola room to grow. The house had been rebuilt as well, with several elaborate touches added by the brownies. Agad had also engineered a direct road from the Fablehaven house to the old manor, which had been refurbished and enchanted with new protections.

Seth was currently off watching TV with Hugo, Mendigo, and the satyrs. Grandpa Sorenson had reluctantly caved after the agreement had been explained, and instead of a generator, the satyrs had electrical lines that ran to their nearest cottage. Grandpa hoped that endless television would help the technology cease to be such a novelty, but so far, the flat screen with surround sound was widely considered the greatest wonder at Fablehaven. Newel and Doren had never been more popular, or more jovial.

Seth still complained that he had not been present when Agad and the dragons had reclaimed Fablehaven from the centaurs, although he got to visit not long afterward in order to dismiss the wraiths. Bracken and several astrids lent some assistance, and Bracken had been surprised to discover that the unicorn horn the centaurs prized actually belonged to him. As punishment for their rebellion, he reclaimed his horn, and Agad reduced their roaming privileges and territorial holdings. The wizard left Grunhold protected by strong enchantments, but nothing quite so powerful as the shielding once provided by the forfeited horn.

Bracken had already gone by the time Kendra used the Translocator to return to Fablehaven. When they had said their good-byes at Living Mirage, he had promised to visit before too long. She understood that the Fairy Queen needed his help transforming Zzyzx into a paradise, but Kendra often wished he could have lingered longer. Before he left, he had used his powers to sever the narcoleptic hold Vanessa had on the Sorensons and their friends. After visiting Fablehaven, although he broke Vanessa's hold on some of the centaurs, he had left her connected to Cloudwing and Stormbrow.

"I'm making lunch," Mom called out the window. "Turkey sandwich okay?"

"Sure," Kendra replied.

"You want to try some avocado on it? Or cranberries?"

"No thanks, just cheese."

Her parents had moved the family to Fablehaven. They were still debating whether Kendra and Seth would return to public school or simply receive their schooling at home. While Grandpa and Grandma Sorenson continued to live in the main house, Grandpa and Grandma Larsen had taken up residence in the old manor. Dale had been found alive and well in the stables, and continued in his role maintaining the rebuilt preserve. Kendra enjoyed the new dynamics at Fablehaven. After so long, in ways she could never have imagined, her family was all around her, and their lives had become calm. Almost too calm.

Kendra looked to the woods. The fairy Shiara had visited Kendra this morning, bubbling with excitement. She had twittered about a surprise visit around noon, but refused to relate any hints or details. Her excitement had left Kendra curious—and quietly hopeful.

Kendra checked her watch. Noon had come and gone. Perhaps Shiara had it wrong. She wasn't the type of fairy to pull a prank.

As Kendra began to wander toward the house, a silver-white dragon came gliding over the treetops. Tucking and diving, he spiraled down to the yard, slowing at the last instant and landing with a flourish of his gleaming wings.

"Hi, Kendra," Raxtus said. "How was that for an entrance?"

Kendra was happy to see Raxtus, and his arrival made sense. Shiara was the fairy who had cared for him as a hatchling, so of course she would be excited for him to visit. But Kendra's heart sank a little at the same time. She had been hoping the surprise might be somebody else who tended to make fairies excited.

"Very impressive," Kendra said. "It feels like it has been a long time."

"I've been helping with the rebuilding," the dragon said. "You already wouldn't recognize Zzyzx. Those fairies can work when they set their minds to it. I think it has been good for everyone. I haven't seen most of them so lively in years. And it's great to have the astrids back."

"I'm glad," Kendra said. "Are you here to visit Shiara?"

"Yeah."

"She must be so proud of you."

Raxtus craned his head away shyly. "You know, my dad is finally treating me like a real dragon. He saw me take out a couple of demons when we attacked Orogoro's rear guard. I'm really small, and my breath weapon is a joke, but my scales are almost as hard as his, and my teeth and claws are unusually sharp. I had no idea. I'd never really tested myself. Now that he runs Wyrmroost, my dad has this whole training regimen planned when I get back from helping the Fairy Queen. He taught my larger brothers lots of tricks that I missed out on. He will help me become a more effective fighter. But I promise I won't let it turn me into an idiot!"

"I'm sure it will just make you more confident with your friendly side," Kendra said.

"And maybe a little scarier?" Raxtus hoped.

"Definitely."

"You know, I didn't come here alone."

Kendra held her breath. She tried to keep her expression composed. "You didn't?"

"He wanted me to bring you to meet him."

"Are we talking about Bracken?" Kendra asked.

"No, Crelang. Remember him? The astrid? He was one of your bodyguards."

Kendra stared at Raxtus blankly.

"I'm kidding. Of course, Bracken! But don't mention I told you. It was supposed to be a surprise."

"I promise to look surprised." Her pulse raced. What if he sensed her excitement? She didn't want to seem pathetic. But she had missed him! It had been weeks since she had last seen him.

"He's been talking about you a lot," Raxtus informed her in a confidential tone. "Go easy on him. I'm going to fly you to him, then get out of your way. You two deserve a little privacy."

"I should tell my parents," Kendra said.

"I'll come back and tell them," Raxtus assured her. "This should be quick. He has a surprise for you. I keep saying too much! Mind if I take you? Don't tell him how much I blabbed!"

"Sure," Kendra replied.

Raxtus snatched her and took flight. "Agad left me with

free roam of all the preserves he restored," Raxtus said. "I think he wants me to help be his eyes and ears among the dragons. He's given me a lot of trust."

"That's great," Kendra said, her thoughts on the upcoming reunion.

"This will be a short flight," Raxtus said.

As the prospect of seeing Bracken became real, Kendra felt startlingly conflicted. It was one thing to daydream about romance, and another to confront it in the light of day. What could the surprise be? What if he proposed! She was so not ready for something like that! Sure, he was cute, and brave, and loyal. Best of all, he was someone she could really trust. But she was fifteen, and he was older than most countries, no matter how young he seemed.

Anxiety knotted her insides. She shouldn't leap to conclusions. There was no way he was about to propose. But what if he wanted a romantic relationship? It was one thing to snuggle a little when the world seemed about to end, and quite another to explain to her parents that she wanted to date an ancient magical horse.

As the dragon glided down toward the circle of gazebos around the former shrine to the Fairy Queen, Kendra struggled to calm herself. It would be good to see Bracken. She would try to wait and hear what he had to say before freaking out. They passed over a hedge wall and landed in the field near the whitewashed boardwalk that surrounded the pond.

Bracken stood on the steps up to the boardwalk, dressed

in a loose white shirt and jeans. Devastatingly handsome, he jogged toward Kendra once she had landed.

"I'm going to go visit Shiara," Raxtus said. "I'll be back soon. Have fun."

The dragon took flight.

"Hi, Kendra," Bracken said, looking pleased, clearly expecting her to be surprised.

"It's you!" Kendra said, trying to play the role. "What are you doing here? How are you? How's your father?"

"My dad shows subtle signs of improvement. He still hasn't spoken. Our best healers feel he will eventually recover, although perhaps not fully. I'm happy to see you!"

"I feel the same way."

"Come here," Bracken said, waving Kendra forward. "I want to show you something."

He took her hand and led her up the steps to the board-walk. He pulled her along the walkway, then down to the little pier beside the boathouse. Together they walked almost to the end of the pier.

"What did you want to show me?" Kendra asked, taking a step forward, gazing across the water at the little island that had once housed the shrine.

"Haven't you wondered how I got here?" Bracken asked, stepping up a little behind Kendra.

"Raxtus?"

"Sort of. Try again."

"The Translocator?"

He shook his head. "Agad has already gathered the arti-facts to start hiding them. Guess again."

Kendra gasped, whirling around to face Bracken. "Did you fix the shrine?"

"This is our first new shrine," Bracken said with a smile. "The second entrance to our kingdom. In the coming years, we hope to create many new shrines. But Fablehaven got the honor of hosting the first. Agad helped us lay the groundwork. Now I can visit whenever I want!"

Kendra felt her face flush and turned back toward the water. "That would be really nice."

"I hope to visit quite a bit," Bracken said. "Get to know your parents and grandparents better. Hang out with Seth. He's an interesting guy."

"He's pretty cool," Kendra said, trying to manage her expectations.

"He still owes the Singing Sisters a favor," Bracken said. "I want to help him make sure everything goes all right."

"My family will be relieved to hear that."

"He may yet find an opportunity to use his tower and his leviathan."

"He was so mad he didn't get to use them at Shoreless Isle," Kendra laughed. "He's thinking of planting the tower here at Fablehaven, to give Hugo an official home."

"Never hurts to have such items in reserve," Bracken said. Smiling knowingly, he stepped closer. "As much as I enjoy your family, I have other reasons why I want to visit Fablehaven."

"How come?" Kendra asked, heart pounding. She was way too nervous to turn and look at him again.

"I haven't been drawn to a girl in a long time," Bracken

said. "Against all odds, this time, my mother actually approves!"

He turned Kendra toward him, hands on her shoulders. "I mean, you know," he added softly, smiling, "what kind of unicorn wouldn't be drawn to a virtuous maiden?"

"What kind of a girl doesn't like unicorns?" Kendra teased, looking up at him.

"Here's the problem," Bracken said, eyebrows scrunched. "I feel young. My mind doesn't get beaten down by the passing years, and neither does my body. It's part of my nature—time does little to sap my youthfulness. But let's face it, however I may feel, I've existed for a long while. Chronologically, I make your grandparents look like infants. And you're not an adult yet."

"You don't seem old to me," Kendra said, unsure how much she believed her words. He looked young, but his manner sometimes betrayed glimpses of an older soul.

"I've been around long enough to recognize the importance of timing," Bracken said. "I care for you deeply, Kendra. A few years will give you time to mature, and offer me time to help my mother rebuild her kingdom." He took her hands in his. "This is the first shrine we restored. As I already made clear, I'll visit, and we'll see where the future leads."

Kendra felt like a weight had been lifted. It was clear that Bracken liked her, just as it was clear that she would have time to sort through her feelings without getting pressured into an official relationship.

Still, as she gazed up into his adoring eyes, she had a

suspicion the crush might linger and grow into something more. After all, hadn't Patton married a naiad? Maybe in time she and Bracken could find a way to make a real relationship work. Maybe when the time was right, she could become an Eternal, and they could remain ageless together, protecting the world from evil.

"I understand," Kendra said. "It makes sense."

Bracken smiled, a candid blend of relief and joy. "Want to know the best part? Once we get things more how my mother wants them, I have permission to bring you to our kingdom from time to time. You'll be the first mortal to set foot there!"

"That sounds perfect," Kendra said. And she meant it.

Is This Really the End?

I sometimes get asked why I don't add an extra book or two to the *Fablehaven* series. From the start, this series was designed to contain five books. Based on my plan, I felt I could keep the story growing with each installment, so that the books would build on each other in fun ways and hopefully never get too boring. To write more would have meant stretching the narrative in a way that I felt would harm the overall story.

In other words, this really is the last book in the *Fablehaven* series. Will I ever revisit the *Fablehaven* characters or preserves in a future book? Possibly. I see opportunities for other stories using the characters and situations introduced in *Fablehaven*. But it would be organized as a fresh book or series, not a sixth book added to this one. I have no plans to write such a book in the near future. However, I will be writing other fantasy adventures that should appeal to the type of readers who have enjoyed *Fablehaven*.

I'm currently working on a three-book series called *The Beyonders*. The story deals with a couple of kids from our world who cross over to a strange, imperiled land where a corrupt emperor is systematically getting rid of all the heroes. All of my books up until now have dealt with fantasy elements in our real world. I'm excited to take readers someplace else! I have been planning this new trilogy for over ten years, and feel confident that it will take readers on a terrific ride. I hope that readers who have enjoyed *Fablehaven* will check it out, starting in 2011.

I also have plans to create a sequel to my novel *The Candy Shop War*. A sizable chunk of my readers tell me that *The Candy Shop War* remains their favorite. Even though it was originally planned to be a single book, I have now developed what I feel will be an engaging sequel. Although still a couple of years away, it represents an important part of my short-term writing plans.

Speaking generally, over the next several years, I intend to write a book or two per year. I believe I am improving at what I do, and feel I have not yet explored my best ideas. I will focus on creating a variety of family-friendly fantasy novels. To keep an eye on my upcoming projects, sign up for the newsletter at BrandonMull.com and swing by my Facebook or Twitter pages. I'm pleased with how my *Fablehaven* books have unfolded, and I'm indescribably excited to tackle future projects. If you enjoyed the *Fablehaven* series, please spread the word, and watch for my future stuff!

Reading Guide

1. If you could visit any magical preserve described in the *Fablehaven* series, which would it be? Why?

2. If you could follow the story of any character in the series beyond Book 5, who would you most like to hear about? Explain.

3. Why do you think Seth helped Graulas? Was it a good decision? Why or why not?

4. Do you believe the Sphinx will be trustworthy as an Eternal? Why or why not?

5. How has Seth changed since Book 1? How was his decision to help Graulas different from his decision to open the attic window on Midsummer Eve?

6. How has Kendra changed since Book 1? How is she the same? What did she do in this book that she might not have done when we first met her? How did her rational, obedient nature help her in Book 5?

7. In the Beckoning Grove, Kendra, Warren, and Bracken had to resist the alluring scent of fruit that they knew would harm them. Is there anything like that around us in the world today? Explain.

8. The wizard Morisant used evil means to extend his life and failed to remain good. Seth tried to befriend a

demon and was betrayed. Are there certain types of dangers or evils around us today that can never be trusted? Explain.

9. If the Sorensons had not interfered, do you think the Sphinx could have released the demons of Zzyzx on his terms and successfully controlled them? Why or why not?

10. Many magical creatures participated in the *Fablehaven* series. What were some of your favorites? Why? Were there any creatures not included in the series that you would have liked to have seen? If so, which ones?

11. If you had the opportunity to become an Eternal, would you take it? Why or why not?

12. Agad suggested that the difference between heaven and hell was not a matter of location. He claimed the difference had more to do with the people around you. How was this true in the story? Can this sometimes be true in our lives? If so, how?

13. Who is the coolest author ever? Is it the guy who wrote *Fablehaven*? If not, what's the matter with you? Explain.

Acknowledgments

I'm so glad the Fablehaven series finally exists outside of my brain. So many people helped that happen, especially the folks mentioned in the dedication, all those who have enjoyed and shared the books. I've thanked most of the following people before. This time, the way the page count worked out, I have to keep it condensed.

Family: Mary, Sadie, Chase, and Rose.

Early readers: Mary, Pam, Gary, Cherie, Summer, Bryson, Chris, Emily, Jason, Natalie, Mike, Liz, Wesley, the Freemans, Gladys, Jaleh, Simon, and Tuck.

Publisher folks at Shadow Mountain and Aladdin: Chris Schoebinger, Emily Watts, Roberta Stout, Richard Erickson, Gail Halladay, Patrick Muir, Lowell Oswald, Sheri Dew, Jeff Simpson, Boyd Ware, Lonnie Lockhart, John Rose, Lee Broadhead, Anna McKean, Liesa Abrams, Bethany Buck, Mara Anastas, and Bess Braswell.

My agent, Simon Lipskar. My film agent, Matthew Snyder. The awesome illustrator Brandon Dorman, who knocked this cover out of the park and also made our picture book, *Pingo*, look amazing. The audio book guys E.B. Stevens and Kenny Hodges.

Families who have hosted me: the terrific Rosenbaums in Spokane and the wonderful Toluta'u family in Hawaii.

Crazy young people making silly YouTube videos: Angela, Brett, Micah, Isaac, and Kathy.

People who meant to help: my sister Tiffany, my nephew Dalton, and my brother Ty, who almost made it through Book 4 in time to help with 5.

050987255